Brad Steiger has long been one of the leading experts on the UFO mystery and the enigma of alien contact. Such bestselling books as *Project Bluebook, Mysteries of Time and Space,* and *The Gods of Aquarius* have set the standards for presenting scientific and technical information in a popular, accessible format.

Steiger discovered that Edgar Rothschild Fouché had in his possession the unanswered questions that the highest levels of government have protected without reservation, without regard to law or constitutional rights, and without accountability.

Presented herein are a myriad of never-before-released astounding facts about the secret government's covert conspiracy not only to cover up alien and UFO contact, but to reverse engineer these "alien artifacts" in a race with the devil to protect our species from alien control.

Alien Rapture

The Chosen

Edgar Rothschild Fouché
and Brad Steiger

1998
Galde Press, Inc.
PO Box 460, Lakeville, Minnesota 55044–0460, U.S.A.

First Edition
First Printing, 1998

Disclaimer

This is a work of fiction. All of the characters, names, dialogue, incidents, incidental references to public figures, and products or services of companies are imaginary and are not intended to refer to any living persons or to disparage any company's products or services. Any resemblance to actual persons or businesses, whether a similarity of description, name, or event is entirely coincidental.

The top secret government documents are alleged to be authentic. However, we believe the U.S. government would disagree. Existing top secret military science and technology, facilities, government reverse engineering of alien technology, and government abuses are also alleged to be authentic. Historical quotes by public figures are accurate.

Library of Congress Cataloging-in-Publication Data
Fouché, Edgar Rothschild, 1948–
Alien rapture : the chosen / Edgar Rothschild Fouché and Brad Steiger. — 1st ed.
p. cm.
ISBN 1–880090–50–3 (trade pbk.)
I. Steiger, Brad. II. Title.
PS3556.0779A79 1998
813'.54—dc21 98–2961
CIP

Galde Press, Inc.
PO Box 460
Lakeville, Minnesota 55044

Contents

This "science faction" novel is dedicated to my loving wife, Rebecca McCollum Fouché, who is a terrific writer, editor, and president of Fouché Media Associates. To the most wonderful daughter any man ever had, Kimberly Alison Fouché, and to Rebecca's terrific children, Chad, Jane, and Sam, and her parents, Sam and LaNell.

A special thanks to my good friends Brad and Sherry Steiger and my incredible agent and friend, Bob Silverstein.

To my long-term supporters who read and made many suggestions over the years of research and writing: J. Elerick, R. De La Garza, F. Jones, M. Woodson, B. Ayola, S. Galus, M. Garcia, Dr. R. Duncan, and to all their families.

And to Robert Cullen and Page Gray (deceased), who gave me input and words of wisdom and to their families. Also to Brad Grubbs of Grubbs Graphics in Dallas.

To each of you and all my other friends and family, I sincerely thank you and love each of you. To those who requested that their names never be mentioned, I acknowledge their input and promise to work diligently to uncover and reveal and truth that our government has suppressed. (To M.G., P.M., M.C., L.L., and the Group.)

In Everything You Do, The Truth
Should Bring You Honor, Not Shame.

To Marvin and LaVon With respect and affection.

The Rapture

by Edgar Rothschild Fouché

Sleeping gods track our fate,
Silently guarding the inner gate

While no harm may come to be,
Myriad manipulations you cannot see

Protect those souls as old as Earth,
A blending and merging of Karma's birth

Beyond the stars comes the source,
A strength, a power, of unknown force

Deities, mentors, abductors, more,
A synergy of long lost lore

The sound of all we cannot hear,
The sum of which we mortals fear

An endless journey towards Rapture's path,
The secrets revealed upon Revelation's Wrath!

Foreword

My co-author, Edgar Albert Rothschild Fouché, is a descendent of Joseph Fouché, Napoleon's prime minister and the head of his secret police. Joesph Fouché is credited with beginning the world's first organized intelligence and spy agency, and many of Ed's ancestors and recent relatives have historically been involved with the military intelligence and classified electronics and communications programs.

During the Vietnam war, Ed volunteered for Pararescue training while in the Air Force, but a broken ankle got him shipped off to the electronics, communications, intelligence, and cryptological schools. Thus his adventure began.

Ed served in Southeast Asia, is a Vietnam veteran, and spent anywhere from an hour to a month at many Southeast Asian military bases. From his training and experiences in intelligence, special operations, and cryptology, he received other government assignments. He filled positions as Major Command Liaison, Headquarters Manager, and Department of Defense factory representative for Tactical Air Command, Strategic Air Command, Air Training Command, and Pacific Air Forces following the Vietnam war. He was assigned to many special secret development programs and classified "Black Programs" during his military-government career.

Later as a civilian Engineering Program Manager for defense contractors, Ed dealt with classified programs, developing state-of-the-art electronic countermeasures, avionics, cryptological, and satellite communications test equipment, and technical and logistics support. Ed is now retired from the defense industry.

Ed gives us an insider's view of Dreamland and numerous secret and classified military projects. As can be seen by Ed's background, this present work had to be written as "science-faction." Many of the episodes described in the novel are Ed's true-life adventures in disguise.

The book will be catnip for the UFO and conspiracy buffs. And while "The X-Files," "The Visitor," and all the others are dealing with fantasy and a few facts, *Alien Rapture* is presenting *many* facts with a little fiction to protect the guilty and shield the innocent.

—BRAD STEIGER

Chapter One

From Darkness Comes Light

He was floating face up, bobbing up and down with the ocean swells, staring at the dawn sky overhead. Suddenly he was aware of something with him in the water, something grabbing at his arm.

"Joe, wake up. Wake up!"

The ocean swells continued to swirl around him for one crazy, disorienting moment—and then he was squinting into dim light and slowly displacing an ocean with his bedroom curtains, the wallpaper, the nightstand, his bed, light blond hair, a woman.

"Cathy?"

"You must have been having another of those drowning dreams."

"I'm sorry." He shook his head, rubbed a cupped palm roughly over his stubbled, unshaven chin and moustache as if to restore circulation to his face. "I'm sorry I woke you up."

She crinkled her face into an exaggerated pout as she sat up and swung her legs over her side of the bed. "You were really threshing around, like you were going crazy. I was afraid you were going to hit me."

"I'm really sorry, babe."

Cathy nodded her forgiveness before she stood up and reached for her skirt draped over a nearby chair. It now was apparent that she was not going to spend the night.

"Where you going?" he mumbled as he swung his own long legs over the side of the bed. "It's after three."

"I really have to go, Joe. You know I have to get to work early tomorrow."

What Joe knew for certain was that another relationship was about to go down the crapper. It was these damn dreams. It was these goddam, half-assed memories that had separated him from any hope of a normal life and a sustained relationship with a woman.

"It's pretty late," he made an attempt at reconciliation. "Sure you're not too tired to drive back to your place? I could get up and make you a terrific breakfast. I'm sure I won't have another of those dreams again tonight."

"Joe, honey," she said over her shoulder as she pulled her sweater over her head. "I'm really sorry you had another drowning dream."

"Yeah, thanks." He recognized the sound of a kiss-off disguised as sympathy.

But he wasn't drowning in those damned weird dreams. Joe didn't really know what happened to him that day in the South China Sea. The best the experts could say was that he had experienced "rapture of the deep." Nitrogen narcosis. Down too deep, too long under the ocean waves.

After Cathy left him with a half-hearted peck on the lips and an even less enthusiastic invitation that they should get together for lunch sometime soon, he grabbed a beer from the refrigerator and turned on the bright light over the kitchen table. He knew that his hands were shaking. Hell, his whole body was shaking. He was glad that Cathy had gone. He would hate for anyone to find out how afraid he had become of the dark.

Dear Jesus! He stood a shade under six-foot-three, weighed in at a little over 210 pounds, was forty-three-years-old—and he was as afraid of the dark as when he was seven.

The cold beer felt good going down, but he would soon pour himself a shot of bourbon. He figured that he probably needed a shrink, but the liquid psychiatrist would have to do for the time being.

He had hoped that after he left the military he would somehow be able to squelch some of the insecurities that had pursued him most of his life. But his fear of the dark had reached the point where he insisted on working the night shift so he could sleep during the daylight hours. He felt unprotected, vulnerable, when he slept during the darkness.

He had moved to Tonopah, Nevada, in 1989 as an engineer for the Lorale Corporation. Work on the Aurora Program had, at first, been challenging, but the assignment had done nothing to quiet his night fears. EG&J managed the top secret Air Force ranges in Nevada, and its primary subcontractor, the Lorale Corporation maintained the massive amount of electronics and computer equipment. Joe had worked on the secret program to develop advanced aerospace vehicles since the first manned prototype flew in 1990.

When Joe started the program, he thought the task of replacing the aging but mystical Air Force SR-71 was the most exotic research program in the United States. But he never dreamed that his work would take him inside "Dreamland," Area 51 of the Nellis AFB Range at the Top Secret Groom Lake facilities.

He had received a promotion to Senior Engineer during the Flight, Operational Test, and Evaluation of the SR-75, but the bizarre rumors that filtered down to him from the Papoose Lake facilities had begun to distract him from full attention to his work. There was strange talk of UFOs, space vehicles, and alien technology being incorporated into advanced aerospace prototypes. He wanted to go there and investigate for himself, but he learned that he would need a clearance classification higher than the one he carried for Area 51.

But why should he care about such weird rumors? Why had he become increasingly obsessed with the notion that someone—perhaps an unknown group of scientists, a secret agency of the government, or a select number of ordinary people—had made contact with alien intelligence?

He splashed a generous shot into a drinking glass, tilted his head back to enjoy the burn in his throat that would eventually bring him some calm. As he raised his chin and clamped his lips to the rim of the glass, the bright light from the ceiling fixture hurt his eyes.

"The light," he whispered in a flash of revelation. "The goddam light still wants me."

He sat back down in the kitchen chair, puzzled by his own declaration, and thought about his dream, the "drowning dream" in which he did not drown.

The dream scenario always recalled his last mission for the National Security Agency in Asia when he was on assignment for the Tactical

Reconnaissance Engineering Assessment Team (TREAT) in Southeast Asia. A division of the National Security Agency TREAT was unknown outside of certain top echelon circles in the NSA and was essentially part of the special operations network that utilized selected personnel with diverse talents. Joe had been chosen because he was an intelligence and communications officer in the Air Force, a degreed electronics engineer, and the holder of a commercial diving license.

A Russian trawler—a notoriously known cover for Soviet communications monitoring devices—had mysteriously disappeared in a storm. The NSA's satellites had locked on to the ship's distress signal and tracked it from above until the storm cracked her hull and sent her to the depths of the East China Sea where it settled just south of the Gulf of Tonkin. The Russians had a dozen ships searching for the trawler for weeks until they gave up without achieving any success.

The National Security Agency knew that the searchers had been a good twenty kilometers from the sunken vessel, and they saw it as an opportunity to recover the Soviet crypto devices, code books, and logs. As a result, the TREAT team divers were assembled, briefed, and outfitted at the NSA's Special Operations Compound outside Washington, D.C., in eastern Virginia.

Joe had been pulled into the National Security Agency years before when he worked at the Sandia National Laboratories in Los Alamos, New Mexico. He had been the Communications Security Officer on a secret nuclear detection satellite designed by TRW and MITRE and built by Hughes for the NSA. From then on, he was called upon a number of times to assist in NSA Special Operations in Southeast Asia. When he was approached for the last time in early 1975, he was contemplating getting out of the Air Force.

On his final NSA operations assignment, the TREAT team was using a forty-foot sailboat registered under the French Maritime Commission. They were posing as oceanographers who were testing the waters of Vietnam's Gulf of Tonkin for toxic chemicals and oceanographic information. The team had embarked from the Philippines, specifically Subic Bay, a western inlet of the South China Sea, west of Manila Bay in central Luzon. Subic Bay was the home of a large U.S. naval base established in 1901 that had been very popular with the GIs for its cheap young whores until it was closed in 1993.

They were positioned just outside the maritime boundary for North Vietnam, awaiting the forecasted weather disturbance that was needed as a cover for their mission. Three divers—Joe would be one—were to place transponder marker beacons near enough to the downed Russian trawler so a deep submersible Navy vehicle could go in and search the vessel for classified equipment, code manuals, and anything else of interest to national security.

The marine biologist assigned to the team, Boris Cherkov, a White Russian immigrant from the Ukraine, had been borrowed from Okinawa's Foreign Broadcast Intelligence Service. The TREAT team found that it took them only a few hours before they were calling him "Boris Jerk-Off" behind his back. To say that he was obnoxious was an understatement, but he was the Russian linguist and an expert on local marine biology, so he would have to be tolerated.

Joe had read the briefing jacket on each of the team members provided by his NSA contact and knew that each man was more than qualified for the job. Diving with him would be his old buddy Mike Crawfoot, an Army Special Forces operative assigned to the Defense Intelligence Agency (DIA), and Owen McKean, who was CIA.

As far as Joe was concerned, the CIA was an agency full of giant egos run amok. He had first heard of McKean when he was assigned to the U.S. military's Military Assistance Command-Vietnam Special Operations Group (MAC-VSOG), and he hadn't heard anything good. Joe had been the liaison for the NSA on a couple of operations with the CIA in Laos and Cambodia, mostly planting and monitoring covert listening devices and other intelligence gathering operations.

On the other hand, he was pleased to see that Mike was on the team. They had a special bond, one that had been formed a few years before in South Vietnam. Joe had been on a sensor drop across the western border into Laos near the Ho Chi Minh Trail when his helicopter picked up a distress from a ground position on the way back to Da Nang. His Warrant Officer hadn't wanted to turn around, but Joe pulled rank. They flew into heavy ground fire to pick up a wounded Special Forces Sergeant, the sole survivor of his reconnaissance team, and needless to say, Mike, a fellow Texan, remained eternally grateful for the lift.

Joe, Mike, and Owen had carefully discussed their mission. The sunken trawler lay in North Vietnam international waters, just north of the DMZ. The three of them would dive toward the coordinates provided and would each activate a portable transponder at the appropriate time. The Russians used a satellite transponder system that identified itself with the proper codes each time it transmitted and received satellite information. The United States, thanks to the code breakers at NSA, knew all of the USSR codes.

The Soviet transponder was a sealed system, impervious to water and containing a back-up battery unit. Technicians at NSA had determined that the transponder's reply underwater would be greatly attenuated and carry only a short distance. The advantage to the TREAT divers was that there would be no surface emissions from the transponder transmission for Russian satellites or surface vessels to pick up. The disadvantage was that one of the men would have to be almost on top of the downed vessel in order to receive a response. The divers agreed that this problem was minimized by their own satellite tracking information being accurate as hell and the supercomputers having simulated the current drift of the mass and specific gravity of the sunken vessel.

It was quickly turning dark and everyone on board was busy with some activity or another which contributed to the quickly approaching deadline.

Suddenly Boris Cherkov snapped an order, taking the divers off guard. "Okay, men, let's do it by the book. Strip!"

Joe could see that McKean greatly resented the dictatorial attitude that Boris had unexpectedly assumed.

"You will wear nothing except the equipment provided," Boris told them.

"You mean I can't wear my custom made snorkel and flippers," Crawfoot sneered. It was obvious he was a man unimpressed by ostentatious authority figures.

Boris wisely ignored the slur as each diver inspected his equipment for damage and efficient working order.

"Booties and pants only," Boris instructed, as if he were dealing with first-time divers.

The men complied, passively allowing the man to check the fitting of their dive booties and pants.

"McKean, your leg zippers are not supposed to be exposed!" Boris snapped officiously.

McKean's temper had risen to very near its boiling point. "Look, Cherkov, I was a Navy fucking Seal," he growled, sticking out his chin defiantly. "I've made a thousand goddam dives. I don't need a trainer or an nursemaid. Got it?"

Boris stepped forward and glared up at McKean. Although he was much shorter and only came up to McKean's angrily twitching mustache, he seemed not at all intimidated by the larger, younger man.

"This is my mission," he began in a quiet, calm voice. "I have selected the equipment carefully—for sturdiness, function, and fit. I have taken extreme measures to ensure that each piece is the best available commercial gear so that it can't be traced if any of you screw up and get yourselves compromised."

The Russian paused, contentedly watching McKean turn a unique shade of red, then continued. "I am the leading marine biologist in the NSA, and I was a master deep sea diver in the Russian Navy before you, sir, were born. I can still out swim, out dive, and out think any of you in the water. Mister, do you have any doubt who is in charge here?"

Joe saw that McKean's jaw muscles were bunched so tight that he couldn't get the words to flow during his first attempt to answer Cherkov. Something muffled came out, but then he carefully and slowly projected his response. "You're in charge, Cherkov. I will follow your orders. But that doesn't mean that I have to like your bullshit!"

McKean undid his calf zippers, rolled down his booties, then redid them so the tops were on the outside.

Boris, ever the martinet, did not miss a beat. "These gloves go on the inside of your wrist zippers. Put them on next."

Crawfoot winked at Joe. They were both thorough professionals, neither of them interested in raining on Cherkov's little parade. They understood McKean's objection, but didn't consider his bitch worth making an issue. They were there to do a job. Why make it any harder than it had to be?

The divers complied with the Russian's orders and within minutes they had each pulled on their wet suit jacket, the hood, leg knife, dive watch, weight belt, lights, wrist compass, and depth gauge.

Boris approved with a broad smile of satisfaction. "Your air tanks are dual eighties and are integrated into your buoyancy compensators," he said, turning on each tank in order to check the regulators and total pressure. He explained again how the transponder slash marker beacon worked. He was definitely redundant, but he was thorough and knowledgeable.

McKean, Crawfoot, and Joe sat on the edge of the port side ready to enter the water on command. Boris watched for the navigator's hand signal and looked at his watch. When the navigator held up three fingers, Joe, the first diver, would enter the water in three minutes. The mission timing called for each diver to enter the water at five-minute intervals, which would place them about a mile apart on their westward journey.

Joe sat silently, preparing for the dive by doing deep breathing exercises. Every special operations or intelligence operative had his own method of handling stress at the beginning of a mission.

The navigator held up three fingers.

"Joe, put on your mask," Boris said.

Joe continued doing his deep breathing. It seemed as though a great deal of time passed before Boris put an arm on his shoulder and yelled into his ear: "One minute!"

While he watched his chronometer, Boris counted off the seconds. "Twenty...fifteen...ten...Go!"

Joe rolled gently backward into the water.

The darkness of the ocean at night can be horrifying for anyone who is even the slightest bit prone to symptoms of claustrophobia or nyctophobia. Joe felt the bubbles rise above his face as he slowly descended into the water. The wave motion was moderate, and he could feel his weight move gently up and down in slow cycles. Once he was down below thirty or forty feet, the motion let up a bit.

At first he didn't turn on his lights. Instead, he checked the luminosity of his gauges, which had to be directly in front of his mask in order for him to read them.

When he switched on each of his lights in turn, it had the same effect that he would experience if he turned on his automobile headlights in an extremely dense fog. The lights illuminated the water for about thirty feet.

Most divers Joe knew had to have the lights on for reassurance. At the fringes of visibility, he could see thousands of tiny reflections from marine life that appeared to be a myriad of star-like eyes watching him. But if he turned the light off, he wouldn't be able to see the end of his finger—even if he were to poke himself in the eyes trying.

Joe reached his coordinates and activated the transponder.

Nothing.

He reset the unit and waited two minutes.

Still nothing.

Joe swam a hundred yard square, trying the transponder at each position. At the last position, which, theoretically, was supposed to be near his first, he tried the unit one last time. The response light lit up and began to flash bright white at even intervals.

He checked the number of flashes against his dive watch, counted them for one minute, then repeated the count twice more. The number would tell approximately how deep the sunken Russian trawler lay beneath the surface.

He disconnected the tether from the transponder/marker beacon and prepared to drop it into the dark depths below him.

But something was wrong. It suddenly struck him that the light was supposed to be flashing red. He was seeing white.

He turned off the unit and looked at it with his dive light. The lens over the bulb was indeed bright red.

He switched the unit back on and once again saw a white light.

"What the hell?"

How could it be white? Was he confused by something obvious? The plastic was red, so the light coming through the red lens cover should also be red. Only impaired visual acuity or something in the water could cause a change in colors.

Joe switched off his dive light and pressed the illuminator on his watch. The little red light clearly appeared red. The effect was not being caused by something in the water.

But how could a red light appear white to his photoreceptors?

Slowly he covered the light with his right hand. His stomach knotted up. He could still clearly see the white light.

He shut his eyes, and the light went away. When he opened them, he hoped the effect would be different.

It wasn't. He could still see the white light on the box that was covered by his hand.

"The hell with it," he said to himself. Then he dropped the box.

Within a second the box disappeared into the darkness of the sea.

But the light was still there beside him.

"I'm hallucinating," Joe decided. His breathing rate accelerated. As he had been thoroughly trained to do, he automatically increased the positive pressure on his buoyancy compensator. With the added inflation, he should slowly be floating toward the surface—but his depth gauge indicated that he was going down.

The light flashed about two feet in front of his face. He turned away and kicked his flippers violently in rapid succession.

The light casually floated by him and stayed two or three feet in front of him.

Joe unhooked his weight belt, dropped it, and repeated the evasive maneuver in several directions.

Nothing changed. He was still sinking deeper into the ocean and the damn light—whatever the hell it was—was relentlessly tracking him, following him.

He pulled one of two emergency cords on his buoyancy compensator and heard the CO_2 cartridge discharge with a swooshing sound. He should now be rapidly rising to the surface.

He wasn't.

With the wet suit on and a fully inflated buoyancy compensator, he should be floating up on the surface. Without the weight belt, he couldn't possibly be sinking.

But he was.

"I'm either crazy or hallucinating, but how the hell can I tell which it is?" he asked himself in near-panic.

His depth gauge was calibrated to a negative two hundred feet, and all of his gauges would function down to at least a negative five hundred feet. His gauge read one hundred feet.

Why was he sinking?

He was completely winded from the energy that he had wasted attempting to escape from the light.

"I'm a dead son of a bitch," he thought as his depth approached two hundred feet.

While he was being drawn down, deeper and deeper, Joe tried to remain calm. He had tried all of his options, and he could only wait to see if he was in some kind of mental state that had somehow totally disoriented him.

Perhaps he really was rising. Or better yet, maybe he was floating on the surface in the darkness. He just had to wait until his mind cleared.

Joe knew that nitrogen narcosis was a state of stupor or confusion resulting from increased levels of soluble nitrogen in the blood stream, brought on by a diver being too deep for too long a period. Or not so deep for really long periods of time. If his depth gauge was defective and he had gone a lot deeper than he thought while getting his target coordinates, then he might be experiencing the rapture of the deep, nitrogen narcosis.

Joe checked his air gauge. He had less than one quarter of his available air supply remaining. His air would be used up long before his lights ran out of juice. That was not a comforting thought.

He switched off his dive light and could see nothing but the little white star shining in the blackness of the ocean. He noticed that the light appeared to be of the same brightness no matter if he had his dive light on or off.

Some unseen force pulled him deeper and deeper as the minutes of air remaining slowly flowed out of his tanks. Far off in the depths below him, Joe thought that he could make out another much larger light.

He shut his eyes for a moment, and when he opened them, it seemed as if the far-off light was becoming brighter, and the little twinkle light was growing dimmer. Or was it moving farther away from him?

Joe knew that he was just along for the ride—whether the lights were real or imagined, whether he was experiencing euphoria, confusion, hallucination, or stroke.

The smaller light appeared to be drawn toward the larger illumination at an ever-increasing speed. It flashed momentarily as it seemed to merge with the more distant and much brighter light.

Joe finally panicked and began violently to kick his flippers and flail his arms. It was his last desperate effort to go anywhere but down.

But the pain and fatigue were more profound than anything he had ever experienced. The physical misery was nonspecific. Every part of his body hurt.

As he spent his energy, his legs and feet were cramping horribly. His movements slowed, becoming exaggerated and uncoordinated. Then the air bubbles stopped.

Joe had a flash of clear thought: I am either dead or soon to be dead.

His muscles started jerking in involuntary tremors.

A ringing began in his ears.

If he had any orientation left, it would soon be completely gone. He couldn't tell if he were falling or rising, and his vision was blurred to the point where he couldn't read his gauges. The ringing in his ears had become a slow, gentle, low-frequency beat.

The light flared brilliantly, filling all of the water around him with incredible brightness. Then it engulfed him.

Please, God, let me wake up from this nightmare!

Little celestial beings floated around him. They had large childlike heads and eyes and small bodies, and they displayed great interest in him.

Three-dimensional reality blurred into an abstract interpretation of what was—and for just the very thinnest slice of linear time, Joe saw the light and knew it for what it was. Then he succumbed to the irresistible pull of the moment and gave himself up to an ultimate sense of peace.

At the predetermined time, the forty-foot sailboat cruised past the pickup coordinates, but Joe Green wasn't anywhere to be seen. It would be daylight soon, and Boris Cherkov would have to decide whether or not to keep searching for the missing diver and to take the risk of being discovered. McKean and Crawfoot had completed their mission and had been recovered on schedule, but there was no sign of Green.

As the sun rose in the east toward Japan, Cherkov decided to pull out and depart. At the moment that he was about to give the orders to turn around and head back to Subic Bay, Crawfoot spotted something in the water. It was Joe, floating face up, unconscious, bobbing up and down with the ocean swells.

Crawfoot was in the water immediately, swimming toward his team member. Joe regained consciousness just moments before Crawfoot grabbed his arm and began to pull him toward the boat.

"Rapture," Joe said as he gasped for air. "I'm going to rapture!"

"You're all right, buddy," Crawfoot told him. "I've got you."

The Navy doctors diagnosed Joe's strange experience as an unexplained blackout, something akin to rapture of the deep. Whatever had happened to Joe Green, he had somehow survived the ordeal.

Boris Cherkov couldn't understand how Joe had suddenly appeared just as they were about to leave. For hours there had been no sign of him—then, presto, there he was floating on the water.

How could Joe Green have been somewhere down in the deep for hours and hours after his air tanks had to have been thoroughly emptied?

But what had really bothered Cherkov was the fact that Joe's air tanks were still full and his transponder was missing.

Dawn was streaking the skies over Tonopah, Nevada. Joe had lost count of the shots of bourbon that he had sloshed into the drinking glass.

Two weeks previously, Joe had taken a sabbatical from Lorale and the Aurora Program at the Groom facilities. In the 1950s, the government had built the super secret Groom Lake facilities in the north central part of the Nellis Range and designated it Area 51. Insiders referred to the Groom facilities as the "Ranch" and "Watertown," and curious outsiders circulated rumors about aliens and extraterrestrial technology that had been utilized to accelerate the various programs at Area 51.

The Top Secret SR-75 had far exceeded the classified military speed and altitude records set by the old SR-71. Lockheed's Advanced Developmental Projects Division, known as the "Skunk Works," had developed the A-12 or SR-71 for the CIA in the early sixties. For the last few years, high-tech buffs speculated that at least one new and exotic aerospace vehicle existed.

One of the Aurora vehicles, the SR-75, had gone operational after two years of flight testing and modifications. The SR-75 attained altitudes of over 120,000 feet and speeds exceeding Mach 8, or 5000 miles per hour. From take-off to landing, the stealthy 75 could make the round trip to Northeast Russia and back in under three hours.

The explosive Pulsed Detonation Wave Engines that pushed the huge SR-75 greatly awed Joe. He had watched the first flight of the big black Air Force SR-75 carrying the little unmanned SR-74 piggy-back on its upper raised platform. The small 74, called "the Scramp" because of its exotic scramjet engines, couldn't take off from the ground. It could only launch from the SR-75 mother ship at an altitude above 100,000 feet, and then it could attain orbital altitudes. The Air Force used the Scramp to launch small, highly classified, ferret satellites for the National Security Agency. The NASA Space Shuttle was an antique by comparison. Joe found little humor in this, knowing that the joke was on the U.S. taxpayers.

Joe sprawled out on the couch, feeling the effects of lack of sleep and too much booze. He wrapped a Navajo blanket around him as if it might protect him from the unseen demons that beset his psyche.

"Dear God," he prayed silently, "please do something to lift those awful dreams from my memory."

One day Joe's prayer would be answered, but not before the blight of his chaotic memory and fevered dreams had evolved into a terrible waking nightmare that was only now about to begin.

Chapter Two

Majestic Twelve

"Damn fools," Eli Jerrold said contemptuously as he looked out of his Washington, D.C., office window at the crowd of demonstrators that had assembled on the mall near the Capitol. "End UFO Secrecy! Stop the Cover-up! ET is Here!" he read aloud from the placards and banners of the chanting multitude.

Jerrold, an exceedingly wealthy attorney, a former Director of the National Security Agency, shifted his weight in the large, over-stuffed leather executive chair that gave him a clear view of the protesters. "If those simple-minded sheep only knew that they were asking," he sighed.

The demonstrators moved as a single entity, surging and waning in unison. The men and women seemed almost to be in a festive mood as they chanted anti-government clichés about conspiracies and cover-ups. Here and there, people dropped out at random, yielding to the stifling humidity of the late summer heat wave.

Page St. John, once an Episcopal priest in a wealthy suburb of St. Paul, was now head of the Church of the Celestial Prophet. It was he who had organized the march to demand a release of all UFO secrets allegedly held in the government's hidden vaults. He had shouted his demands through the Sony megaphone until he had grown hoarse.

General James Van Grouse, U.S. Air Force, retired, entered Jerrold's office with his usual exaggerated air of urgency. "Aren't those weirdos becoming a bit troublesome, Eli? Perhaps we should encourage the police to disband them."

Jerrold shifted once again in the overstuffed chair, trying his utmost to find a comfortable position. He preferred an orthopedic chair—and his arthritic back agreed.

"It's the Labor Day weekend, Jimmy," Jerrold snorted derisively. "It's customary for the freaks and fanatics to assemble to shout their protests at this time of year."

Van Grouse sniffed and clucked his tongue. "I suppose so. But..."

"Quiet, please, Jimmy," Jerrold hushed the man. "I want to hear what that bastard St. John is babbling about now."

Page St. John, his voice rasping and dry, had lost none of his mesmerizing power over his followers. The loudspeakers carried his message over the assembled masses and into Jerrold's office.

"Blessed is he that heareth and heedeth the prophecy of St. John. Know that the time has come to take on the cloak of the one true faith. I am Alpha and Omega, the beginning and the ending, sayeth the Lord, which is and which was and which is yet to come.

"Since the dawn of humankind, you have been endowed by God with power and strength and greatness of spirit. You, whose ancestors were the very prop of civilization, must suffer the indignity of having your elected leaders erect a barrier against the progress of the faithful. Your very own elected leaders are withholding from you the truth about the strangers in our skies, the UFOnauts who have visited our planet since the beginning. I call upon you to rise up against these tyrants, who blaspheme against the Most High and who suppress knowledge from today's prophets. Take charge of your own destiny!"

Jerrold's practiced eye scanned the crowd milling around St. John's speaker's platform. Basically, the man attracted a mixture of UFO buffs, New Agers, new-wave religious types, the usual curious shoppers at the latest spiritual supermarket, and government conspiracy addicts—with a few stray Trekies and the disenfranchised thrown in for good measure. The New Age prophet's rap was a curious blend of Asian and Christian religions, combined with a little divine mysticism, seasoned with a heavy dose of UFOlogy. In Jerrold's opinion, the man was dangerous.

"...band together for strength in unity," St. John was rambling on. "In Revelation it is foretold that the time is at hand for the 144,000 faithful to rise up and to embrace the Rapture, for the end of civilization is at hand. Behold, He will come from the clouds. Every eye shall see Him and all kindreds of the Earth shall wail because of his wrath. The seventh seal will be opened in the year 2000, and the Four Horsemen—War, Revolution, Famine, and Pestilence—shall rule the Earth. This fast-approaching Apocalypse will cleanse the evil from humankind forever, and it shall be called God's wrath."

Since the cold war had thawed, the liberal press, the electronic media, and the film industry had fought with frenzy to be the first to release classified information, confirmed or not. Eli missed the USSR as much as he missed booze in his diet. He often lamented the days when U.S. operatives could blame everything on the Reds and the public would believe their lies.

In the last six months of 1994 a disturbing trend had developed. Eli monitored with apprehension the number of popular and respected news organizations that addressed the subject of government spending on secret black programs. Ten years ago no one would dare to print or to acknowledge publicly such secret agencies as the NSA, the NRO, or—God forbid—the MJ committee. To make matters even worse, the UFO controversy had been resurrected with a vengeance and tied in with some deep, dark government conspiracy. Now the UFO believers group and Page St. John's Church of the Celestial Prophet were attracting the New Agers, the normal run of weirdos, and, surprisingly, a large following of average, middle-class people. The Church had even hired a Washington lobbyist.

It was becoming a nightmare, Eli groused. How much closer to the truth would these fanatical troublemakers get?

Eli didn't have a lot of use for religion in general. Cults tended to depart from conventional norms of society, and in his view, that was a form of anarchy. Even though he knew most cults were transient movements that tended to proliferate during periods of social unrest, the recent rise in militant antigovernment groups disturbed him greatly. If he had his way, he would put all the Sun Myung Moons, the Jim Joneses, the David Koreshes in prison cells and throw away the keys. Violent conflicts with the law were a by-product of a cult's insularity and distrust of society and its government. St. John's Church had had a phenomenally rapid growth in a short period of time, due, in large part, to the chaos of contemporary culture and its lack of strong leadership.

Admiral Michael Sullivan, for many years Director of the C.I.A., had entered Jerrold's private office and was peering out the window with a bemused grin on his face. "Shit! It looks like every UFO buff, anti-government anarchist, shaved-head Aryan, and fucking weirdo in the US of A is outside. Eli, I don't know why we tolerate this shit. These people are an impediment and an irritant to our course of action."

"Why, Michael," Jerrold scolded in mock exaggeration, "they have a right to express themselves according to the First Amendment."

"First Amendment, my ass!" Admiral Sullivan roared. "Those dumb shits out there don't realize that the world as they know it would cease to exist if they got what they wanted. If it weren't for patriotic watchdogs like us, St. John's ass would be cosmic grass!"

Elden B. Neal, once chief assistant to the director of the F.B.I., had joined them. "I sometimes fantasize about what would happen to the general public if we told them the whole truth about UFOs. Just how would Joe Lunchpail and Betty Stationwagon really handle it?"

Jerrold nodded toward Page St. John. "There's your answer, Neal. Apocalypse, revolution, famine, and pestilence would descend upon us and all of the bulwarks of our once great civilization would collapse around us."

"And the Page St. Johns of the world," Admiral Sullivan laughed. "What of his God, his Judgment Day, if we released all the files he screams about? What, indeed, would become of organized religions, the Pope, the Vatican? If that fool out there only knew the truth, he would be thanking his God that we are running interference for him."

Cover-ups and conspiracies were the ways of governments, religions, and powerful people, Eli Jerrold thought. He knew that the Vatican had, since its very inception, kept ancient artifacts and writings hidden in their vast underground cellars, prohibiting the outside world access to them. These controversial treasures of religious import were suppressed by the Vatican because they would damage the Church's credibility and cast doubt over their official doctrines and scriptures.

Eli often wondered if the faithful really wanted to know the truth about the origins of their beliefs. It was doubtful, he had decided. He felt the same way about the Program.

Eli spoke to no one in particular when he quoted a passage from his nearly photographic memory: "And I saw a new heaven and a new earth, for the first heaven and the first earth were passed away."

Admiral Sullivan failed to suppress a smile as he inquired if Jerrold had been listening to Page St. John a bit too much.

Jerrold returned the smile, then replied. "It's from the other St. John. The one who wrote the last book in the Bible. It's Revelation 21:1."

St. John's apocalyptic vision was Jerrold's worst nightmare. He was seventy-two, a reformed alcoholic, arthritic, balding, and overweight. His doctor thought he was a hypochondriac with more complaints than Abbie Hoffman.

He looked again at the mall across from the Capitol and observed the crowd of thousands. It was unlikely that even one individual in that teeming mass of men and women protesting a government cover-up of UFOs knew who the hell he was. Not a single one of them knew that it had been his responsibility as Director of the National Security Agency to keep the lid on the subject of UFOs. He had been with the NSA since its founding by Executive Order of President Harry S.Truman on November 4, 1952.

Many years before he had gone with the NSA he had been a bright and enterprising young captain with the forces of occupation in Germany. He had been at Peenemuende at the close of the war, a twenty-one-year-old engineer assigned to the War Department Intelligence group who had breached the super-secret German research center.

He had entered the rocket base with the U.S. Army's infantry, looking for evidence of the mysterious "foo fighters" and other exotic aerospace vehicles that had plagued Allied aviators during the closing days of World War II. He discovered numerous plans having to do with the construction of rockets, but nothing that dealt with the eerie aerial fire balls. His subsequent interrogations and debriefings of German, Japanese, and Allied military men confirmed his suspicions that the mystery objects had not been manmade.

Just before a former Nazi general died an unfortunate death by suicide in January of 1946, he revealed the secret location of a cache of gold bullion to Captain Jerrold. Always one to heed his own counsel, the young captain decided that the Nazi gold should remain a secret from his commanding officers, and it wasn't long before discreet investments had made him an extremely wealthy man. Now, fifty years later, Eli Jerrold was one of the wealthiest men in North America.

Until the end of the Cold War, NSA and its inner workings had been the best kept secret in the government. It was the premier intelligence agency in the world, and yet the average citizen had no idea that it was larger than the F.B.I. and the C.I.A. combined in personnel, resources, budget, and, most of all, power.

There were those who thought that Eli Jerrold should have retired or been forced to retire in the late 1960s, but, damn it, he outlived or destroyed his opponents and kept his power until he was ready to leave active service in 1985.

General J.A. Stewart, once Chairman of the Joint Chiefs of Staff, and Chief Justice Artemus S. Artabrae arrived at the same time. Now the six members of the top secret group MJ-12 who had been available for an emergency meeting were all present in Jerrold's office.

"Sorry I'm late, gentlemen," General Stewart apologized, pausing to wipe the sweat from his forehead and cheeks. "I had to wade through that mob of nuts out there. If I had my way, I would call out the National Guard and run those freaks off with fire hoses and tear gas."

Chief Justice Artabrae agreed. "I think the Capitol police force on duty was far too few in number to maintain proper order. I think the Guard should have been called. I also think this Page St. John character has been allowed to rant and rave for far too long."

Elden Neal told General Stewart and Chief Justice Artabrae that the former Director of National Security, Eli Jerrold, had just reminded them that Page St. John and his followers had a right to express themselves according to the First Amendment.

Jerrold allowed a few moments of laughter at his satirical jest, then raised a hand for silence. He indicated that his fellow committee members should take a seat around the comfortable round table that had been equipped with bottled water, cigars, and small sandwiches.

The fate of human civilization rested in the hands of these powerful men, members of the MJ-12 Committee, who sat at the table. Eli looked at the red-jacketed folder lying in front of him. He knew its contents by heart, for he had been its primary author while in the position of Director of the National Security Agency (DIRN-SA)."I know that you must all be wondering why I called an emergency meeting of all available committee members," Eli Jerrold acknowledged. "It surely was not so that we might gather and observe the protesters demanding the release of additional government documents and listen to another sermonette by our favorite fanatic, Page St. John."

The five men before him chuckled politely, but it was easily apparent that they wished him to cut to the chase.

"Gentlemen, NBC and *Newsweek* are both releasing classified information on the Aurora project."

Neal, at age fifty-seven the youngest member of the MJ-12 committee—whose average age was seventy—raised his voice above the chorus of mumbled curses and gasps. "How much do they know?"

Jerrold glanced at his watch. "We'll know in about twelve minutes. NBC is featuring the project on their popular series, 'Exploring the Unknown.' "

Neal shrugged. "So what? *Popular Science* already brought our newest 'secret' reconnaissance aircraft out of the black and revealed that it was developed at the Air Force test facility at Groom Lake, Nevada."

Jerrold admitted that this was so. "But NBC, *Newsweek,* and other network programs and newsstand publications are going to attempt to document our using alien technology to build our Mach 6 spy plane and a number of other black projects still undeveloped."

Neal buried his head in his hands. His nine-hundred-dollar hand-tailored suit could not hide his discomfort."Oh, shit, shit. This is not good. What do we do?"

Jerrold shook his head. "I've already talked to the senior vice-president of NBC, who refuses to pull the segment. Says only the president of the network can make that decision, and he is off fishing somewhere in the Caribbean."

Admiral Sullivan wanted to know how NBC and *Newsweek* got their information.

"We are certain that it originated from an independent reporter named Blake Webster, who put the story together with the help of a number of informants."

Director Neal was certain that he had heard that name before.

Jerrold allowed that he probably had. "We've known about Webster's activities for about six years, but he appeared to be just another crackpot that nobody paid very much attention to—except the UFO buffs. He's worked for half a dozen small-town newspapers, done independent material for the wire services, worked for a few defense contractors as a technical writer. He's been working out of the Las Vegas area for the last year or so."

"So how did this asshole get the goods on alien technology?" General Van Grouse asked, his left hand nervously rubbing the bald spot on the back of his head.

"Apparently some insiders talked...or he has a damn good spy network of his own," Jerrold said.

Chief Justice Artabrae was very pale, and his hand was shaking as he poured some water into a glass. "Eli, shouldn't we bring the President in on this? I mean, President Truman set up the original MJ-12 committee in September of 1947, right after the alien bodies were recovered from Roswell, New Mexico."

Jerrold shut off the Chief Justice's argument. "We do not bring the President into any of this. You know I have been vehemently opposed to our keeping any President informed about our secret alien involvement since we made the mistake of letting Truman in on this in the first place."

General Stewart raised what he thought was a legitimate point of order. "We really did need Truman at the beginning to put the official imprimatur on things."

Jerrold shrugged. "Possibly. But you know that I argued against his involvement even then. And I was proven correct in my fears when in order to smooth General MacArthur's ruffled feathers over being relieved of command in Korea, Truman confided in him and informed him of the greater threat from another world. Then what did that doddering old soldier do but blab to the *New York Times* that Earth must begin preparing for a war of the worlds?"

General Van Grouse agreed with Jerrold. "That was how far MacArthur could be trusted to keep a secret. He actually went around warning people that we were about to be invaded by beings from other planets. In 1962 when he addressed the graduating class at West Point and advised them to prepare to deal with the sinister forces of some other planetary galaxy, I thought for certain that MJ-12 would be exposed."

Jerrold winced at the memory. "That's why I insisted that we cut off all MJ-12 intelligence to the President after we made the horrendous mistake of bringing Eisenhower to inspect the alien craft at Muroc Dry Lake in April of 1954. Too many personnel at Edwards Air Force Base got a glimpse of the space vehicles and the alien crews. We had to plug too many leaks after Eisenhower got his mind blown. That Kansas boy may have seen Paris, but he could never really deal with having seen alien technology for himself."

General Stewart clicked the stem of his pipe against his bottom teeth in a brief moment of reflection. "Yes, from that time on, MJ-12 no longer existed as far as the President of the United States was concerned. We went deep underground and officially became a footnote in history. We gave the UFO nuts and the curious the Air Force's Project Bluebook to keep them quiet."

Chief Justice Artabrae was still not completely satisfied. "Jimmy Carter saw a UFO for himself. The UFO groups leaned heavily on him to launch an investigation into alleged government cover-ups."

Director Neal chuckled. "Yes, but he had the good sense not to push the matter once he was in office. Besides, the hostage situation in Iran gave him more than enough to keep him busy."

The Chief Justice shifted uncomfortably, then decided to speak up with another argument. "What about Ronald Reagan? He knew. I know he knew. Who told him?"

Jerrold stood his ground. "Reagan only thought he knew."

Chief Justice Artabrae was still not finished. "Reagan must have known when he spoke to Gorbachev about the threat to our planet from another species in the universe."

Jerrold was growing impatient. "Reagan was speaking hypothetically to the Soviet leader. He said that their job as peacemakers would be easier if Earth suddenly were threatened by an invasion from outer space. He said that humans would forget their petty differences if attacked by a common foe from another world. Believe me, Ronald Reagan had no actual facts about the alien technological tradeoff or MJ-12."

General Stewart growled contemptuously. "If only it was as fucking easy as Reagan thought! We would only create mass panic if we announced to the general public that the aliens are not just among us now, but that they have always been with us!"

"What of Reagan's remarks in September of 1987 to the entire United Nations General Assembly that 'an alien threat' was among us?" Chief Justice Artabrae persisted. "Who leaked that little tidbit to him?"

Jerrold's face was getting red with controlled anger. "The man was imaginative, but he was not informed of the workings of this committee. Nor will our present leader learn of our activities."

Elden Neal wondered how, then, if the material telecast that night should prove to be embarrassing, would the various committee members cover their asses when the President or a Senate investigating committee wanted to know what in hell was going on?

"We handle it like we always do," Jerrold said. "We simply lie and blame it on a scapegoat we can easily discredit. This plan has worked since Roswell, so why change?"

"But there's never been this much information flying around in the media before," Neal pointed out. "We have fifty or more cable channels and the Internet flooding the average American family of 2.5 television sets and 1.2 computers with an endless array of speculative crap on UFOs, government conspiracies, and aliens."

Admiral Sullivan stood and began to open the wall panel that contained six television monitors. "It's time," he said as he switched on one of the sets.

NBC's "Exploring the Unknown" opened with a history of the UFO phenomena around the world. Acknowledging that most so-called "flying saucers" were found to be misinterpretations of natural phenomena, top secret military prototype projects, or simple misidentifications, the program then focused on a number of cases in which the sightings of unidentified aerial vehicles could not be so easily explained away. The third segment of the program featured interviews with former Air Force and commercial pilots who had close encounters with UFOs, followed by a physicist—whose face was darkened and his voice altered—who claimed to have seen space ships while working in Area 51 of the Nellis Range. The teaser for the final segment announced that Blake Webster, an independent investigator, had provided "Exploring the Unknown" with astonishing video footage of a UFO and a top secret Air Force vehicle.

"Video footage of a UFO?" General Van Grouse echoed. "What in hell is he talking about, Eli?"

"Here's where we get clobbered," Director Elden Neal said, referring to the upcoming segment. "If they can produce as advertised. If not, it's all bullshit, and not to worry."

"It has to be bullshit," Jerrold said with full confidence. "But I wonder what they'll use to try to snow the gullible public?"

After what seemed to the MJ-12 committee members to be a small eternity of commercials, the segment opened with a pan of the desert, mountains silhouetted in the background, slowly sinking into dusk. Out of the dying embers of the sun, a dark shadow suddenly appeared above the horizon, approaching in a blur from the west and turning, without banking or braking, making a massive G turn to the north. Then it came to a sudden stop and hung in the air above the desert, motionless.

The zoom on the camera enlarged the flat black craft so it appeared cigar-shaped from the side, then slowly rotated counterclockwise. The viewer could tell that the vehicle was triangular, shaped almost like a huge black Vicks cough drop.

The narrator explained the evolution of stealth aircraft and spoke of the exotic materials used in such vehicles. He told of the Hillary platform, the Avro saucer, the Northrup wings, the SR-71 and 75, the Lockheed Skunk Works, and finally the F-117 stealth fighter and the B-2 stealth bomber. He discussed what was required in reconnaissance aircraft, the remarkable materials used in such types of vehicles.

An explanation of radar and low observable stealth technology followed. The black triangle twinkled with red and green lights along its three leading edges, and the low-profile canopy became clearly reflective in a gleam of silver-blue.

"What you are witnessing," the narrator continued, "is a nuclear-powered prototype aerospace vehicle with indefinite loiter time. The TR-3B is a high-altitude stealth reconnaissance platform developed by the top secret Aurora Program. The Aurora is the most classified aerospace development program in existence, and it is funded and operationally tasked by the NSA and the National Reconnaissance Office. And now, watch this!"

And then, seemingly from out of nowhere, and at a speed unmatched by the TR-3B, a huge, silver-blue triangular starship approached the prototype U.S. craft and came to a complete stop beside it. A thin silver line of light glowed around the circumference of the massive ship that dwarfed the TR-3B.

"Jesus!" General Stewart nearly choked on his pipe stem. "It's one of theirs!"

"How the fuck did they get that video?" Admiral Sullivan demanded of whomever might have an answer.

"Shut up and listen!" Jerrold ordered.

"What you are seeing now is an actual alien spacecraft from another world," the narrator proclaimed. "Many UFO investigators have claimed that since the late 1940s certain select military and government scientists have been working side by side with extraterrestrial intelligences in a kind of exchange program in which alien technology has been bartered for certain artifacts of Earth. It is further maintained that such scientific alien\Earth interaction has occurred at secret installations north of the Nevada Test Site at the Nellis Range, or Area 51, also referred to by insiders as the Ranch or as Dreamland. In this amazing film footage of an extraterrestrial spacecraft, we have proof of these allegations. Our government and military scientists have been working secretly with aliens in order to accelerate the timetable of Earth technology."

"Look at the size of that mother," Director Neal said in awe. "I've never actually seen one before."

"It's as if it suddenly appeared there to mock us," General Stewart said.

"Or to warn us," Chief Justice Artabrae suggested.

Everyone seated around the table in Eli Jerrold's office took random glances at the former director of the National Security Agency, each trying to read something from his body language and changes in expression.

Eli held his tongue, but his mind raced ahead with actions that would have to be taken to mitigate the severe repercussions of this dreadful security leak.

As the camera held fast on a blowup of the alien space vehicle, the narrator continued: "Our confidential sources state that an even more secret area exists, called Papoose Lake, just south of Groom Lake. Here, according to informants, an ultrasecret group of the shadow government known as MJ-12 has been directing and funding research with alien technology, right under the very noses of unsuspecting military personnel working on more conventional projects."

The frozen picture of the UFO on the television screen suddenly dissolved into live video footage of the alien craft soaring off at speeds and sharp-angle turns that lay far beyond the technology represented by the TR-3.

"If we've been incorporating alien technology, when will our aircraft be able to maneuver like this remarkable vehicle?" the narrator asked. "And are we watching a captured alien craft under our control? Or an extraterrestrial vehicle under the control of an alien crew?"

"Jesus Christ," Admiral Sullivan wheezed through clenched teeth. "How the fuck did Blake Webster get ahold of that film?"

General Van Grouse was furious. "We'll see to it that every asshole at NBC associated with this program is put in jail...until hell freezes over."

"Can't do it," Chief Justice Artabrae said firmly. "They will say the program is intended only as speculative entertainment. They'll air a disclaimer as to the factual authenticity of the video tape."

"Hey, guys," Elden Neal cut off their discussion. "Now they're trying to rouse the ire of the American taxpayer."

The narrator began an impassioned wrap-up:

> Our sources estimate that up to thirty-five percent of the SDI funding was siphoned off to provide primary expenditures for the Air Force's

most secret "Black Project." The Aurora Project reportedly cost five billion per vehicle—and only three have been produced to date. Several other smaller Remotely Piloted Vehicles and Independently Piloted Vehicles have been built and tested using this advanced alien technology.

What this taxpayer wants to know is whether a five-billion or five-thousand-million-dollar expenditure for such exotic military toys can be justified during peacetime.

I also want to know how much of the tax dollar has been spent on exploiting alien technology since the late 1940s. Is this why our nation has been moving deeper and deeper into debt?

And if we do have access to the technology of an advanced super science, who says the military gets to keep it all for themselves? This same technology that produces vehicles for military intelligence could also revolutionize civilian air and space transportation, thus developing tens of thousands of jobs and thereby helping to reduce our trade deficit.

How long, Mr. and Mrs. Taxpayer, do you want to support thirty-five billion dollars being spent annually by the Defense Department on the black budget? And, in the final analysis, are we supporting E.T.'s long-distance calls home to Alpha Centauri?

"That's enough of that horseshit!" Admiral Sullivan shouted, advancing toward the television set and angrily snapping it off. "I'd love to know how that liberal anarchist puke Webster got such a good video of the craft."

Chief Justice Artabrae turned to Eli Jerrold. "What are we going to do?"

Jerrold smiled almost beatifically and answered in a calm voice. He was still very much in control of the situation. "Above all, we keep our heads and don't overreact. As long as we remember who we are and what we stand for, I am confident that we can effect proper damage control.

"Gentleman, as always the primary objective of the MJ-12 committee is to limit and control public information regarding alien technology.

"First of all, we inform our contacts at CBS, ABC, CNN, and Fox to suggest on all of their most significant newscasts that the video footage was an obvious hoax. Our people at the wire services will be provided with a news release stating that Blake Webster has long been known as a true believer in UFOs and he used some of his Hollywood contacts to provide him with some excellent UFO-type special effects to prove the reality of aliens walking among us."

General Van Grouse liked Jerrold's plan so far. "Hell, Eli, you're absolutely right. This is the age of *Star Wars, Close Encounters, 2001: A*

Space Odyssey and all the rest of those weird science fiction things. The public is used to seeing a hell of lot more convincing special effects than they saw for real on that video!"

Jerrold paused to sip a glass of mineral water. "The public's main concern about our using any kind of advanced technology is that it might be radioactive and dump nuclear waste on them. We will tell our people at all the Department of Defense branches to leak disinformation about its use of nuclear power in aerospace vehicles as impractical and prohibitively dangerous to pilots and the public in general. That's what the public will want to hear—and that's what we'll tell them."

Eli knew that the government had to be sensitive to the public's irrational fear of nuclear-powered aerospace vehicles because the Russian nuclear-powered satellite, Cosmos 954, crashed and littered radioactive debris over Canada in 1978. All that was required was just another plausible lie to distract the public from the truth.

Neal nodded his head vigorously. "Good, good, Eli. Then we'll track down the leak that resulted in that untimely and unauthorized video."

Jerrold said that he would take care of that problem.

"I'll call our old friend Karl Sturgeon, our official UFO debunker, and see about getting him on with Ted Koppel or Tom Snyder," Admiral Sullivan said.

Jerrold looked pleased. "That's a damn good idea, Sully. Do it!"

General Stewart also rose to the challenge. "I'll fax our folks within the civilian UFO groups to start spreading the rumor that Blake Webster is a C.I.A. agent. They love to spread that shit about each other. They're always denouncing each other in those groups."

Jerrold praised the men as though he were a satisfied schoolteacher grading his students' homework. "Good going. I know you'll keep coming up with more great ideas. We'll soon put a cap on all of this. In no time at all, we'll be laughing about it."

On his way back to his mansion outside of the city, Eli Jerrold reflected on the new challenge that had been placed before MJ-12. The dedicated men on the committee truly were the modern counterparts of the nation's early patriot leaders. It was they, just a noble handful of stalwart guardians of the American way, who truly knew what was best for the country—and had since 1947!

As soon he arrived home, he would immediately call Colonel Ty Trent. Trent, a decorated Marine Special Operations and intelligence officer, had worked directly for him at the NSA, and he knew the workings of the NSA and the military better than anyone other than himself. Trent was a man of action who effected positive results in a timely manner, and unofficially of course, he still took care of awkward situations for Jerrold and MJ-12. Trent did a damn good job of plugging leaks. Even big ones such as this.

PRESIDENTIAL ORDER

(Unnumbered Order)

President Ronald Wilson Reagan

(Authorized By Proxy)

REVISED CHARTER

MARS JUPITER - TWELVE COMMITTEE

February 22, 1987

Presidential Order, February 22, 1987

By virtue of the authority vested in me as Chairman of the Mars-Jupiter Twelve Committee, an Ultra Secret Committee established by President Truman, with full consent of the permanent voting members of the Mars-Jupiter Twelve Committee, this Presidential Order by Proxy is established and ordered as follows:

1. CHARTER: There is hereby established the strategic group of key government personnel called the Mars-Jupiter Twelve Committee (referred to as MJ-12) with authority to take any action, to the maximum extent possible, in relation to Foreign or Alien data, materials, information, technology, artifacts, and Extraterrestrial Biological Entities (EBE), hereafter referred to as Foreign Artifacts (FA), which may bear upon the national security of the United States of America. Amendments to this Charter, and Foreign Artifacts materials and information shall be classified to the highest levels available to the US Government. The MJ-12 committee's actions and directives will be referred to as "The Program" outside the MJ-12 membership.

The MJ-12 Committee shall have sole United States governmental authority to direct each FA aspect or substance, and to make such FA available to the President and/or to each member of the MJ-12 committee, and to such departments and officials of the Government as MJ-12 Chairman may determine; and to carry out, when requested by the MJ-12 Chairman such supplementary activities as may facilitate the securing of FA important for national security not now available to the Government and direct the acquisition, use, disposal, storage, and research as deemed necessary for current and future national security of the United States. All US laws, regulations, and directives are secondary to achieving these goals, not subject to the boundaries of the US proper, of providing for the integrity of the US national security and protecting the sanctity of the US Constitution.

2. CONTROL: The several departments and agencies of the Government and Department of Defense, as identified by the MJ-12 Committee, shall be notified by Departmental Directive to consider any FA as highly classified and alert the DoD Foreign Technology Division (FTD) immediately on the occasion of any incident, happenstance, or encounter with FA. Directives will be developed by the MJ-12 Committee, the DoD, the DIRNSA and the President, as determined by the MJ-12 Chairman, detailing coordination, handling, transportation, isolation, quarantine, security, research, storage, and disposal of any and all aspects of FA; make available to the MJ-12 Chairman any and all such reports of FA, or any other pertinent (undefined) requests relating to national security as may be requested from this date forward.

ULTRA TOP SECRET MJ-12 EYES ONLY Page 03 of 03

The MJ-12 Committee Chairman has the authority to make any decision, without regard to Civil or Federal law, or take any action in order to provide for national security of the U.S.

3. VOTING MEMBERS: The Director of the National Security Agency (NSA) shall be the Chairman and the current President of the US the Co-Chairman, if the President is a member, of the MJ-12 Committee. The MJ-12 Chairman has the authority to exclude unstable subsequent permanent members, including but not limited to the President of the United States. The MJ-12 Chairman may appoint subsequent members to the MJ-12 committee, as may the Committee by majority consensus. Each member must take an oath to the United States, and swear to abide by this Charter and the MJ-12 Chairman's directives; and to further provide plausible deniability, deny culpability, action, association of, by, and for this charter to any and all outside the permanent membership. Permanent voting members shall be selected from the highest ranks or positions from these various departments and agencies of the US Government: President or Vice-President (Executive), National Security Agency (NSA), Federal Bureau of Investigation (FBI), Central Intelligence Agency (CIA), Secretary of Defense or Chairman of the Joint Chiefs (DoD), Military Chief of Staff (Armed Forces), Chief Justice of the Supreme Court or Attorney General's Office (Justice). No "elected" official shall be appointed without a majority vote of the MJ-12 Committee. Religious or spiritual leaders shall be forbidden membership.

4. NON-VOTING MEMBERS: Additional members, up to twelve, may be chosen by the same method, for their appropriate political influence, skills, or industry position as non-voting members. Non-voting members will not be privileged with information not directly needed to accomplish their intended goal, research, or objectives previously delegated by a MJ-12 voting member.

5. BUDGET: Within the limits of such funds as may be allocated to the MJ-12 committee, the Chairman may employ necessary personnel and make provisions for supplies, services, facilities, equipment, and as needed to provide for national security in relation to FA. Funding will be acquired from DoD Black Budgets and supplemented from US Armed Force's intelligence and security programs at the discretion of the MJ-12 voting members.

Admiral Eli A. Jerrold, the Director of the National Security Agency, is hereby designated as permanent Chairman of the MJ-12 Committee, by Presidential Order, by Proxy.

Ronald Wilson Reagan, By Proxy
President of the United States
THE WHITE HOUSE

Eli A. Jerrold, Admiral (Ret)
Director of the National
Security Agency (DIRNSA)

ULTRA TOP SECRET (MJ-12) EYES ONLY Page 03 of 03

Chapter Three

Joe's Search Begins

Joe Green lined up four shots of Cuervo in front of him on the bar, then carefully selected one of the glasses to drink down past his bushy mustache. He achieved this movement with the smooth action that came from lots of practice. He had dispensed with the customary lime and salt years ago. He had decided that they were an unnecessary accouterment to his purposeful imbibing.

In the background buzz of shrill voices, shifting feet, alcoholic laughter, and the drunken babble of a few loudmouthed rednecks, Joe could hear fifties music pulsating from the ancient jukebox in the corner of the Pilot Club. He often drank at the Pilot, a bar frequented by retired military veterans, government contractors, and active duty types who worked at the Air Force's top secret Nevada test site and Nellis Range.

Even before the waitress made the announcement, he knew that last call was just ten minutes away.

He watched as his cigarette burned to a stub, the last trail of smoke drifting over his fingers and up into the stubble bristling his fair-complexioned cheeks.

He downed another Cuervo, followed it with a hearty swallow of a Corona. He was drinking to keep his nervous stomach quiet before he left

Tonopah and drove in the darkness to Las Vegas. He knew he didn't drink to forget. Hell, he had forgotten so much of his life that he wasn't certain of the memories he had left.

He still didn't understand what had happened to him earlier that evening when he was watching the television program, "Exploring the Unknown." He remembered seeing the incredible video of the alleged alien spacecraft zooming up to the prototype aircraft TR-3B. Then he was off somewhere in a kind of dream memory.

He was back in the Green family automobile on a night in June of 1960 when he was seven years old and crammed into the back seat of the old Buick. His mom and dad sat up front. They were moving from Americus, Georgia, to San Antonio, Texas, because Pop was out of work again.

Joseph Gordon Green had worked as a carpenter, a livestock wrangler, a farmer, and at a seemingly endless list of semi-skilled jobs. Joe knew that his father was smart enough, even personable at times, but he just couldn't seem to land a good job. He blamed it on bad luck.

When he had too long a stretch of bad luck, he could become abrasive, short-tempered, and very impatient. These mood swings and periods of unemployment seemed to coincide with his bouts of heavy drinking.

Joe remembered the night, that strange night of the Light.

Pop preferred driving in the coolness of the summer evenings. Everything the family owned had been packed into the big, black four-door Buick that was still caked with red clay and dust—the last vestige of rural living in southern Georgia.

"We're going to have our own place in San Antone," his father said loudly, repeating their family mantra for better times. "No more living like a bunch of damned sardines in a can."

Joe couldn't imagine what it would be like to be in a house without Mom, Pop, and his aunt, uncle, and cousins all under one tin roof. What he wondered was how could they afford a bigger place when Pop was out of work.

Joe couldn't remember ever meeting his mother's parents. His mom, Mary Katherine, referred to them as "your grandparents, the Whittles." His father referred to them as "your holy-roller grandparents." Joe was not at all sure what a holy roller was or why his mother took such offense at the words.

Joe had no idea what time it was. He would doze off, lulled by the motion of the car and the unrelenting boredom, then be jerked awake by a rut in the road or by his father cursing loudly at some "damn, stupid, lousy driver." Pop pretty much preferred kids to be seen and not heard, and he seemed to feel the same way about women, especially his wife.

When Joe opened his eyes just before it happened, he remembered yawning and noticing that they were driving through heavily wooded hill country.

His mom was talking in hushed tones, more or less enumerating their options for work, housing, school, and survival in general when they arrived in San Antonio.

Joe listened with little interest, surveying the scene through drowsy eyelids—until Pop let loose some sarcasm about Mom's holy-roller parents and a shrill argument flared for three or four minutes and brought him fully awake.

Because there were no street lights, Joe could look up at the night sky and see countless stars. He liked that. He would lay his head back on the wide shelf behind the overstuffed back seat. The large rear window of the Buick became his own personal skylight, providing him with a clear view of the heavens above and the outside world passing away in the distance behind them.

But he didn't like the smoke from Joseph Gordon Green Senior's cheap cigar that wafted around inside the car and seemed directed by some unseen hand to crawl up inside little Joe's nostrils, thus enhancing his propensity to motion sickness.

In fact, when he first noticed the strange red glow outside the car, he thought maybe he was getting dizzy again from the cigar smoke and starting to see things.

No, clearly, something off in the distance, something in the woods, was moving toward the Buick.

A white-tailed buck ran from the underbrush, startled by the light. Joe watched the animal frantically charge around until it ran head on into a large tree, buckling both forelegs to the ground.

"Mom, Pop, look!"

His mother glanced over her shoulder. "What is it, Sweetie?" She always called Pop, Honey, and little Joe, Sweetie.

"Look in the trees...there!"

The white tail was awkwardly rising to its feet.

"Yes, Sweetie, it's a deer."

"No, Mom, the light. Look at the...."

"You act like you've never seen a damned deer before," Pop huffed from the side of his mouth and dislodged ashes into his lap.

"The light scared the deer, Pop," Joe said, pointing at the red glow.

"Of course," his father nodded. "The car's headlights scared it."

Suddenly his mom spoke in an alarmed tone. "Wait, Honey, I see what Joe means. Look at the trees. There's a red glow in the forest. You don't suppose there's a forest fire, do you?"

The senior Green was growing weary of the distractions to his peaceful night driving, but he knew that his wife was not easily alarmed. He slowed the Buick by lifting his foot off the accelerator and coasting silently down the dusty back road.

Joe's excitement grew, for now both of his parents were looking at the deep red light filtering through the trees.

"I don't think it's a fire, Kathy," Pop said, always having to sound authoritative.

"What is it, Pop?" Joe remembered being frightened for no reason he could verbally express.

The car coasted along at about fifteen miles per hour. The light's deepening reddish hue brightened.

Joe hated to concede to his wife that he might be wrong, especially in front of little Joe, but he said in a thoughtful voice that the light could be a fire. "Probably just some farmer burning trash or some brush."

"Pop, look it's getting brighter!"

"Honey, it is. It is getting brighter. And it's coming closer to us."

"Just settle down, you two," he said, assuming the calm, in-control position expected of a father. "We're safe."

And then the car's engine stalled and its headlights and panel lights were extinguished.

Joe remembered the red glow coming nearer and nearer the stalled Buick that sat all alone in the middle of nowhere. The Light—bright, blood red, pulsating, foreboding—filled the forest, consuming every shadow in its path.

And then it was inside the car.

Joe could still hear his mother screaming first...then his father's coarse shout.

Then he remembered only the Light.

Joe wiped the cold alcohol sweat from his forehead and into his receding blond hairline. Damn those memories! Memories that were at times vague illusions and at other times vividly real.

Earlier that night as he had sat watching television and had seen the UFO—the alien craft from another world or dimension—he had entered a weird, trance-like state. He was seeing the Light again. The Light that had lured him to the ocean depths. The Light that had engulfed him and his parents when he was a boy of seven. The Light that haunted his dreams nearly every night.

If he were to remain sane, he must discover the cause. It was as if something in his brain, some bizarre timing mechanism, some psychic alarm clock, was set to go off very, very soon—and he was afraid that whatever it was would destroy him.

Somehow—he could not explain why—Joe knew that the renowned scientist and eminent theoretical propulsion expert Dr. Carlton Farr had some of the answers he wanted. Joe had met him at a propulsion seminar a year before, and he had sensed that the man knew a lot more about the ultra top secret, black government projects than he let on. Joe planned to drive to Las Vegas that very night and fly out of McCarren the next day to San Antonio, where he had recently learned that Dr. Farr lived after taking an early retirement from the Brooks Advanced Research Center.

In moments of fear and melancholy such as this, Joe often thought of Karen, the beautiful strawberry blonde who had promised to wait for him until he got back from Vietnam. She had waited, and they had married. But even Karen with her love and support and desire to understand him could not conquer the personal demons that tormented him. She didn't divorce him as much as she escaped from the curse that blighted his every attempt to lead a normal life. Joe knew that Karen was the only woman that he had ever really loved—and it seemed as though she would be the last.

"So's how it going, Joe?"

With his mind wandering in the past and his grasp of his immediate surroundings blurred by the alcohol, Joe was slightly startled until he recognized the older man standing across the small bar table from him.

"Mind if I pull up a chair and join you?"

"Sure," Joe paused for a moment, then the name came to him. "Sure, Red, have a seat."

"Buy you a drink?" Red asked as he slid the wooden chair back to take a seat.

"No, thanks. I've got to drive to Vegas yet tonight," Joe said. "Just having a few to calm my nerves and collect my thoughts."

"Must be a bad case of nerves," Red said, chuckling as he motioned with his beer bottle toward the half dozen empty shot glasses and full ashtray.

Joe smiled and nodded. "Bad day, I guess."

"I've had a few of those myself," Red admitted before he took a swallow of beer.

"Actually," Joe shrugged, "it's more like a bad year. Hell, it's actually a bad lifetime."

"Life can be the shits," Red agreed.

Joe hadn't really wanted any company, but on the other hand he was tired of thinking about his own sorry mess. He had seen Red a number of times in the couple of years that he had frequented the Pilot Club. He had even had a couple of beers with him. Red did a little mining, a little prospecting, and sold rocks and gems to lapidary shops throughout Nevada. He seemed to be the sort of guy you could spill your guts to and who wouldn't be judgmental.

"I know this isn't any of my business, Bud, but are you in some kind of trouble? I mean, like at work or with the law?"

Red's question seemed out of line and out of place. "Trouble?" Joe frowned his annoyance. "Not that I know of. I'm on a leave of absence from Lorale so I couldn't have pissed off anyone at work...at least not recently."

"No lawsuit or litigation?"

Joe was getting a little perturbed with the off-the-wall personal questions. "Why are you asking about such shit?"

Red shrugged. "Don't intend to be personal or ruffle your feathers, Joe. The reason I ask is the last time I saw you in here, three maybe four days ago, some dude who had been hanging around the bar started asking questions about you after you left."

"The hell you say. What kind of questions?"

"Like who were your friends, how much you drank, how often you came in, did you come in and leave with any women. Those kinds of questions."

"Any idea who he was?" Joe wanted to know.

"Not then," Red shook his head. "Later I found out that he was one of those Wackenhut security assholes. I know they keep a close eye on you guys that work in Area 51, but this was different."

"Different how?"

Red pursed his lips and narrowed his eyes as if summoning deep thought. "This was more personal, more intense. And this guy was your typical, low level, rent-an-ex-GI type. Someone is watching you, amigo. That's why I ask if you are in some kind of unpleasant situation."

Joe laughed. "Red, if you didn't look so damned serious, I'd figure that you were pulling my leg. I can't imagine what any of those Wackenhut goons would want with me. I've had top secret special access security clearance for over twenty years. I haven't even had a speeding ticket in fifteen years."

The bartender shouted that it was closing time.

Joe swallowed the last shot of Cuervo. He waved good night to the waitress, shook hands with Red, and made his way carefully to his truck. Now he was headed toward Las Vegas where he planned to catch the first available flight to San Antonio.

As he drove into the night, his stomach slowly churned with bile. His tall frame shifted uneasily from nervous energy and tension—and too much liquor on an empty stomach.

His instincts told him that the answers he sought from Dr. Carlton Farr could open a Pandora's box that he might not be prepared to confront. But at this point in his chaotic and confused life, his instincts were the only things that he trusted.

The bile rose without warning and flooded his mouth. He just managed to pull off the road before it spewed out of him like a geyser. The foul tasting vomit emptied his body of the alcohol, but it was unable to purge the emotions that contaminated his soul.

It was then that he fully realized that he could no longer live without knowing what had manipulated—and so profoundly affected—his life since he had first encountered the Light.

Chapter Four

Silver Dollar Respite

Joe looked at the odometer and mentally calculated that it was 215 miles from the Pilot Club to the Showboat Casino. It had been a little after midnight when he left the bar, and the trip had taken him three hours and forty minutes.

He pulled wearily into a parking lot across from the casino and lay back against the headrest for a moment. Whatever the outcome of his journey, the fact that he had taken an active step toward possible depletion of chaos in his life lifted his spirits. He would close his eyes for just a moment or two....

The sound of a car backfiring caused Joe to jump involuntarily. Morning light stabbed his eyes. When he squinted at his wristwatch, he saw that it was almost seven. He had obviously fallen asleep for over three hours, and every muscle in his body ached from sleeping in an awkward position.

His head pounded from the previous evening's hours of over-indulgence. He wished he had a drink and some aspirin.

He was across the street from the Silver Dollar Casino, and he had plenty of time to catch some breakfast and a little hair of the dog.

The Silver Dollar was a country western bar that served pretty fair food, had better than average country bands, and best of all, like most places in

Vegas, it was open twenty-four hours a day. It didn't get a lot of tourist traffic and that was what made it draw the locals—the dealers, showgirls, waiters, and bartenders that worked the myriad of gaming facilities in town. It was also the favorite hangout for law enforcement types and the city's shop and store owners.

Out of nervous habit, Joe lit up another cigarette as he entered the Silver Dollar. There were six male customers sitting at various points around the U-shaped bar in the center of the casino. An old woman in a red sweat suit sat near the entrance, pulling off a nickel slot machine with a near trancelike expression. Two flashy young ladies, attractive enough to be showgirls or high-priced hookers, sat in a booth near the back dance floor.

Joe chose a stool at the back side of the bar, facing the front, waiting for someone to take his order. By this time of the morning, the bands were long gone, the normal people were home in bed, and the lost souls sat out the early morning hours, contentedly avoiding going where they should be.

Joe recognized one of the two morning bartenders as a former electronics countermeasures technician on the F-15 Eagle fighter aircraft stationed at Nellis Air Force Base.

"Hey, there, Hank, Hank Carswell. How's it going, man?"

Hank grinned at him as he turned from having served his previous customer. As he approached him, Joe noticed that he had a natural swagger about him that was almost comical. He was about the same height and build as Joe, but Hank didn't have any hair on top. Getting older. But then he didn't have the extra ten pounds around the middle that Joe had. The thing about Hank that always surprised Joe was that the man could out-eat and out-drink any man alive and still remain the same weight. He was either a bulimic or had one helluva lightning-fast metabolism.

"Amigo! Long time no see." Hank reached out with a friendly hand.

"How are you doing Hank, really?" Joe asked in a quiet voice.

Hank shrugged. "Same old shit. Work, pay bills, fight with the old lady, and try my damnedest to stay out of trouble. And you, amigo?"

"I've been pretty busy at work," Joe said, tapping ashes from his cigarette into the tray at his elbow. "This is the first time I've been in Vegas in months."

Hank smiled, hands on his narrow hips, towering above the bar. "Same old happening place, ain't it? What will you have this morning?"

Joe ordered a breakfast drink, a screwdriver, and a couple of eggs over easy with toast.

Hank shouted in the food order, then made Joe's drink. When he saw that none of the other customers needed anything, he placed the screwdriver and a clean ashtray in front of Joe and leaned forward in a conspiratorial manner. "You still working out in Area 51?"

Joe nodded. "It's still the same old, isolated, paranoid grind as when you were there." There was no need to mention his taking a sudden sabbatical.

"I don't know how you handle that kind of bullshit—day in and day out, year after year. I'm surprised I lasted six months. Those security assholes, the early flight every morning before daybreak from McCarrin, coming home after dark, couldn't talk to anyone about my job. No thanks, amigo."

Joe grinned over the top of his screwdriver. "I don't blame you for bailing out. You always were a free spirit."

Hank leaned forward again and spoke in a whisper. "I've been hearing about all kinds of weird goings-on out there. You would not believe some of the far-out stuff I hear from some of the drunks that wander in here."

Joe raised an eyebrow. "Such as?"

Hank gave a I-don't-really-believe-but chuckle. "Well, basically, there's talk of out-of-this-world technology. And I don't mean, like super modern, I mean alien, like from outer space."

Joe sipped at his screwdriver. "I've heard some of it."

Hank studied Joe's face for a moment, then seeing that he was not going to contribute any additional comments, he continued. "There's two basic stories, you know. One, that we've got a crashed UFO and we've had it since the late 1940s. Or we've actually got aliens, you know, ETs, working with our scientists."

"I haven't see any bug-eyed scientists walking around," Joe said."Other than the usual nerd-types who have always worked there, that is."

Hank gave a peculiar snort of feigned amusement. "C'mon, amigo. You must have heard something. There is that physicist, what's-his-name—who went public not long ago. Went on television and said that he had been working on projects at Groom Lake that he believed originated from alien crashed saucers."

A kitchen bell told Hank that Joe's breakfast was ready. He was back at the bar in a few seconds, prompting Joe to respond.

The eggs were good, Joe thought, just a touch of some kind of spice to quicken the taste buds.

"Yeah, I've seen him, the guy you mean," Joe said, smearing grape jelly on his toast. "And I've heard some the wild local talk on the radio call-in shows. I know what you're talking about."

Joe had heard rumors that several scientists had suffered from some kind of mental breakdown. He had also heard that workers with Top Secret Q clearances and above had disappeared after breaching security. According to one undocumented account, the technology developed at Papoose far exceeded any known within the world scientific community. With each new rumor that he heard, Joe's nightmares had become more frequent.

One night, he had been able to watch the SR-75 take off for its round trip to northern China and eastern Russia.

And he would never forget the sight of the alien looking TR-3B based at Papoose. The pitch black, triangular-shaped TR-3B was rarely mentioned—and then, only in hushed whispers—at the Groom Lake facility where he worked.The craft had flown over the Groom Lake runway in complete silence and magically stopped above Area S-4. It hovered silently in the same position for some ten minutes before gently settling vertically to the tarmac. At that moment he knew the technology expressed in that aerospace vehicle could not have been developed by human ingenuity alone.

Joe had many reasons for wanting to know more about the secrets associated with the TR-3B and the Papoose Lake's Area S-4. The sabbatical that he had taken proved that he was willing to risk a lot to discover the truth.

Hank left to fix a drink for another customer, and Joe had finished his eggs by the time he got back to him.

"Some of the wildest shit that I've heard has to do with underground bases where human scientists employed by a so-called shadow government are working openly with alien technicians," Hank said after he had lit a cigarette and hung it on his lower lip.

"Oh, yeah?" Joe tapped his empty glass, signaling his request for another screwdriver.

When Hank returned, he spun a bizarre story about an alleged underground base somewhere near Dulce, New Mexico. According to what he had heard, even the secret government had tried to renege on their deal with the aliens when they learned that the ETs were conducting experiments with human genetics and exploring the possibility of crossbreeding a new species of mutants. A confrontation had erupted between the scientists and their extraterrestrial counterparts. In order to ensure extended cooperation from the secret government, the aliens had taken a number of scientists as hostages. In response, crack troops from Delta Force were sent into the vast underground tunnels to rescue the scientists.

"But the Delta Force was no match for the super mind-control weapons that the aliens had been concealing," Hank shook his head sadly. "Some say from about a hundred to several hundred humans were killed during this confrontation."

Joe skewered his face in skepticism. "And we didn't see this on CNN or read about it in the papers?"

Hank rubbed his hands on his apron. "Joe, all this alien and UFO shit is controlled by the secret government that runs this country from behind the scenes. Cover stories to explain the deaths were provided to all the families of the deceased."

"So now the aliens have conquered us and rule the secret government way behind the scene?" Joe's brain was spinning. "Why bother to have elections if some jerk from Andromeda is really running the White House?"

Hank leaned forward, lowering his voice. "You got to understand. There's the regular government stiffs that the people elect—senators, congressmen, the president and vice-president—and then there's the secret government behind the scenes that calls the shots about the things that really matter—like making deals with aliens that can turn this planet into a crisp, black cinder."

Joe caught himself just before he opened his mouth. What about the Light that he had encountered on at least two previous occasions? Why hadn't the Light burned him to a crisp? Or his parents? Or the crew in the Gulf of Tonkin?

Hank was going on with his creepy narrative. "This big bloody battle at Dulce was supposed to have happened a couple of years back. According to what I hear, some of the secret government's head honchos, an ultra black group called MJ-12, reconciled with the ETs—but now they knew that they couldn't completely trust them. The aliens obviously had their own secret agenda."

"Keeping secrets from the secret government," Joe interjected. "Sounds like something nasty monsters from outer space would do."

"Exactly! So even though these projects at the underground bases and Groom Lake, Area 51, and so forth are back on target, the MJ-12 is trying to keep a tighter lid on things, because they no longer totally trust their alien buddies."

Joe had finished his second screwdriver. "And the little alien bastards with the huge insect eyes that some of the UFO buffs call the 'grays' are supposed to be mixed up in all this in some way, right?"

Hank nodded. "And what about 'Exploring the Unknown' last night? Did you see it?"

Joe indicated that he had.

"What did you make of that fucking UFO leaving our latest super bird behind in the dust motes, man?"

Joe felt cold sweat bead his forehead. "If the video was authentic, it is mind blowing."

"How the hell did this Webster guy manage to get that footage? I mean, Joe, you know how tight security is out there."

Joe laughed. "Old buddy, even as we speak, some Air Force and DOE security stiffs are getting their asses reamed out good and proper."

"You can bet on it," Hank grinned. "And Wackenhut, too. I still wonder how Webster got the film. You know they already have the tightest security system in the world out there. I heard they even have one of those stationary satellites over Area 51 just so they can watch themselves. Can you imagine that?"

Joe could imagine that and much more.

He knew that the satellite in question was a specially modified TRW KH-13 launched by the giant Titan 4 boosters in 1992 from Cape Canaveral Air Station's Pad-41. Its purpose was to monitor Department of Defense and Department of Energy installations for intrusive threats. Hydrazine fuel was burned to position the KH-13s for imaging and for making the constant critical course and altitude adjustments necessary to keep them on target and to avoid their drifting or spinning out of orbit. When the KH-13s weren't imaging, the hydrazine-powered thrusters kept them high enough to reduce atmospheric drag.

The solar powered TRW Stationary High Orbital Reconnaissance Electro-Optical Satellite (SHOREOS) was a computer linked telescopic system that utilized solid-state CCD array sensors to scan and to provide real-time infrared and visible wavelength images of objects of less than two inches—even through heavy cloud cover and darkness. Real-time data was provided by a Burst Laser Encrypted Compressed Digital Signal Transmitter (BLEC-DST).

The ground-based computers at the Nellis and Groom facilities received surveillance, acquisition, tracking, and assessment data that tracked movement by type, speed, direction, size, mass, and infrared signature for the western United States. What made the SHOREOS unique was that the data transmittals could not be intercepted by anyone outside of Area 51 because of the laser transmitter and other unique provisions of the system. SHOREOS allowed the operator to differentiate between a rabbit and a coyote, to read tail numbers off aircraft, and to identify license plate numbers on ground vehicles. The surveillance system's only weakness lay in areas experiencing severe weather-related electrical disturbance.

Even that single flaw was a fluke, or FLUC, something of a bad joke inside the NSA special operations arena. NSA operatives had switched the Hubble's 94-inch light-gathering mirror at NASA with one that had failed the manufacturer's quality control, along with a space fuzzy logic Unix computer (FLUC). They needed it for the SHOREOS satellite; the mirror was perfect, but the FLUC was flawed.

Hank was summoned by a patron standing at the other end of the bar. "You know, amigo, you work in one spooky kind of place."

"It can get to you if you let it," Joe agreed.

And the reason that he was sitting there in the Silver Dollar killing time before his flight to Dallas was that it most certainly had got to him—and he was on his way to find some answers.

As Joe left the saloon and got back into his car for the drive to the Vegas airport, he considered the "spooky place" where he worked.

Groom Lake held many secrets. At twenty-eight thousand feet, it had the longest paved runway in the States. It also housed one of the largest hangers in the nation, big enough to house four huge C-5 transports.

During the week, two thousand personnel came in daily via unmarked 737 aircraft. One hundred sixty double-occupancy duplex apartments provided quarters for the current 370 permanent staff. Four apartments were on reserve for visiting VIPs.

Dreamland was a man's world, where testosterone ruled, where big men played with their big toys. Traditional wisdom among the upper echelon military held to the belief that women were too unstable to be trusted with such deadly secrets. Joe often thought that the male chauvinists in charge of Area 51 and Groom Lake made the Navy assholes at Tailhook look like feminists.

At lunch break on the night shift at the Groom facilities, Joe occasionally sat with Oscar De La Garza, the Air Force's head of security for

Dreamland. One recent night stood out in Joe's mind. The usually upbeat and cheerful engineer had seemed distant and somewhat depressed as the two of them munched on chicken salad sandwiches, potato chips, and Cokes. After some prompting, De La Garza admitted to Joe that he was having some trouble with HIDA, the Holographic Intruder Detection Alert security system.

Joe had always been told that the security around Groom and Papoose was state-of-the-art. Visual, aural, motion, heat, vibration, metal, and mass sensors were utilized in addition to the SHOREOS satellite.

De La Garza confirmed Joe's data. "But somehow there's a glitch somewhere. We've been getting too many security alerts, and the security chiefs are really riding my butt about it—especially Agabarr, the head Wackenhut honcho. You ever meet the asshole? I think he's really the devil. I'm not shitting you, man. That bastard is evil."

Joe laughed, asked his friend to define the problem as best he could.

"I think it's a sensor problem, but the DOE consultant thinks it's a software problem."

De La Garza explained that they were using seismic motion sensors (SEMS) along roads, pathways, mountain trails, and flats leading into the area.

"They measure ground vibration and alert to anything weighing over one hundred pounds," Oscar continued. The Biological infrared detectors (BIDS) pick up body heat of 98.6 plus or minus five degrees. Magnetometers and gravitational sensors detect movement of masses of more than ten pounds.

"Strategically placed on mountain tops within Area 51 are telescopes coupled with digital format CCD cameras hooked up to the HIDA system," he continued. "When an intruder is detected by the HIDA, the central processor alerts the master security computer and sounds an alarm on a computer display. The operator can then turn on a camera at the end of a telescope on a strategic mountain location and achieve pin-point acquisition for closer detail. The communications security and physical security data is also fed into the HIDA computer."

From his perspective as an engineer, Joe didn't assess the system as all that complex.

"I know what's causing the problem," De La Garza told him. "But I don't know how to solve it. The sensors are very high tech, and the slightest changes in underground and surface stress can set off the alerts."

Joe knew that Oscar had to be talking about micro-quakes, vibration of the earth caused by shifting of the underground tectonic plates, lightning, sonic booms, and the like.

While they continued eating, Oscar opened up a bit more about the details of the system—and suddenly Joe had an idea.

"What if you set up a line of sensors further away from the present perimeter and use the signal to normalize the alert input. That way you could eliminate the natural underground causes and external explosions."

De La Garza paused in mid-bite, considered the strategy for a moment or two, then broke into a broad smile. "That would work. We could place them a mile on either side and use the delay time to alert to anything within a two-mile perimeter of the sensors."

His face clouded momentarily as he thought of another aspect of the problem. "Hey, Joe, what about lightning and sonic booms?"

Joe sipped at his Coke before he answered. He knew that optical blocking of sensors occurred when a visual or infrared sensor was overloaded by an extreme light or heat input.

"You could program your software to shut down alerts that happen concurrently with optical blocking."

Oscar was pleased with Joe's solution. "Hey, my man, you are pretty good. You should come work for me in security."

Joe laughed away the compliment, but he was flattered by Oscar's enthusiastic acceptance of his solution to the problem.

"No, thanks. To me, security would be boring. And I don't think the Air Force or Wackenhut security engineers get paid as well as we contractors do."

Oscar shrugged. "True. We're peons compared to you dudes. We just do our boring little jobs and serve as support personnel to you weenies on the special dark projects."

Joe finished his lunch. It was time to get back to work.

"Just teasing you, Oscar. As a matter of fact, I think my work is boring. I'm thinking of getting completely out of the Black Program business for a while. Thought I'd try something normal for a change. Something outside of the DOD military-industrial complex."

De La Garza put a friendly hand on Joe's shoulder. "Naw, Joe, you're too much of a company man. You think too much like you belong here. Hell, I had spent the better part of a month working on this fucking problem, and you solved it over lunch. Because of you, our saying in security is once again true: 'You can't hida from the HIDA.'"

The two men laughed together at the unbelievable amount of abbreviations, acronyms, and technical jargon that smothered the personnel who labored in the dark programs. With it came a high-tech humor that provided a stress relief of sorts.

Once he was finally seated on the airplane, Joe drifted into a deep sleep almost immediately after takeoff. Too many drinks and not enough shut-eye had made him extremely susceptible to the hypnotic hum and vibration of the jet liner.

"You can't hida from HIDA or the sandman," he mumbled to himself before he closed his eyes.

At that exact moment, an intruder into Area 51 was discovering for himself that same awesome technological truth about HIDA and learning just how effectively Joe Green had solved a security problem for his friend Oscar—and for the devil known as Agabarr.

Chapter Five

No Man's Land

Red had been on the trail of flying saucers since his stint in Korea in 1953, and during the last couple of years he had taken his private war against UFOs to a productive level by providing footage of secret alien activity in Area 51 to independent investigator Blake Webster.

No one knew Red's real name, and at times he had trouble remembering it himself. Clive Redding Teller didn't have a driver's license, a credit card, or an accurate social security number. Since the end of the Korean War, the big prospector with the scruffy red beard had become a non-person as far as the government was concerned. To anyone who would meet him in his present identity, he was nothing more than a secretive, crusty, sweat-grimed, half-crazy desert rat.

Born five years before WW II, the Big One, he had lied about his age and under the name of Charles Redding—Red to his friends—had entered the Army Corps of Engineers at seventeen. The worst days of fighting during the "police action" were over by the time Red touched soil in South Korea. In fact, he had seen only two months of active duty before the armistice was signed at Panmunjon in July.

Although his youthful eyes had been spared the carnage of the brutal hand-to-hand fighting that had marked so much of the Korean campaign,

Red had witnessed the most gruesome sight of his life when he was detailed to help search for survivors of a B-29 bomber that had gone down after frantic communications were received that they were being attacked by a large bright light.

When that little tidbit of intelligence was passed on to the guys in the detail, they had begun to joke rather nervously about flying saucers, as they were called in those days. Troops on sentry duty during the late-hour shifts had often talked about having seen some weird things in the sky. And nearly all the guys had seen movies like *War of the Worlds* and *It Came from Outer Space* and had passed a lot of idle barracks time with speculations about alien invasions. So maybe Martians had attacked the bomber.

They all stopped their wisecracking when they found the bomber intact in the hills where it had gone down. There were no piles of rubble, no furrows of plowed-up earth to indicate a crash landing. Only the bottom of the fuselage showed any damage.

But the crew! Red would never forget what had happened to the men in that ill-fated bomber. Although they were still sitting in their safety harnesses, they had all been mutilated. Their anuses had been cored out of their colons. Corkscrew patches of skin had been sliced from their necks and jaws. Their eyes and genitalia had been removed by extremely precise surgery, yet not one drop of blood had been spilled anywhere—nor was any trace of blood left in their bodies.

Red and most of the men on the detail had puked up their breakfasts as they body-bagged the victims of an atrocity that they knew would never find its way into any official report.

Not long after the ghastly incident, Red found himself sharing some beers with an ace fighter pilot, who, after many drinks, spilled his guts in confidence about his aerial encounters with flying saucers.

"I'm up in the wild blue yonder in my F-86A Sabre jet, the ultimate in technology, the cutting edge of aeronautical science, man," the pilot recalled with grim humor. "I am a fighter pilot—God's own special gift to women, America, and the U.S. Air Force. And then these weird things—these fucking flying saucers—come swooping out of nowhere and make me look like I'm flying a goddamned piece of shit. I mean, they zoom past me like I'm parked at the side of the road taking a piss."

Red asked the pilot if the saucers had taken any hostile actions toward him. "No, thank God. With their obvious technological superiority, they would have pulverized me. Thank Jesus, Mary, and Joseph that they seemed contented to humiliate me."

The fighter pilot swallowed most of another bottle of beer before he added: "What really pissed me off, man, is that my commanding officer told me to shut up about the whole business. I mean, it was obvious that he knew what the hell I was talking about, but he told me that it was U.S. Air Force policy that, officially, these things didn't exist. I told him that I felt like a damned fool being made a horse's ass by something that 'officially' wasn't even there. But he told me that I would be in for one helluva lot of fucking trouble if I told anyone what I had seen."

After he was discharged, Red had become a full-fledged beatnik. Or at least that was what his grandmother had called him. Red's mother had been an Irish whore in the Goldfield and Tonopah red-light establishments and his father had most likely been one of her customers. She had long since been lost in a world of booze and drugs, so she didn't really notice if Red was still on the planet.

Red studied yoga, transcendental meditation, Eastern religious philosophies, Tai Chi, and the mental discipline of a number of the martial arts. But he could never forget those eyeless crew members of the B-52 who had been so gruesomely mutilated by what could only have been alien invaders from another world. He read every UFO book he could get his hands on, and he became increasingly angry at the massive government cover-up of the flying saucer mystery. Somehow, damn it, it all had to stop, and he became determined to do whatever he could to expose conspiracy and reveal the truth of the UFO enigma to the masses of the world who were being deliberately kept in ignorance.

Red became a regular fixture at UFO conferences up and down the West coast. Within a few years, he was on a first-name basis with most of the prominent researchers in the field of UFOlogy, including Blake Webster.

It was when rumors of weird goings on in Area 51 began to circulate that he and Webster came up with the plan of his heading back to the Nevada desert country and going undercover as a weathered old prospector.

As a kid, he had pretty much raised and educated himself and devoured books on mining, desert lore, and survival. Whenever he had the chance, he would pick the minds of the miners, geologists, and adventurers who patronized the Bouncing Betty brothel, and he absorbed a lot of valuable information about exploring and surviving in the high desert and mountains.

According to Red's estimate, the Nevada Test Site and the Nellis Range each had to cover over thirty thousand square miles. The area stretched from Las Vegas to Tonopah bordered by U.S. Federal Highway 95 on the west. The highway snaked through the creosote bush toward the high Great Basin. On the north, the sites were bordered from Tonopah across to Ash Springs, via Warm Springs along U.S. Highway 6 and Nevada State Highway 375. From there the inverted irregular triangle of the site continued south along U.S. Highway 93 into North Las Vegas. The road that actually meandered through the region was a collage of old Indian and mining trails, wagon routes, game paths, and railway roads.

During the early part of the century, Tonopah had been the largest city in Nevada, and though primarily a silver town, it had yielded its share of gold. Highway 95 south to Goldfield, Rhyolite, Mercury, and into Vegas was still dotted with dozens of ghost towns.

Although he was not yet sixty, Red soon convinced the military security personnel patrolling the area that he was just a senile old coot with a mangy pack donkey at his side. As long as he didn't get too close to their facilities, they let him be. And with his familiarity of the area to guide him, he seldom allowed them to see him snaking closer and closer to vantage points where he could observe and film the testing of secret weapons and vehicles.

Almost at once he was able to provide Webster with plenty of mind-boggling information for his articles and electronic media appearances. Their ultimate coup was the video of the alien spacecraft that had been shown the night before on "Exploring the Unknown." Red knew that the sight of that incredible vehicle on network television must have really singed somebody's balls, and he would have to watch himself for the next few days.

As it was, the Wackenhut goons had recently started harassing him. He had his donkey run off by ominous black helicopters on three occasions. Last month, he had been apprehended and turned over the Lincoln County sheriff in Alamo for trespassing. After two days in the calaboose and a stern warning from Sheriff Pete Burke to "stay the hell of the Nellis Range and the Nevada Test Site," he was turned loose.

Red was crossing Papoose dry lake when three Wackenhut security thugs roared up beside him in their black Jeep Cherokee and shouted at him to halt.

"What can I do you for, boys?" Red grinned in his half-wacko prospector persona. "You lost your way?"

The grim-faced men were not in the market for any bullshit this day. Right out in the open, they grabbed him, clubbed him, and bound him.

Even after he had regained consciousness, he feigned helplessness and confusion. They had placed a blindfold over his eyes, and two guards, one on either side, supported him under each arm.

Every instinct within Red's body told him that his life could be at risk. The fact that military security would club down a civilian who was only walking near the site convinced him that they could easily dispose of his body in the desert without anyone questioning his demise. Except Blake Webster. And he had to keep absolutely mum about his association with the journalist.

He wondered if he should try to make his escape when his captors dragged him into an elevator that began to descend into the earth. He decided to continue to play it limp and weak. Although it might cost him his life, he had to satisfy his curiosity.

Over the years a massive amount of construction had taken place at the Groom, and to a lesser degree, the Papoose facilities. Local newspapers had claimed that over five hundred million dollars a year had been spent on the Groom and Papoose facilities for the last decade. Many scoffed at the notion, but Red had seen the military transports, the Army Corps of Engineers, the Air Force Red Horse construction teams, and the massive amount of dirt shifted to make room for more construction.

From what certain curious area residents and independent researchers had observed from secret natural watchtowers in the mountains, most of the construction was not above ground. One excavation and foundation that was completed in 1990 could hold a ten-story building with each underground floor covering approximately forty thousand square feet. During the last decade, many elevator shafts and underground tunnels connecting subterranean buildings had been completed. Red figured that fifty percent of the Groom facilities and eighty percent of the Papoose facilities were now underground to protect their post-Cold War secrets from prying satellites and high-altitude aircraft.

When the elevator stopped, the men pushed him into a room that smelled like a doctor's office. Red felt his stomach lurch involuntarily. He hated doctors' offices.

The guards lifted him to a heavy wooden table and strapped down his arms and legs.

Someone removed the blindfold, and Red blinked against the bright lights. A tall, slender, nearly bald man in his fifties was bending over him and checking his vitals. The characteristic white smock that he wore added to the clinical atmosphere and increased Red's anxiety.

Red's attention was immediately drawn to a dark complexioned man who sat watching the doctor with an air of authority and ill-concealed impatience. By the way the guards kept their respectful distance, the dude was obviously the man in charge. His jet-black hair was slicked straight back, and his color was that of a Latino.

Red was uncomfortable, but not frightened of the man's sadistic sneer and deep-set brooding gaze. Red began at once to work on controlled breathing. He would remain calm and centered. He would remain in charge of his sovereign being.

"Is our guest now ready to answer some questions for me, Dr. Quinlin?" His accent was more South American than Mexican. Maybe Chile, Argentina.

"Your men gave him a pretty solid whack on the head," the doctor told him, his words tinged with disapproval. "But he seems all right. I'll just administer some antiseptic and…"

"Don't bother," the sinister man said curtly, rising to his feet. "He won't be around long enough to need it." He motioned to Quinlin to step aside. "Leave his blindfold off. I don't want him to miss a thing."

For just a moment, he stood quietly beside the table on which Red had been strapped, then he leaned over him and said in a theatrical whisper, "Welcome to Oz, Dorothy."

The chuckle that followed was guttural, almost inhuman, and it made Red's skin crawl.

"I am Raul Agabarr. We've invited you here to ask why you have been snooping around these facilities. Perhaps you are the one who took the video that we all saw on television last night."

Red didn't move a muscle or flick an eyelash.

Agabarr smiled, as if he were the perfect host. "Take our guest to holding cell five," he said to the guards. "It is one of our most luxurious suites."

Red maintained his expressionless stare, but inwardly he was stifling a small scream. Dear Jesus, he had drawn the proverbial short straw. His host was none other than the much feared and hated Chief of Security for Area 51, Raul Agabarr—an unprincipled soldier of fortune who sold his services to the highest bidder and who loved his gore so much he would have worked for free.

Two guards half-dragged and pushed Red to his cell. None of the other doors opening into the main corridor that had been cut into the natural bedrock appeared to be cells for prisoners.

The cell was about average size for a large walk-in closet. An old sagging steel cot with spring steel webbing was bolted to the wall. A stained sink and a filth-encrusted ceramic toilet, dark from use and age, were hung on the bare rock walls. Cobwebs laced around the cell, creating the overall effect of a tomb. It was a safe guess, Red decided, that the cell had been around for over thirty years.

When the guard shut the steel door, a harsh clang reverberated down the corridor. The cell was dark, with darker shadows on the walls and floor. The only illumination came from small red lights along the corridor. It was just enough for Red to make out his surroundings.

After he had bruised his fingertips raw exploring the rough walls of the cell, he made contact with something smooth and loose under a rock touching the floor. It was flat, metallic, and pointed at the narrow, tapered end. He snorted when he realized that it was nothing more than an old flatware knife, worn down to a point at the end from prolonged use. Red smiled grimly at his discovery. Would he be able to fight his way to freedom with such a mighty weapon?

Red used his jacket to knock a layer of dust off the steel cot, then he rolled it up to use as a pillow.

"I will now lie down," he told himself. "I will not allow fear to permeate my inner self. I will meditate and move deep into the silence. I will transcend this reality. I will not allow anyone to remove me from my center—no matter what they may do to me."

Chapter Six

Contract Predator

M. D. Crawfoot sat in the back corner of Baltimore's Best Barbeque near the rest rooms. He shifted his weight on the balls of his feet, feeling his calf muscles tighten ever so slightly. Mother, his control, was late and his bottled water was empty.

He toyed with the idea of having a plate of baby back ribs and a cool mug of beer, yet he resisted the urge. He hadn't eaten red meat in years, sustaining his need for protein with dairy products, fish, nuts, tofu, and legumes. His body was bereft of body fat, and since high school he had kept his weight at 185, which was appropriate for his build and height of five-eleven.

Crawfoot had been a contract agent for the National Security Agency since his last tour in Vietnam. He had served his government well, first with the reconnaissance pukes—and then he found his forte as a Marine forces sniper. Three tours, two as a sniper with the Phoenix Rural Pacification program and one as Special Operations for MAC-V assigned to I Corps in northern Vietnam. And then the war was over, too soon to suit him.

Six years in the Marines seemed a lifetime away, but his short service career had served his purpose well in establishing his true talent as a paid assassin, a vocation that he had practiced for the last twenty years. It wasn't the money that drove him. He could make a hell of a lot more hawking out his skills on the international market. No, it was the game, the contest of wit, brains, and physical capabilities. He thought of it as a great cosmic shell game.

Crawfoot noticed a dusty American flag on one of the walls. It was funny, he mused, it just didn't mean the same thing to him as it had when he was a kid. He had gone to Nam to serve his country. He didn't protest. He didn't burn his draft card. He felt that any patriot should serve when called.

He remembered coming home on a flight that landed at Travis Air Base and taking a shuttle to the San Francisco airport with other soldiers and airmen. They were met by antiwar demonstrators who called them baby killers and murderers and who had further humiliated each of them by pelting them with rotten food and eggs, desecrating their uniforms.

He sat alone on the plane home, reeking of filth and unable to muster his emotional defenses as the outward rejection wormed its way into his soul, demoralizing his self-worth and leaving shame in its wake. How could his fellow Americans be so stupid as to blame the guys in uniform for the war? They sure as hell hadn't started it. It was all the fucking politicians.

From that day on, he had loathed the common man and felt that they were little more than sheep that should be led like animals. The general public had no greater worth than that which the leaders of the country had assigned to them. They were the mindless pawns that could be moved about on the cosmic chessboard of life at the whim of their leaders.

Crawfoot looked up. A large silhouette, illuminated by a blaze of sunlight, filled the door frame. Mother looked around the bar, waiting for his eyes to adjust to the dim light, noting the long oval bar with tables evenly spaced for patrons.

Crawfoot couldn't go to Washington, D.C., or the Puzzle Palace, so Mother had to meet him at a place of his choosing. Baltimore's Best Barbecue was on the northern fringe of the city. He had discovered "B's," as the locals called it, ten years previously on an assignment to tag a Westinghouse scientist who was selling advanced radar information to the Russians. The errant scientist was a Jewish immigrant with political ties to Israel, so the agency didn't want a trial or any publicity. The unfortunate man was killed by a mugger—or so the police and the press had determined.

Mother took off his charcoal-gray suit coat before he joined Crawfoot, loosening his tie as he wedged his bulk into the booth.

"I'm always overdressed for this place," Mother said as he shook Crawfoot's hand. "By now I should know enough to change before I meet you here."

B's had been at the same location on York Road for twenty-five years, and it wasn't too far for Mother to drive from the NSA compound.

Mother, aka Colonel Ty Trent, noticed that Crawfoot wore his usual off-the-shelf clothes, nothing that would be traceable or noted as anything but the ordinary, mass-produced, nondescript norm. When the waitress approached him, he ordered a Sam Adams lager and another bottled water for Crawfoot.

When the waitress was an appropriate distance from their table, Crawfoot asked what Mother had for him.

Trent slid a manila envelope the size of a three-inch diskette across the table. "It's all in there," he said, tapping the disk with a forefinger. "The dossier, his picture, psychological profile, and a map and layout of his house on Medina Lake."

"Texas?"

"Yes, outside of San Antonio, about twenty miles."

"I know where it is." Crawfoot's body language showed no emotion when he spoke, and his eyes were impossible to read behind the dark glasses he wore so religiously. "What are the parameters?"

"Elimination in the shortest practical time. It has to look like an accident. Your backup cover, if you're caught, is that you are a deranged, disabled Vietnam vet who's wandered away from the Audie Murphy Veteran's Hospital in San Antonio. There's also a Mexican passport that you will use to re-enter the U.S. You should fly to Montreal from Washington, then fly to Mexico City before your last leg to San Antonio. Upon arrival in San Antonio, you will dispose of the Mexican passport and ID, then use the deranged vet's ID."

"Any input on how the accident should look?" Crawfoot asked.

Trent pulled another envelope from the inside pocket of the suit coat that he had hung on the side chair. "Yes. Ostensibly you are there to hunt deer. Your license is with your ID package. The area around the lake is zoned for hunting, and you will arrive during the season. It starts next week," he paused, looked at his chronometer, "in five days."

Crawfoot nodded. "All right. Is this assignment related to the..." He paused and looked around before continuing. "...Project?" forming the word with his mouth but allowing no sound to escape.

"Yes."

"Are the old men getting more paranoid or what?"

"What's your point?"

Crawfoot grinned and shook his head indulgently, as if he were dealing with a slow learner. "Well, after the two scientists from British GE and those three soldiers last year, and the ex-congressman and the Air Force pilot this year, old Eli and the magic twelve have kept me pretty busy."

"National security has priority, and each one of those people knew the risk they were taking," Trent replied brusquely, scowling his annoyance. "Never forget that those men whom you so often malign have had a great and awesome responsibility placed upon them. Never forget that those men are true patriots."

Crawfoot snorted his disrespectful opinion. "Patriots as opposed to me, a fucking assassin. Is that your less than subtle point, Trent?"

"I mean that they are patriots forging a new tomorrow for all of us. But let's not argue," Trent requested as he set the menu aside.

Crawfoot laughed a bit louder than he had intended. "In order to argue with you, I'd have to give a shit one way or the other."

The waitress returned and they ordered dinner. Trent ordered baby back ribs and another beer. Crawfoot stayed light with a salad and grilled shrimp, both with lime juice.

"Crawfoot," Trent challenged with a sly grin, "how do you know that this place isn't bugged?"

"Because, Mother, see those two guys in the telephone repair uniforms at the bar? For one thing I noticed that they're wearing loafers, not the work shoes repairmen usually wear. And I can see from here that their nails appear to be manicured. Their van outside is new, fresh paint, not a scratch or dent on it. Hell, it doesn't even have a speck of dirt on it. Oh, and another thing. They're carrying nothing in their large double shirt pockets. I'll lay money that they're your monkeys and that they swept the place before your arrival."

Trent made a coy expression and winked. "Just testing, smartass."

Crawfoot put one hand behind his back, the other across his chest, and took a mock bow. "I will assume that's an affirmative."

The colonel took a deep swallow of his Samuel Adams and leaned closer. "You know, Crawfoot, Eli Jerrold and MJ-12 are really steamed about this new leak, the video that showed on NBC's 'Exploring the Unknown' last night. Did you see it?"

Crawfoot shook his head. "Negative. But I heard about it."

"Too much information is leaking out too soon. They expect damage control to be immediate and permanent."

Crawfoot chuckled softly. "What would your new boss at NSA do if he found out you were still taking orders from your old boss? I often visualize the scenario. Could I ever blister your collective asses if I whispered a few of my dark little secrets."

Trent's cheeks turned red with controlled anger. "We call on you because we know that you can be trusted to keep a secret. You've proven your loyalty to us time and again. My involvement with MJ-12 is one of the greatest secrets in the whole of United States intelligence. I'm really shocked that you would even make a cheap joke about playing traitor to a cause to which you have given so much."

Crawfoot pursed his lips. If Trent expected an apology, he would still be waiting when hell froze over. "I would submit, my colonel, that an even bigger secret is how many fucking scientists, researchers, UFO buffs, and nosy military personnel I've killed for Eli and the boys of MJ-12."

Trent displayed a rare, and extremely fleeting, moment of regret. "Sometimes I have nightmares about the things that I have asked you to do."

Crawfoot shrugged. "Forget it, Mother. Just keep feeding me these assignments and telling me that they are necessary for national security. That's all I require. I don't lose sleep. I have a good appetite. And my conscience doesn't bother me."

Trent waved his beer bottle emotionally at figurative punctuation in the air. "I cannot imagine how that could be true, man. You're a human with human emotions."

Crawfoot studied his contact's face. Trent was fat, balding, bearded, and a master of bullshit. Excessive bouts of alcohol abuse and female scandals had sidetracked his once brilliant career at the NSA. If Eli Jerrold had not become the director and sponsored Colonel Ty Trent, the man might have been out on the streets as a contract agent.

"Naw, Trent," Crawfoot answered. "It's all just a fucking job to me." He knew if he had shown the slightest signs of emotional disturbance or weakness of any kind, he himself would be next on old Eli's scratch list.

The food came and Colonel Trent consumed two more beers, an enormous plate of ribs, and a shovel of fries. After stuffing himself, he looked at the mess he had made, smiled, belched, and laughed at Crawfoot. Trent had managed to spot his tailored white dress shirt in at least a dozen places.

Crawfoot sensed that Mother was about to deliver his parting speech, the traditional Spartan send-off: Come back with your shield or on it.

"Crawfoot," he began, building the intensity, "I don't have the whole picture, and for security reasons you know even less. But, man, I want to go on record here that I truly believe that the security of our country is at stake and that what we are doing is essential to protect the freedom of our nation—and our world. Eli Jerrold calls MJ-12's Project a race with the devil to reclaim humanity's destiny. I really don't know exactly what that means, but I respect and trust Eli Jerrold more than I would God when it comes to matters of national security."

Crawfoot maintained a respectful silence, but he suspected that Colonel Ty Trent had a damned good idea of what MJ-12 was up to and that he had a very clear view of the total picture. He had listened quietly to Trent's little speech, but he knew it was just one of those great-sounding lies that intelligence people told and half-believed themselves.

"Colonel Trent," Crawfoot addressed him formally, lifting his water glass in a salute, "you may tell Eli Jerrold, your personal prophet of the new millennium,that my present assignment will be carried out successfully—and that I wish him luck in his race with the devil."

He'll need it, Crawfoot thought to himself.

Chapter Seven

Return to San Antonio

Joe Green didn't recognize the sprawling metropolis as they flew the approach pattern to San Antonio International Airport. He had not been in the city since he had completed basic training at Lackland Air Force Base in the late sixties and departed unceremoniously to Fort Benning for jump school training before being sent to Vietnam.

Joe scratched the bristle on his chin and contemplated the fact that he had just completed another circle in his life. He was born in Americus, Georgia, moved to San Antonio as a kid, then back to Georgia for jump school at Fort Benning, and now he returned to San Antonio some twenty years later to search for scattered pieces of the jigsaw puzzle of his life. He wondered if he had any relatives or friends still living in the area.

There were half a dozen major military bases and dozens of government-oriented research and engineering companies in San Antonio. To outsiders, the city was known as a tourist town, but the locals knew it as a military town in every sense of the word. The largest employer was Uncle Sam, and the majority of retirees living in the area were military veterans and former civil service employees.

Later, after he had picked up a white Ford Taurus rental, Joe stretched out on the bed in his motel room and pulled his personal phone book from his luggage. Luckily he and Farr had exchanged telephone numbers, for the scientist would be certain to be unlisted.

He picked up the receiver, checked his wristwatch. It was five o'clock. Should be a good time. Catch him before dinner. He punched in the numbers on the phone's cradle.

One ring. Another. "Hello, you've reached 210-555-999. There's no one here to answer your call. Leave your name and number, and your call will be returned at the earliest opportunity."

Goddam answering machine.

Joe slammed the receiver down and tried again after smoking another cigarette. This time he left a message:

"Dr. Farr, this is Joe Green from Tonopah, Nevada. We met at the Propulsion Seminar in Tonopah, the one sponsored by the NRC and JPL. Look, I'm staying at the Best Western near the Brooks Advanced Research Center. I'm in room 126. I'd really like to talk to you about your research work in Nevada. This would really be important to me. Please call...."

His time had run out on the answering machine's tape, and he held the receiver listening to the dial tone.

"Let's hope he doesn't hear it and wonder why he should give a shit," Joe grimaced.

Later that evening, Joe drove the rented Taurus over to the southeast side of San Antonio. In the fifties and early sixties, this side of the city had been dotted with little bedroom communities of blue collar works of Polish, Czech, and German descent.

When he was a kid, he and his maternal grandfather, Cecil Reid, who had quite a sweet tooth, wandered the neighborhood making major decisions, such as whether to have a Black, Brown, Orange, or Purple Cow at the Pig Stand. Vanilla ice cream floats with cola, root beer, orange, or grape soda made for a cool treat.

Sometimes the two of them walked down to the little green and white Texaco station with the tin Bardahl signs on the corner of Holmgreen and W. W. White to buy a nickel cola. After a few sips, Grandpa Reid would pour a bag of peanuts into the bottle. Little Joe preferred a Moon Pie with his soda pop.

Joe chuckled at his nostalgia time. He had come to San Antonio searching for truth, and here he was wondering if they still bottled Barq's Strawberry Cream soda.

As he drove east on W. W. White Road, little seemed familiar to him. But when he turned onto Holmgreen Road, the past came rushing back.

The little wooden frame homes hadn't changed that much, and he held his breath when he saw the old Nazarene Church on the left. He pulled onto the gravel apron that served as a parking lot for the small church and shut off the ignition.

His grandfather had earned a living as a carpenter and cabinet maker before turning his life over to religion, so before he put his tools away, he had built the little L-shaped church. With the help of some church members, Grandfather Reid had also constructed the modest-sized parsonage to the right of the church—which was now painted an ugly brown, not the white with green trim that Joe remembered.

Another flash of memory hit him. It was a sunny day, and he and Grandfather Reid were cruising down W. W. White Road.

"This is your last day of vacation, Little Joe," Grandfather said. "Monday we're going to take you down to the elementary school and register you."

"What grade will I be in?"

Grandfather frowned at him in a manner that told Joe that he should have known the answer. "Second grade."

"Second grade?"

"Sure," Grandfather said impatiently. Joe was beginning to feel uneasy. Somehow he had angered the old man. "Second grade. Don't you remember going to the first grade?"

Joe shook his head. "Where?"

Grandfather was quiet for a while before he answered. "Americus. You went to...Wheatly Elementary School in Americus, Georgia."

"I...I don't remember, Grandfather."

And, try as he might, Joe never did remember. All he could recall whenever he tried to think back to Americus was the Light. The Light that had confronted them on their move to Texas.

He remembered the Light very well. And that's when the nightmares, the cold sweats, and the bed wetting started.

His problems increased the next year when his father died, leaving his family penniless. Joe was convinced that the Light had returned for his father, and for many years he was terrified that it would come back for him, too.

His grandparents somehow made room for him and his mother in the small parsonage. At night when he lay in bed listening to his mother speak to her parents in hushed tones, he overheard bits of conversation such as "too much stress" and "he just couldn't handle being a failure" and "shotgun blast" and "unforgivable sin." Joe's life changed dramatically when he was suddenly surrounded by his grandparents' fevered brand of religion and expected to embrace it.

Grandfather Reid had assessed young Joe as being weak like his father. It was clear to the patriarch that the boy lacked direction in his life. Joe's father drank hard and smoked relentlessly, and Grandfather Reid took it as his personal mission to see that the son didn't follow the father's misbegotten path to sin and damnation.

By the time he was twelve, Joe was confused by the conflicts in his life. He hadn't done well at school, and his grandparents' old- time religion was consuming his life.

The week began with Sunday school, noon church services, afternoon family togetherness, evening services, and family prayers at night before bedtime. Without fail, Joe, his mother, and grandmother listened to Grandfather read from the Holy Bible, starting at 9:30 in the evening, progressing through family prayer on their knees in the living room, then to bed with prayers by ten. On Tuesday nights there was choir practice; Wednesday nights, prayer meeting; Thursday, missionary meeting; Friday, visitation; Saturday afternoons, youth functions at the First Nazarene Church. Such a rigorous schedule of prayer, Bible passages, and a disciplined pilgrim's progress left little time for Joe to make friends.

At night he would lie awake, praying to God to make the Light that filled his nightmares disappear.

Joe sat in his room at the Military Inn, smoking his second pack of cigarettes, looking out at the night, and sipping coffee from the thermos that he had filled at the motel's restaurant. Somewhere around six in the morning, he nodded off.

He awoke with a full bladder at 9:10 A.M., but instead of going directly to the bathroom, he dialed Carlton Farr's number.

Farr's machine answered, and once again at the sound of the beep, Joe introduced himself. He heard a voice from the receiver just as he was about to hang up.

"Hello, are you there?"

Joe jerked the receiver back to his mouth and blurted, "Yes, I'm here. Is this Dr. Carlton Farr?"

"What do you want?"

"I thought we might meet and have a drink."

Farr chuckled softly. "I don't drink with strangers."

Joe forced himself to be patient. "We're not strangers, Dr. Farr. We met at the classified propulsion symposium in Tonopah, and I asked you if the prototype advanced technology aerospace vehicles were often mistaken for UFOs."

"Hmm, yes, I seem to remember now," Farr said. "I told you the probability was quite likely nonexistent."

Joe smiled. The man was being cautious. "No, as a matter of fact, you said the probability was about ninety-six percent."

"Did I now?"

"You did. Then I asked you, if UFOs exist, then who do the vehicles belong to? Your answer was, 'Others, not us.'"

There was a long silence. "Look, Mr. Green, I'm not at all comfortable talking about such matters over the telephone. I'll call you back shortly."

"Wait, I'm staying at…"

"I have your message from last night. I know where you are." And Dr. Carlton Farr cut off their connection.

Joe took a shower, then ordered a pitcher of coffee from room service. When the phone rang two hours later, he picked it up on the first ring.

"I'm at a place named Pat's at Medina Lake," Farr told him. "If you'll get a pencil and paper, I'll give you directions. I assume you have transportation."

"I do," Joe said, digging pen and notepad out of a drawer in the nightstand. He wrote fast and asked only one question. "When?"

An hour later, Joe spotted a liquor store next to the HEB grocery on Culebra and Tezel. He decided to pick up a bottle of unblended single malt whiskey. He chose a quart of Glenfiddich and was certain that Farr would appreciate the quality.

As he drove to meet the scientist, Joe mused that once again he seemed drawn to life's events as if he was being summoned by some relentless, unseen force.

Chapter Eight

The Devil's Domain

Sometime during what he guessed to be the early morning hours, Red was awakened by the abrasive sound of metal grinding against metal. Disoriented at first from waking up in the dark in a strange place, Red's eyes finally managed to make out a food tray, an aluminum mug, and a personal hygiene kit with a roll of toilet paper.

He figured he knew pretty well the psychology the mean-eyed honcho Agabarr was trying to work on him. First they brought him blindfolded into what looked like some kind of laboratory, spread-eagled him on a table, made threatening noises, then brought him to a dank, dark cell to get good and nervous.

Red laughed. It was like the time his teacher locked him in the clothes closet in third grade so he would promise not to disrupt the class when she let him out. These military dorks were just trying to scare him. Let his fears work on him during the night. Secret air base or not, there was no way that they would lay hands on a civilian. He would be in for a first class ass chewing by Agabarr, then he would be turned over to the county sheriff to cool his heels in jail until Blake Webster came to bail him out.

He tasted the food on the tray. Bland and uninteresting, but he was hungry. The mug contained some tepid liquid that tasted vaguely like coffee.

Red stepped over to the dark-stained sink to wash his hands with the small bar of soap. He had pretty much wolfed down the food and quickly swallowed the coffee without considering that it might be drugged. His hands hadn't even worked up a lather when the dimly lighted cell began tipping peculiarly to one side.

He managed to lie down on the steel cot before he slipped back into darkness.

When he was next awakened by the harsh, scraping metallic sound of the food tray being unceremoniously delivered to his cell, he had no idea how many hours—or days—had passed.

He considered avoiding the bland food and the awful coffee, but he had awakened with an unrelenting thirst.

This time there was a voice to accompany the tray: "Eat up, old man. We're going to have some fun and games…soon."

The voice had a sneering tone to it that suggested pain and unpleasantness. Just what they wanted him to think, Red told himself. They wanted him bewildered and bothered. In some ways he felt like the proverbial Thanksgiving turkey being fattened for the kill.

He took a hearty swallow of the coffee. There would be no drugs this time, he reasoned. They wanted him alert, but docile. He chuckled to himself. They were about to learn that the word "docile" had never been in his dictionary.

He had just finished his meal when he heard voices in the corridor. The cell door slid open, and two guards motioned for him to get to his feet.

Before Red could speak or react, one of the men raised his hand and fired a trailing-wire electrovoltaic weapon at him. The thousands of disabling volts running down the wire were set to stun, not to kill. Red crumpled into a heavy pile on the floor, his body shaking in spasms from the electrical shock. He was dimly aware of the two guards lifting him by his arms, pulling him out into the corridor, and strapping him onto a gurney. Then he blacked out.

When Red regained consciousness, the doctor was just completing his examination. His clothes were lying on the floor; he had been stripped naked while he lay on the gurney.

Red's body belied his age. He still had the stamina of a twenty year old from treading the Nevada mountains and deserts foot by foot during the past several years. Although his body was scarred from bar fights and gave evidence of hard mileage, he had an inner source of energy driven by an iron will.

Agabarr, wickedly smiling like a demon who brought with him a portable hell, stepped into his line of vision. "Enough," he snapped at Dr. Quinlin. Then to the guards: "Put our guest in the chair."

Red saw that the interrogation room was a large stone room that contained a desk, a chair, a stool, and something that looked like a dentist's chair hooked up to many wires running to a console directly behind it. There was a light above the strange chair and a lamp on the desk.

Agabarr watched silently as the men strapped Red into the chair. Red saw that the thin, dark-haired man's eyes had an evil squint. His pupils were like twin black vortexes that could absorb light.

"Secure him well," he advised the guards.

As one of the men pulled a strap tight around Red, he muttered, "He won't be going anywhere."

Agabarr's voice was as cold as death. "Your life depends on it."

The guard with the loose mouth swallowed hard and averted his attention from Agabarr's dark stare.

When Red was strapped in tight, Dr. Quinlin stepped forward and gave him an injection.

"What's that?" Agabarr demanded.

Red noticed that the doctor seemed both impatient and disgusted with Agabarr. "It's a psychohypnotic. It will make him alert mentally, but passive, disassociated from reality. He will be easier to question."

Red relaxed. Fucking amateurs. He was certain that he would be able to resist the drug. He had studied numerous mind control systems and yoga techniques, to say nothing of the time that he had spent with the shaman of a Native American Church who had taught him the mysteries of Mescalito, peyote. He had participated in more than sixteen services in which he had chewed the peyote buds, puked up his guts into a tin pail,and soared to blend with the Great Mystery. On his own, he had experimented with mescaline, psilocybin, and the sacred mushrooms. After dozens of trips to in-between universes, he had learned to control an objective, observer aspect of his mental faculties even while ostensibly under the influence of psycho-hallucinogenic drugs.

Red would employ passive cooperation, not passive resistance to Agabarr's questions. Passive cooperation would permit him to answer any queries explicitly, implicitly, literally, figuratively, and from any other point of view that came to mind—without giving up any usable information.

"What were you doing in Area 51 when you were apprehended?" Agabarr asked him.

"Doing what a man ought to be doing. Minding my own business, minding my donkey, and minding my father's business," Red answered. "Know ye not that I must be about my father's business?"

"Who is your father?"

"The Lord of Heaven and Earth. When you go into the city, you will see a man with the colt of an ass. Tell him that the Lord has need of it. It is Hosanna time in the streets of Jerusalem!"

Agabarr scowled at Dr. Quinlin. "What the hell is going on here?"

"What is going on," Red answered, "is the logical process inverted as common man confronts his existential leap of faith into the vortex of contemporary soap operas."

"What the fuck did you give him?" Agabarr shouted. "Do you know your business, Dr. Quinlin? Or shall I do it my way?"

Dr. Quinlin stepped forward with another needle and Red felt a rush. The additional shot of joy juice would make it harder, but he knew he could block the drug's full effect.

For four grueling hours, Agabarr questioned Red about what he knew about the Project and Area 51.

Why had he been spotted on more than one occasion spying on the Groom and Papoose facilities?

Had he taken any pictures or videos?

Had he been providing anyone with information about Area 51?

Red assumed completely the role of the desert prospector. If anything, the drug made it easier for him to role-play and to draw upon the knowledge of the area that he had been accumulating since he was a boy outside of Bouncing Bertha's.

He told Agabarr that he didn't know anything about what was going on with all the military goons running around the desert and he really didn't care—as long as they stayed the hell away from him. And the only reason that he was ever seen near their fucking facilities was the fact that their fucking facilities were on the routes that he had been taking to desert mining sites for years.

Although his answers seemed solid and truthful, Agabarr still didn't like the way that Red responded a bit too flippantly.

For the next twelve hours, with the doctor and the interrogator popping uppers to stay awake, Raul Agabarr and Red fought a battle of wills.

For a total of sixteen hours, Red had bored the pants off his captors and his interrogator. Each question brought a deluge of minute details about the life of a desert prospector instead of the quick information that Agabarr wanted to hear.

Red's iron will was too great for the drugs that Dr. Quinlin administered to be effective. Agabarr sat slumped at the desk. After sixteen solid hours of confrontation, captive and captors had worn each other down.

Red was taken back to his cell for rest—and then brought back as soon as he had fallen asleep. At least that was what it felt like to him, but he really had no way of knowing for certain how long his recess period had lasted.

When he was brought back to the interrogation room, Red discovered to his great dismay that Agabarr had decided to give up on drugs. He was holding two electric probes in his hands.

Chapter Nine

The Two Greatest Conspiracies Ever

When Joe Green arrived at the small bar called Pat's Place, it was nearly three in the afternoon. The sky was filled with a hazy, gray cover and was full of the kind of moisture that made the skin tacky to the touch.

Humidity in the high desert of central Nevada averaged around fifteen percent, with the exception of the rare rainstorms. In San Antonio, it was the exception when the humidity dropped below fifty percent for two days in a row. Joe didn't remember the humidity being so oppressive as a child growing up there, but adults rarely reconcile the past with the present.

Dr.Carlton Farr sat at a picnic table under the covered patio behind the bar. A slightly overweight man in his mid-fifties, he was holding a small brown dog and nursing a long-neck bottle of Lone Star beer.

"Dr. Farr." Joe presented himself with an outstretched hand. "I'm Joe Green from Tonopah. Remember me now?"

"Vaguely. Maybe." He motioned for Joe to join him at the picnic table. "This is Albert," the scientist said, indicating the hunk of fur sitting on his lap and panting against the heat.

"Guess I didn't make much of an impression at the symposium." Joe laughed nervously.

Farr narrowed his eyes, studying Joe's features. "Do you want a beer? They were out of my favorite, Shiner Bock. The coldest brew they had was a Lone Star, so I ordered that. Do you want one?"

Joe nodded, and the scientist called for a waitress.

Farr raised his bottle to his forehead and relished the feel of the cool glass against his skin.

"I thought you might remember me," Joe said, "because I asked you so many questions about…things you didn't want to discuss in public at the symposium. We didn't really have time for an actual conversation, so I guess I can't be surprised that you don't remember me."

Joe's beer came and, as he smiled at the waitress, he self-consciously ran a hand through his damp hair.

"Aha!" Farr laughed. "Now I'm getting the image of you at the symposium. A seemingly quiet young man with disheveled blond hair, dressed in a long-sleeved white shirt with the cuffs turned up, a loosely knotted tie, faded jeans and loafers, who suddenly came alive with a dozen uncomfortable questions."

Joe breathed a sigh of relief. "Sounds like a fair description."

Farr lowered his gaze and grinned impishly. "I recall that I rather tactlessly brushed you off."

Joe nodded. "I deserved it the way I kind of jumped at you with a lot of questions about black projects."

"Is that why you're here, Joe Green? You want to pursue the conversation that you tried so hard to initiate in Tonopah?" Farr shook his head in wonder.

"You've got it," Joe admitted.

"Then let's finish our beers and get out of this humidity," Farr said. "Poor Albert has been panting up a storm. My place is just a short distance from here. We'll go there. I have air conditioning and a dehumidifier."

Carlton Farr accompanied Joe to the rented Taurus and got in on the passenger's side. Albert sat obediently on the scientist's lap as Farr directed Joe to turn off on a narrow dirt path that cut across the inlet between Pat's Place and his home.

Farr's house was on a hill that overlooked Lake Medina. Five acres of the heavily wooded land that surrounded the home also belonged to him. The structure sat atop a base that elevated the floor about eight feet in the rear. A large deck wrapped itself half-way around the compact, three-bedroom, white wood frame house.

From the inside, the house assumed the ambiance of a cabin, with oak slat walls, wooden floors, and dropped beam ceiling. The living room contained two overstuffed chairs, a small sofa, and a table that had been placed around the brick fireplace in the corner.

Joe noticed that there wasn't a single picture or knick-knack in sight. There were two large bookshelves. A very quick glance at a number of the titles indicated primarily history, religion, and scientific reference.

Joe took the fine bottle of Scotch out of his shoulder bag and presented it to Farr, who was feeding Albert in the adjoining open kitchen area.

Farr grinned. "The persistent fellow also bears gifts."

It was obvious that he appreciated the gesture. "But do call me, Carl. I really don't like to drink with people who call me Doctor."

Farr accepted the bottle, holding it as gently as if he were entrusted with someone's baby. "Would you care to open this fine single malt Scotch and have a drink? Or is it too early in the day for you?"

"Not at all," Joe said. "I take mine on the rocks with a splash of water."

Farr nodded approvingly. "I take mine a la natural. I have some bottled artesian water if you like. It's better than the lake water that comes up in my well."

Joe told him that ought to be about perfect, then asked how long he had been retired. "I gathered from your presentation at the symposium that you were doing some research for the Department of Defense and the Air Force."

"I took an early retirement about two months ago. Just couldn't deal with the stress anymore."

Joe noticed that Farr did indeed take his liquor neat, for he had filled half of an eight-ounce glass with the amber-hued scotch. He was glad that he had opted for the quart bottle rather than a fifth. When he tasted his own drink, he decided that Farr had forgotten about the artesian water. Fortunately, Farr had filled his glass with ice before adding the scotch and a dash of water. He made a mental note to mix his own drinks for the remainder of his visit.

Farr had picked up the scruffy mutt and with his free hand he raised his glass to Joe. "To your health."

Joe returned the salute. Farr looked healthy enough for a man in his mid-fifties, and he looked too young to retire. He was about twenty pounds overweight, but his legs and arms still had plenty of muscle.

Farr pushed the graying strands of hair back over his balding scalp. "Let me show you the rest of my humble abode."

Joe followed him to small bedroom which contained only a queen-sized bed and one dresser. "This is my bedroom, as if you couldn't guess," Farr smiled. "And this," he pointed to the open door next to the bedroom, "is the bathroom and next to it is the spare bedroom."

He set Albert back down, took Joe's arm, and gestured toward the spare bedroom. "In there is where I spend most of my evenings."

Joe could not help wondering about the significance of a room with a high grade Higgens cipher lock on the door. What could merit such security when it appeared that the most valuable artifact in the entire Farr household was a small Braun espresso-cappuccino machine in the kitchen? Other than that one indulgence, Dr. Carlton Farr appeared not to possess a television set, a stereo, or any electronic gadgets. The furniture in the house could very well have been purchased at a garage sale. There were no magazines lying around. No people-pictures of friends or family. It was a totally depersonalized dwelling.

Joe followed his host into the living room, then paused at the front door to enjoy the view of the lake. Two small bass fishing boats bobbed lazily on its surface.

Farr plopped down in the light-gray, two-cushioned sofa and indicated that Joe should take the stuffed recliner nearest him. "Tell me something about yourself before we begin this conversation that you have come so far to have."

Joe sat back in the recliner. From what he knew about Carlton Farr, he was the kind of man who didn't trust anyone. The scientist might be pure intellect in the laboratory, but it was obvious that he relied on his instincts to inform him about the people he met. He thought that Farr liked him, but it was obvious that he also had his own ghosts to reckon with.

Joe told the scientist that he had been born in Georgia and raised in San Antonio. "I went into the Vietnam conflict right out of school and got out of the service shortly after it was over. I worked in communications, intelligence, and crypto. Then I put on civilian clothes and did the same thing for the government for the next ten years before I went to work as a government contractor in the defense industry."

Farr chuckled as Albert jumped up onto his lap. "Joe, you are the only person that I've ever met who can tell his life story in one minute flat. Come on, man, is it modesty? You surely could not have had a boring life if you were in Southeast Asia and worked for the NSA."

"Some of it is from working so many dark programs," Joe said. "And I guess I am a private kind of person. What makes you think I was with the National Security Agency?"

Farr laughed, idly stroking Albert's head and ears. "Come on, who do you think you're kidding? All communications and intelligence personnel and especially—or should I say, 'exclusively'—cryptologists have had prior connections with the NSA. And you do live outside of the Nellis Range or Area 51, don't you?"

Joe acknowledged that his assumptions were correct. "Were you connected, Carl?"

Farr set the dog back on the floor and dismissed it with a playful swat on its little rump. "The DOE and DARPA funded all of the research projects in which I was involved. They don't do anything that the NSA isn't aware of. And most of the stuff we worked with was so classified that the software and records were encrypted."

Joe had done his homework, reading or skimming through Farr's published books, articles, and papers. Dr. Carlton Farr was one of the leading theoretical propulsion experts in the United States. He had worked at Sandia, Los Alamos, and Lawrence Livermore National laboratories for twenty-nine years before transferring to the classified Brooks Advanced Research Center at Brooks Air Force Base for the past couple of years. In addition, Farr had been an MIT physicist, an NSA mathematician, and a Stanford materials scientist. The only personal element that Joe had been able to isolate in all of the man's writings was his apparent interest in Sumerian archaeology.

"I found your fascination with the ancient culture of Sumer to be quite interesting," Joe ventured. "An interest in the past seemed so much in contrast with all the futuristic projects you've been involved in."

Farr's eyebrows arched, surprised by Joe's sudden introduction of one of his passions into the conversational flow. He studied his empty glass for a moment. "You ready for a refill?"

Joe indicated that he was fine. He had only taken that initial sip from his drink.

When he returned with a fresh supply of scotch, Farr responded to Joe's interest in his Sumerian studies. "What began as a hobby evolved into an obsession. The ancient Sumerians were an astonishing people. Did you know that they settled in Mesopotamia—or Iraq as we would call it today—about 4500 B.C.E.?"

Joe nodded. "I also find it interesting that the Sumerian civilization precedes 3760 B.C.E., the first date on the Jewish calendar, which is also the date that certain Christian fundamentalists acknowledge as creation. However, even that is predated by 4236 B.C.E., which is the first date in the Egyptian calendar."

The look on the scientist's face showed that he was surprised that Joe had his dates correct.

Farr went on to deliver an impromptu lecture of sorts, telling how the Sumerians had established their civilization on an agricultural basis and had built the first true cities known to humankind. They had fine buildings, large monuments, public water systems, and sewage drainage.

Warming to what was his self-confessed obsession, Farr stated that the first known hieroglyphic writings, or cuneiform, came from the Sumerians. Tens of thousands of clay tablets had survived and had been translated.

The Sumerians had built an impressive empire of city states made up of craftsmen, administrators, farmers, herders, fishermen, doctors, lawyers, pharmacists, and religious leaders. They reigned supreme until, eventually, somewhere around 2200 B.C.E., their empire was slowly absorbed by the Semitic people from Arabia.

"The Sumerians believed that the gods had taken an active hand in the development of their civilization," Farr said, "and they also believed that these gods actually coexisted with them on Earth. Do you find this at all interesting, Joe?"

"Yes, surely," Joe answered politely. In truth, he considered it a diversion from the subject that he really wished to pursue with Farr, but he didn't want to offend him.

Farr winked knowingly. "Well, you will find there is a point to all of this. For example, the Sumerians believed that there were twelve planets. The nine we recognize, our sun and moon, and another between Mars and Jupiter."

Joe was confused. "I can see how they would have classified the sun and moon as planets—and I'll take your word for it that they knew about the other nine—but there is no planet between Mars and Jupiter. That's where the asteroid belt lies."

Farr readily conceded the location of the asteroid belt. "Although most astronomers theorize that the asteroids are residual matter left over from the formation of the planets, some of them believe that the belt was formed when a planet was destroyed after a celestial collision with another large object. Asteroids were discovered in 1801, and Clyde Tombaugh discovered the planet Pluto in 1930."

Farr sucked on a piece of ice from his glass, waiting for what he had said to sink in.

Joe's brow wrinkled. "And?"

Farr laughed at Joe's confusion. "The point that I'm trying to make is that the Sumerians knew about Pluto's existence over five thousand years ago and that, according to their astronomy, there was once a planet where the asteroid belt now exists."

Joe smiled. "So how did these early geniuses figure all this out?"

"They were taught by beings from outer space that they thought to be gods," Farr said bluntly.

Joe shook his head and grinned broadly. "Are you talking about the ancient-astronaut theory? Gods in flaming chariots? Jesus in a spaceship?"

"Don't be so quick to dismiss what I am suggesting, Joe," Farr told him. "In the Judeo-Christian book of Genesis, we read that God said, 'Let us make man in our image, after our likeness.' Doesn't that sound like God was talking to others like him at the time of creation?"

"You definitely have a different slant on scripture than my Church of the Nazarene preacher grandfather," Joe laughed.

Farr spoke on about the "sons of God" taking wives of the "fair daughters of men."

Joe was afraid that he may have reached Dr. Carlton Farr a bit too late for the once brilliant physicist to be of any help to him. He was spouting a theory that sounded like the headlines in the supermarket tabloids. There had been dozens of books written on the "God was an ancient astronaut" theme. Television documentaries had explored the subject time and again. These pseudoscientific explorations could always be counted on to boost the ratings, but no respectable scientist took them seriously.

"How can any thinking person deny that our species had a little help from our cosmic friends during the course of our evolution?" Farr said, his voice rising with his convictions. "Two million years passed between advanced Australopithecus and Neanderthal, yet their tools were virtually of the same primitive type. Then forty or fifty thousand years ago, Cro-Magnon and his cousin, Homo sapiens, appeared from nowhere and seemingly swept Neanderthal man from the face of the Earth. Another thirty or forty thousand years go by and the Sumerians have a thriving civilization. Forty thousand years from the appearance of Cro-Magnon until the Sumerian culture is only two percent of the time between Australopithecus and Neanderthal. In the next six thousand years, we went from wooden wheels and clay tablets to artificial intelligence and genetic engineering. Don't you find it pretty hard to believe that a nice, steady progressive evolution could take such a miraculous leap forward without a little cosmic goosing from somewhere else?"

Joe glanced at his watch. It appeared that he had come a hell of a long way for a drink.

Farr immediately sensed that he was losing his audience. "Joe, I have copies of the documents that I am about to refer to on computer disk."

Out of courtesy Joe decided that he would give Farr another forty-five minutes or so. An hour, tops.

Farr began his story: "In the autumn of 1947, Miles Copland, the station chief in Damascus of the newly formed CIA, was presented with a cache of ancient parchment scrolls by an Egyptian trader. Copland proceeded to photograph these scrolls, and afterwards a CIA associate, an expert in Hebrew studies and Semitic languages, identified the major significance of the parchments. One scroll was later identified by scholars as the book of Daniel. Other texts, although photographed, have never surfaced for open examination by scholars."

Joe wondered if Farr was talking about the famous Dead Sea Scrolls.

"Some of the parchments were later released and were given that name by the scholars who received them," Farr said, "but there were other texts, perhaps as many as seven, that were secreted away."

"After all these years, we hardly know what is contained in the Dead Sea Scrolls," Joe said, taking another sip of his drink.

"From what I have learned, the early involvement of the CIA with the scrolls was to screen those that dealt directly with the life of Jesus of Nazareth," Farr continued. "Harry S. Truman was the president then, and shortly after the discovery of the Dead Sea Scrolls was officially announced, he was quoted as saying, 'There is nothing new in this world except the history you do not know.'"

Farr paused, took another swallow of Scotch. "Joe, a lot of history, especially in these United States, has been suppressed since Truman authorized the formation of the CIA and the NSA."

"So you think that Truman was involved in suppressing discoveries made from the Dead Sea Scrolls?"

Farr shifted uncomfortably. "The man who said that dropping the atom bomb was no great decision, that it was merely another powerful weapon in the arsenal of righteousness, was more than capable of directing the CIA's involvement in every aspect of our lives, from politics to religion."

Joe leaned back in the chair. "But you're talking about suppressing information that affects millions of Christians. That's supreme arrogance."

"Arrogance?" Farr said slowly, as if he were tasting the bitterness of the word. "In 1945, Truman said, 'The human animal cannot be trusted for anything good except en masse. The combined thought and action of the whole people of any race, creed, or nationality will always point in the right direction.'

"Joe, what may seem like arrogance to you, may, to someone in power, seem like a benevolent protective measure. Truman, who certainly considered himself to be a good man, a benevolent despot with the good of his people foremost in his mind, may have sincerely felt that he was doing the right and proper thing to protect the masses. There may, in fact, have been a number of good men who felt that they must protect the tender American psyche after it had just survived the ghastly terrors of a savage world war."

"Noblesse oblige," Joe said. "The moral responsibility of the leader to care for his people."

Farr shrugged. "Something like that. When an entire world has just had so many of their ideals and belief structures turned upside down by the devastation of the most destructive war known to recorded history, why knock out what underpinnings they have remaining by telling them that some of things that they most dearly cherish may not be so? Why destroy what little faith they have left?"

Joe was becoming intrigued. "If there is a conspiracy to keep these scrolls hidden away, what revelations do you think they contain?"

Farr poured himself another shot of Scotch. "The scrolls declare that many prophets and teachers of ancient times received their teachings directly from gods."

"I thought that's what the old prophets always claimed," Joe said. "That they were receiving messages from God."

Farr's voice was becoming slightly slurred. "Not God, my boy. The gods. Beings that we today would call aliens. Astronauts from another world. The guardians of our faith and our political structure could not have the great church-going masses believing that large parts of their religion had been dictated by entities from another planet.

"The two greatest conspiracies conducted by church and state have to do with the suppression of all evidence of the ancient 'gods' and their involvement in the creation of humankind...and the fact that these so-called gods have returned."

Now Farr had Joe's full attention. "Carl, would I be making a quantum leap if I were to ask you if you believe that what is going on in Area 51 has anything to do with your ancient gods and your obsession with Sumer?"

"Possibly," Farr shrugged. "You came to me looking for answers, Joe, but I suspect that you have the truth somewhere inside of you."

"I've got all kinds of things inside me, Carl," Joe blurted. "That's why I came here, hoping you might give me a few answers. What do you know about what is really going on at Area 51?"

Farr looked at his watch. "Damn, it's nearly eight o'clock. I didn't know it was so late. Tell you what, Joe, I've got some leftover chili and corn bread in the fridge. Let's eat. You can sleep on the sofa, and we'll continue our conversation in the morning."

Joe spoke honestly. "I'm more hungry for information than I am for food."

Farr teetered as he got to his feet. "Look, we've killed half a bottle of Scotch this afternoon. I'm too tired to play host any longer than supper time."

Joe had barely had more than two shots all afternoon, but he decided to humor Farr and eat his homemade chili and corn bread. It was fairly tasty, if a little hot.

After dinner, about nine, Farr threw a blanket and pillow on the sofa for Joe and went to his room.

About ten-thirty, Joe got tired of sitting on the porch overlooking the lake and decided to walk over to Pat's Place. Except for a couple of old men drinking beer, a stocky Hispanic in hunter's clothes, and an old woman behind the bar, the place was empty.

Joe ordered a cold beer and made eye contact with the Latino, who seemed to be staring at him as if he recognized him. But then the man looked away.

Joe went outside to sit on the patio. There was a slight breeze, making the humidity more bearable.

Out of the corner of his eye, he saw the Hispanic fellow watching him from the doorway of the bar. A few minutes later, when Joe went in to pick up a cold six-pack to take back to Farr's place, the man had gone.

As Joe turned off the paved road onto the gravel road that led toward the house on the hill, he thought he heard the scuffle of feet behind him. He stopped and the noise behind him stopped.

He waited a few seconds and heard nothing other than the breeze rustling through the tops of the trees. He continued walking down the gravel road.

He certainly hoped that Farr would open up to him tomorrow and trust him with his secrets of Area 51. If only…

The crunching of gravel interrupted his thoughts.

The sound was definitely behind him. He kept walking, listening carefully. Without question, something or someone was following him.

Joe gently set the six-pack down on the side of the road, then abruptly turned and began to run back the way that he had come. He heard someone scramble on the gravel road just ahead in the darkness—and then something crashed into the heavy brush to his left.

Joe stood still and listened. Whatever—whoever—had been following him was working its way farther into the undergrowth. There was no doubt in his mind that he had been followed. But why?

Chapter Ten

One Truth at a Time

When Blake Webster, freelance journalist and UFO conspiracy buff extraordinary, crossed the California-Nevada border around sunset on Sunday in his thirty-foot Dodge RV, he was still on a natural high from the telecast of "Exploring the Unknown" on Friday night. He knew that the video of the alien starship had really socked it to MJ-12. Anonymous though they may be, Webster knew for certain that they did exist and that they were conducting the most extensive cover-up by any government in the history of the world.

Nevada called itself the silver state, the battle-born state, and the sagebrush state. A more appropriate motto, he thought to himself, would be the conspiracy state. Of the 111,000 square miles of land in Nevada, more than eighty percent was controlled by the federal government—the highest percentage of any state in the union. If it were not for the gaming industry, the federal government would be the largest employer in the state, with eighteen thousand federal and military personnel and another twenty thousand government contractors and suppliers. The Nevada Test Site, Nellis Air Force Base and Gunnery Range, Fallon Naval Air Station, the Hawthorne Army Ammunition Plant, and the aerospace industry ate up a lot of U.S. tax dollars.

Webster wondered about Red Redding, his private undercover man in the desert. He hoped that he'd had the good sense to lay low after the video had aired on Friday night. This was no time for any stupid heroics. Let's not push our luck, Red baby.

It was nearly midnight when he drove into Las Vegas, and he was surprised to find the traffic bumper-to-bumper, even on a Saturday night. He turned off the strip, explosive with the myriad garish, brilliant lights from the casinos, and pulled into the back lot of the Holiday Suites Motel. He often stayed at this particular motel. It was centrally located and had a few unadvertised RV hookups in back.

As he left the RV, he glanced down at the Nevada license plates that he had hurriedly placed on the Dodge before crossing the border. Nevada was run by the federal government, the gaming board, and organized crime—all of whom watched out-of-state vehicles closely, especially where he was going.

Webster's schedule allowed eight hours sleep before his three-hour drive to Rachel, Nevada, the following morning to connect with Wayne Newsome, protector of the environment, endangered species, and a host of other causes, primarily Extraterrestrial Biological Entities (EBEs), UFOs, and the secrets of Area 51.

Webster hoped there would be a message waiting for him from Red. If there wasn't, he would be damned worried.

Pops Feldman was at the front desk in the lobby. Once a notorious get-rich-quick, alcoholic skirt chaster, Webster knew that the old man had been reformed for nearly twenty years, due in major part to the efforts of Pops' loving Jehovah's Witness wife and ex-stripper Cherry Feldman.

"How's the night life, Pops?"

Pops pulled a deep drag from his cigar and blew a series of rings at Webster. "Same old, same old. The hustlers, pros, and tourists are passing through in droves. And they say that near four thousand families are moving to LV every month."

"Sounds like the same old gold rush fever," Webster said. "Pops, you got any messages for me?"

"Matter of fact, I do," he nodded. "If I can just find it in this pile of shit."

He rummaged through the thick pile of papers, bills, and memos on the top of his desk, peering intensely through his bifocals. "Here it is, by ginger! I'm not completely senile, after all."

The message was from Dr. Charles Farr. Webster had been in a very quiet, very secret contact with the top scientist for several months. The journalist knew that if he were to get his ass in a wringer over the video shown on "Exploring the Unknown"—or if the Air Force should try to convince the public that it was faked—Dr. Farr was prepared to come out of the closet and back him up with substantiating documents.

For obvious reasons, the message was cryptic and terse: "You want it, come to me."

Fair enough. He would drive to Medina Lake. Dr. Farr had already told him that he was convinced that the MJ-12 committee or the NSA would not hesitate to eliminate him if he chose to reveal the information that he possessed concerning the ultra-secret projects with which he had been for so long involved.

As the scientist had told him early in their association: "The truth is horrendous. The truth is an abomination to everything that you believe and have been taught throughout your life. If you want to tell people the truth, find out all you can about MJ-12, the Rapture, Hangar 12, and the twelfth planet."

Blake Webster loved mysteries, and he loved it even more when he knew that an enigma was starting to unravel. As a kid he had devoured the Hardy Boys, Sherlock Holmes, Doc Savage, James Bond, and Agatha Christie. His passion was discovering clues, developing leads, and tracking down an elusive story.

He was five feet seven in his stocking feet and he weighed 145 on a dry day, but he had never avoided conflict, controversy, or strife. The UFO mystery was an enigma within an enigma—perhaps the greatest mystery that humankind had ever attempted to solve—and if he could play even the smallest supporting role in cracking the puzzle, he was willing to die for the chance.

Now in his late thirties, Blake Webster had inherited a large sum of money when he turned twenty-one and had graduated from Berkeley with a MS in journalism when he was twenty-three. His type of gonzo journalism, specializing in UFOs, government conspiracies, consumer frauds, corporate buy-offs, and corrupt politicians' pay-offs, did not pay enough in itself to lift him much above the poverty level. Fortunately for him, he was in a financial position to supplement his income with his inherited wealth and was thus able to buy such necessities as the Dodge RV so that he could stay on the move and avoid being tracked by agents of the shadow government. And even before developing his obsession to expose the government's coverup of UFOs, he had been a practicing anarchist, a fervent anti-bureaucrat, and a super-patriotic liberal Democrat who enjoyed being a permanent thorn in the backside of the Establishment.

Webster had had a large computer system with backup power installed in the RV. He also had a GPS and a microwave dish mounted on the roof. Programmable wide-band scanners and multi-band transmitter were mounted in the front end. He wanted his Conspiramobile to be as self-contained as possible.

He was unusually tired that night, so he drifted off a few minutes after two. A little before three, a noise awakened him, and he instinctively reached for his nine-millimeter semi-automatic. He always slept with the blinds open when he was alone so he could keep an eye on his surroundings.

After studying the lot around him, he decided that he had only heard an alley cat scavenging for a late night snack in the garbage pails behind the Holiday Suites Motel.

The next morning it took Webster three hours to drive the 150 miles to Rachel (population one hundred) from downtown Las Vegas. In the old days, when Nevada didn't have an speed limits outside of the cities, one could cross the endless miles of desert and barren hills at blinding speeds.

It was eighty degrees and very dry and clear when he pulled his RV into the lot in front of the Little A-le Inn with its "Welcome UFO Crews" painted on a board attached above the entrance. Wayne Newsome would be driving down from Tonopah to meet him there for lunch.

Webster sat at a table where he could watch the front door. The lunch and dinner menu were both printed on a single folded sheet of white paper. When folded, it displayed a drawing of a mature gentleman and lady holding a menu seemingly unaware of a large-headed alien peering over their shoulder at the bill of fare.

The walls of the cafe were filled with photographs of UFOs, aliens, aircraft, news articles about saucer sightings, and maps of the local area, including the Nevada Test Site and Nellis Range. The Little A-le-Inn took full advantage of its location on the northern edge of the Nellis Range and the persistent rumors of aliens and alien vehicles being sighted just south in Area 51.

A few minutes before noon, a tall, slender, distinguished man in khaki pants and shirt entered the cafe. When the two men made eye contact, he walked over to Webster's table.

"Newsome?"

The man nodded.

"Blake Webster," he offered with an outstretched hand.

Wayne Newsome shook his hand and joined him at the table.

"I figured that it was time that we met in person," Webster said.

Newsome agreed. "Especially since we are fighting the same crusade."

Webster glanced nervously toward the door as two men in dark sunglasses and brightly colored, gaudy shirts entered the cafe.

"Just tourist types," Newsome told him. "You're pretty jumpy."

Webster nodded. "I've heard that they've got some Wackenhut goons working with the DOE stiffs to tighten security in the area."

"Surely do," Newsome confirmed Webster's concerns. "Did you see any of the white Jeep Cherokees yet?"

"Not yet."

"If we go for a drive near Area 51, you will see them appear like magic," Newsome chuckled. "Relax while we have some lunch, man. I can spot the goon squad a hundred yards off. You know, they all have low IQs and high testosterone. They're typical paramilitary types—overaggressive, anal-retentive, Type-A personalities with little pricks and big guns."

"Charming as all hell," Webster laughed. But then he sobered when he thought of Red falling into the hands of such gorillas. "I'm worried about a…friend."

Newsome looked up from the menu, his look of concern indicating that Blake should continue.

"He's a crusty old prospector. Maybe you've seen him in the area. Red hair. Walks beside a shaggy mule."

"Red? You talking about old Red?"

Webster smiled. "Yes, do you know him?"

Newsome studied Blake's eyes. "How is it an obvious city dude such as yourself is a concerned friend of an old crusty desert rat? Did you search together for El Dorado? I don't think so. Or did you surf together in Hawaii? I don't think so."

Webster shifted nervously in his chair. He had just met Wayne Newsome, but he had known of his work for years. His investigation of Area 51 and his own research into the government UFO coverup was well known. But could he dare trust him with even a hint of Red's undercover work?"

Newsome chuckled and buried his face for a moment behind the menu. "That old fart. I always felt there was something not quite right about Red. Or I should say I always felt that he was more than he seemed."

And then it struck him. Newsome lowered his voice and leaned closer to Webster. "Blake, it was old Red who got the video footage of the UFO they showed on 'Exploring the Unknown,' wasn't it? He's been working with you all along."

Webster felt his heart thudding against his chest. "Have…have you seen him? I mean, since they aired the footage on Friday night?"

"Jesus," Newsome winced. "You don't think the goons got him, do you?"

"I don't know," Webster said. "I pray to God not. But there should have been a message from Red waiting for me at the motel last night when I got into Vegas."

The two new allies decided to eat lunch and take a drive into the desert.

"Likely as not, we'll spot old Red and his mule walking through the desert just as big as life and twice as ugly," Newsome said.

After a quick lunch of hamburgers and fries, they decided to take Newsome's Land Rover and let him do the driving since he was familiar with the area. Newsome pulled a Dallas Cowboys baseball cap over his unruly gray hair to protect his scalp from the broiling sun, and the two men were soon speeding down an old mining road.

"The Department of Defense has seized thousands upon thousands of acres of public and Bureau of Land Management land for the Nevada Test Site and Nellis Range," Newsome said above the road noise. "Like the ninety thousand acres annexed in the early 1980s, and then Whitesides in '95. Since the fifties, miners, ranchers, desert dwellers, and recluses by the hundreds have been unceremoniously evicted from their land without benefit of the judicial system's support."

"So I'm naive," Webster conceded, "but how the hell could they get away with such a major land grab?"

"The Feds just look the other way, and they will continue to do so as long as the military needs to hide, develop, and test its most secret of secrets," Newsome replied. "Illegal testing and disposal of nuclear and toxic propellant materials, the testing of expensive, exotic aerospace vehicles, amount to just the tip of the iceberg—as does the mysterious disappearance of a few citizens who represent a threat to the cloak of secrecy."

As the two men bounced over the desert road, they compared notes.

The Aurora Project at Area 51 had funded several top secret prototypes of aerial vehicles dating back to 1986. The primary purpose of the program was to create a replacement for the SR-71 Blackbird that would combine the latest stealth technology, advanced propulsion, radar avoidance, electronics countermeasures, and advanced composite technology. The result was the SR-75, which went operational at Groom Lake in 1990. The SR-74, or Scramp, was a smaller spy plane that could ride piggy-back on the 75. It had gone operational in 1994.

The TR-3B, which Red had photographed being outclassed by a UFO, was a tactical reconnaissance vehicle that had the ability to hover indefinitely over a target—for days or even weeks if necessary—at a very high altitude.

How could the craft stay indefinitely suspended over a a target?

Newsome explained: "The TR-3 is a reconnaissance platform with an indefinite loiter time. Indefinite because it uses a nuclear reactor for power. The TR-3 is a wedge-shaped vehicle, apparently responsible for many recent UFO sightings. The primary rocket fuel for the craft is hydrogen. The propulsion is provided by three multimode thrusters mounted at each bottom corner of the triangular platform. Supposedly the TR-3 is a sub-Mach 9 vehicle until it reaches altitudes above one hundred thousand feet—then God knows how fast it can go!"

Blake remembered interviewing a theoretical propulsion scientist who informed him that, in a liquid oxygen/hydrogen rocket system, eighty-five percent of the propellant mass is oxygen. The nuclear thermal rocket engine uses a hydrogen propellant augmented with oxygen for additional thrust. The reactor heats the liquid hydrogen and injects liquid oxygen in the supersonic nozzle so that the hydrogen burns concurrently in the liquid oxygen afterburner. The multimode propulsion system can operate in the atmosphere with thrust provided by the nuclear reactor, in the upper atmosphere with hydrogen propulsion, and in orbit with the combined hydrogen\oxygen propulsion.

The two men talked incessantly, desperately exchanging information, just in case something should happen to one or the other of them.

"We know that the scientists in Area 51 are able to make these quantum leaps in technology because of the deal that MJ-12 has made with alien intelligences," Blake Webster said.

"Or because of the alien technology that they've recovered from saucer crashes," Wayne Newsome said. "I'm not really certain in my own mind which it is. But it is one or the other. Do you know about the MFD technology?"

Webster shook his head. It was a new term to him.

"The MFD is technology that is so far ahead of anything ever before developed that you cannot use this information without fear for your life, man. The government will go to any lengths to protect this technology."

With Blake's full and undivided attention, Newsome stated that a circular accelerator ring, about two feet wide, called the Magnetic Flux Field Disrupter, surrounds the crew compartment of a vehicle and contains a mercury-based super-conductive plasma doped with barium, calcium, and gold. The MFD generates a magnetic vortex field that disrupts or neutralizes the effects of gravity on mass within proximity.

According to Newsome's informant, Sandia and Livermore laboratories had developed the MFD—nicknamed the Motherfucking Disrupter because of its technological challenges and the problems associated with its development. The plasma, mercury based, was pressurized at 250,000 atmospheres at a temperature of 150 degrees Kelvin and accelerated to 50,000 rpm to create superconductive plasma with the resulting gravity disruption.

"I've heard rumors of a new element that acts as a catalyst to the plasma," Newsome said, "but I can't get any confirmation of that. With the vehicle mass reduced by ninety-nine percent, the craft can travel at Mach 9, vertically or horizontally. My sources say the performance is limited only the stresses that the human pilots can endure. Which is a lot, really, considering along with the eighty-nine percent reduction in mass, the G forces should also be reduced eighty-nine percent. A prototype remotely piloted vehicle (RPV) called the Tier-4B is currently being developed that will eliminate the need for a manned crew and allow flight characteristics associated with alien UFOs."

Blake Webster reached over to squeeze his companion's shoulder. "They must have an almost unlimited access to alien technology. You're talking antigravity devices, crafts hovering indefinitely. This is alien technology, man. This is what we've been watching the fucking UFOs do for fifty years."

Newsome laughed at Webster's excitement. "It would seem that science fiction has become reality, wouldn't it? The aliens not only walk among us, they work among us, creating a new world of alien/human technology."

Webster scowled. "Yes, at taxpayer's expense while they deny everything. While they lie to the public. Do these high-level assholes really believe that the masses cannot accept the most exciting news flash in history? That there's not only life on other planets, ladies and gentlemen, it's right here building better flying machines in Area 51."

They had arrived at what seemed to Webster to be the end of the Earth. As he stepped out of the Blazer with Newsome, he knew that he had absolutely no idea where he was.

In the thin desert air, a chill beyond what could have been expected from the dropping temperature gripped Blake Webster to the core of his being. He shook it off as fatigue and anxiety and stood looking at a ranch about three hundred yards in the distance.

"Wayne, how did you find out about this antigravity device they're using in Area 51?" Webster wanted to know.

Newsome offered him a bottle of water, then explained that the Magnetic Flux Field Disrupter was not truly an antigravity machine.

"Antigravity provides a repulsive force that could be used for propulsion. The MFD creates a disruption of the Earth's gravitational field upon mass. The mass of the circular accelerator and all mass within the accelerator, such as the crew capsule and the nuclear reactor, are reduced by almost ninety percent. This causes the effect of making a vehicle extremely light and able to outperform and outmaneuver any craft that we've yet built."

Newsome took a large swallow of his water. "Hell, Blake, I am no fucking scientist. The man who could really explain it all to you, a top physicist who was working on the TR-3 program, got so paranoid that he retired early and went to hide out in Texas."

Webster felt a tickle of excitement in his solar plexus. "Might you be speaking of Dr. Carlton Farr?"

Newsome seemed startled. "I might."

Webster gave him a rather smug grin. "Just as soon as I find Red and get his ass out of this desert, the two of us have an appointment with Dr. Farr."

"An appointment? For when?"

"Just as soon as we can get down there."

Newsome puffed up his chest. "You bozos are not going without me."

Webster laughed. "Be glad to have you, Wayne. But can you just up and leave like that?"

Newsome scratched his chin and looked toward the sunset. "My Dorothy, God love her soul, passed four years back. My daughter is married and lives in Albuquerque. My son is attending grad school in San Francisco. I can pick up and leave whenever I damn well please."

Webster gave the much larger man a friendly slap on the back. "Then let's go on about finding old Red, so we can head for Texas."

Chapter Eleven

The Killing Room

Agabarr was furious. "This is simply not working, Dr. Quinlin. You are keeping the old bastard so drugged up that he's not feeling enough pain—even when I am using maximum power. Put the Aplastacabezas on him."

The doctor swallowed so hard that Red could hear him.

"Damn it, Raul, you are being too hasty. You could kill him with that and not get the information from him you need. Besides, we still don't really know that he has seen or told of things that are classified. He may be just what he seems—an old prospector. For God's sake, man. We don't want to kill him."

"That's why you're here, Dr. Quinlin," Agabarr said. "It is your responsibility to keep him alive long enough for me to obtain the information we need to determine exactly who and what this man really is."

"Then isn't the use of the Aplastacabezas hasty?" The doctor's voice became a bit shrill with his barely restrained repugnance for Agabarr.

"No!" Agabarr snapped back. "I know how to use the device as well as any interrogator alive. I do not have any more time to play games with the likes of this alleged old desert rat. His social security number is bogus.

The computer has no records of this man other than that he served in Korea. Then he officially disappeared…like the man who never was."

Agabarr leaned forward and spit in Red's face. "Your mind is too agile, too facile for you to be the entity that you wish us to believe that you are. You are no fucking prospector. You are a very clever, very good undercover agent. And I will find out who you're working for."

"Raul, I'm logging my protest over your use of the Aplastacabezas in my report of this interrogation," Quinlin told him.

"Put your protest up your ass," Agabarr sneered. "And stay the fuck out of my way."

The Aplastacabezas was the contemporary derivative of the horrible Venetian head crusher that had been developed by zealous priests during the Spanish Inquisition. Modern technology had improved upon the monstrous device a hundredfold. The modern instrument consisted of a face and head apparatus and an electrode-riddled strap that ran from the helmet down the back, under the crotch, back up to the chin and into the headpiece. It was worn over the victim's naked body and essentially linked all of the central nervous system via the head gear to a computer that was designed to deliver a menu of tailored pain.

The Aplastacabezas was the undisputed king of torture instruments. The interrogator, as if he were a perverse puppet master, could make the victim thrash about and scream in a violent dance of pain. Or if he chose, he could fry his victim internally. Or make him suffer a heart attack. The limitations of the Aplastacabezas were only those of the torturer, since the device was engineered for an infinite variety of pain. Agabarr was a master of the instrument.

Red had his own thoughts of torture and murder. Although he had never tortured anyone, he had seen his share of gore and death. Given even the slightest opportunity, he knew that he would rip Agabarr's throat out, pop his eyes like over-ripe grapes, crush his windpipe into mush, and drive his testicles up into his spine. He feared the opportunity would not present itself.

He hadn't felt remorse for his killing of Chinese communists in Korea, rationalizing each in the line of duty for service and country. His only remorse was for the innocence he lost after the first killing.

"Let's probe his jaw first," Agabarr ordered the doctor.

Dr. Quinlin felt as though he had sold his soul to the devil. He was powerless to disobey, for his orders expressly stated that he was to assist Raul Agabarr, and they made it very clear that he was to be subordinate to the interrogator.

The nerve centers that supplied the lower jaw molars were the largest and most sensitive nerve bundles in the parasympathetic nervous system. The means for stimulating these nerve centers was accomplished by inserting a glass microcapillary probe directly into the gum surrounding the fifth lower molar. The probe was filled with a conductive solution of potassium chloride and manganese chromate. When a small electric current was administered to the microscopic opening at the capillary end, it would cause an enormous neurological pain reaction directly on the main nerve bundle.

The doctor adjusted the micro-dial gauge on each side of the jaw on the helmet in order to set the probes into the proper nerve bundle.

"Now, Mr. Wise Ass, let us see what you are made of," Raul Agabarr said gleefully as he flipped the switches on the console.

Instantly Red's brain exploded. He felt an indescribable pain that evolved quickly into an infinite horror of unrelenting, overwhelming torment.

The pain shredded Red's integrity of consciousness and caused his fingers and toes to contract violently. His heart palpitated wildly. His eyes were blinded in a cascade of intense neuron firing.

His mind crawled on its belly like a snake into a cesspool of unholy hideousness.

Red danced with Satan, whose true name was Agabarr, as demons played a dirge of emotions for the dead and the yet undead.

In addition to the unfathomable anguish unleashed on his jaw, Agabarr used the electrodes placed along the body strap to stimulate other key nerve endings which elicited still more excruciating torment, thus making the effects of the torture multidimensional.

The pain was so unbearable that Red's subconscious mind knew it was time to shut down the central nervous system, thereby eliminating the need for conscious awareness. From Red's iron will, his subconscious diverted the encroaching shock. The result was a cleaving of his mind into an abstract medley of paranoid-schizophrenic behavior and basic survival instincts.

"This is getting boring, old man," Agabarr screamed at Red. "Tell us what we want to know, and we will let you go."

Even if Red had been able to hear or understand—which he could not—he would know better than to trust or to believe anything that Raul Agabarr promised.

Red now saw his tormenter from a narrow visual peephole, restricted by his own central nervous system. He could only perceive a blurred myopic vision of a monster. The thing that stood before him was revealed as a devilish fiend masquerading in human form.

Agabarr was actually laughing with pleasure at Red's body squirming and thrashing in pain.

Red's hoarse screams were unintelligible and constant. And then his eyes rolled back in his skull as he escaped to a world of his own making.

Dr. Quinlin jumped at the sudden silence and screamed at Agabarr. "Cut it off! Cut it off!"

Agabarr was lost in his own frenzy of monstrous glee.

Dr. Quinlin hit the emergency off switch on the console and the hum of high voltage whined down to quiet.

Red's body slumped back on the chair when his taut muscles collapsed. His body was dripping with sweat. His bladder had released urine to run in rivulets into the chair's splash pan. Blood trickled out of both sides of Red's mouth, and his face was drained of color underneath his tan.

"You crazy, fucking madman," Dr. Quinlin shouted at Agabarr. "We almost killed him. You stupid idiot! The NSA will murder us if we screw up on this job."

Raul's face became a mask of rage, and he pointed a menacing forefinger at the doctor. "Careful, little man. You could be next! You don't really know who I'm working for. I can have your fucking liberal bleeding heart for breakfast if I want."

Red was babbling the childish gibberish of a full paranoid-schizophrenic attack. "Domo arragoto! I'm going to get you vato! I'll try harder, bossman. Scream a little scream of me, ta da de da."

Spittle dribbled down his beard as his broken mind responded with nonsense. "He cut open the cadaver and pulled a live-er. No, no, he cut open a seam…he pulled out a spleen. No, no. He split him apart, pulled out his heart, and said, oh, what a good boy am I."

Agabarr slapped the console and the power came back on.

"What are you doing!" Dr. Quinlin shouted as he lurched for him.

Agabarr pushed the doctor away, knocking him to the floor.

Red screamed anew, then raced further into the depths of blackness.

Agabarr tripped the off switch with disgust. "Guess I was wrong."

The doctor was on his feet, shouting his rage. "You bet you were wrong, you stupid asshole! You're going to kill him if you're not careful. And who the hell do you think you are, putting hands on me?"

Agabarr shot the man a look of utter contempt. He was not used to working with anyone when he was brought in to interrogate a subject. It was a great annoyance to him to have to deal with a weak-kneed medical doctor burdened by cumbersome professional ethics.

"I really thought the son of a bitch was acting," Agabarr growled.

He kicked the torture chair in frustration, then pulled a crumpled cigarette pack from his pocket, listening impatiently to Red's schizophrenic nonsense while he lit his smoke.

Red began to giggle, as if he were a child. His teeth gleamed with wet, red blood that oozed from his mouth in trickles.

"Talk, you son of a bitch," Agabarr shouted, "or you'll never see the light of day."

"The poor bastard can't hear you," Dr. Quinlin told him. "Can't you see that for yourself? Look at his eyes. He's somewhere else entirely."

Red's head was rolling in circles, and only the whites of his eyes showed. "Rat soup, rat soup, rat soup. Yes, please, I'll have some more. Snakes slither silently over my bones."

Agabarr grabbed Dr. Quinlin's tunic and bunched it up in his fist, pulling the man closer to him. "Listen to him! If the dumb fuck can talk, then I know he can hear me!"

The doctor jerked the man's angry fist from his tunic. "That's not the way it works! Can't you hear he's babbling out of his head?"

Red was stuck somewhere between shock and complete shutdown. "The void is great, the rift is high. The cycle of time repeats…the beginning will occur…the past is over…the rapture is coming."

"You've fried his fucking brain," Dr. Quinlin said angrily. "He's dumping gibberish. Can't you see what's happening? Can't you see what you've done?"

"What we've done," Agabarr corrected in an icy tone. "You're the doctor who's supposed to prevent such a thing as this from happening."

"You cold-blooded son of a bitch!" Dr. Quinlin cursed. "I ought to have the guards arrest you and place you in house arrest until an inquiry into this entire affair has been conducted."

Agabarr laughed. "These men," he indicated the two impassive guards stationed on either side of the entrance to the interrogation room. "These fine fellows and I work for an agency above yours. I would suggest that you do not try any kind of power play, good doctor."

Dr. Quinlin frowned, glanced questioningly toward the guards. "What are you talking about? We were both assigned to this unholy task by the NSA."

Agabarr laughed again. "You poor, stupid shit, you have no idea of what's really going on here, do you? You have no idea of who's really in charge here."

Red moaned on the chair and began another meaningless litany. "Hickory, dickory, dock. My life runs off the clock. Can you change a cow for two chickens? Stop the clock! Stop the dock!"

The shattered man coughed up blood, but it didn't still his incoherent monologue. "Rubber shirts…goose grease…apple knockers…"

"Bring him around, Doctor," Agabarr commanded.

"Listen to him, you vicious ass! You've fried his brains! There's no bringing him around. It would take several days of rest before we could even get him coherent again."

"We don't have days," Agabarr's eyes narrowed malevolently. "We must find out within minutes if he has had anything to do with the video of the spacecraft. We must find out if he has been working with Blake Webster."

"Blake, flake, cake," Red mumbled.

Agabarr leaned over him. "Did that name ring a bell in your supposedly fried brain? Tell me about Blake, about Blake Webster. Is he your friend?"

Red's eyes rolled crazily. "There was a young lady from Mars, whose tits were shaped like stars."

Agabarr turned to give the doctor a fierce look. "Incoherent, my ass! Brain fried, my ass! If that were true, how would he be able to come up with a fucking limerick? He's somewhere inside of his skull laughing at us. He's not going to make a fool of me!"

Before Dr. Quinlin could interfere, Agabarr had pushed the level forward on the console.

Red violently strained against the chair restraints with every muscle in his large-boned body. A low animal howl, a primordial scream from deep within his very soul built in intensity.

"Oooooooh, nooooooo! Auuuuwagh! Stop! Stop! Noooo mooore! God, oh, God…please…stooop!"

Dr. Quinlin's stomach turned sour with bile. He knew that the last vestige of Red's mind was escaping within while his subconscious tried desperately and unsuccessfully to hold on to shards of reality and whatever sanity he had left.

"Unstrap him!" the doctor ordered the guards. "Unstrap him and place him on the examining table. Do it now!"

Neither man made a move to answer the doctor's commands.

Agabarr kept the power turned up high.

Red's mind had backed into a pit deep within himself, into the darkest and safest corners of his unconscious.

From far away, he could see a bright light. Someone was walking toward him. "Grandma," he called. "I hurt, Grandma. Make it stop."

His grandmother reached out a hand for one of his. "Come home, honey. You come home with me now. Come home where there is no pain."

Red's body slumped forward.

"Stop the power!" Dr. Quinlin shouted. "Cut the goddam juice now!"

"When I say!" Agabarr shouted back. "When I wish!"

"I think he's dead!"

Agabarr scowled his disbelief, but he cut the power. At his signal, the two guards unshackled Red and lifted his body onto the examining table.

A quick examination of Red's vital signs reversed the doctor's visual diagnosis. A flicker of life still pulsed within Red's tormented body. "He's still alive, you goddam sadist, but you've fried this man's brains for good. You'll not get anything more out of him."

"Shit," Agabarr grimaced. "The son of a bitch beat me. The tough old bastard never told us a fucking thing."

Dr. Quinlin's mouth dropped incredulously. "That's it, you heartless bastard? You have just destroyed this man's mind, a man who may have been exactly who and what he claimed to be. And that's as close to regret as you can get? The son of a bitch beat you?"

Agabarr wiped the perspiration from his forehead with a damp paper towel. "My regret, Doctor, lies in the grim fact that I was assigned by my superiors to get this man to talk, to be one hundred percent certain that he was not somehow involved in any of the leaks regarding the alien technology being used in certain of our dark projects. And I failed. I did not succeed in making him talk. For that I am remorseful."

Dr. Quinlin shook his head in astonished disbelief. "Raul Agabarr, you are the most evil scumbag I have ever met. And you're crazy, too. Alien technology? You demolished this man's mind because you believe in UFOs? You are fucking nuts."

Agabarr opened his mouth in mock horror. "Oh, awful me. It appears as though I might have breached security. You mean you aren't working for MJ-12?"

"MJ what?" Dr. Quinlin shook his head. "I work for the NSA, the same as you."

"Wrong. I told you earlier that these two men and I work for a group above the NSA."

The doctor took such talk to be but another indication of the man's dementia. "At any rate, I am writing up a full report of your...destruction of this man during your needlessly brutal interrogation."

Agabarr sighed impatiently. "That's two good reasons to kill you. You now know too much, and you keep insisting that you're going to write this negative report about my work habits."

He turned to one of the guards at the entrance. "Sergeant Kandowski, do you think we should kill this whining, narrow-shouldered, skinny-assed mother fucker?"

Kandowski seemed startled by the question. He glanced nervously from Agabarr to the doctor, trying desperately to perceive whether or not he was serious.

"You arrogant son of a bitch!" Dr. Quinlin snarled. "I'm reporting you to General Beauharnais."

"Please don't do that, Doctor," Agabarr laughed in a dismissive manner. "I don't like having my wrist slapped."

The guards shifted uneasily, awaiting a definitive order.

Agabarr sighed deeply. "Men, take this piece of shit to the medical center."

Then with an air of noblesse oblige, he told Dr. Quinlin, "Keep him alive. Perhaps his stubborn old brain will manage to unfry itself in a few days. If it does, we shall have another encounter. If it does not, then he is certainly no longer a potential threat to security, and I have, in a real sense, done my job to the best of my ability."

The guards hoisted Red's limp body, draped his arms around their shoulders, and headed toward the elevator to the surface.

"Now it is up to you to work your medical miracles and wonders," Agabarr challenged the doctor.

Chapter Twelve

I'm Here to Help You

Joe Green had turned in a few hours before sunrise, making himself as comfortable as possible on the sofa in Dr. Carlton Farr's living room. About noon the smell of fresh brewed coffee and small noises in the kitchen woke him.

A few minutes later, Joe sat across the table from Farr sharing coffee and stale doughnuts. Once again, the scientist began to expound on the evils of bigotry, the dictatorship of organized religion, and the suppression of various historical documents.

Joe found it ironic that the man who had at first been reluctant to speak with him could not stop talking. "Carl, last night I asked you if these powerful ancient alien gods and their presumably advanced super science had anything to do with the advanced technology being developed in Area 51."

Farr dunked a piece of his doughnut into his coffee before placing it in his mouth. "First I want you to tell me what has happened to you personally that drives you to seek out this information?"

Joe studied his host for a long moment before he responded to the request. "This isn't something I usually talk about, partly because of my high security clearances and partly because people would probably think that I was crazy. I guess it all started for me when I saw this weird Light during my family's move from Georgia to San Antonio when I was seven years old."

Farr barely moved or blinked while Joe related the strange incident with the Light and his mother, dad, and himself out on the lonely stretch of country road.

"That was the first experience I had with lost memory, so-called missing time, and the Light," Joe concluded the account. "Since that initial encounter, I have had several other incidents of lost memory—or whatever the hell it really is."

Farr reached down to set Albert on his lap. "Tell me more," he urged.

Joe shrugged, becoming self-conscious. "Well, there's not a great deal to tell. It wasn't until the last few years that I really began to realize that the fast pace of technology in this century, especially during the past couple of decades, has far exceeded the mathematical probability that it should. Somewhere along this same time, I also became interested in UFOs and in our government's alleged use of alien technology. I suppose by now I've read nearly every book on UFOs published. I've also been reading a little science fiction—and a lot of books on ancient civilizations."

Joe paused to take a couple of sips of coffee. "Carl, it's really difficult trying to get my experiences and beliefs and my quest into words. I guess the bottom line is that something happened to me, and I'm looking for answers."

Farr smiled and nodded as he stroked Albert's neck and back. "I'm glad you've come, Joe."

Joe grinned, feeling more at ease. "I guess I've pretty much come to the same conclusions you have. I mean, about there being an outside alien influence on our civilization."

Farr asked him if he had ever heard of or listened to the Reverend Page Saint John.

"You mean the cultist preacher?"

Farr nodded. "Are you aware of the premise of his Church of the Celestial Prophet?"

Joe admitted that he had only heard excerpts of a couple of St. John's sermons.

"It would seem that he would agree with our contention about aliens having influenced the development of our civilization," Farr said as he poured them each a fresh cup of coffee. "And I guess he would add our religions, as well. His particular spiritual dogma contends that our ancient

God Yahweh or Jehovah was actually from a superintelligent, technologically advanced race of aliens."

Joe ran his finger around the rim of his cup. "Do you think this St. John has had some special experience or insight? Or is he just combining his Bible-thumping with flying saucers?"

Farr shook his head and lifted his hands palm upward in a gesture of open wonder. He got up from the table and looked at his watch. "How about a drink?"

Joe told him that he would wait until later for a drink, but he would welcome a sandwich.

Farr hauled some ham slices and a package of cheese out of the refrigerator. "I've also got some homemade salsa, not too awful hot, and some tortilla chips."

Just before he placed the food on the table and joined Joe, Farr made himself a healthy drink. Joe was a little disappointed to observe that the serious drinking was beginning early that day.

Joe ate his sandwich and sipped his coffee, but the salsa was so God-awful hot that he couldn't imagine how anyone could eat it.

After their lunch, they moved out on the patio that overlooked Medina Lake. Joe reached for a cigarette, but caught his host's disapproving frown and put the crumpled pack back in his shirt pocket.

"Where are these aliens from?" Joe asked. "Why did they come here? And, the biggie, where are they now?"

Farr set his drink on a picnic table and leaned over to scratch Albert's ear. "There are roughly six possible places of origin for our visitors—from a parallel universe, another star, from the past, from the future, from another planet in this solar system—or from our own mental aberrations and hallucinations."

Joe nodded. "I, personally, have to strike your number six. I suppose we could substitute angels, but I don't think we are talking about heavenly beings."

"Those skeptics who insist that all UFO sightings are the product of hallucinations have certainly never seen one—nor have they studied the history of the phenomenon," Farr agreed. "I have to cast a negative vote against the theory that the aliens arrived here from another star or a parallel universe. The transition from a parallel universe would be tantamount to going through a black hole. Anything material attempting such a passage would be crushed back to primordial energy."

Joe agreed. "Unless they're nonphysical beings of some sort."

Farr dismissed the brown dog with another of his affectionate swats on its butt. "But they certainly appear to be physical entities when they are in our world. We know that their crafts are material enough."

Joe considered this, then suggested that the aliens could be multidimensional beings, somehow capable of materializing and dematerializing as both physical and nonphysical entities.

"Who knows," Farr shrugged. "Such a technology might one day be achieved by our own superscience. Kind of like, 'Beam me aboard, Scotty.'"

The two men laughed at the physicist's *Star Trek* allusion.

"As we understand our Earth version of physics," Farr explained, "the amount of material energy required to propel a large space ship to another planet-bearing star, together with the amount of time to make such a trip, plus a logistics support system to maintain the technology once it reached here would seem to make visitors from another solar system extremely improbable."

Farr got to his feet and turned his back to Joe while he refilled his drink from the bottle on the picnic table. "Ready?" he motioned to Joe with his glass.

Joe shook his head. "And, you know, while the concept of time travelers from the future is an intriguing one, I just can't buy it. There have been some fairly good science fiction films that deal with this theme, but it has seemed to me that even the very best always contain some internal contradiction."

Farr took a sip of his fresh drink. "I know what you mean. Even beyond the cliché, what-if-you-killed-your-own-grandfather type of science fiction time-travel tale, there would seem to be physical laws that would prevent different dimensions of time from interacting. Perhaps one might be able to observe the past, as if you were visiting a live-action history museum, but there would have to be strict rules against touching the living exhibits."

Joe decided to pour himself a small shot of the remaining Scotch. "Which leaves us, via the process of elimination, with the conclusion that these ancient gods came from another planet within this solar system."

Farr agreed enthusiastically. "And that planet existed, at one time in ancient prehistory, between Mars and Jupiter, where the asteroid belt now lies. And it is very probable that Mars served as a temporary home base for the aliens before they visited Earth."

Farr held up his hand, as if he were a cop halting the flow of traffic. "Let's take a break so my dog and I can stretch our legs and take a pee."

Joe walked off a bit toward the woods and had a cigarette. As he looked down toward Pat's Place he remembered the night before when he had heard something or someone following him back to Farr's cabin. That had been an eerie experience, but everything certainly looked innocent enough in the light of a hot, humid Monday afternoon.

Joe sat on a tree stump and watched the scientist playing with Albert, tossing the ball, then teasing and praising the little mutt.

After a few minutes, Farr was out of breath. "I think old Albert and old Farr have had enough exercise. Let's go back in the cabin. I want to show you something."

Farr ushered them back to the kitchen and poured himself the last of the Scotch that Joe had brought. Joe reached in the refrigerator and snagged a cold beer from the six pack that he had bought at Pat's Place.

Without a word, Farr led him to the mysterious locked spare bedroom. He paused, then entered a six-digit number into the electronic lock. A heavy deadbolt retracted and the door swung open.

Joe was dumb-struck by what he saw. Hundreds of tiny lights, dials, computer displays, and other immediately unidentifiable light sources emitted a complex pattern of illumination and eerie shadows dancing across the walls and the ceiling.

Here was a house that for all appearances didn't have a television or stereo set in the living room, an electric can opener or toaster in the kitchen, and not even a clock radio in the bedroom. But there, inside a twelve-by-twelve foot area, was a room supporting wall-to-wall electronics of the most sophisticated kind.

The lengthy work surface nearest the wall to the left contained no less than six monitors. The first displayed what appeared to be a real-time satellite image of the northwestern United States. The second displayed a digital drawing of Area 51.

With a rush of realization, Joe knew that Dr. Carlton Farr had just opened his most private inner sanctum for his examination. He had won the reclusive scientist's trust.

"Go on in and pull up a chair," Farr invited.

Joe took a seat in one of the two swivel chairs nearest the back wall and decided to focus on one area of the room at a time.

The end monitor was hooked up to a wide-band scanner that digitized the speech from the analog output and converted it to text via voice recognition software. The software sophisticated enough to accomplish this had to have been "borrowed" from the government.

From what Joe could quickly determine, Farr had to be tapping into at least three different government satellites. When he glanced up at the shelf above the work surface, he saw that he was looking at a security system that monitored each side of the cabin, displaying the exterior on four different monitors.

Farr laughed at his friend's astonishment. "I'm monitoring Milnet and Internet using keyword/phrase data files and user address lists. I keep up on the latest scientific research, black budget dollars and contracts, and I managed to backdoor a number of interesting government systems."

Joe still had not found his tongue. Farr probably had at least one or more satellite dishes and various antenna arrays hidden around his property. They could easily be camouflaged amongst the dense trees crowding the cabin.

"I haven't seen a room like this outside of a government facility," Joe managed at last. "You must have an incredible amount of money tied up in this room."

"I saved my lunch money for years. A nickel here, a dime there," Farr chuckled, then disappeared for a moment.

Joe was afraid that he had gone to fetch another drink. His concern was realized when the physicist returned with two glasses and a bottle.

"This isn't as elegant and fine a Scotch as you brought, but it is several steps above rotgut, and it will do," he said, sloshing some in a glass for each of them.

Joe feared that it would do to put Farr in the bag again before he had learned what he had come to find out about Area 51 and the alien technology.

"You know, Joseph Green, you should feel honored that you are the only other human that has ever been in this holy room, this sanctum sanctorum."

They sat opposite one another in the dimly lighted room. "I do feel honored, Carl," Joe said.

"And I can completely trust you?"

"Yes, you can."

"Then tell me more about yourself. There's something I am waiting to hear from you."

Joe was puzzled. Was there some magic word that he was supposed to utter? "Well, I took a leave from Lorale. I've been working on the Aurora Program funded by the NSA, NRO, and ARPA. Specifically, I have been involved with the SR-75."

Farr slid up to the computer next to the scanner system and typed in "Joseph Green, Top Secret, Area 51." The CD-ROM booted up and hummed to life. It was soon apparent that Farr had the CD-ROM that the Defense Industry Security Clearance Office used for listing civilians with security clearances within the Department of Defense industry. The display read:

Joseph Gorden Green, Jr.
6400 S. Air Force Road
Tonopah, NV 89409
DISCO FILE 89-4127 TS/MJ: FT & AA
Previous: USAF-1969, NSA-74, Lorale Corporation 1989
SSN 349-82-4127
Born June 24, 1953
Americus, Georgia, Sumpter County USA
Top Secret/EBI/SI Aurora; Clearance issued March 11, 1989 Lorale Corporation

Farr spoke in a loud and firm voice. "Now tell me something I don't already know, Joseph."

It was now obvious to Joe that if Farr had not already pulled up his file, he wouldn't be sitting here with him in his secret domain. He quite likely would not have met with him in the first place.

"I want to know more about the Light, Joe."

Joe pulled back. "But why?"

"Goddam it! I don't have time to bother with explanations. Tell me about the Light."

Joe felt perspiration dot his upper lip and forehead. "I…I have had a fear, an apprehension all of my life since my experience with the Light. So much of it is so blurred in my mind that I really don't like to talk about it."

Farr slammed his fist down on the worktable. "Tell me about the Light or get out of my house! Don't you have any concept of how little time we have?"

Joe was stunned by the scientist's persistence and by the importance that he seemed to affix to his encounters with the mysterious, frightening Light. "I can't be certain where reality stops and nightmares begin."

"Just talk." Farr's tone allowed no room for argument.

"Ever since it happened, I have never felt as though I was in charge of my own destiny. I feel like I'm living out someone else's life. Or maybe like I'm playing a part in some weird movie."

Farr nodded before he took another swallow of his Scotch.

Joe couldn't begin to imagine what demons that Carlton Farr was attempting to drown with the liquor. He only knew that he had his own ugly mind-creatures that he had never revealed to another human being in his life. And now here he was with a stranger, a half-drunken stranger, who insisted that he spill his guts to him. He was, however, willing to make the tradeoff, because he suspected that this stranger, Dr. Carlton Farr, had some sorely needed answers for him.

"All right, Joe," Farr prompted. "So you had nightmares and the sense that your destiny was being controlled. What else do you remember?"

"Ghostly images in my dreams. Things like that."

"Have you ever seen a professional about these dreams and nightmares?"

"No, never."

Joe decided that he did need some Scotch after all. He took a generous swallow from the glass that Farr had placed beside him. He felt the liquid burn the back of his throat before he answered: "I guess I never sought professional help because of my clearance—and because I didn't want any verification that I was losing my mind…or worse."

Farr asked him if he knew anything about entrainment, the ability of the brain to synchronize with external light or sound.

Joe considered the definition for a moment. "Such as when epileptics are around a strobe light they might have a seizure."

"Exactly. But there is a scientific use for the phenomenon." Farr turned to the smallest computer monitor between Joe and himself. He pulled out a pair of goggles attached to a cable and plugged them into the computer interface.

Joe became wary. He could see that four red light-emitting diodes were mounted around each eye of the goggles with a circular hole in the center. "What are those?"

"You place these over your eyes and the flashing lights assist you in entraining your brain waves," Farr explained, handing the goggles to Joe. "This top-of-the-line unit was made by Neurosync Systems."

Joe remained unimpressed. "You better tell me something more about entrainment. Other than epileptics having seizures, that is."

Farr laughed at his friend's reluctance to experiment with the system. "Joe, you have heard of Buddhist monks and Hindu fakirs going into trances from meditating, and you have heard of biofeedback."

"Yeah, like when you want to learn to relax or sleep better, that kind of thing."

"With this system," Farr said, pointing to a menu on the computer screen," you can achieve in an extremely brief period of time what may take weeks, months, or years to achieve through meditation—or even biofeedback."

Joe wasn't certain where Farr was going with this. "Like how long with this system?"

"Usually thirty minutes or less. It's a lot like a hypnotic state at the lower levels of entrainment."

"I don't think I can be hypnotized," Joe said.

"Of course you can," Farr said firmly. "And to be certain, I'm going to give you this hypnotic to relax you. It increases the effect of the entrainment process."

Joe studied the small pill that the scientist had handed him. "Carl, what does all this have to do with what we were talking about?"

"I can set this machine for a programmed mode that will take you to a state where you could be hypnotized. Understand, you will be aware of everything that's going on around you, and you will remember everything afterward."

"Okay, go on."

"Joe, you cannot remember what happened to you during your contact with the Light. With this machine, you may remember more."

"I don't know, Carl. Maybe I'm not supposed to remember anything about the experiences."

Farr found such a response unacceptable. He moved the mouse and the pointer on the screen to meditation, then he picked up a head cap from the shelf above the computer. "Put this on."

Joe looked at the cap, a glorified shower cap in many ways, made of some kind of synthetic material with dozens of round, inch-wide rubber-like suction cups inside.

"The ribbon cable attaches to the base of the computer," Farr explained. "The cap measures the electrical state of your various brain waves."

Joe slipped on the head cap. His curiosity was growing.

“Look,” Farr said as he adjusted the oscilloscope, “this is your present state at twenty-five cycles per second. From fourteen to thirty cycles per second is called the Beta, or awake, state.”

Joe saw that the computer had commands for a number of modes: Relaxation, Sleep, Visualization, Energize, Normal Consciousness.

“See there, Joe,” Farr grinned. “This cap proves that you are conscious. It doesn’t hurt, does it?”

Joe agreed. He reached for the glass of water that Farr handed him and took a sip to wash down the pill. He might as well go through with the experiment. Maybe after all these years of fearing the Light, he was about to get some answers.

Chapter Thirteen

On the Scent of Death

M. D. Crawfoot pulled his Jeep to a stop on the gravel surface in front of Pat's Place. He had been in the area for two days, reconnoitering. It was approaching the time when he would fulfill his assignment from Mother.

He had memorized his briefing file and destroyed all materials before he left Montreal for Mexico City. There he used his Mexican passport and identification to purchase a ticket to the San Antonio International Airport.

He arrived from Mexico City as Ricardo San Juan on the noon flight of Mexicana. Crawfoot's father was a Cherokee from Oklahoma, his mother a Creole from Louisiana. His heritage easily permitted him to pass as Hispanic.

He entered Pat's Place and took a stool at the short bar, once again taking in the ambiance, the fading white plastered walls decorated with a colorful assortment of flyers, maps, photographs, and advertisements. Everything was yellowed and dusty with age, but fairly clean as these places went. A strong smell of hamburger and fried potato grease wafted about the bar.

He had entered the bar the night before, quietly, a dark shadow that had a beer and simply observed the local characters in Pat's Place.

A stocky woman behind the bar in a flowered cotton dress had finished preparing two hamburgers with fries for the two older men at a table. She plopped the orders onto two paper plates and cheerily delivered them to the men who greeted her and their food with loud guffaws of pleasure.

Within seconds she was back behind the bar and approaching Crawfoot with a smile and a small, stained white towel with which she methodically wiped the aged laminated surface of the bar as she walked toward him.

"Hi, stranger. I'm Betty Bock. Everyone calls me Mammaw. What can I get you today?"

Crawfoot didn't need the menu. "Coffee, glass of orange juice, and an order of whole wheat toast without butter."

"Not much food to keep a man going," she felt obliged to inform him. "Especially if you going tromping after a deer today. Folks say we got the best burgers in the county."

"I am certain that the food must be wonderful here. I am just not so hungry right now," he smiled.

"Suit yourself," Mammaw shrugged her generous shoulders.

She didn't bring his coffee or his juice until the toast was ready. Crawfoot picked up his order, explaining that he wanted to sit at one of the outdoor tables on the back patio.

The table he chose provided him with a clear view of the narrow gravel road entrance to the trailer park, which was part of Pat's Place. Behind him was Medina Lake. Across the little inlet to his left, he could see the scientist's small frame cabin sitting high up the hill, directly across from the patio where he sat sipping his warm coffee.

From the file provided by Mother, Crawfoot knew that Farr was single, something of a recluse, and very attached to a small, brown dog. While he sat checking out the lay of the land, a man who was quite likely the scientist stepped out onto the porch overlooking the lake. He was accompanied by a younger, taller man, the same man that Crawfoot had followed the night before.

Who the hell was this guy? Farr should have been alone, according to the file. He wished that he could take out his small Bosch digital monocular and get a better fix on both men on the porch, but he didn't want to draw attention to himself.

Crawfoot took a bite of his dry toast. It didn't matter who was keeping Dr. Charles Farr company. He would take the scientist out if he were in the middle of a country square dance. That was his assignment. And his superiors knew that he always got the job done.

A tall, lean, white-haired older man appeared at the door of the patio and seemed to be looking for company. Crawfoot frowned at the obvious distraction walking toward him.

Walter Dean Ray, a retired Air Force colonel, kept himself occupied by working on his lakeside house, deer hunting, and fishing. Ray had been an F-15 Eagle fighter pilot who knew everyone within five miles of Pat's Place. The widowed sixty-year-old was very active in the surrounding community and was considered a dashing, charming ladies' man. In Ray's social philosophy, he had never met a stranger, only a previously unknown person who was about to give him an opportunity to talk about himself.

Crawfoot gave him a practiced go-to-hell look, but the man extended his hand, undaunted by the stranger's obvious lack of interest. "Howdy. Don't believe that I've had the pleasure. I'm Walter Dean Ray. Everyone calls me Walt."

Crawfoot stood and shook Ray's hand. "Hello, Walt. My name is Richard."

"Hello, Richard," Ray pumped his hand enthusiastically and invited himself to a seat opposite Crawfoot. "May I ask what brings you to our modest community?"

Crawfoot took to his cover as one might slip on an overcoat. His personality changed in an instant. He would extract himself as quickly as possible from this unwanted meeting. The less he interfaced with the locals, the better off he would be after he terminated the scientist.

"Came up to do a little hunting. Thought I would take a look at the lake and some property while I was in the area."

"You'd like it here, Richard," Ray smiled. "I can tell you anything about the area that you might like to know. For instance, you are now in Bandera County, and that out there," he pointed to the water behind them, "is the north shore of the lake."

Ray leaned back in his chair and made an expansive, sweeping motion with his right arm. "This is a beautiful area here, Richard. It's abundant with white-tailed deer, gray squirrels, red and gray foxes, and our famous—or should I say, infamous—rattlesnakes and armadillos."

Since the man had paused for a reaction, Crawfoot obliged with a curt: "I guess it depends whether or not you like rattlesnakes."

Ray laughed loudly, as if he had heard a retort of great wit.

Then he continued with his monologue of the wonders and glories of the area: "The mesquite, live oak, Texas red oak, elm, cedar, and possum haw trees, along with the red berried agarita shrubbery, prickly pear cactus, and red yucca provide good cover for the wild animals. Sometimes I think that it's like we've got a natural game preserve here, Richard, but with the best of both worlds, because we still get to hunt all we want. At least so far."

Ray paused to take a breath, then was back on the case. "In the spring, the Texas state flower, the wild bluebonnets, bloom everywhere, along with..."

Crawfoot had had enough. The guy was a walking encyclopedia.

"All that is very interesting," he said, interrupting the travelogue, "but I'm more interested in finding out about property values and which properties might be for sale."

Ray nodded. No problem. He would just shift topics. "Well, I couldn't help noticing that you were looking at the houses across the inlet. That big stone one is for sale. It's about two thousand square feet with a lot of enclosed porch space. I hear they're asking $140,000 for it. Damn good buy."

Crawfoot winced. "That's just a bit out of my price range, Walt. How about that smaller place, that cabin up on the hill, the one right across the inlet? Something like that is more my style."

"Well, you're out of luck there, Richard," Ray told him. "That one's not for sale. That's Carl Farr's place. He's a retired scientist."

"Must have been a biologist to want to live all the way out here, near the river, lake, and woods, and all," Crawfoot suggested.

"Nope," Ray narrowed his eyes in recollection. "Think he was a physicist. He's not very sociable. Lives alone with a scruffy little excuse for a dog and feeds every stray critter that comes along. I never see anyone at his place, no visitors at all. I guess he's what you would call a recluse. Guess that's the way he likes it."

Crawfoot pointed to the cabin's wraparound porch. "Looks like he's got some company right now."

Ray squinted and leaned forward, as if to shorten the distance between his eyes and Farr's cabin. "Sonuvagun. He does indeed. Well, I'll be damned. He does know someone besides that mutt of his. I wonder who the hell it is?"

"Maybe a relative."

"Could be," Ray agreed. "Maybe we'll get a chance to find out if they walk down and get a drink or something later."

Crawfoot chuckled. "Well, I'll be long gone. I've got to bag my limit while I'm here or Mother will be on my butt."

Ray smiled. "Your mom really likes venison, eh?"

"Actually, to tell you the truth," Crawfoot leaned forward as if in confidence, "I think she just wants another trophy to hang on her wall."

Chapter Fourteen

Thanks for the Memories

Dr. Carlton Farr told Joe that he would first take him to the alpha state, between nine and thirteen cycles per second.

"That will relax you. You will experience a pleasurable or floating sensation. You will feel very calm, and you might have some lucid daydreams."

Joe said it sounded good so far.

"Next I'll program the computer to take you on down to the theta state, between four and eight cycles per second," Farr said. "This is a very relaxed state, similar to a hypnotic state, and you will be open to suggestion. This is the state utilized in twilight learning and subconscious problem solving through intuitive or creative imagery. You will also experience REM, rapid eye movement. At four cycles per second, you will enter a deep, dreamless sleep called delta."

Joe cleared his throat. "So it sounds like we'll be working in theta."

Farr confirmed his conclusion. "While you're in theta, I will ask you a series of questions about your lost memory and the Light, as you call it."

The scientist had a small recliner in the corner of the room, and he motioned Joe to sit in the chair. The cord to the headset and goggles was conveniently long enough to reach. Joe suspected that Farr had used the device many times before to relax or to meditate.

"Get comfortable, then adjust the goggles," Farr told him from his position at the computer.

Joe leaned back in the recliner, slipped on the headset, and adjusted the goggles until they felt comfortable. His field of vision was completely black. He could not detect the least bit of light. "Now what?" he asked the scientist.

Farr told him that the headset was picking up his brain waves, his pulse rate, and his blood pressure. Everything seemed normal.

"First I will set the light patterns in motion. After a few minutes I will start the sound. Don't think about anything other than the lights and the sound. Try to remain comfortable and breathe normally. Once we reach theta, I will reduce the sound volume so you can hear me talking to you. I'm recording everything on videotape. Ready?"

"Go for it."

Almost at once, the series of lights mounted inside each eyepiece of the goggles were flashing at about twenty to thirty cycles per second.

"The lights...hurt my eyes a little. They're too bright."

Farr told him the threshold was normal. "Joe, are your eyes shut?"

"Of course not. How could I see the damn lights if my eyes were closed?"

Farr laughed. "Joe, your eyes are supposed to be shut. I'm sorry. I should have made that clear. The effect of entrainment isn't on the photon receptors of the eyes. The rhythm and phasing of the light sequencing is the critical part. It bypasses the part of the brain that processes visual information. Are they still too bright?"

"They're okay."

"What color is the light?"

"At first it was red," Joe responded. "Then a few moments after I shut my eyes, different colors started to appear. Now I see complex patterns and many different colors."

Farr told him that was normal. "The brain is interpreting the signal and creating the colors. As you probably know, the LED lights are red, and the color from them remains constant. The lights at times will appear to be synchronized, and at other times they will be out of phase."

A deep resonate tone of low-frequency audio filled Joe's ears. The lights now appeared to be synchronized. He adjusted himself more snugly in the reclining chair and tried to relax.

When he next heard Farr's voice, it seemed to be coming from very far away. "Joe, I've turned down the volume a bit. It's been twenty minutes, and you are approaching the alpha threshold. Everything is normal, and you are at fourteen cycles per second. When you reach theta and stabilize, I will begin to ask you questions. Now just relax and enjoy the experience."

The wall of sound increased and returned to its former volume. The deep resonate bass had slowly turned into a medium frequency that sounded like warbling. Joe's body felt as if it weighed at ton. He couldn't tell if another minute or an hour had passed. The lights seemed to slow and flash out of sequence.

Farr alternated watching the computer monitor readouts and Joe. Everything seemed to be all right, even if it was taking Joe a little longer than normal to entrain. He watched the audio sound wave as it increased in frequency until an underlying bass frequency joined it in what was termed a binaural beat. The complex sound added to the entrainment effect of the flashing lights.

The binaural beat was as old as civilization. It was the beating of drums, the chanting of shamans, the Gregorian chant, the deep bass of rock music.

Although the sound was important to the process, eighty-five percent of the entrainment effect came from the lights. It had taken Joe twenty-eight minutes to reach high theta.

While Joe was "cruising" at eight cycles per second, Farr quietly slipped out to the kitchen to make himself another drink. The bottle he had brought with him into the laboratory had held only a few final shots, so it was time to draw another from his reserve in the cabinet above the refrigerator. Albert the poodle was asleep on the living room sofa, oblivious to the bizarre machinations of his human companions.

Farr settled himself once again into the computer chair, took a sip from his fresh drink, and checked the monitor readouts. Joe had reached a deep theta state, and his pulse and respiration had slowed appropriately.

The scientist hooked a microphone into the breakout box next to the computer and adjusted the volume to Joe's headset to a lower setting.

"Joe, you should be able to hear me," he spoke softly into the microphone. "You've reached a stable theta state. Raise your index finger on your right hand slightly if you hear me at a comfortable level."

Joe slowly raised his finger about half an inch.

"Joe, you are in your parents' car. You are somewhere between your old home in Georgia and your grandparents' home in San Antonio. You are lying in the back window of the car. Everything is quiet and peaceful.

"Now you see some kind of light coming out of the woods on the side of the road. Your father has slowed the car. Tell me what happens next."

Joe was somehow back in time, listening to Farr's voice, able to speak with him and answer his questions without disrupting the flow of memory.

"Pop is stopping the car. Mom is afraid. She has her hand over her mouth, the way she does when something is really bothering her. Pop looks funny. He can't take his eyes off the Light. It's getting brighter, and it's coming closer to the car. I can feel the hair on the back of my neck standing straight out."

Joe's voice became more agitated. "The Light is above the car. The air in the car is warm and stuffy. Mom is screaming. Pop is just sitting there, staring like he sees a ghost. I'm afraid. I'm afraid something terrible is going to happen. I can't get the car door open, and the window won't roll down. Oh, no! Dear Jesus!"

Joe stopped talking.

"Just relax, Joe. You're all right." Farr checked Joe's pulse rate and found that it had increased slightly. It was clear that he was recalling something stressful. It was not at all uncommon for memory to produce physiological functions of the body just as reality would.

"Joe, nothing bad is going to happen to you. I'm here with you. I won't let anything bad happen to you. This is just a memory. Joe, tell me what happens next. What was it that startled you?"

"Mom and Pop are sitting there, like they're sleeping with their eyes open. The car is full of creepy shadows, dancing around like crazy spiders or ghosts." Joe was telling his experience from the viewpoint of a seven-year-old boy with his adult intellect narrating.

"I hear the door latch open. The door is slowly opening, but I can't see outside. The Light is outside...all around the car. It is too bright. It hurts my eyes. I'm afraid something bad has happened to my parents. I think we're all going to die.

"Oh my god! Someone is opening the door. I'm trying to move away, but I can't move my arms or legs. I can only sit in fright, just like my parents.

"Someone is pulling me off the seat and out of the car door! The Light has filled the inside of the car. All I can hear is the sound of my heart beating in my ears. I think my heart is going to explode. I can't look. I don't want to look. I shut my eyes. And then I feel like I'm being lifted up into the air."

Farr had set his drink aside and was listening intently to Joe Green's story. He did a double take when he glanced at the monitor. All of a sudden Joe's brain wave had taken a dip to two cycles per second. He had slipped down to a mid-delta state and stopped talking.

"Joe, this is Carl. I'm here with you, boy. Everything is all right. Please go on. Please continue telling me what's happening."

"I can't tell you. I'm not supposed to remember."

"Joe, you can remember. Tell me what happens next."

Joe's voice was almost robotic, mechanical. "Yes, I can see what's happening, but I can't tell you. I can't say the words."

Farr sat back in his chair and took a stiff drink. Joe had reached a memory block that was quite likely caused by the trauma of the experience. He would ask Joe some questions and walk him past the memory block.

"Are you out of the car, Joe?"

"Yes."

"Are you on the ground?"

"No," Joe responded, his voice filled with wonder. "I'm floating. I'm floating above the ground. I'm about as high as the top of the car."

"Is there anyone around you?"

"Not that I can see. The Light is so bright. I can barely see the top of the car. My whole body is covered with goose bumps, and the hair on the top of my head is standing straight up. I feel sleepy. I can't ever remember being this tired."

"Are you moving as you are floating? Or are you just hovering there next to the car?"

Joe's voice was becoming very excited. "I'm moving up. I'm moving up toward the source of the Light!"

Farr took a moment to calm him, to soothe him. "What happens when you get to the Light?"

"A tunnel opens up, and I'm being pulled into it. The Light is moving away from me, leaving me in the tunnel."

Farr asked him to describe his surroundings.

"The tunnel is shiny…metal. I think I'm still floating. I can't tell which direction I'm moving. I hear a humming noise, and I see a light at the end of the tunnel. I think something is pulling me near the end of the tunnel."

"As you near the end of the tunnel, what do you see?"

"Angels," Joe said in the awe-filled voice of the boy of his memory. "Beautiful, beautiful angels!"

Farr wanted a more detailed description than "beautiful."

"Kind of pale, kind of light gray color. They have halos and big, big eyes."

"Are they big angels?"

Joe shook his head. "Naw, they're small. Not much bigger than me. They have skinny arms and legs like tubes."

Joe suddenly began to giggle.

"What's so funny, Joe?"

"They don't have any clothes on. But I can't tell if they're boy or girl angels."

"Why can't you tell?"

"'Cause they don't have anything between their legs. It's just all smooth. None of them have any hair on their bodies, either."

"How many angels are there?"

"Four. They just stand there looking at me with their awful eyes. It's like they don't have real eyes. Or like maybe they're wearing some kind of thick, black sunglasses. But their eyes don't reflect light the way sunglasses would. I think I'm still floating."

Joe shuddered. "One of them reached out and touched me with a long, skinny finger. Something is wrong with its hand. I don't think they have the right number of fingers. I don't think they're angels anymore. They don't seem beautiful anymore. They don't look like they did when I first saw them."

Farr wondered if they communicated with Joe in any way.

"One of them," Joe hesitated, "I think somehow that it's a he...he's speaking to me. I can't see his lips move. In fact, none of them seem to have any lips. Just a thin line, a little groove where their lips should be, kind of like a snake's or a turtle's mouth. It's really weird..."

"What is he saying to you?" Farr prompted.

"He saying that they are friends...that they don't want to hurt me. They want to help me. 'You're special,' he says to me. 'You are one of the chosen ones.' His voice sounds really funny, like it's coming out of a tin can and right into my head. It's kind of like I'm thinking the words that he wants to tell me."

"Does he tell you why you are there? What does he mean when he says you are one of the 'chosen ones'?" Farr had read stories about UFO abductions, but he had never met an abductee—until now. Joe Green was apparently abducted by aliens as a child. He had to know why.

"He's telling me that I will help when God comes back to the people," Joe said. "I have been chosen to lead...to lead someone? He says that they are here…that they have always been here to assist humankind on its quest. He says that humankind is very close to the rapture."

Farr took another swallow of his drink. What the hell was this? It sounded like a combination of a near-death experience and an alien abduction. And the rapture? That was born-again fundamental Christian religious dogma.

"Did these angels, these helpers, say where they were from, Joe?"

"My head is getting fuzzy," Joe complained. "I can't see anything but clouds, and it feels like they stuck a bug in my brain. They stuck something in my head. Something tiny, crawling around inside my skull. My stomach feels sick. I think I'm going to throw up."

Farr calmed him once again, assured him that he was there to help him. After Joe's pulse and respiration had lowered, he asked him about the thing that the angels had put inside his head.

Joe gritted his teeth. "I don't like the feeling of that bug crawling around inside my head."

"But that bug is telling you something, Joe. Tell me what it is saying."

Joe mumbled something unintelligible, then his words became clearer. "They're from a place that no longer is. Men and women are supposed to tend the garden…be good gardeners of Earth. God is ashamed of us. We are His bad children. We were supposed to be better than animals. God was so ashamed that He went away and left the angels here to teach us how to find Him again when we are ready. When we grow up."

"What else, Joe? Is there anything else?"

"I'm not supposed to tell anyone about them. For a long time I will see them only in my dreams. But they will see me again someday."

"What else?"

"I'm outside in the night air. I'm standing beside the car."

Farr wanted more. "How do we find this God? Where did God go? When is He coming back?"

The scientist fired off a rapid series of questions to Joe, but he just sat silently.

"Joe, did the little gray angels tell you the answer to any of the questions that I just asked you?"

"No."

Charles Farr followed the obvious line of questioning. It was logical to attempt to determine if the aliens had ever come again for Joe Green. If so, document as thoroughly as possible where, when, and why.

Over the course of the next three hours, the physicist found little to list under the "why" column, but he did discover that Joe had been abducted by these same entities six times in his life. He typed up a thumbnail sketch of each of the abductions on the computer file.

1. Georgia-Alabama state line. Summer of 1960. With parents in family automobile. Age 7.
2. Georgia at farm for family reunion. Summer of 1965. In the corn field. Sixth grade, age 12.
3. Louisiana in bayous along airline highway. Age 15. 1968.
4. Longview, Texas, out on Lake Cherokee. High school. Age 18, 1971.
5. South China Sea, toward end of Vietnam conflict. Age 22.
6. Idaho, up at the Trinities lakes. During vacation. Age 31. 1984.

Joe seemed certain that he would not see the aliens again, that they were through with him until he was ready to find God.

Farr was convinced that Joseph Green had interacted with something quite extraordinary, something quite outside of the normal mundane human experience. But how much of it was real and how much was a dream, a distortion of reality by Joe's subconscious during an altered state experience?

He knew that he must bring Joe back to full consciousness. But first he would try something.

"Joe, this is Carl again. You are resting easily, very relaxed, and you feel wonderful. As time goes by, you will remember more and more of your dreams. Each time you dream, you will remember more about the angels and why they came for you. When you awake from your dreams, you will remember everything that you have dreamed. You can now safely remember everything that happens to you in your dream state. Your memories will no longer disturb you or frighten you.

"When I awaken you now, you will remember fully everything that we have discussed and everything that you have experienced. You will not forget any of these experiences. In fact, you will remember more and more details as each day goes by.

"I have now turned off the entrainment system and removed your headset and goggles. On the count of three, you will open your eyes and be fully awake. Fully awake and feeling better than you have in weeks and weeks, months and months."

Joe admitted to Farr that it had seemed as though he were asleep and in a dreamlike state. He remembered the angels, the Light, the abduction experiences. But could they all be real? Or were they fantasy experiences somehow mixed up and blended with his real-life turmoil and confusion?

But he knew deep down that something had happened to him the first time that he had encountered the Light. He knew that it was real and that it had directly and significantly affected his life.

And now, after the session with Dr. Charles Farr, he knew more details about the disturbing elements in the nightmares that had plagued him since he was seven years old. Somehow, now that he had faced his demons, they seemed less threatening, less frightening.

He no longer felt overwhelmed by the haunting terror from his childhood—even if he had really talked with angels or little gray aliens. He felt better equipped to face reality, no matter what form it would take. And he knew that he would not rest until he found the full truth of the greater reality that lay beyond his dreams.

But for now, he was exhausted. Although it was only ten o'clock, he had spent nearly five hours under the headset and the flashing goggles. He was drained.

After a stiff drink with Carl, even the lumpy sofa in the living room felt good—and for the first time since he was seven years old, he wasn't afraid to fall asleep in the dark.

In his dream that night, Joe was twelve, visiting his grandparents on the farm near Americus for the Green family reunion. Although both his mother and his grandparents had been reluctant to allow the nearly-thirteen-year-old to make such a long bus trip by himself, Joe considered his safe arrival to be the biggest triumph of his young life.

Joe was excited to be back in the old farmhouse where he had been born and where his dad and his nine brothers and sisters had been raised. Now Uncle Junior, his wife Sadie, and their daughter Kelly, two years younger than Joe, lived in the big house alone.

Uncle Junior let Joe join him plinking at rusty tin cans in the trash pile with a worn Remington single-shot twenty-two. Joe learned to disassemble, clean, and reassemble the old rifle; and on the third day of his visit, as a sign of trust, Uncle Junior suggested that Joe get up before dawn and police the corn fields for the pesky rabbits that were destroying the crop with their relentless nibbling.

Joe slept so restlessly, tossing and turning with pride and anticipation, that he got up hours before dawn, even before Aunt Sadie, who started the wood cooking stove an hour before sunrise. The old farmhouse that had held five previous generations of the Green family didn't have indoor plumbing, but since Joe and his parents had left, Uncle Junior had acquired electricity from the Georgia rural electrification program. The family room, the kitchen, and the bedrooms each had one white ceramic light fixture mounted in the center of the ceiling.

Joe made his way downstairs without turning on a light, stopped in the kitchen to grab a leftover biscuit and a glass of buttermilk, then stepped out the back door onto the large back porch. Two of the farm hounds slept near the well on the cool ground where the large, square baking pans lay cleaned of their dinner. He filled his lungs with the cool, fresh air of the early morning and got goose bumps with the chill in the air from the moist dew.

Joe's bare feet were tough with calluses, and the packed red clay under his toes felt cool as he rounded the back side of the farmhouse and checked the pocket of his overalls for the half-box of twenty-two shells Uncle Junior had set out for him. He wore a pair of his uncle's old overalls pinned up at the cuffs, for they were a good four inches too long for him.

The chickens were all silent in the coop. An old bloodhound snoozing under a giant pecan tree in the front yard yawned and stretched at Joe's approach. A bright full moon shed enough light on the familiar surroundings—the huge old hay barn, the fenced-off natural springs that fed the hog wallow, the tractor shed—for him to make his way across the wooden bridge to the acreage with the newly sprouting corn stalks.

He stopped on the bridge to lean over a railing to see if any green turtles were visible on the river bank. He hoped to see one, knowing that Aunt Sadie loved to make soup with them.

Joe yawned, disappointed that the hard-shelled snappers were still asleep in their watery beds. As he stretched, he surveyed the fifty acres of cotton behind him. He had heard the stories so often about how his family had been proud to have been part of the Free French who had abhorred slavery and who had remained neutral during the Civil War, in spite of the fact that the Confederacy had seized most of their lands as a result of their beliefs and neutrality.

Joe figured that it must still be about an hour before daybreak. He would be certain to be on patrol when the pesky rabbits came up to nibble at the stalks. Then, if he were lucky, he would bag one or two of the tasty critters to take home for the evening's meal.

The morning fog hugged the ground and was uncommonly thick. It was kind of eerie out in the field alone in the silence, and Joe started to hum to himself to break the stillness around him.

And then he realized that it was suddenly getting bright all around him. But the light couldn't be from the sunrise; he was facing west, not east. He froze in fear, knowing that a terrible unnamed entity had found him again.

He heard a high, frantic buzzing in his ears. He stepped backward a few steps and a field of energy charged him with enough static electricity that every hair on his young body stood straight up.

The predawn shadows fled from the onslaught of the Light. Just like the first time, the Light filled everything. The Light was everything.

Joe sat up, sweat pumping from every pore. His breath was coming in short gasps.

Carlton Farr had been sitting in an overstuffed chair watching him. He handed him a glass of cool water. "Are you all right, Joe?"

Joe nodded and gratefully took several deep swallows of the water.

"I thought it was likely that you might have a dream about one of the visits of the Light," Farr explained. "I wanted to be here for you in case it got tough."

Joe expressed his appreciation for the scientist's concern, then briefly summarized the dream memory that had surfaced: "Uncle Junior found me that morning, standing mute in the middle of the corn field. I was naked, my clothes folded in a neat pile, the single-shot twenty-two carefully placed on top of the clothes. Country folk back then kept their skeletons in the closet. I doubt if my uncle even told Aunt Sadie. And he probably just forgot about it, figuring his nephew had just gone a little nuts."

"You're going to start remembering a lot more in the days and nights to come," Farr told him. "Think you can get back to sleep? Want a drink?"

Joe took a deep breath. "Thanks, Carl, I'll be all right. I feel as though I'm beginning to take my first real steps to solving my problems."

Farr smiled, said another good night. What Joe Green didn't fully realize, the scientist thought to himself, was that his problems might be those of all of civilization.

Chapter Fifteen

One Lone Bullet

As a Marine sniper, M. D. Crawfoot had used the M40A1. Now he favored a Remington model 700 BDL Varmint bolt- action rifle with a twenty-four-inch barrel, chambered for .308 caliber. He could punch a three-inch group in a target at five hundred yards.

Crawfoot selected his bullets by weight for maximum penetration. He wanted a flattened taper for kinetic energy transfer and a core lock metal jacket deforming compound bullet for ultimate killing effect. Maximum damage to the target was accomplished by the largest hole; ergo, the wider the diameter and the heavier the bullet the better. He had used the firing range and the lab at Quantico to match the best possible combination of size, shape, and weight of bullet with an optimum load.

He lay in the dirt sighting in the prone position, first determining the range to the back porch of Carlton Farr's cabin to be 180 yards. He had checked his rifle, scope sight, and custom grade ammo three times and resisted the compulsion to check them yet again.

He had memorized every detail of the Farr compound and the surrounding landscape. Wind, humidity, and heat rising from the ground were all factors that could distort his sight and affect the trajectory of the bullet. He checked the wind, noting that the breeze was toward him and could cause the bullet to rise or fall just like an airfoil. The high humidity would slow the bullet slightly. He adjusted the center point elevation on his scope for the correct distance.

He munched on the last of a candy bar and remembered surviving in the southeast Asian bush off of worms, snakes, rice bugs, and plump rats. He didn't think of himself as a vicious predator, though he'd prefer to assassinate a human than have to kill an animal. The concept of hunting for sport offended him.

Carlton Farr was late for his routine play time with his dog. Neither the scientist nor his mysterious visitor had shown themselves outside yet that day. It was apparent that they had put in a late night and were slow getting going. It was almost two in the afternoon. A door had opened around noon to let the dog out to relieve itself on a bush near the cabin, but neither man had stepped outside to supervise.

If he was lucky, Crawfoot could finish the contract and make his way back to San Antonio along the country roads and secondary highways. His stress from the heat and the humidity was building. He took several deep breaths and focused his vision on the petals of a lone wild flower several yards away. Slowly, with controlled breathing, he relaxed.

No one was safe from a competent sniper—no president, no pope, no citizen. And the price of a person's life was no greater than the price of a bullet.

Regardless of competent and effective professional military training, not every soldier can kill. Crawfoot knew why. The first thing you saw when you sighted your scope on a man was his eyes. It was not the same as coming down on a silhouette practice target. It took a special kind of man to be a contract assassin. It took an intelligent, resourceful, iron-willed, patient person, a real lone wolf. He liked being that kind of lone wolf—no commitments, no ties, no baggage, just a dedicated patriot with a clean conscience.

Crawfoot waited patiently. He would lie silently in the deep, humid heat for as many hours as it would take.

About three o'clock, the back door to Farr's cabin opened. The outside of Crawfoot's lips turned slightly upward in a smile.

The little brown mutt bounced and bounded around the man, begging him to throw the little red ball to fetch. Predictably, Farr picked up the ball and threw it some thirty yards toward the boat dock.

Crawfoot pulled the butt of the rifle snug against his shoulder, drew a deep breath, exhaled halfway, then gently stroked the trigger. The full-metal-jacket, Teflon-coated, 180-grain Black Talon Winchester .308-caliber bullet left its copper shell casing as the powder exploded. It traveled down the rifled barrel at nearly three times the speed of sound and exited the muzzle at 2,400 feet per second.

The sound of the rifle's discharge could be heard for over a mile as it shattered the afternoon calm. The speeding bullet caused a sonic ricochet off the surrounding trees, dispersing the sound so that it became difficult to determine the source of the explosion.

The bullet dropped less than one inch in the 180 yards to the target. It entered the left side of Carlton Farr's chest level with his heart, creating lethal damage as it ripped through his left lung, thoracic aorta, and heart before exiting.

The scientist first appeared startled. Then he placed his hand to his chest and watched the foaming red blood gush out between his fingers. He flailed his arms desperately for balance, then fell, arching his torso upon impact with the ground. Within seconds after he lay trembling with his life's blood spilling out of him, he knew that he had been shot—and he knew why.

Joe heard the report of the rifle; he hesitated for a second when he realized that it was deer-hunting season. But his trained ears suspected that the rifle shot had sounded suspiciously close. He set his drink on the kitchen table on his way to the back door that led out onto the porch. As he moved toward the back rail, he saw Farr lying sprawled on the grass, his dog, confused and frightened, nudging at his fallen master.

Within seconds he was at the man's side. "Carl! Dear God!" He pulled a clean handkerchief from his back pocket and stuffed half of it into the gaping wound. Farr was pale and appeared to be going into shock.

Joe rolled him back onto the side where the bullet had entered to keep pressure on the wound and to keep the fluid that was collecting in his lung from interfering with his labored aspiration. He brushed Albert back, trying to keep him out of the blood oozing into the dry grass.

Joe saw several people gathered on the back patio of Pat's Place. He shouted at them for help, then realized that, at a distance of over one hundred yards, they couldn't hear him.

He started to rise from his knees, but Farr had caught his shirt in an iron grip. "Carl, let go. I've got to call 911. I've got to get help."

As he gently tried to pry open Farr's fingers from their determined hold on his shirt, Joe saw that the man's mouth was moving and he was trying to say something. He leaned closer. "What are you saying, Carl? Tell me so I can get some help."

"My wallet," Farr said in a barely discernable voice. "You…get my wallet…from bedroom. You get…"

"You don't need your wallet. You need help!"

"Wallet!"

It occurred to Joe that Farr might have pictures of his loved ones in his wallet and that he might want to see them for what might be the last time.

"All right. You let go of my shirt, and I'll go call for help and bring you your wallet."

With his strength diminishing, the last embers of his life flickering and dimming, Carlton Farr looked at Joe Green with the clarity of vision given only to the psychically gifted and the dying. He saw that there truly was something special and unique about Joe.

Joe squeezed his hand."Just hang on, Carl. You're going to be all right."

Farr relaxed his grip, allowing Joe to dash into the cabin. "Chosen one," he whispered after him.

By now a number of the locals at Pat's Place had been able to figure out that something was amiss at Carl Farr's place. By the time that Joe had called for emergency help and had returned to Farr's side, three men and a stout woman stood around the fallen scientist with looks of shock and disbelief on their faces.

"My god, this is terrible, terrible…"

"Goddam deer hunters. They should outlaw the bloody sport…."

"Did you see who did it? Did anyone see who…"

The stout woman reached down and picked up Albert, then started crying.

Joe stood there helplessly, confused, numbly wiping some of the blood on his hands on his jeans.

The sound of an approaching vehicle distracted Joe from the jumble of his anguished thoughts. At first he thought it might be emergency help from his 911 call, but he was dismayed to see that it was not when a medium-sized recreational vehicle slowly pulled into the open clearing near his rental car.

The gravel under the large truck tires popped and crunched as it settled to a stop. Joe was surprised to see that the RV bore Nevada plates.

A slightly built man hopped down to the ground from the driver's side of the RV and a tall, rangy man let himself out of the passenger's side.

"My sad guess is that the unfortunate fellow lying bleeding on the ground over there is Dr. Carlton Farr," the smaller man said. "Am I correct?"

"There's been a terrible accident," Joe said. "What do you want here?"

"We've driven nonstop from Nevada to meet with Dr. Farr," the taller man replied. Then, turning to the driver: "The bastards killed him! What do we do now?"

The smaller man offered Joe his hand. "I'm Blake Webster. This is Wayne Newsome. Who are you?"

Joe knew who both of the men were. He had listened to Webster talking about UFOs and the government conspiracy on a number of radio talk shows. Newsome was a well-known environmentalist and UFO activist from Tonopah who specialized in reporting on rumors about Area 51.

Joe shook Webster's hand. "My name is Joe Green."

"Joe, we might not have much time. Who are you and why were you here?" Newsome asked bluntly.

Hesitantly, Joe told them that he was on leave from his civilian contract work at Area 51. He had met Dr. Farr at a seminar and they had begun a friendship that he had wished to continue. He had just been visiting.

Newsome was direct. "Did you come here to kill Dr. Farr?"

Joe was stunned. Who did this jerk think he was?

"Wayne, Jesus, man!" Webster shouted at his companion. "Look at Joe's eyes. Those aren't the eyes of an assassin. Those are the eyes of some poor bastard who's as driven as we are."

Then, turning back to Joe, Webster explained, "Farr said that he had some important information that he would give to me only if I came down to Texas to get it in person. Before we started out, we tried our damnedest to find my undercover man so we could bring him along out of harm's way. We feel just terrible, but we finally had to give up. We figure some goons from MJ-12 jumped him and are holding him prisoner."

Joe was feeling more disoriented by the moment.

"And now the murdering assholes have taken out Dr. Farr," Newsome said, his large hands bunching into fists of anger and frustration. "He was our last hope to find out the truth about what's going on at Dreamland."

Joe narrowed his eyes in a sudden thought. "Webster, you were responsible for the video clip of the UFO on 'Exploring the Unknown' last Friday night, weren't you?"

Now it was Webster's turn to be wary. "You saw the program?"

Joe nodded. "It's the reason I'm here. The program…I don't really know how to say it, but when I saw that UFO…I mean, it was like something…"

Newsome tried to fill in the blanks for him. "It was like something was triggered inside your head, maybe prompted some old memories?"

Webster grinned in private triumph. "So you're one of them. One of the chosen. That's what I had hoped the telecast would accomplish. Activate people like you all over the world."

"And now the three of us better get the hell out of here," Newsome advised. "You'd better come with us, Joe."

Joe was getting dizzy listening to the two of them. He saw that the local sheriff's car and an emergency medical van were arriving on the scene, their warning lights flashing.

"I can't leave. I've got to see about Carl," he told them. He also remembered his promise to bring him his wallet.

"Joe," Newsome called after him, "this is no hunting accident, man. They were out to get Farr because he could substantiate Webster's video footage. By now they know who you are."

Webster added his advice: "Don't volunteer any information. Keep it as simple as possible."

On his way back to the alleged accident scene, Joe stopped by Carl's bedroom and got the wallet from on top of the dresser. He slipped it in his back pocket.

While the paramedics were examining Farr, Joe spoke to the sheriff, following Webster's advice to keep it simple. He told him that he was a casual professional acquaintance of Dr. Farr's from Tonopah and that he was in San Antonio on vacation. He had called up Farr for a drink a couple of nights ago, and Farr had invited him to the lake. They ate, drank too much, and Joe had slept over. He had seen no one after he heard the shot. It was probably a careless deer hunter.

But Walter Dean Ray didn't think it was a hunting accident and boldly offered his opinion. He described, in exacting detail, the peculiar Hispanic-looking man who had been hanging around Pat's Place off and on for nearly three days. He could also describe the stranger's vehicle, and he even remembered the license plate number.

The paramedics lifted Farr into the ambulance, and Joe heard one of them tell the deputy that it didn't look as though he would make it alive to the hospital.

Carl's wallet! Joe tried to get to the medical van before the doors clamped shut. The sheriff seemed more interested in taking Walt's statement and calling in the license plate numbers to the Texas Highway Patrol. The retired Air Force colonel was the center of attention. Everyone wanted to hear what he had to say, and he was relishing every second of his moment in the spotlight.

While everyone was distracted, Joe stepped back in the cabin and looked through Farr's wallet. There were a couple of credit cards, his Texas driver's license, sixty-seven dollars, and a few receipts. No pictures of loved ones.

But when he stuck his forefinger behind the side panel that had held the credit cards, he felt something hard. He pulled out a key that was wrapped in a small piece of paper.

The paper bore a crisp message: "Key for Blake Webster. Green box under kitchen sink."

Joe had been trying to decide whether or not to trust Blake Webster. If the journalist had won Dr. Carlton Farr's confidence, then the decision had been reached.

"That's it!" Webster shouted when Joe handed him the key. "Farr told me he would hand over some disks that would blow down the walls of the government cover-up about the use of alien technology at Area 51."

Newsome gave Webster's shoulder a gentle shove. "Then let's get the box out from under the kitchen sink and tear ass out of here."

"You're right, man," Webster agreed. "We have to boogie big time."

"I'm coming with you," Joe said, reaching his decision.

Webster nodded approvingly. "I didn't take you for a fool."

"If you'll follow me back into San Antonio, I'll check out of my motel and turn in my rental car. Then I would be much obliged if I could ride back to Las Vegas with you," Joe asked.

Newsome clamped a big hand on Joe's shoulder. "You got it. And then, my friend, you are going to do the lion's share of the driving, 'cause the two of us are beat."

Chapter Sixteen

A Demand He Couldn't Refuse

General Jean-Claude Alexandre Beauharnais was a direct descendent of the famous French general who had fought in the American Revolution and the French Revolution. General Alexandre Beauharnais de Vicomte's widow married Napoleon I and became the Empress Josephine. His son Eugene de Beauharnais was also a general who served with distinction under his stepfather, Napoleon, and was later made Viceroy of Italy. His daughter Hortense married Louis Bonaparte and became queen of Holland in 1806.

Alex, as he preferred to be addressed by his peers, had made his rank the hard way, not by ass-kissing, but by consistently getting results. He had made a career of turning around troubled Black programs of the greatest secrecy.

His positive results had influenced the promotions of many colonels and generals above him. They didn't like him, but they needed him, so they pulled him along up the promotion ladder until he was currently Director for Defense, Special Projects. He reported to the Secretary of Defense and monitored the National Reconnaissance Office (NRO), Space & Missile Systems Office (SAMSO), and the Advanced Research Projects Agency (ARPA) Black projects, which included research and development at the Groom and Papoose facilities.

He wondered why the old bastard Eli Jerrold had summoned him to his spacious offices near the Capitol.

Jerrold had never given him the time of day when he was Director of the National Security Agency. Why the hell did the crusty old son-of-a-bitch need him now? He wasn't even certain what it was that Jerrold did. He had heard rumors that he served as the legal representative of some international consortium of multimillionaires, but for all he knew, the tough old shit could be running a kiddie porn ring.

Alex's salty attitude toward authority figures came from his conviction that his government and military leaders had betrayed the fighting men and women during the Vietnam war. He had survived the Hanoi Hilton as a prisoner of war. He would never totally trust the Establishment again. Where the fuck was Eli Jerrold when he really needed him? Where was any high-ranking official when he could have used a little help?

As a major, Beauharnais had flown the General Dynamics supersonic swing-wing F-111A fighter-bomber from Nellis Air Force Base, Nevada. During the holiday season of 1972, the Air Force and Navy flew some five hundred aircraft from Guam, Thailand, Navy aircraft carriers, and bases in South Vietnam to bomb Hanoi and Haiphong under Operation Linebacker II. The bombing intensity wasn't equaled again until the Desert Storm war.

He commanded a cell of three F-111As over Hanoi. They flew two missions a day from the 18th of December until he was shot down.

U.S. aircraft had taken heavy losses from the North Vietnamese SAMS (surface-to-air missiles). Hanoi was ringed with radar-lined SAMS and MIG aircraft. Some eighty-one American craft were downed during the twelve days of bombing. His aircraft was Number 4,029 shot down since 1964, and he fell to earth just as thousands of tons of napalm, white phosphorous, and anti-personnel mines, high-explosives, defoliants, and bombs had before him. He was twenty-nine years old that Christmas Eve.

For the duration of the war, his home was the Hanoi Hilton, where torture, starvation, humiliation, and propaganda were served up daily. He would never forget the scrawl on the concrete wall of his cell that Christmas. It was trite and silly, but he would never have another Christmas that it didn't play in his head:

"On the twelfth day of bombing my government gave to me—twelve fearless politicians, eleven pilots flying, ten aircraft soaring, nine whores a sucking, eight bombs a bursting, seven Americans dying, six draft cards burning, five mothers weeping, four star generals kissing ass, three grieving widows, two POWs crying, and a traitor named Hanoi Jane."

He had served a tour in hell and survived. But he was changed for all time. He would never trust his government again, never have another family that would desert him, never grieve another dead buddy. In March of 1973 he was with the last of 591 American POWs to be returned.

The final conclusion of the lessons that he had gained from his experiences in Nam never varied from his moment of revelation in the Hanoi Hilton: The military leaders, the politicians, and the DOD contractors had all wanted the war for self-serving reasons. The military leaders wanted power, recognition, promotions, and a place in history. The politicians wanted PAC contributions, gratuities from DOD contractors, and to be reelected. The DOD contractors and the military-industrial complex wanted wealth, job security, and promotions.

Those insiders who objected to the war believed that the military-industrial complex's influence over the politicians and military leaders with their high-tech weapons was evil for having perpetuated a deadly hoax on the nation. Money was power, and in 1972 alone over ten billion dollars were spent on replacement aircraft for the Vietnam war. And that was just the tip of the iceberg. All three of the groups—the military leaders, the politicians, and the DOD contractors—manipulated public opinion, whipped up the brand of patriotism, and used the fear of world communism to bolster their arguments. What pomposity, what guile, what greed had fueled the self-serving motivations that resulted in the loss of over fifty thousand soldiers, airmen, and sailors.

Two dark-uniformed security guards were stationed outside the elevator bank. They checked his identification and directed him to Room 916 on the ninth floor of the office building.

The moment he got off the elevator, a heavy-set colonel seemed to be waiting to greet him. "General Beauharnais?"

"Yes," Alex glanced at the officer's name tag on his dress blue, "Colonel Trent."

Trent stretched out a hand. "It's a pleasure to meet you, General."

Alex nodded. What the hell was another officer doing here? Was Jerrold headhunting for officers to join his firm after their retirement?

And what was a man like Colonel Ty Trent doing here? The man had a reputation in the Special Operations world. In Alex's mind, Trent could be described in three words: "Cold," as in ruthless; "hard," as in conscience-free; and "connected," as in he knew his way around the intelligence business.

Jerrold's office was decorated in hardwoods and leather furniture. Alex crossed the room and shook Jerrold's hand.

"General Beauharnais, it's a pleasure to see you again," Eli smiled as he pumped the man's hand. "It has been a long time, and I appreciate your coming on such short notice."

Alex nodded. "This is a great office, Jerrold. Of course I never saw your office at the NSA. You never invited me to that one."

He couldn't imagine it could have been more plush than this one, and he resented the opulent excess.

Eli Jerrold chose to ignore the general's mocking tone. "Would you care for a drink? Anything at all?"

"Just some bottled water for now, thank you."

Colonel Trent poured him some water and Eli Jerrold tried to seize the initiative. "We're both busy men, so I'll get right to it. I understand that you have some objections to the security measures that have been ordered for Area 51 of the Nevada Test Site. I also understand that you wrote a memo to the Secretary of the Air Force and Secretary of Defense stating your objections."

Alex's face flared a deep red. "With all due respect, Jerrold, but what the hell business is that of yours? You're no longer Director of the NSA, so where the fuck do you get off even bringing the matter up with me?"

Ty Trent squirmed in the oversized leather chair, wishing that Eli had been more subtle and had exercised a bit more tact in dealing with the volatile general.

Jerrold's eyes narrowed, fighting to control his own anger. "I still serve…in an advisory capacity. You see, I have your memo here on my desk."

Alex rocked back in amazement. "What's going on here?"

Jerrold held up the memo as if he were an attorney presenting Exhibit A in court. "I still have the final say-so over several matters of communications security and physical security for the Nevada Test Site and Nellis Range, which encompasses your Area 51."

General Alex Beauharnais sat quietly in his chair. After his initial outburst, he had regained his calm. He had been caught off guard. It wouldn't happen again. He would show no emotions or body language at all, something he had learned from days of interrogation by his North Vietnamese captors.

He raised his glass and slowly took a drink. He would remain calm, but he would get to the bottom of this perplexing situation and find out just what Jerrold was up to.

"If I violated any protocol, Mr. Jerrold, it was because I was unaware of this secret chain of command that you now claim exists," Alex told him, keeping his voice almost at a monotone. "But it was my sincere intention to go on the record about my objections to these harsh security measures. As a responsible military officer, I am not about to commit felonies against the private sector without justification."

Eli Jerrold sipped at the bourbon and water he had poured for himself. "Go on, General, I'm listening."

Alex sighed as if he were speaking to an idiot who had no knowledge of the law. "We are a democracy. We have a constitution. We have laws. You have asked me to break these laws. There is no way that I will have United States citizens killed. I will never infringe upon the constitutional rights of American citizens."

Jerrold responded sharply. "You have no concept, no idea of the scope of the national crisis that we are facing. If we don't keep a lid on it, our society—our world—will come apart."

Alex was becoming increasingly uneasy. "What crisis are you talking about? A few nosy civilians crawling around the desert trying to get a peek at our Black program prototypes hardly classifies as a crisis. Good God, man, you are overreacting.

"According to my understanding of the Posse Comitatus Act, the military is prohibited from enforcing civil law. What the DOE/Wackenhut security personnel are doing is in direct violation of that law. This Offensive Security policy is an offense to the Constitution and the rights of U.S. citizens!"

"Offensive Security" was a concept that had been created by Eli Jerrold. He sat up quickly in his chair and leaned forward in a threatening manner. "General, don't you give me any of that pompous, self-righteous bull shit! You will follow these orders, or I'll have you retired before you go to bed tonight."

Alex met the man's cold stare. Did Eli Jerrold still wield that much power from behind the scenes? Or had the power-crazy martinet gone completely mad in his retirement?

Colonel Trent broke his silence. "Eli, perhaps the general needs clarification on some matters."

Alex nodded. "Indeed I do. For example, the Wackenhut personnel have been authorized to aggressively pursue and protect military and Department of Defense agencies outside the normal protective zone perimeter. At the Nevada Test Site they routinely patrol Bureau of Land Management, county, and state roads outside the government's property. They have harassed citizens, seized private property, and detained the curious who have ventured too close to the restricted area's protective zone perimeter. These goons have got to be toned down."

Eli Jerrold sat angrily pointing a forefinger at General Beauharnais as if it were a loaded pistol. "You stupid prick, you have no idea what we're up against."

Alex was puzzled by the man's continued vehemence, and he felt his face becoming red with waves of rising anger.

Colonel Trent decided to take the ball away from Eli and run with it. "General, with all due respect, since the end of the Cold War, even the Russians have been telling our secrets. *Popular Science* magazine placed a satellite picture of the Groom facilities on their cover. CNN, "The X-Files," "Unsolved Mysteries," and last week "Exploring the Unknown" have produced programs about the Nellis Range, Area 51, and the Groom and Papoose facilities. And popular magazines like *Omni, Time, Newsweek,* and *U.S. News and World Report* have all carried detailed articles on Area 51. We have been using Offensive Security for over two decades, and look at the leaks we have. If we relax these security measures, it will only get worse. In the interest of national security, we cannot allow that to happen. Surely, you agree."

The general looked down at the rows of medals on his uniform. "You see this one? I received it for my last and third tour of Nam. I was flying an F-111A swing-wing fighter-bomber and a surface-to-air missile shot us down. I was a prisoner of war in Hanoi, and I had lots of time to think about the military's responsibility to the nation. I was in a goddam war that we should never have been in. Our generals lied about our progress and our achievements, and they covered their jaded interests to promote and to prolong the war. It was a national disgrace, and many soldiers were killed needlessly."

Alex paused to take a sip of water. He held up a palm for silence when it appeared that Colonel Trent was about to interrupt him. "The reason that I'm telling you this is because I made myself a promise that if I was ever to return to the military that I would never be a yes-man or a self-serving asshole like the generals that ran the Vietnam war."

Colonel managed to get his word in. "I understand your concerns, but…"

Alex winced. "I don't think you do, Colonel. You see, I have been asked to detain and interrogate U.S. citizens who cross over protective zone perimeter in Area 51. I know for a fact that the DOE and the Wackenhut agency have done this on numerous occasions. I have ordered them to stop this practice, but I know they ignore my orders. I can't prove what has happened to the citizens who were detained, but I have my suspicions."

Eli answered the general's suspicions. "They were turned over to the CIA or other top-secret agencies. Executive Order 12333 issued by President Ronald Reagan in 1981 allows the CIA to conduct 'special activities' within the United States as long as such action does not involve efforts to influence the domestic political process, media, or public opinion."

Alex pursed his lips thoughtfully and shrugged. "Well, I'm sorry Eli, but your extremely forceful request just doesn't cut it for me. And unless the Secretary of Defense or the Secretary of the Air Force orders me to do otherwise, I respectfully decline to obey your orders."

Eli Jerrold looked at Colonel Trent, then General Beauharnais. He took a swallow of the bourbon, then set the glass down on his desk. His voice was low, controlled. "All right, General, I will lay all my cards on the table."

"Eli," Trent cautioned. "Are you certain?"

Eli sighed, then nodded slowly. "In his own way, I know that General Beauharnais considers himself a great patriot. And several times within the past hour he has expressed his single, abiding, overwhelming concern to be the welfare of United States citizens. Is that not true, General?"

Alex answered in the affirmative, not certain where Jerrold was going with this.

"Then," Jerrold continued, "it most certainly stands to reason that General Beauharnais would be most vigilant and eager to protect these same citizens if he understood that they faced the greatest threat to their welfare, their safety, their very existence that one could ever imagine."

Alex shifted uncomfortably. My God, he wondered, had some outlaw third-world nation perfected nuclear power to the point of aggression against the United States?

"General, do you know anything about the source of our technology in the Aurora Programs?" Jerrold asked him, once again throwing him off balance.

"Why, no, I have never had a need to know," Alex replied. "Of course I've heard those rumors that we claimed some of it as spoils of war from the Nazis at the end of World War II. Or that we stole it from the Russians or the Japanese. I've even heard that crazy story about how we captured or recovered an alien spaceship."

Eli smiled, feeling once again in control of the situation. "Have you ever heard of the MJ-12 committee?"

"No, I don't think so."

Colonel Trent cleared his throat noisily. "General, I am reminding you that you enjoy top security clearance. At the same time, I am cautioning you that what you are about to hear is way above top secret. It stays in this room. Understood?"

Alex studied the faces of the two men. Whatever the hell this was all about, he had never seen two more deadly serious faces in his life. "Understood, Colonel."

Eli Jerrold leaned back in his desk chair. "Shortly after Secretary of Defense James V. Forrestal resigned in March of 1949—and before his mysterious suicide—Secretary Louis Johnson issued a Top Secret Directive establishing the Armed Forces Security Agency, which was placed under the control of the Joint Chiefs of Staff. This was the forerunner of the National Security Agency. The CIA and DIA were also established at this time. On December 29, 1952, President Truman in one of his very last acts as president, signed approval on NS-CID No. 9, approving the establishment of the NSA."

General Beauharnais sat quietly with a look that said, "And so?"

Eli opened a drawer, removed a red folder. "Unexplained phenomena, sights of unidentified aerial objects, and other mysterious occurrences around government and DOD installations resulted in the birth of the MJ-12 committee."

Jerrold handed the general the red folder stamped with the classification Top Secret, MAJIC ONLY, MJ-12 Eyes Only in large, bold black letters.

"I would like you to read this, General Beauharnais," he said. "I am certain that after you do, you will understand our need for ultimate security. I am also certain that you will want to join our band of patriots."

Alex opened the folder and proceeded to read the contents.

The papers definitely had caught General Beauharnais' interest.

He glanced up at Eli Jerrold and Colonel Trent. Eli was sitting back in his chair, his arms crossed above his head. Trent paced the floor.

They were waiting for his reactions.

Alex never liked to be predictable, so he stopped reading and asked what had happened to Secretary of Defense Forrestal. Why had his death been important enough to be mentioned in a Top Secret briefing for the president?

Eli informed him that James Vincent Forrestal had been born in 1892 in Beacon, New York, and had died by his own hand in 1949. He was Secretary of the Navy from 1944 to 1947 and Secretary of Defense from 1947 to 1949.

As Secretary of Defense, he had been chairman of the original MJ-12 committee established in 1947 after a series of bizarre UFO sightings and incidents. Mental illness had forced his resignation.

He later committed suicide by jumping backward out of the sixteenth floor window of the Bethesda Naval hospital. His suicide occurred less than a year after he created Project Sign to investigate alien technology.

"His medical records are sealed to this day, even to the exclusion of his heirs," Eli concluded.

Alex accepted the refill of water that Colonel Trent offered him. Later, he knew that he would need something stronger. For now, he wanted to keep his wits about him.

"I'm assuming that the suicide of Forrestal was the reason that you, as the Director, or former Director, of the NSA now head the committee instead of the Secretary of Defense?" the general asked Jerrold.

Eli shook his head at Colonel Trent, who appeared about to answer the question in too great detail. "We'll get into that later. Please read on, General."

NATIONAL SECURITY INFORMATION

****
* TOP SECRET *
****

EYES ONLY COPY <u>ONE</u> OF <u>ONE</u>

BRIEFING DOCUMENT: OPERATION MAJESTIC 12

PREPARED FOR PRESIDENT-ELECT DWIGHT D. EISENHOWER:
(EYES ONLY)

18 NOVEMBER 1952

<u>WARNING:</u> This is a TOP SECRET-EYES ONLY document containing compartmentalized information essential to the national security of the United States. EYES ONLY ACCESS to the material herein is strictly limited to those possessing Majestic-12 clearance level. Reproduction in any form or the taking of written or mechanically transcribed notes is strictly forbidden.

****
* TOP SECRET *
****

EYES ONLY T52-EXEMPT (E)

****
* TOP SECRET *
****

EYES ONLY COPY ONE OF ONE

SUBJECT: OPERATION MAJESTIC-12 PRELIMINARY BRIEFING FOR PRESIDENT-ELECT EISENHOWER.
DOCUMENT PREPARED 18 NOVEMBER 1952.
BRIEFING OFFICER; REAR ADM. R. H. HILLENKOETTER (MJ-1)
NOTE: This document has been prepared as a preliminary briefing only. It should be regarded as introductory to a full operations briefing intended to follow.

* * * * * *

OPERATION MAJESTIC-12 is a TOP SECRET Research and Development/Intelligence operation responsible directly and only to the President of the United States. Operations of the project are carried out under control of the Majestic-12 (Majic-12) Group which was established by special Classified Executive Order (CEO) of President Truman on 20 September 1947, upon recommendation by Dr. Vannevar Bush and Secretary James Forrestal. (See Attachment "A".) Members of the Majestic-12 Group were designated as follows:

Rear Adm. R. H. Hillenkoetter*
Dr. Vannevar Bush
Sec. James V. Forrestal*
Lt. Gen. Nathan F. Twining
Lt. Gen. Hoyt S. Vandenberg
Dr. Detlev Bronk
Dr. Jerome Hunsaker
Mr. Sidney W. Souers
Mr. Gordon Gray
Dr. Donald Menzel
Gen. Robert M. Montague
Dr. Lloyd V. Berkner

The death of Secretary Forrestal on 22 May, 1949, created a vacancy which remained unfilled until 1 August, 1950, upon which date Louis A. Johnson was designated as permanent replacement. Gen. Walter B. Smith replaced Rear Adm. R. H. Hillenkoetter upon his reassignment to the Pacific Seventh Fleet.

****
* TOP SECRET *
****

EYES ONLY T52-EXEMPT (E)

****
* TOP SECRET *
****

EYES ONLY COPY ONE OF ONE

On 24 June, 1947, a civilian pilot flying over the Cascade Mountains in the State of Washington observed nine flying disc-shaped aircraft traveling in formation at a high rate of speed. Although this was not the first known sighting of such objects, it was the first to gain widespread attention in the public media. Hundreds of reports of sightings of similar objects followed. Many of these came from highly credible military and civilian sources. These reports resulted in independent efforts by several different elements of the military to ascertain the nature and purpose of these objects in the interests of national defense. A number of witnesses were interviewed and there were several unsuccessful attempts to utilize aircraft in efforts to pursue reported discs in flight. Pubic reaction bordered on near hysteria at times.

In spite of these efforts, little of substance was learned about the objects until a local rancher reported that one had crashed in a remote region of New Mexico located approximately seventy-five miles northwest of Roswell Army Air Base (now Walker Field).

On 5 July 1947, a secret operation was begun to assure recovery of the wreckage of this object for scientific study. During the course of this operation, aerial reconnaissance discovered that five small human-like beings had apparently ejected from the craft at some point before it exploded. These had fallen to earth about two miles east of the wreckage site. Four were dead and badly damaged due to the crash trauma, action by predators and exposure to the elements during the time period which had elapsed before their discovery. A special scientific team took charge of removing these bodies for study. (See Attachment "D.") Civilian and military witnesses in the area were debriefed, and news reporters were given the effective cover story that the object had been a misguided weather research balloon.

****
* TOP SECRET *
****

EYES ONLY T52-EXEMPT (E)

****
* TOP SECRET *
****

EYES ONLY COPY ONE OF ONE

A covert analytical effort organized by Lt. Gen. Twining and Dr. Bush acting on the direct orders of the President, resulted in a preliminary consensus (19 September, 1947) that the disc was most likely a short range reconnaissance craft. This conclusion was based for the most part on the craft's size and the apparent lack of any identifiable provisioning. (See attachment "D".) A similar analysis of the five bodies was arranged by Dr. Bronk. It was the tentative conclusion of this group (30 November, 1947) that although these creature are human-like in appearance, the biological and evolutionary processes responsible for their development has apparently been quite different from those observed or postulated in homo-sapiens. Dr. Bronk's team has suggested the term "Extra-terrestrial Biological Entities", or "EBEs", be adopted as the standard term of reference for these creatures until such time as a more definitive designation can be agreed upon.

Since it is virtually certain that these craft do not originate in any country on earth, considerable speculation has centered around what their point of origin might be and how they get here. Mars was and remains a possibility, although some scientists, most notably Dr. Menzel, consider it more likely that we are dealing with beings from another solar system entirely.

Numerous examples of what appear to be a form of writing were found in the wreckage. Efforts to decipher these have remained largely unsuccessful. (See Attachment "E.") Equally unsuccessful have been efforts to determine the method of propulsion or the nature or method of transmission of the power source involved. Research along these lines has been complicated by the complete absence of identifiable wings, propellers, jets, or other conventional methods of propulsion and guidance, as well as a total lack of metal components. (See Attachment "F".) It is assumed that the propulsion unit was completely destroyed by the explosion which caused the crash.

****
* TOP SECRET *
****

EYES ONLY T52-EXEMPT (E)

****
* TOP SECRET *
****

<u>EYES ONLY</u> COPY <u>ONE</u> OF <u>ONE</u>

A need for as much additional information as possible about these craft, their performance characteristics and their purpose led to the undertaking known as U.S. Air Force Project SIGN in December, 1947. In order to preserve security, liaison between SIGN and Majestic-12 was limited to two individuals within the Intelligence Division of Air Materiel Command whose role was to pass along certain types of information through channels. SIGN evolved into Project GRUDGE in December, 1948. The operation is currently being conducted under the code name BLUE BOOK, with liaison maintained through the Air Force officer who is head of the project.

On 06 December, 1950, a second object, probably of similar origin, impacted the earth at high speed in the El Indio Guerrero area of the Texas - Mexican border after following a long trajectory through the atmosphere. By the time a search team arrived, what remained of the object had been almost totally incinerated. such material as could be recovered was transported to the A.E.C. facility at Sandia, New Mexico, for study.

Implications for the National Security are of continuing importance in that the motives and ultimate intentions of these visitors remain completely unknown. In addition, a significant upsurge in the surveillance activity of these craft beginning in May and continuing through the autumn of this year has caused considerable concern that new developments may be imminent. It is for these reasons, as well as the obvious international and technological considerations and the ultimate need to avoid a public panic at all costs, that the Majestic-12 Group remains of the unanimous opinion that imposition of the strictest security precautions should continue without interruption into the new administration. At the same time, contingency plan MJ-1949-04P/78 (Top Secret - Eyes Only) should be held in continued readiness should the need to make a public announcement present itself. (See Attachment "G.")

****
* TOP SECRET *
****

<u>EYES ONLY</u> T52-EXEMPT (E)

****
* TOP SECRET *
****

<u>EYES ONLY</u> COPY <u>ONE</u> OF <u>ONE</u>

ENUMERATION OF ATTACHMENTS:

*ATTACHMENT "A" ....Special Classified Executive Order #9892//B/CEO/EO. 20/9/47 (TS/EO)

*ATTACHMENT "B" ....Operation Majestic-12 Status Report #1, Part A. 30/10/47. (TS-MAJIC/EO)

*ATTACHMENT "C" ....Operation Majestic-12 Status Report #1, Part B. 30/10/47. (TS-MAJIC/EO)

*ATTACHMENT "D" ....Operation Majestic-12 Preliminary Analytical Report, 19/9/47. (TS-MAJIC/EO)

*ATTACHMENT "E" ....Operation Majestic-12 Blue Team Report #1-5. 30/6/52. (TS-MAJIC/EO)

*ATTACHMENT "F" ....Operation Majestic-12 Status Report #2-4. 31/1/48. (TS-MAJIC/EO)

*ATTACHMENT "G" ....Operations Majestic-12 Contingency Plan MJ-1949-04P/CEO: 31/1/49. (TS-MAJIC/EO)

*ATTACHMENT "H" ....Operation Majestic-12, Maps and Photographs Folio (Extractions). (TS-MAJIC/EO)

****
* TOP SECRET *
****

<u>EYES ONLY</u> T52-EXEMPT (E)

Chapter Seventeen

Offensive Security

General Alex Beauharnais scanned the several dozen pages of attachments to the MJ-12 files. He had occasionally imagined such possibilities as those documented within the text to be true, but he had rejected such premises according to the dictates of his superiors that they were all nonsense and unsubstantiated allegations.

"Now do you see the dilemma we face in regard to security?" Eli Jerrold asked him.

Alex was not yet ready to commit himself to declaring open season on civilians regardless of the reason. "What has been accomplished since the MJ-12 committee was established?"

"My God, man," Eli leaned forward excitedly, "the breakthroughs that we have made in the five decades since the Roswell crash are astounding.

"To name only a few, we have, of course, the quantum leap forward in aerial technology; the accelerated development of computers; genetic breakthroughs, breaking the human genome, seeking to discover just what has been manipulated within our species since Neanderthal. And then there's lasers, fiber and solid-state optics, bio and nanotechnology, certain advanced types of composite materials. All these concepts and advances were directly related to artifacts and data gleaned from UFOs."

While Jerrold paused to catch his breath, Colonel Treat picked up the ball. “The so-called Cold War was exaggerated and manipulated by both sides to justify the huge defense expenditures funneled into these extraordinary technologies. The Russians went broke, and our country has accumulated a huge debt. We’re borrowing money against our future, racing against the devil for survival.”

“Who the hell are they, these aliens?” Alex wanted them to answer the two most obvious questions. “And where are they from?”

Colonel Treat shrugged. “We don’t know their initial point of origin, but they would have us believe somewhere not in this solar system. They also claim to have had a base on Mars longer that humankind’s history. That should explain to you why both the Russians and ourselves have lost probes in the Mars orbit.”

“Yes, but we did finally get to Mars in July of ’97, and the little rover didn’t discover anything earth-shattering. If these ‘aliens’ sabotaged the Russians’ and Americans’ previous attempts, then why was the latest one successful?

“Simple answer. We didn’t shield our computers and they could see that our targeted landing zone was the most remote part of Mars, equivalent to the most desolate part of the earth’s Sahara desert. Our landing wasn’t a threat to their presence on Mars.”

“Then why spend five hundred million dollars to go again?”

“To quell some of these alien rumors; alien facilities on Mars; aliens control outer space; NASA faked all the previous landings, and a myriad of similar rumors.”

“Expensive PR or disinformation.”

“Worth every penny, I assure you.”

Jerrold poured himself another bourbon and made a gesture of offering the bottle to the general. This time Alex nodded his acceptance of a drink. He was definitely ready for something stronger than bottled water.

“They claim to have been on our planet since before Neanderthal man,” Eli said as he poured a shot of bourbon for General Beauharnais. “To be frank, though, our only communications from them come through occasional thought projects or brief radio transmissions. We have yet to be able to decipher their writing.”

“Why’s that?” Alex wondered as he accepted the glass of bourbon and water from Jerrold.

"They use pictographic characters," Colonel Treat said, as he crossed the room to the liquor cabinet to mix himself a drink. "Tens of thousands of different ones. The alien vehicles are piloted by androids..."

General Beauharnais interrupted the Colonel with an unrestrained burst of laughter. "Androids? This is starting to sound like an episode of *Star Trek,* gentlemen."

Colonel Treat smiled grimly. "This is science fiction come true, General. These androids aren't robots or machines, they're some kind of biological entity. They call themselves the 'Jexovah,'* and we call them Extraterrestrial Biological Entities or EBEs, because we have never seen the aliens who created them."

"And these...androids are flying in from Mars?" Alex asked before he took a large swallow of the bourbon.

"We suspect that the smaller scout ships and the considerably larger research craft are probably based on much larger interplanetary or interstellar vessels. They, in turn, may be controlled by a massive mother ship manned by the Jexovah. We haven't been able to gain much intelligence from the androids themselves, for, unfortunately, we discovered that when an android-piloted craft crashed or became otherwise disabled, the entities rapidly biodegraded or autodisassociated, and this autodegradation process is not fully understood by our scientists."

"What about their hardware, the crafts themselves?" Alex asked. "Apparently we've been able to gain a lot of practical knowledge from an examination of these vehicles."

"But it hasn't been easy," Eli answered. "A great deal of the recovered crafts' computers and other instrumentation were structured of organic-like material, so they also degraded. We can now match a great deal of the alien technology, but they can still come and go at will with little regard from our defense systems. We are hoping that the Aurora and SDI-like programs will change all that. We intend to make them have more respect for us as a species."

General Beauharnais set his empty glass on the edge of Jerrold's desk. "But obviously these...Jexovah entities must be peaceful, even benevolently inclined toward us. Otherwise they could have blown us to atoms long ago. Or, if it is true that they have been around since before Neanderthals, then

---

*Pronounced "ye-ou-va." The *x* is silent.

they could have raised our entire species to be their slaves if that had been their desire."

Eli nodded. "We have considered all of these things, General."

"I would expect that you had," General Beauharnais said. After all, they had had fifty years to think about these things.

"The problem is," Colonel Treat interjected, "we don't really know their game plan. We don't know what kind of timetable they might be running on. Hell, they might consider us and the whole planet as their property. They could be waiting for just the right moment to enslave us. Maybe we were too dumb for them before. They didn't want a bunch of hairless monkeys to do their bidding."

Alex wanted to know if there was any solid evidence of the alien's hostile intentions.

"There have been incidents that certainly indicate a callous disregard for human sensitivities," Jerrold said. "And there have been more serious incidents that indicate a rather serious disregard for human life."

Colonel Treat pulled up a chair so that he might sit closer to the general. "That's why we must maintain a strict policy of maximum security. We just don't know what the aliens are up to. They could turn on us at any time."

Eli chuckled. "Think of all these well-meaning, but naive, environmentalists running around trying to save the planet. General Beauharnais, tell me, is there is no viable, free civilization, then what good is the planet? The logic of MJ-12 is to first protect our species, then the environment."

"But in the fifty years that our government has been interacting on one level or another with these alien creatures, MJ-12 must surely have learned more than you have told me thus far," General Beauharnais reasoned.

Colonel Treat turned to face Eli Jerrold. As the present head of MJ-12 whatever intelligence disclosed to the general was completely up to him.

"From our studies since 1947, we have discovered that a good many of the legends of gods, angels, and miraculous occurrences reported through human history have been based on the activities of the Jexovah aliens," Jerrold said. "Every religion and culture has been profoundly influenced by these aliens and their androids. We believe that the Sumerian civilization was directly programmed and directed by these alien entities."

Colonel Treat felt a tacit permission had been granted to provide General Beauharnais with as much intelligence as he could absorb in a few hours sitting. "We have learned a considerable amount about their technology from our examination of four crashed vehicles—the first of which was the one at Roswell. We theorize that our contemporary technology may now be close to where the aliens were roughly six thousand years ago—except they had a form of interstellar propulsion."

Eli Jerrold pushed back from his desk, stood, then walked to the large wall safe behind him. The instant he opened the safe door, the curved, teardrop shape of an alien android head came into view. The bust, with its grey skin and deep black bulging eyes, was secured in a hermetically sealed clear plastic bag. He removed the bust and a small metal box containing crash residue.

"Eerie looking son of a bitch, eh?" Jerrold asked the general.

Alex nodded, fighting back a feeling of revulsion. "I assume it's not real. A mounted trophy for the wall. You said their bodies rapidly biodegraded."

Colonel Treat confirmed his assumption. "It's a silicon copy, very exact in detail. The color, a light gray with subtle blue highlights, is also accurate. So are the measurements."

Eli removed the bust from its plastic seal, then pushed it toward General Beauharnais across the top of his hand-carved mahogany desk. "It's enough to give a guy the willies, right? Have a closer look, General."

Alex ran a forefinger over the alien's smooth forehead. "Those big bug eyes could really get you, huh? A kind of hypnotic quality."

He turned the bust in his hands. No jaw. Small holes for the nostrils. A thin line for a mouth. Tiny bump where one would expect the ears to be.

"I've heard the alleged accounts and descriptions of these creatures by people who claimed to have been abducted by aliens," Alex admitted. "They say that the creatures are only about four feet tall. However, that doesn't mean they couldn't be a threat to us. A helluva lot of Viet Cong were under five feet tall, and they managed to kill over fifty-eight thousand U.S. soldiers."

Eli had poured himself another small shot of bourbon. "The greatest threat need not be a physical one," he said quietly. "I will confess something to you, General. We have alluded to the alien's ability to communicate mentally. I don't know if it was just my imagination, but when I was called to Groom Lake to inspect the largest of the four intact alien vehicles that we had recovered, I actually felt as though I received some kind of communication from them inside my head."

"What kind of communication?" Alex prompted.

Eli shook his head. "I'm not certain. Maybe my will was too strong to pick up actual thoughts that could be translated into words, but my brain was filled with the most extraordinary images. It was as if I had somehow been transported to another world, another dimension where the things of our world made absolutely no sense. I got the hell out of there as fast as I could to clear my head."

Colonel Treat cleared his throat as he got up to fix himself another drink. "Probably damn good thing you got out of there when you did. Remember Secretary Forrestal."

Eli lowered his eyes for a moment before he continued. "It was after Forrestal had observed the autopsy of the dead aliens from the Roswell crash that he was driven mad by the images and the voices he claimed to see and hear in his head."

Treat sat down again next to General Beauharnais. "He wasn't the only one."

Eli lifted his eyes and looked directly at the general. "No, he wasn't. Since the first crash in 1947, 237 male and eighteen female personnel who have worked on these projects have been placed in high security mental institutions spread throughout the United States."

"Holy shit!" Alex exclaimed, throwing his studied calm to the wind.

Jerrold and Treat emitted mirthless laughter at the general's emotional and unexpected response.

"Holy shit, indeed," Jerrold continued. "Each of these individuals—all 255 of them—claimed to have received some kind of communication from the alien corpses."

"Or from alien spaceships and living android crews," Treat added.

"The colonel is correct," Jerrold agreed. "But whatever they claimed to be the source of their mental communication, some became comatose, withdrawn from reality, while others turned into blathering, drooling idiots."

Colonel Treat added another interesting detail. "Some, though, exhibited strange, new mental powers. You know, being able to predict future events, picking up details about strangers. We're studying these particular people very carefully. The others we keep heavily medicated."

General Beauharnais was finding all of this difficult to absorb. "Surely not everyone who dealt with the alien corpses or technology went mad."

"Of course not," Eli said. "We soon found that it was personnel who held strong literal or fundamental beliefs about God or Christ who were the most tragically and extraordinarily affected."

Colonel Treat shifted his thick body in his chair and crossed his legs. "This is one of the reasons for tight security. If a lot of people knew the truth about the aliens, it would destroy their orthodox and conventional belief structures. We might have millions of men and women to put into institutions."

"That's possible," the general conceded the point. "But what if we began a massive educational program to acquaint our citizens with the truth?"

Eli disagreed. "In this case, General, we do not believe that the truth would set them free. Let me explain what we have gleaned from the images that those men and women we had to institutionalize shared with medical personnel in their moments of lucidity. It gives us a composite of the aliens, their world, their intentions. It may well have been that each of these wretched people were given a piece of some great cosmic jigsaw puzzle that we were challenged to assemble."

Eli began unraveling the composite picture of an alien world for the general by stating that it appeared the beings' once earth-like planet had become barren and dead of all life forms. A planet once inhabited by millions of species of diverse plants and animals had become a graveyard in space, because its dominant species had sacrificed their world's future for a technology that had turned on them.

"The Jexovah had exhausted their natural resources. They had manipulated their world with a super science beyond anything we humans can now understand," Jerrold continued. "They literally took their planet apart. They altered nature, tested bizarre theories, and wreaked havoc to their fragile ecosystem in the name of progress. Without the discovery of the magnetic flux field plasma vortex propulsion system, it is certain that they would have perished in their own ashes. Because of this advanced propulsion system, vast numbers of the Jexovah were able to leave their sterile rock planet and condemn the rest of their kind to deal with a noxious liquid muck filling its oceans, an atmosphere storming out of control, and a deadly mixture of toxic gasses blowing about."

Eli paused a moment, sipped at his drink. It was clear that he had the general's undivided attention. "The Jexovah explored and expanded through the universe," he said, resuming the account that had been pieced together from hundreds of individual visions. "They possessed the technological ability to move from one universe to another and back again through artificially created 'worm holes' in space. This capability they created through the use of quasi-crystals, which allowed for what Einstein called in still-secret papers a 'quantum time domain flux field transference.'"

According to the composite mental impressions received by the government personnel who had been driven mad by the alien communications, the Jexovah discovered that they only aged in their universe of origin. When they explored other universes, they enjoyed a glorious immortality. Thus being able to explore literally forever, never aging except in their home universe, they appeared to have evolved to the point where they could live the ultimate dream that any scientifically advanced civilization could hope to achieve.

Their space probes, passing through the outer limits of our solar system, detected a planet between Mars and Jupiter that was compatible with their needs.

Excitement infected the Jexovah when their probes alerted them to the existence of natural quasi-crystals on this faraway world. When this planet was destroyed through a series of natural cataclysms, they found Earth to contain other precious metals that they needed and an environment that was kinder to their biological and logistical requirements.

"And now we come to the part wherein the Jexovah came to our lovely green oasis in space," Jerrold said, feeling the anger rise within him. "We come to the part where they decided to interfere with our planet's natural evolution and pump some of their genes into Neanderthal man."

General Beauharnais scowled his objection. "Are you suggesting that the first true human, the Neanderthal, would never have evolved if it were not for the Jexovah intervention?"

Jerrold answered without hesitation. "From what we have pieced together, it seems apparent that Homo erectus would have been a dead end for the hominid species if it had not been for the Jexovah. They arrived on this planet bearing their gifts of science and proceeded to alter a species by genetic manipulation. They planted their seed within us."

Colonel Treat spoke up. "So you can see, General, why those who take their Bible and their religion literally would be knocked for a giant loop to learn that they had not been created by a god who placed them in a Garden of Eden, but by an alien species who wished to perpetuate their own kind. We were not created in the image of God, but in the image of the Jexovah."

This was getting to be a bit much for General Beauharnais. "I guess, whether I wish to or not, I think I would be upset by such an allegation—especially if it could be proved."

Eli seemed satisfied with the general's response. "You are beginning to understand more clearer why MJ-12 and those of us who know the truth about aliens and UFOs have been so protective of our weaker brethren. It really is up to us to assume the role of shepherds for the masses of humankind."

General Beauharnais took a really stiff drink. He had more questions, but he decided to allow Eli Jerrold to continue with his narrative.

"We are, in essence, an attempt of the Jexovah to correct the overmanipulation that their species had made in their own genetic engineering for hundreds of eons," Jerrold said. "They started their gene manipulation with primates; and as Homo erectus evolved into Homo sapiens, the androids have continued their work."

Eli paused, leaned forward to emphasize his point. "And understand, General, understand this well: The work of the Jexovah is not yet finished. We are not the linear descendants of Neanderthal man, nor are we Jexovah. We are something in between. We are some goddam abomination of nature."

General Beauharnais had moved to the edge of his seat. "When you say that the Jexovah are not yet finished…"

"It is apparent that during intermittent but regular periods of time, the Jexovah supervise the genetic examination and/or manipulation of Earth's higher life forms as a quality control measure, making certain that the target life forms are evolving in the direction of their plans."

Colonel Treat stood. It was time to refill his glass. "General, a well-read man such as yourself is certainly aware that since humankind's earliest memories and most ancient records, the gods have appeared in fiery chariots and other fantastic vehicles. Since the beginning, they have abducted certain earthlings, manipulated their genes through selective impregnation, and left them with weird stories or suppressed memories."

General Beauharnais declined another drink. He wanted to be certain that he was understanding all of this.

"We've also learned that there is particular EBE known as a seed android," Jerrold said. "In effect, this entity is a changeling, carrying a complex geo-organ in which is stored most of the Jexovah genetic material. This organ is capable of duplicating other of the target species' genetic material while carefully inserting Jexovah genes. Being a mimicked life form, the seed androids converted to human and mated with humans."

The general shook his head slightly, as if to sharpen his mental machinery. "If I am following all of this, then the offspring would bear human genetic material as well as the Jexovah genes."

Jerrold nodded. "Since the seed androids were, in essence, living machines—gene factories, so to speak—they could mate again and again, inserting the Jexovah genes at planned intervals, each time forcing the evolution of our species to become a civilization of pseudo-Jexovah."

A thought occurred to the general. "Since these seed androids are human in appearance, they would live among us unnoticed."

Eli shrugged. "Possible. But from the fragments of information that we've pieced together, we really have no idea if there are seed androids walking among us."

"But perhaps that's what all these abductions are all about," General Beauharnais suggested.

Eli paused, collecting his thoughts before answering. "We only know the seed androids existed at one time. There is both the ancient historical documentation and the alien thoughts that some have received. These abductions are another matter. They are performed by androids that seem intent on a kind of genetic manipulation that involves the stealing of sperm, eggs, or fetuses from us for some kind of quality control process."

The general sat for a moment in quiet reflection. "How far are we from becoming true Jexovah?"

Eli Jerrold considered the question. "No intelligence in the universe, except the Jexovah, can answer that question."

Eli got out from behind his desk and began to pace. "Now, General, do you have a clearer picture of the awesome, the terrible responsibility that those of us on the MJ-12 committee carry around with us every moment of the day and night? There are times when my head actually aches from the secrets that I carry inside my brain!"

Colonel Treat agreed. "But we have not just been wringing our hands over this nightmare. Thanks to the brilliant and resourceful leadership of Eli Jerrold, we have spread the research to catch up to the Jexovah technology throughout the Department of Defense and commercial industries. The prime movers in this research are such national laboratories as Sandia, Los Alamos, Livermore, and Bell. The government laboratories heading up the research on alien technology are Armstrong, Philips, Rome, and Wright Patterson."

General Beauharnais was puzzled. "But I've been to most of those laboratories, especially the four government laboratories that are on our air bases. It is becoming increasingly clear to me that this research is not generally known to the rank and file—or even to those of us with extremely high rank and security clearance."

"Only those who consider themselves patriots of the highest order are aware of these projects," Jerrold explained. "Others are recruited as their services are required. That was why you were invited here today."

"And because I protested against such severe security measures as I see being enforced on certain Black programs," the general said.

"And now you understand the need for such extreme measures," Colonel Treat said, adding with just a slight taint of threat or, perhaps, merely earnest prompting, "don't you?"

"I suppose I do," Alex answered. "My mind, though, is still unsettled from all of this sudden, astonishing input."

Eli continued to outline the current research that they hoped would enable the secret government to protect its citizens: "Under the Department of Defense's supervision, Los Alamos works with Livermore on nuclear weapons and nuclear propulsion. Los Alamos also works with the materials associated with containment of the prototype magnetic field disrupter and the downsized reactors. Livermore developed the plasma containment and superconductors."

General Beauharnais interrupted. "When you say the DOD supervises this research at Los Alamos, you are, of course, referring to select administrative personnel who have already joined your band of patriots?"

Colonel Treat confirmed his deduction. "That's correct. All military and civilian underlings are under their oath not to disclose any details of these Black projects. And because most of them only work with bits and pieces of research, few of them could figure out what the hell was going on anyway."

Jerrold stopped his pacing and took his seat behind his large desk. "Our people at Rome Laboratories are providing us with research on electromagnetics and magnetic field generation technology, as well as energy weapons and the phenomenal quasi-crystals. The Rome Laboratories at Griffiss AFB NY research the alien communications and provide intelligence techniques for monitoring alien movements.

"Our contacts at the NSA work closely with these laboratories to provide guidance to the National Reconnaissance Office for satellite surveillance and Space Command for tracking UFO movements outside of the atmosphere.

"Wright Patterson works on the airframe and materials reverse engineering from artifacts recovered from the four crashes, as well as efforts in developing avionics, flight dynamics, and atmospheric propulsion systems.

"Philips Labs at Kirtland AFB gave us research on rocket propulsion, ramjet, and scramjet technologies. They have done a great deal with advanced weapons development, also.

"So you can see," Jerrold concluded his rundown, "we have spread the technologies and research around in a desperate effort to be prepared for a possible all-out alien invasion. In addition, dozens of university and private research contracts have been discretely let to assist the prime movers."

Alex sighed and leaned back in his chair. "Then I guess all those rumors about alien bodies at Wright Patterson are really true after all."

Colonel Treat knew that the general was referring to the alien bodies found in the wreckage of the 1947 Roswell, New Mexico, crash. "The remains of the alien space vehicles were taken initially to Los Alamos, for the simple reasons that they had developed the A-bomb, they were closest to the crash, and they could provide the necessary security. The materials, debris, and later some of the vehicles' pieces were taken to Wright Patterson. The bodies were never taken there."

The general smiled. "Okay, then, let me guess. But you have to tell me if I'm correct. Could they have been taken to the Armstrong Aerospace Medicine or Human Systems Laboratories at Brooks AFB facilities in San Antonio?"

Colonel Treat laughed. "You win the cigar!"

"Sandia Labs at Kirtland also assisted," Jerrold added.

Alex knew the moment of truth was fast approaching. "How do I fit into all of this?"

Jerrold seemed only too pleased to answer his question. "Most of our actual ground and air testing is done at Area 51. There are, as you know, areas that even you have not been allowed to enter. Although we used to do a lot of testing at White Sands, Los Alamos, and the high desert around Edwards AFB, our last bastion for ultra-secret testing is Area 51.

"We want you to tighten security, double the Wackenhut and military personnel," Jerrold emphasized his request by slapping his palm on his desk in rhythm to his spoken words.

It was now doubly clear to the general why he had been summoned. But even the threat of alien invasion did little to soften his opinion of the Wackenhut paramilitary security personnel funded by the DOE. He despised them.

"I now understand your position," Alex told Jerrold. "What you have told me explains a lot of what I never before understood about a lot of things."

Jerrold told him that they had some new security technology that would soon be installed in the area. "General, if we can just hold off the media, the cultists, the UFO buffs, and misguided government officials who are all sticking their ignorant noses into our vital defense efforts for another four years, we'll be able to set up a solid bulwark against the Jexovah. Do we have your commitment to be a true patriot and to join our noble cause?"

Alex nodded. "I will support you, Eli. But I will not support the torturing or detaining of U.S. citizens. We will just have to tighten security so we won't have to resort to such extreme measures."

Eli Jerrold seemed satisfied. "We've expanded Area 51 to include the Whitesides and Freedom Ridge areas near Rachel. We will now be able to accelerate the testing of our secret prototypes. The UFO buffs, especially the pain-in-the-ass types like Newsome and Webster, have severely hampered our testing schedule the past two years. We've already put a massive disinformation campaign into gear that will 'prove' the video shown on 'Exploring the Unknown' to be a fake created in a special effects lab."

General Beauharnais stood and saluted the two men. "I'll begin implementing the new security measures at once."

Jerrold shook his hand. "It means a lot to the MJ-12 committee and to me personally that you are with us now and that we can count on you."

The general excused himself and left the elegant offices of Eli Jerrold. The MJ-12 committee needed his support, but he knew with a grim certainty that he could be replaced if he didn't follow their orders and conduct himself as a proper superpatriot. It was clear to him what he must do. He must find out more about what was really going on with MJ-12 and how extensively the alleged alien threat truly extended itself into the lives of the average citizen.

Chapter Eighteen

A Lost Memory Regained

Joe Green put in the first long shift at the wheel of the RV on the drive back to Las Vegas while Blake Webster and Wayne Newsome did their best to catch up on some sleep.

After a few fitful hours of trying to find a comfortable position for his tall, lanky body, Wayne Newsome gave up and joined Joe in the front seat to listen to the radio. The Reverend Page Saint John's "Cosmic Revival" seemed to be on every other station. They had heard his signature hymn so often that once, just before they stopped for coffee to soak up the cobwebs in their brains, they even sang along with the radio as a lark:

When earth was in its darkest hour
The Jexovah bequeathed their power
From vaulted heavens they came to stay
And with the daughters of man they lay
The hybrid race, their fate unknown
Flesh of their flesh, bone of their bone
In innocence fulfilled their plan
Yet evil dwelt in heart of man
No prayers or rituals purged their fate

God's servants toiled from heaven's gate
  Beyond man's hope, beyond man's dream
A plan was formed to man redeem
  Rapture from touching the Chosen One
A million years of peace, begun

"Stupid hymn," Blake Webster mumbled from the back seat, his sleep punctured by his companions' enthusiastic, but off-key, rendering of Page Saint John's musical credo.

"Hell of a rousing band, though," Newsome laughed.

They decided to get some breakfast at a twenty-four-hour restaurant. It was three o'clock in the afternoon, but they all agreed that it felt like seven in the morning.

When they climbed back in the RV, the men began to compare notes and share their individual interpretations of the UFO enigma. Joe was rather well-informed about the various escapades and theories of Webster and Newsome, but he was a complete nonentity to them. By the time that he had confided in them about his experiences with the Light and the experiments that he had undergone with Dr. Carlton Farr's supervision, they were listening to him with keen interest.

Around six o'clock that evening they picked up the first of the news bits exposing the videotape that had been shown on "Exploring the Unknown" as a fraud. While they greeted such obvious government-planted misinformation with hoots of derision, their obscene analyses were quieted by the official allegation that Wayne Newsome was involved in the hoax.

"Chet Haynes, producer of the popular NBC series, 'Exploring the Unknown,' reminded reporters of the disclaimer that precedes each airing of the program. 'Ours is strictly an entertainment show,' Haynes said. 'We make every effort to substantiate and to validate the authenticity of each program, but we make no claims to be presenting solid scientific truths when we deal with such topics as UFOs.

"We accepted the video film provided us by Blake Webster and his associate Wayne Newsome in good faith. We knew that both men were well-known UFO buffs and government gadflies, but we took their word as to the film's authenticity. We have since learned that the film was a hoax, a mock-up done in a Hollywood special effects studio. We apologize for any embarrassment this may have caused the U.S. Air Force or anyone else. But we did present the segment as speculation, not scientific fact."

There was more, but the three men had caught the essence of the coverup.

"The two of you hadn't even met before you went searching together for Blake's undercover guy," Joe said. "How did they toss Wayne into this?"

Webster's features had become very serious and somber. "Because they are really out to get us. They're tired of fucking around with us. Jesus, they did God-knows-what to my friend Red. They blasted a hole the size of a tomato can through Carl Farr. Now the bastards are after us. Big time. For keeps."

Newsome stretched his cramped arms, then quickly dropped them back on the steering wheel. "Sure looks that way."

Webster turned to point a finger at Joe. "You can bet they know who you are by now. And they figure since you were with Carl Farr for a couple of days, you know too damn much to walk around loose. We have to take all this very seriously. We are all in real danger. I just hope that Red is still alive."

Joe had been meaning to ask about Webster's undercover man. "This Red, I think I know him. Might even have had a few beers with him at the Pilot Club. Older guy, but in good physical shape. Works at a little prospecting and sells rocks to lapidary shops around the state."

Webster smiled and nodded. "That's my man. You know him, eh?"

Joe shook his head in wonder. "I never figured him for anything other than what he appeared to be."

"That's why he is so damn good at his job," Webster said. "Or at least he was. I know the bastards must have made him. But old Red will never give me up. He'll die first. That's why I have to do something to get him out of there."

"You're certain they have him at Area 51?" Joe asked.

"Where the hell else?" Webster argued. "Newsome and I did a damn good job of scouring Red's desert hideouts before we headed to Texas to see Dr. Farr."

Newsome folded a piece of chewing gum into his mouth. After a few moments, he spoke as much to himself as the others: "For the first time since she passed on, I'm glad my Dorothy's no longer with me. You know, it's when the bastards can lay a threat against a man's family or friends that they can really put the squeeze on him. I don't think the assholes will try to hunt down my kids. At least I sure as hell hope not."

Webster nodded vigorously. "That's why I haven't tied the knot with my fair lady Rainey. We've been going together steady for three years, and

I've never even mentioned her name to anyone. Newsome's right. They can get to you through the people you love most."

Newsome shifted his gum. "But isn't that where you told me we were going to lay low for a while? At your girlfriend's place?"

"Just for a very short while, man," Webster said. "She wouldn't have it any other way. Rainey is a tough cookie, and she's into all of this shit as much as any of us. She's been my right arm in researching the whole frigging government coverup. She's a conspiracy buff of the highest order."

Joe leaned back in the seat. It suddenly occurred to him that he hadn't slept for well over thirty hours. He yawned, settled into the cushion of the back seat. It was raining slightly and moisture streaked the windows, distorting the lights of approaching cars.

He yawned again. There was really no reason to fight off sleep. Newsome was taking his turn at the wheel. Webster would relieve him.

Joe started thinking about the Greyhound bus trip he had taken to Kilgore, Texas, in 1971, shortly after he had turned eighteen. By then, his father and his grandparents on both sides of his family were dead and buried. Just before his mother entered a long-term health facility, she arranged for him to live with her sister Ida and her husband Glenn Whittle in Kilgore so he could finish his senior year in high school. Joe wasn't told as much, but he knew that his mom had terminal cancer.

He hadn't seen Aunt Ida or Uncle Glenn for years, but he remembered his uncle as a giant of a man with a loud, boisterous manner. He had shoulders as wide as a door, hands with large knuckles, and a big red Okie nose, and he stood six feet five inches in his bare feet. Joe had heard all the stories about Uncle Glenn having played college baseball and boxed professionally. He was now the owner of a small fleet of sixteen-wheelers.

On top of all that, the man could do anything with his hands. If Aunt Ida wanted the stains and tears in the sofa covered, he upholstered it for her. If she wanted new cabinets for the kitchen, he built them. If she felt like something spicy for supper, he prepared a zesty cajun gumbo.

Joe was intimidated just from hearing all the stories about Uncle Glenn Whittle. How would he be able to please a man who could do so many things so well?

Joe smiled and allowed his eyelids to drop shut. Uncle Glenn had become a role model the like of which few young men had ever been blessed.

Who could be dour around the ebullient Glenn Whittle? In his early forties, he wore the kind of flat-top hair cut that had been popular in the late 1950s. He dressed Western style with wide-buckle belt and cowboy boots—and added a light gray dress Stetson when he wanted to gussy up. Joe couldn't believe his good fortune when it was his turn to drive the new Ford pickup into the high school parking lot. Sure, he knew East Texas was oil, cattle, and resource rich—and many of his classmates drove sports cars and the like—but Joe Green had never dreamed that he would ever have a piece of it.

Uncle Glenn and Aunt Ida owned a small automobile import business, and they had promised to get him a sports car if he had his grades up by summer vacation. Joe had never done well academically, not because he wasn't smart, but he just couldn't concentrate with all the unceasing traumas in his life.

Uncle Glenn insisted on accompanying Joe to the high school on the first day of classes and speaking directly with the principal, Mr. Emanuel, to see that he got settled in properly. Uncle Glenn was like that—embarrassingly bold. But he surely did grow on a person. After a frank discussion in the principal's office, the football coach, Mr. Barnes, escorted Uncle Glenn and Joe around the sprawling high school, the largest in East Texas.

Everyone knew Uncle Glenn—he was the guy who sold those fast, flashy foreign cars. So pretty soon, everyone knew his nephew, Joe Green. Joe found it incredible how friendly everyone was in the community. Everyone he met was jovial, easy-going, not at all like his mother's quiet, strict, and seriously religious family.

His grades came up fast, and he made friends easily. In spite of his being shy, he was filled with emotional insecurities and had a desperate need to be accepted. At first, all he was able to talk about was his tragic early life, religion, and foreign cars, which he was still learning about.

But he smiled a lot, and he watched everyone as though he were a spy infiltrating a foreign nation. He soon picked up on the "in" cliches so that he could be thought witty at all the appropriate moments, and it seemed that almost overnight he became one of the most popular kids in school. He played on the football team, took speech class, joined the debate team, and did just about everything he could to be around other students—especially the girls.

On weekends and whenever he could after school, Joe earned his spending money working at the family car dealership. It was his responsibility to detail the new cars after head mechanic Johnny Ray had signed off on the initial service of each vehicle. And it was hard work removing the thick

Cosmoline that coated every inch of the European automobiles. The stuff was similar to the tar-like coating they put on telephone poles.

"They didn't put that shit on there just to make life miserable for you, Joey boy," Ray told him. "That Cosmoline has to be on there to protect the new car finish from rain, saltwater, and the environment in general, so these expensive play toys can make the trans-Atlantic voyage in good shape."

It usually took Joe three hours to remove the gummy Cosmoline with the solvent—which often took patches of the outer layer of his skin along with it. And then another two hours to polish and wax the little sports cars.

Joe divided his time among the garage, the football field, his studies, and his girlfriend, Karen Foster. His best buddies were Dink Hewes and Lyle Littleton. Dink played football with him, and according to Coach Barnes, he was the best fullback in the state. Lyle's mother ran the Corral, the rec center where the sports rallies, dances, and other important high school activities were held.

By now Joe had nearly reached his full adult height and weight. He stood a little over six-two and weighed a hard-muscled 190. He enjoyed working his body, and he seemed to thrive on the roughest drills that the fertile mind of Coach Barnes could create. At the same time, the hormones that surged through him caused him a great deal of confusion and inner stress.

Almost from the first time that he had seen her in geometry class, Joe had developed a full-sized crush on Karen Foster. She had long strawberry blonde hair that she tied in a ponytail, and she filled out her blouse in a way that made little beads of sweat break out along Joe's forehead and upper lip. Her blue eyes seemed large enough to dive into and float forever, and her full red lips seemed always to be smiling—especially at him.

It wasn't long before Karen was wearing his senior class ring wrapped with a wad of tape around her finger, and he was wearing her class ring around his neck on a gold chain. There were times after football games when they sat watching the moon from the Ford pickup that they got pretty hot and heavy. But even though a lot of his buddies bragged crudely about "getting a piece" and giving their girls "a hot meat injection," he was satisfied with kissing and making out. His Uncle Glenn was not a holy roller like his grandparents, but he had put the fear of God in him about getting a girl pregnant.

And then came that night…

He had been slow dancing with Karen at the Corral after their victory at the football game when Dink grabbed his shoulder. "Joe, come outside. Lyle and Dave are in trouble."

Joe told Karen to wait inside, and he followed Dink through the side exit. When they stepped outside, he saw his skinny friend Lyle and Dave, the team quarterback, ringed by a dozen or so guys on the fringes of the parking lot.

He didn't recognize the three boys who were taunting Lyle and Dave. It was too dark to see their school colors or the lettering on their jackets. But he could hear their hostility in the filth that spewed from their mouths.

Lyle, almost unbearably skinny but uncommonly courageous, was trying to get the troublemakers to leave. Since his mother was in charge of the Corral, he undoubtedly felt the pressure to assume responsibility and to serve as peacemaker.

"Why don't you guys just get in your cars and leave now. Pronto!" Lyle told them.

"Shove it, asshole!" the largest of the three malcontents shouted. His few words were slurred with alcohol.

"Yeah, make us, shithead!" challenged another of the strangers.

Joe and Dink now stood behind their buddies. Their very presence must have been interpreted as an overt act of aggression, because the big guy hurled his beer bottle at Joe, who ducked, stumbled backward, and fell on his butt. With Joe down for the moment, he then jumped Dink.

"Get him, Durwood!" the big kid's buddies urged him on. "Beat the shit out of him!"

In those days teenaged protocol demanded that once a fight broke out, the onlookers were required to stand by to make certain the fight was fair, but participation, other than cheers and curses, was strictly forbidden.

Joe got back to his feet, brushed gravel off his butt, and spotted a fourth stranger, much older-looking than his friends, get out of their black '60 Chevy and edge toward the fight. Joe would keep a close eye on him.

Dink and Durwood fought with much movement, much swinging, and much mouth, without any serious damage being dealt to either combatant.

Dink was strong as a bull, short and stocky, and moved with a slow, stalking motion. His opponent was taller and quicker, but he would have had to have used a baseball bat on Dink to hurt him.

The show came to an end when Durwood nailed Dink twice in the face and really pissed him off. Dink grabbed the kid around the waist and wrestled him to the ground. He got on top of Durwood's chest and rested his full 220 pounds on him. One quick sledge hammer punch was all that was necessary to take the wind and the fight completely out of the invader.

Joe hadn't seen Karen and Dink's girl, Patricia, come out to the parking lot, but Karen was shouting in a shrill voice that the police had been called. "You boys are going to jail if you don't get out of here right now!"

With his attention on Karen, Joe didn't see the older boy moving toward him with the switchblade. A second too late, Dink yelled at him to watch out. Somewhere in the distance of the night a siren screamed.

The blade of the knife cut deep into the sleeve of his letter jacket and into the flesh of his right arm. But he didn't feel the cut. His adrenaline was pumping, his heart was pounding, and there was a peculiar buzzing sound in his ears.

"Way to go, Eric," Durwood encouraged his friend. "Carve us all a piece of the son of a bitch!"

Joe wasn't a fighter. He simply reacted. The older boy angrily slashed and lunged repeatedly at him, but each time Joe would skillfully block the knife or move just enough so the blade would miss him.

Then Dink was there, slamming the mad slasher on the jaw with a punch that Joe thought would knock him into next Tuesday.

Eric was dazed by the powerhouse punch, but it somehow only served to enliven him. Surprisingly fast, faster than either Dink or Joe could react, he dropped down to one knee, scooped up a handful of dirt, and threw it in Dink's eyes.

While Dink coughed and cursed and Joe bobbed and weaved, Eric stood to drive the glistening blade of his knife directly at Dink's throat.

Joe's arm shot out and grabbed the blade in his bare hand. He wrenched it from Eric's angry grasp and threw it to the gravel of the parking lot. Afterward, no one remembered seeing the sudden movement, not even those onlookers who were facing the action, but Joe's right hand was cut deeply.

Before the four out-of-town hoodlums could get into their car and start the engine, Officers Collier and Morphus of the Kilgore Police Department arrived and placed them in custody. Joe was taken to the hospital by Dink, Karen, and Patricia. He needed seven stitches in his hand, five in his forearm. Strangely, he felt little pain, but the two couples agreed that they had had enough excitement for the night. It would be burgers and fries at the Wagonwheel Drive-In, then home to bed.

Joe realized that he was dreaming, but somehow he was now able to step out of the dream and observe the startling subsequent events of that dramatic evening in Kilgore. He could see himself awakening that morning about three…

…with the sunlight glaring into his bedroom windows. But it couldn't be the sunlight. It had to be something else.

Something was calling him, telling him to step outside into the back yard. The Light seemed to be everywhere. And when he obeyed the suggestion to go outside, he felt an energy encircle him.

Then the Light was pulling him skyward. And there was nothing around him but the Light. His skin seemed to be crawling with fire. It was as if he had died, but his brain still functioned.

From out of the Light, long, narrow Jexovah fingers reached out and pulled his body into a large, silver, circular-shaped vehicle.

Joseph Green, we will not hurt you. You have nothing to fear from us. You have been with us before.

The voice echoed in his head. Three other Jexovah moved closer to him as he lay horizontally. He tried to speak, but something was in his mouth. He wanted to tell them to please let him go. He didn't want to be there.

You have to be here. You are one of the chosen. You are the hope of the future for all of humankind. We have to adjust you. When we are finished, we will return you to your people. Try not to fear us.

Fear? Why couldn't they comprehend the overwhelming terror that filled his mind? He lay there naked, caught in a nightmare of unfathomable horror, with these small beings that called themselves Jexovah hovering around him with strange, shiny implements in their hands.

The Jexovah that had spoken to him put his small hand on Joe's forehead, and he felt instantly calm, able to feel detached from the scene.

"Please tell me why you are doing this to me," he pleaded in his thoughts.

Joseph, there will come a time when you will understand. When this time comes, we will assist you. You will understand somewhere after the year your people call 2000. Then the time will be imminent. The Rapture will have begun. When our mission is completed, the time will be at hand.

You will understand the purpose of our mission, and you will remember. For now, be aware that you are the Chosen One.

Suddenly Joe's brain was flashing images of rape, murder, incest, torture, government conspiracies, religious deceit, greed, envy, hate, lust, war. Somehow he understood that he was perceiving the legacy of humankind. Six thousand years of technological and scientific progress had brought humankind to the brink of the destruction of its environment, its planet, and itself.

Something in his mind evolved and energized.

We have placed a sliver of nonmetallic quasi-crystal in your skull. It has two purposes. The first will allow us to track you with a resonant energy device, for the crystal contains special subatomic particle matrix that will also allow us to communicate with you. The other function is more complex.

Joe had another flash of insight that they had placed something up his nasal cavities when he was a child—and as he had matured, a gradual change had taken place in his genetic makeup.

We have genetically engineered deoxyribonucleic acid (DNA) by transplanting genes from our Jexovah species into the cells of Homo sapiens. When the fullness of time is realized, the DNA will become an active part of the Homo sapiens genetic makeup and will be replicated. The DNA is the principal constituent of chromosomes. Chromosomes are the structures that replicate hereditary characteristics.

He had no idea at that time what they were talking about, Joe remembered as he observed his dream from the vantage point of the present. He had just wanted to be away from them.

And then the eighteen-year-old Joe was seeing mental images of the double helix of DNA, proteins, enzymes, and other microscopic elements of the human genome. It meant nothing to him. Nor did the pictures of apelike man creatures working in mines and other structures.

The present genetic makeup of Homo sapiens is defective. When the Jexovah first arrived on Earth, the Neanderthal was the most advanced species. We needed to process organic and inorganic elements to repair our vehicles.

Neanderthals were capable of simple training. Their species had much potential. They needed higher mental functions and understanding. More genetically adjusted Neanderthals were then bred satisfactorily and humans came forth.

Eventually Neanderthals would have advanced, but it would have taken half a million Earth years. They would never have achieved technology. They were limited. Homo sapiens has much more potential. After we finished our building tasks, we left. We gave Homo sapiens civilization. We left the Helpers with a plan that has been difficult to fulfill. You are an aggressive and violent species.

Young Joe witnessed the emergence of the Sumerian civilization, the introduction of writing, laws, religion, technology—all in a blur of rapid montages of colorful images that impressed themselves on his subconscious. And all designed to demonstrate that Homo sapiens was a hybrid Neanderthal-Jexovah being.

The second function of the implanted quasi-crystal in your skull is very important. It is a catalyst for a genetic transformation that we call the Rapture. This process will permit the Chosen Ones to communicate mentally. This will promote harmony and happiness. This will promote peace among your kind. This will begin to prepare all humans for the next stage of their evolution.

Most humans will fear the Rapture. We will assist you. You will be Jexovah after the Rapture. The next stage in your evolution will be a revelation. The collapse of your civilization will be apocalyptic. Those who rapture will become the future of humanity.

When the Jexovah—or Nefilim—arrived in your solar system, they settled on the planet between Mars and Jupiter. This planet was destroyed at a time when giant beasts roamed Earth. The debris from the destruction of this planet caused a cataclysm on Earth which brought about the extinction of the giant beasts. Our masters, the Jexovah, needed Earth's resources to rebuild their flying machines, and as I have told you, while they lived on Earth they created Homo sapiens from the Neanderthal.

Twelve of the Jexovah bred with Homo sapiens. This had been forbidden. The fallen twelve, along with their progeny, were evicted from the fold.

The inbreeding of Homo sapiens and Jexovah destroyed the original intent of the leaders. The children of the breeding were stronger and smarter than the Homo sapiens that had been created through genetic engineering, but they were also more susceptible to acts of violence, greed, and evil. While they had the capacity to develop into an intelligent people, their warlike tendencies could eventually destroy many worlds if they did not destroy themselves first.

The Jexovah chose to ignore the hybrids until they began to dominate the majority. The Jexovah gave your civilization religion, hoping that it would temper humankind's violent nature. Sadly, in many instances, religion made the situation even worse.

The Jexovah studied your species' genetic structure for many thousand years. During this time, your civilization was manipulated to prevent it from destroying itself. In spite of our interaction, we feared many times that we would not succeed.

Two thousand years ago, we developed a new plan. We found a solution that would take two thousand years to complete. When the plan is complete, the Rapture will begin. The genetic structure of humankind will be repaired.

The hybrid Homo sapiens has lacked two Jexovah traits: the ability to communicate mentally and the ability to live indefinitely. The Rapture will correct these deficiencies. The result will be that the human race will evolve into true Jexovah. The children of God will be redeemed in the Jexovah's eyes. We, the Helpers, are the guardians of the plan. It is our task to complete the plan and guide humankind to the Jexovah.

When Uncle Glenn got up at seven o'clock that morning, he found Joe asleep in the back yard, naked except for his jockey shorts.

"You poor kid," he said, helping Joe to his feet. "You had quite an ordeal last night. You must've got turned around during the night and you wandered out here. Let's get you back inside."

Uncle Glenn grabbed for Joe's bandaged hand to wrap his arm around his neck, then pulled back when he remembered the boy's wound.

"Sorry, Joe. Did I hurt you?"

Joe straightened his body in sudden realization. "Uncle Glenn, it doesn't hurt at all!"

As his uncle stood by in stunned amazement, Joe unwrapped his bandages. The stitches were gone. So was any evidence of the cut on his palm. The same was true of his forearm. No sign remained that would indicate that a doctor had carefully sewn fourteen stitches in that area the night before.

"Praise the Lord," Uncle Glenn said, calling out to summon Aunt Ida and Eddie. "We have been privileged to have witnessed a miracle come to pass on our boy, Joseph."

A sudden dip in the highway jolted Joe awake. As the headlights from an oncoming car struck his eyes, he involuntarily emitted a loud gasp. For a split second, he thought it was the Light coming for him once again.

"You all right back there, bud?" Wayne Newsome asked. "Sorry about that dip back there. Woke you, huh?"

Joe told him it was all right. He held up his right palm and studied it for a moment as if he had not really seen it since he was eighteen. Not a scar. Not even a fine line to show where the knife blade had entered.

Carl Farr had told him that their experiment would continue to reactivate old dreams and memories. But Joe had just had an astonishing recall of his interaction with the Jexovah when he was eighteen and he had now remembered the complete message of the beings that had been buried in his subconscious for over two decades.

He also remembered Karen's face when he had shown her his wounds later that same day. She agreed with Uncle Glenn that a miracle had occurred. With the memory of the Jexovah completely submerged in his brain cells, Joe had nothing with which to refute such an interpretation.

"It's because you were willing to sacrifice yourself for a friend," Karen told him. "Jesus said that there was no greater love than that of laying down your life for a friend. Joseph Green, you are really a special person, and I know that God has chosen you to do something really special in life."

Joe smiled at the memory. Karen Foster had also proved herself to be a special kind of gal. She had patiently waited for him to return from Vietnam and to get his act somewhat together before he asked her to marry him. He really had loved her since that first day in geometry class. He would be forever sorry that their marriage had failed.

Chapter Nineteen

The Fallen Conspirator

Michael Crawfoot sat in a truck stop outside Albuquerque, New Mexico, in a stolen white 1989 Olds 98, thinking over his options. He had kept moving since he had terminated the scientist. The hit wasn't as clean as he would have liked it, and there had been at least one witness. The job just hadn't been up to his usual exactingly high standards.

He replayed the assassination at Medina Lake in his mind and tried to resolve the sickening feeling that he had made a major blunder.

Two nights before he offed the scientist, he had spotted a tall Caucasian male about his own age who looked strangely familiar. He had watched him from outside Pat's Place, then followed him as he returned to the house with a six pack of beer. When he had shot the scientist and was tear-assing out of there, he had spotted the other man once again. Who the fuck was he?

It was his habit to always assume the worst-case scenario and hope for the best, but he knew he had been sloppy on this assignment.

He should never have had the bullshit conversation with the nosy old retired officer at Pat's Place. He should have just got up and walked out when the dude started talking to him.

Yeah, right! Then the old fart would have got so pissed that he would remember him forever.

He assumed the authorities would be watching the airports, car rental agencies, and bus and train stations. He had dumped the Jeep he was driving in a ditch and ripped off the Olds in front of a bar.

He didn't dare stop at a motel or hotel. He kept moving, for he knew it was entirely possible that the old bastard had been sharp enough to describe him well enough to enable the cops to put out a composite drawing of him and broadcast a multi-state all points bulletin on his ass.

He looked at his watch. It was Wednesday, September 4, the second day after the job in San Antonio, and at 3:00 P.M. he would contact Colonel Ty Trent at his private number at the NSA. It would be 5:00 P.M. in Washington, and Mother would be awaiting his call with further instructions.

The Olds shook as a semitruck rolled by, and he wondered how many more people he would have to kill before he had his fill. He had enough money saved to live modestly, but comfortably, for the rest of his life if he decided to drop out. In addition, he had a phony VA disability retirement that had been set up by Colonel Trent that would generate almost eighteen hundred dollars a month.

He looked around and guessed that there were at least two dozen long-haul trucks parked around the stop. Most drivers were sleeping or were in the restaurant loading up on grub and coffee.

He walked to one of the outside pay phones and dialed the 800 number that would link him with Trent. It rang six times and stopped. He entered his six digit code number, then waited a minute or so in silence.

He was about to give it up and drive another hundred or so miles before calling back when the receiver on the other end clicked. Trent answered.

"It's me," Crawfoot told him.

"God, man, I've been waiting for a call from you. Where the hell are you?"

Crawfoot told him he was just west of Albuquerque and that he needed an update.

"Well, my ace assassin, you got kind of sloppy this time," Trent said, not sounding at all pleased. "You overexposed yourself in that jerkwater bar. Your identity has been seriously compromised. They've put out an APB on you, and they've got a damn good composite portrait of you to go on. They found the Jeep you ditched, so right now they're looking for a shooter from Mexico City."

"Tell me something nice, Mother."

"Okay, okay. Let me put you on hold for a couple of minutes. Hang on, all right?"

Crawfoot tried to be patient for the five minutes it took Trent to get back to him.

"Crawfoot? You still there?"

"I wish to hell that I was in Bora Bora, but I am still here."

"Listen, I want you to drive up to Kirtland Air Force Base and wait at the convenience store nearest the main gate. I've contacted a CIA case officer at Sandia National Lab at Kirtland. He will have a new identification, credit cards, and special orders for you."

"Orders?" Crawfoot scowled at the receiver. "You're putting me back in the saddle so fast?"

"We've got a couple more problems, cowboy. We want you to head for Nevada. You will report to the base commander at Nellis, and he will arrange for you to receive transportation to Area 51 of the Nevada Test Site. Your orders will identify you as a security inspector for Wackenhut."

"You're sending me to Dreamland?"

"Yes. We have a General Beauharnais who is in charge there. He has been ordered to increase security, but he seems a little reluctant to cooperate completely with MJ-12. You will inspect the Groom and Papoose facilities and surrounding area for security. At the same time, you will keep a sharp eye on the General. If he gets out of line, you will be given direction on how best to take care of him. You'll be on the job with MJ-12 operative, Raul Agabarr."

"The Torture Master? What is he doing at Dreamland?"

"I told you, Crawfoot. We've had some troubles there. Civilians have been breaching our security."

"But Agabarr? Come on, man. Even I have some scruples. I don't want to work with that son of a bitch."

"You'll work with him—or he'll work on you!" Trent laughed at his sick humor.

"Hey, Ty, you know I'm a good soldier," Crawfoot reminded him. "But if that asshole even looks cross-eyed at me, I'll send him back to you in six different special delivery packages."

Colonel Trent laughed again. "I can tell that you two love bugs are going to get along just fine."

"Yeah, sure. How and to whom do you want me to report?"

"You will still report to me," Trent told him. "The Wackenhut Director of Security will be given orders to give you free reign and full cooperation if you need it. I want you to call in every day at the same time if you can. If you miss a call-in, then call the next day at the same time."

"Ty?"

"What?"

"Are we okay?"

"What do you mean?"

Crawfoot cleared his throat. "I know that I screwed up on the hit. But it's the first time in nearly two fucking decades."

Trent was surprised to hear even the slightest hint of insecurity come from this hard-as-nails son of a bitch. "Hey, man, I need you more than ever. You know that you're indispensable to me."

Crawfoot had to ask another question before they hung up. "Ty, there was another guy with the scientist I terminated. Any idea who the the hell he was?"

"We haven't made him yet," Trent answered, "but after your hit, two well-known trouble-making assholes showed up—Blake Webster and Wayne Newsome. Those two—as well as the mystery man—will have to be taken out pretty soon. We'll get back to you on that."

"So we're okay then?" Crawfoot wanted to be reassured.

"Forget about the job in San Antonio, man," Trent said. "Don't keep running it through your head. Let loose of it. We'll clean it up. Now get your ass up to the base and get your new papers."

"You've got it."

"Be certain you destroy all ID you currently have on you."

"Already done."

"Good man. You have two days to report to the base commander at Nellis. Once you get your new papers, check into a good hotel, chow down, get some rest, and rent a proper 'clean' car."

Crawfoot was casing the cars at the truck stop. He would have to dump the Olds soon in case the cops had figured out he might be driving the stolen car that someone must have reported by now.

"Call me when you arrive at Dreamland and get settled in," Trent said, wrapping up the conversation. "Your rank will be a GS-15, giving you an effective rank higher than anyone other than General Beauharnais himself."

"Higher than Agabarr?" Crawfoot asked pointedly.

"You're the man," Trent laughed. "Now get your ass in gear. I don't want to have to bail you out of a New Mexico hoosegow."

Chapter Twenty

Surfing the Collective Unconscious

When they stopped to eat that next morning, they were only about a hundred miles from Las Vegas. Blake Webster was able to tell at once that Joe Green seemed somehow very different that morning—and he was certain that the subtle transformation was due to more than a few hours of sleep.

Reluctantly at first, Joe told Blake and Wayne Newsome about the revelatory dream that he had experienced during the night. He also reminded them that Carl Farr had warned him that the experiments that they had undertaken would be prompting more memories of his interaction with the Jexovah to surface during his dreams.

When they got back into Webster's RV, the men began to discuss the effect of such information upon orthodox religionists, the present political structure, and the public in general.

Webster thought that some of the more fundamentalist churches would be pretty upset to learn that Jesus might have more sheep in his flock than they had been led to believe. And what if other people began to worship the Jexovah as their new gods?

"The Jexovah do not see themselves as gods," Joe said. "They see themselves as creators and explorers. When they arrived in our solar system, humankind did not exist. Then they gave Neanderthal a Jexovah DNA energy boost to create us."

"The Frankensteins from Outer Space," Newsome laughed as he imitated a little ooooeeee science fiction theme music.

"Yeah, but go easy, man," Webster reminded him. "We're the monsters they created."

"That's true," Joe agreed. "The Jexovah androids were left here to correct the mistakes in genetic engineering and crossbreeding of the Jexovah and the Neanderthal which produced us hairless little apes. From what has come to me, their task has been difficult because they don't want to make alterations in our genetic makeup that will destroy our spirit or our soul."

"It's nice to know that we have souls," Newsome said before he yawned and leaned back in his seat. It was Webster's turn to drive.

"Again, from what I'm starting to remember, they discovered the solution to the dilemma sometime around our year of 1935. Their final implementation has been put into operation. Shortly after the beginning of the new century, the change, the solution, what they call the Rapture, will become apparent."

Webster sipped at the coffee that he had brought with him from the restaurant. "Have they ever told you if they have a God?"

"They do, but their concept of deity is not that of a single entity. They believe that every spirit that has ever existed or is now alive is somehow connected together. Essentially, they believe that God is in every being and that all entities, past, present, and future, are God."

Webster considered the alien theology. "Cool. I could accept that."

Joe closed his eyes for a moment. "You know, it seems that when I shut my eyes and talk about these things, I can tap into an ocean of memories. I have more memories and more abilities being activated than I ever could have dreamed of. Obviously, the Jexovah really pumped information into my subconscious whenever they abducted me."

He suddenly realized what he was saying and laughed self-consciously. "I'm glad I'm with you two when this activation of memory is occurring. Anyone else would probably have me locked up!"

"And you think we won't?" Newsome asked, once again making his ooooeeee eerie "creature from outer space" sound effects.

"Seriously, man," Webster wanted to know, "will anyone else, like, maybe, Wayne or me, ever be able to talk with the Jexovah androids?"

Newsome shook his head in mock disgust. "Webster just wants the first network interview with a real, live alien."

Webster protested once again that he was serious, and Joe closed his eyes to receive whatever might come to him.

"What's coming to me is that every spirit, human or Jexovah, is networked with the mass collective unconscious. Apparently every sentient being in the universe is also linked in some way. The spirit of itself is good, and through repeated incarnations, it grows until, at a certain point, it reaches its full potential."

"Oh, boy, here it is," Newsome sighed. "The dreaded *R* word—reincarnation. If Sister Mary Margaret were here right now, she would smack all of our wrists with her ruler."

Joe seemed unmindful of Newsome's irreverent sense of humor. "It's our human genome that is defective. That's what causes us to be violent and to get into the kinds of problems that we keep having throughout history. The human body is flawed, filled with mood-shifting chemistry that causes anger, depression, hate, greed, and other manifestations antithetical to spiritual growth. But the spirit within us is able to evolve through a succession of incarnations."

Joe appeared to be in a some kind of light trance state, so Webster decided to take advantage of the situation. "Can you tell from your newfound abilities if Jesus really existed?"

Joe paused to allow the information to emerge from his Jexovah-charged memory banks. "Definitely. Perfect human genes are a rare occurrence, but Jesus was a chosen one, and he attained the Rapture. And so did Moses, Elijah, Mohammed, Krishna, and many other great religious and humanitarian leaders."

Newsome finally decided to ask a question of his own. "What is our purpose in all this? Our mission seems to be to expose the truth about the government cover-up of UFOs, and now, I suppose, to release information about the presence of the Jexovah; but what then?"

Joe was quiet for several moments before he spoke again. "After the revelation comes the Rapture. If we achieve the revelation and survive, then we will be a part of the Rapture."

Joe opened his eyes, and his companions interpreted that as a signal that the present question and answer session was terminated. Newsome wasn't satisfied with the response to his question, but somehow he felt that they were about to entrust their lives to Joseph Green and his most peculiar advisors.

"What I wish is that you would use all that knowledge coming at you from the universe to tell us if Red is still alive?" Webster said wistfully, his right forefinger tapping the steering wheel for emphasis as he drove. "I just can't get Red out of my mind for a minute. I feel so damned guilty. Almost as if I set him up to take the fall. I'd give anything to know how he is—or if he still is."

Joe shrugged. "I can give it a try."

"Hey, man, great," Webster grinned, placing both hands back on the wheel and pulling himself up straighter. "That would be terrific."

Newsome arched a skeptical eyebrow, but he chose to keep his doubts to himself.

"What's Red's complete name?" Joe asked.

"I know him as Red Redding. I think his real name is Clint or Cliff or something like that."

"If we're not certain about his true name, I'll just visualize him as I know him,"Joe said. He closed his eyes, took a deep breath, held it for a few seconds, then slowly released it. He repeated the process three times.

Joe winced as an image came into his interior mental viewing screen. "I hope this isn't Red."

"What?" Webster wanted to know at once. "What is it that you're seeing?"

"Some poor guy who's really been worked over. He's in really bad shape." Joe took a deep breath, then added: "Oh, dear God! It is Red!"

"But he's alive?" Webster prompted as he accelerated to pass a slow-moving truck.

Joe nodded, his eyes still closed, seeming to squint to gain a clearer mental image. "He's alive, but it's like his brains have been scrambled. He seems to be aware of me, but he can't get his thoughts connected to make complete sense of what's going on around him."

Webster grimaced, as if feeling Red's pain and confusion.

Newsome asked how Joe knew that Red was aware of him.

Joe smiled. "It's as if there's the beat-up Red lying on a steel cot, the physical man; and then there's the real Red, his spiritual self, kind of bobbing just above his material body. It's the real Red that's aware of my spiritual presence."

Webster wanted to know where his friend was.

"I'm seeing what looks like an old jail cell. Man, it's filthy, I'll tell you that. I'm picking up that it's somewhere underground in Area 51," Joe answered.

"How do you know that you're really seeing Red and not someone else?" Newsome asked pointedly, wondering if all this was a fantasy conjured up by Joe's unconscious.

Joe pursed his lips in thought. "I'll ask for a sign." He was silent for nearly a minute, apparently conducting a mental dialogue with the "real Red." At last, he chuckled and shook his head. "I don't know what this means, but he says to tell Blake Webster that he owes him big time, and he's holding up a chicken wing."

Webster laughed. "It's my Red, all right."

"What the hell does that sign mean?" Newsome demanded. "A chicken wing?"

Webster wiped tears from his eyes before he answered. "Red dearly loves those little barbequed chicken wings. The first time we met was in a bar during happy hour. We sat down near a plate of the things, and he gobbled up the whole works in no time. Ever since then, I always buy him an order of barbecued wings whenever we get together. I promised him that if he pulled off a video shoot of the starship that I would buy him the biggest plate of wings known to humankind."

Newsome narrowed his eyes as if carefully considering the validity of Joe's proof of Red's continued existence, but he seemed satisfied with Webster's confirmation.

"Now, my friends," Webster said grimly. "We've got to get Red out of that cell in Area 51."

Chapter Twenty-One

The Secret Autopsy Report

They arrived at Rainey Roberts' place in Las Vegas at a few minutes past two that afternoon. Webster's longtime lady had a small house with two bedrooms and a combination living room-den that she used as a large study.

Rainey was not a glamour puss, but she was young and attractive with a nice figure. And, Joe thought, the most beautiful red hair he had ever seen. She wore very little makeup, just a touch of lipstick, and it was obvious that she was comfortable around men and not the least bit intimidated by any of them.

After embracing her wandering lover and receiving introductions to Joe and Wayne, Rainey and Blake huddled over her computer in the corner of the living room, discussing the box of disks that Farr had bequeathed to them. Newsome was in the kitchen watching a news broadcast on television and drinking a beer. Joe decided to sprawl out on the sofa for a bit to center himself after the disturbing remote viewing of Red in the underground cell.

"None of the disks are labeled," Rainey said. "It's going to take a while to go through all of them."

For the next thirty minutes, she fed one at a time into the three-and-a-half-inch drive.

"They all appear to be 1.4 meg disks," she finally commented. "There are some database files, some spreadsheets. Most seem to be word processing files."

She handed a number of disks to Blake. "Mark these as word processing files." Her forefinger tapped each of the other stacks. "This pile is database files. This one is spreadsheets. Mark 'em, Blake-o."

Newsome emerged from the kitchen. "Hey, everybody," he said excitedly, "Linden Soles on CNN 'Prime News' just told the world what sleazebags Blake and I are for deceiving NBC with the phony UFO film."

Rainey shook her head. "They've blasted the shit out of you for the past three days while you guys were on the road. MJ-12 has worked overtime on this coverup."

Newsome stood up, stretched, and yawned. "What say we send out for some food? Becoming a public menace has made me hungry."

Rainey said that she had enough stuff in the refrigerator to make sandwiches. "If that's good enough for you, help yourself. I want to say at these disks for a while, and I would rather not go out or take time for a big meal."

"I guess a sandwich would work for me," Newsome said.

Webster slipped into the kitchen and returned with a couple of beers. "Joe?" he offered. "This is some good, imported stuff I squirrel away in Rainey's fridge."

Joe smiled, then shook his head. "I'll pass on the beer, thanks. Maybe fix a sandwich, though."

Then it struck him. He hadn't had a beer since they left Farr's place in Texas. Or a cigarette. In any previous two-day period, he would have had two or three six-packs, several mixed drinks, and a couple of packs of cigarettes.

Rainey had decided to take a quick break to fix herself a sandwich and to oversee the mess that Wayne and Blake were making in her kitchen.

Joe walked over to the computer and sat down. He looked at the piles of disks, about forty in all.

He picked up six disks that Blake had marked "database" and fanned them like playing cards. For no apparent reason, he selected the fifth one and popped it into the three-and-a-half-inch disk drive.

He entered the directory command from the DOS prompt and scanned the files. There were eleven, and he immediately selected a file name and entered it.

Rainey had re-entered the living room to ask Joe if he would like her to make him a sandwich. She frowned when she spotted him at her computer.

She crossed the room and put a hand on Joe's shoulder. "Hey, big guy, I don't normally like people fondling my keyboard."

She had hoped to be pleasantly diplomatic, but Joe didn't respond.

She looked at the computer screen, then at Joe's face—then she shouted for Blake.

"What's up, Babe?" he asked with a mouth full of sandwich. "Why did you yell?"

"Joe's acting weird, man. I mean, it's like he's in some kind of trance. He's spooking me."

Blake hurriedly chewed and swallowed. "Oh, yeah, well, he probably is. In a trance, I mean. He...he does that sort of thing. I hadn't had time to explain to you about Joe and his special talents."

"You trying to tell me that he's some kind of medium or psychic or something?" Rainey wanted to know. "If he is, then get him away from my computer before he screws things up!"

Newsome had joined them. "Hold on! First see what he's doing."

Rainey thought that sounded reasonable. "He's in a database file," she told the others, looking over Joe's shoulder. "But he's down in the code. Jesus, Blake, there are some hidden files down in the program software code. He's looking for something."

Newsome grunted. "Then let him look. He's got special help."

"Hey, you guys, look!" Rainey's finger pointed at the screen. A file came up, and the three of them tried to read the text. Joe sat mute as they crowded around him.

OPERATION MAJESTIC-12

PRELIMINARY ANALYTICAL REPORT

ATTACHMENT D.
PART B.
Section 3.

Preliminary Autopsy of Extraterrestrial
Biological Entity (s)

5 JULY 1947

TS/T2/EO/
5 July 1947

Page 02 of 04

From: Dr. Detlev Bronk, Chairman National Research Council
Atomic Energy Commission; Medical Advisory Board: Physiologist, Biophysicist.

To: President Truman

Subject: Preliminary autopsy of unidentified cadavers (multiple).

Time of death: 2330 hours (approximately)
Date of death: 4 July 1947
Place of death: 45 miles north-northwest of Roswell New Mexico
Time of Preliminary autopsy: 1600 hours/ Date: 5 July 1947
Place: Roswell Army Air Force Base, Roswell New Mexico

The purpose of this preliminary postmortem examination is to determine the causes and manner of death, the origin of the entities, and the type of biological life form. Doctor Bronk is assisted by a noted forensic pathologist, Dr. Stanford, an Air Force pathologist, Major J. B. Johnson, Capt. Miser, the base Mortuary Affairs officer, and an anthropologist, Professor Frank Holden. Security personnel are stationed throughout the hospital and outside the operating room. Lt. General Nathan Twining commander of Air Materiel Command at Wright Field and Secretary of Defense (Select), James V. Forrestal are witnesses and will hand carry the report of the initial autopsy to the President of the United States.

Unidentified debris of nonferrous materials was discovered 75 miles northwest of Roswell by a local rancher William Brazel, witnessed by his son and daughter. An early morning aerial search resulted in discovery of partially intact and severely damaged unidentifiable aerospace vehicle and unidentifiable bodies on 5 July 1947.

An intelligence officer, Major Jesse A. Marcel of the 509th Bomb Group Intelligence Office, was the first official of the government to recover debris from the incident. Captain Sheridan Cavitt, Counter Intelligence Officer, of Air Intelligence (T2), witnessed and assisted Major Marcel. Debris will be subsequently transferred to Wright Field in Dayton Ohio, Sandia Base, Albuquerque, New Mexico, and Classified Location.

The bodies appear identical in appearance disregarding the damage sustained. One body appears to be undamaged and the other four are severely damaged from the trauma of the crash, exposure, and predators. The cadavers support a disproportionately large cranium and appear to be mongoloid/oriental by loose comparison. Each is clothed in a single piece metallic material of unusual strength while remaining soft and pliable.

TS/T2/EO/ Page 02 of 04
TS/T2/EO/ Page 03 of 04

No instrument available can cut or pierce the material. The material has a dull sheen and is silver in color. Four bodies have external dermal abrasions and carbonized areas around the face and cranium. The one-piece clothing on two of these bodies has separated in sections that run along a seam from under the arm down to the feet. Another seam with partial opening runs from the neck down the back to the buttocks.

The bodies have been stored in a cooler at the base and transferred to the base infirmary for the post mortem. The undamaged body is uncommonly warm to the touch. This is unusual since the other bodies are near freezing in temperature and all the bodies were removed from the cooler whose temperature is a constant 38 degrees. Some sort of chemical action or reaction continues to take place in the undamaged body in order to produce the 89.3 degree Fahrenheit temperature.

I have ordered each of the four damaged bodies be placed in a hermetically sealed container and packed in dry ice for shipment to facilities more appropriate for examination. The undamaged body will be kept at 89.3 degrees Fahrenheit during shipment.

No heartbeat or palpitation was observed although some background noise or resonance can be heard through a stethoscope. No pulse or respiration can be detected. The bodies all weigh fifty-six pounds and actual height of these beings is 49.4 inches. The limbs are consistently tubular and no joints are discernable. The arms are 5.1 inches in circumference and the legs are 7.5 inches in circumference. The neck measures 10 inches and both the chest and hips measure 31 inches around, consistently from the torso down to the hips. The finger tips reach to where the knees should be, or mid-leg. The hands contain four long slender fingers with some webbing and no opposing digit such as a thumb. Each finger tip has four bumps or wartlike projections with concave centers. Function unknown. The cranium measures 22 inches maximum and there are no discernable jaw or cheek bones. A thin crease 1.25 inches wide, much like a scar appears where the mouth should be. The mouth cavity is tiny and does not appear to function as a means of ingesting food or communications. No ears are visible, but a small 3/4-inch diameter bump protrudes 1/8 inch where the ears should be. Two small openings appear where the nasal cavity should be and no visible structure exists for a nose. The small inwardly tapered nasal openings are slightly less than 1/8 inch in diameter. The head is firm but slightly pliable and responds to pressure similar to the feel of a human without the skin being loose.

TS/T2/EO/ Page 03 of 04

TS/T2/EO/ Page 04 of 04

The eyes are of particular interest. On the damaged bodies, they are wide spaced, teardrop in shape, with the point being at the edge of the skull. The deep-set eyes are without eyelids or eyelashes and the eyes are solid deep dark brown in color. An opaque film, in milky color, coats each eye.

The undamaged body is different. A dark, coarsely textured, flat black, seamless almond shaped apparatus covers each eye with no apparent attachment points. For a lack of better description, eyeglasses or sunglasses comes to mind. Perhaps this apparatus is an aid in distance viewing, blocking harmful solar radiation, enhanced spectrum detection, low-light or infrared vision, or some other unknown use.

There are no visible sexual organs or genitalia or other differentiating exterior signs of sex or mating capabilities, nor are there a urinary or rectal openings. The bodies are bereft of hair, bumps, and scales, and the skin has the texture of fine cotton cloth of an ivory parchment color. Tiny lines run horizontally from head to foot much like record groves but smaller and are only discernable through a magnifying glass or microscope.

Of peculiar note is the fact that Sec. Forrestal reported a buzzing sound in his skull and severe migraine-like pain on each occasion that he touched the undamaged body. He is the only one in attendance that reported such phenomena.

No digestive system, no gastrointestinal tract, no alimentary or intestinal canal, no interior reproductive organs or other recognizable organs are present. One large Geo-organ is present. Cause of death; acute blunt trauma, Blood: colorless viscous liquid oozing which smells like ozone and ammonia.

A more detailed scientific report will be made available to the Secretary of Defense and the President. The follow-on report will address: analyzing fluids, materials, gasses, and biological structures and functions of these beings. Upon examination in person, it does not take a leap of imagination to realize that these beings are alien extraterrestrial biological entities. Acronym EBE should be used as an interim for security measures. A special committee, headed by the Sec Def or a Presidential appointee, should be formed for the express purpose of determining the impact upon "National Security." I hesitate to speculate upon the impact to civilization, religion, government, or individual sanity if this information is prematurely released. The highest security should be maintained by all involved. God help us all.

TS/T2/EO/ END Page 04 of 04

Rainey Roberts' hand was over her mouth.

"It's part of the original report from the Roswell crash. It's the frigging autopsy report on the alien crash victims."

"How in hell did Carl Farr get his hands on it?" Newsome wanted to know.

Webster took a long pull at his beer and sadly shook his head. "No wonder they had the poor bastard killed."

Newsome emitted a sharp burst of dry laughter. "Yeah, and we've got the disks now."

Rainey touched Joe's forehead. "He's hot, like he has a fever or something."

She went to the kitchen and returned with a damp towel to place on Joe's brow. His eyes were shut, and he seemed to be lost in a peaceful dream.

Blake asked Wayne to help him move Joe to the sofa. Much to their surprise, he stood slowly when they lifted him, and he walked like a zombie, following their gentle guidance.

"Let him rest," Rainey said. "I don't think we should try to wake him."

She covered him with a light blanket and motioned for the two men to follow her to the kitchen. The three of them sat up and talked until around midnight. Then, exhausted from the long drive, Newsome excused himself to sleep in the RV. Rainey and Blake split another beer, then retired to her bedroom for the night.

Chapter Twenty-two

Take Me or Else

Joe Green awoke shortly after dawn. When he sat up and looked around, it took several moments to remember that he was in Rainey Roberts' living room and that he had apparently spent the night on her sofa. He didn't really remember much of anything after he had sat down to look at Carl Farr's disks. He must really have been beat to have fallen asleep so early.

In a kind of reflex action, he reached for the crumpled pack of cigarettes in his shirt pocket and started to shake out one of the smokes. But then his stomach turned with revulsion. Once again it occurred to him that he hadn't had a cigarette or a drink since they had left San Antonio.

Nor had he eaten anything since yesterday's breakfast. He was really hungry.

He stood up, stretched, and yawned. He figured that Blake was with Rainey in her bedroom and that Wayne Newsome was bunked out in the RV. He had brought his suitcase in the house last night, so he decided to shower as quietly as possible and slip into a change of clothes.

By the time he left the bathroom, freshly showered and changed, Newsome had gotten up and put on a fresh pot of coffee.

"You put on quite a performance last night, Joe," Wayne said with a broad grin as he handed him a cup of steaming coffee. "You kind of spooked our hostess, though."

Joe gratefully accepted the cup, then self-consciously asked Newsome to explain.

"You cracked the mystery of Farr's disks, Buddy, then unearthed some really hot dope about the autopsy report of the alien UFOnauts."

Joe had helped himself to a couple of cookies from a jar on the counter and was on his second cup by the time Wayne had finished detailing the remarkable events of the previous evening. He was protesting his complete lack of memory when Blake and Rainey entered the kitchen.

Rainey had slipped a terry-cloth robe over her shortie pajamas. Her hair and lipstick were mussed in the telltale manner of a woman who had recently made love.

"Morning, Joe," Rainey teased. "Who are you today?"

Blake laughed. "You kind of surprised Rainey last night, Joe. I hadn't had a chance to tell her about your abilities and your little friends."

Rainey chuckled as she poured herself a glass of orange juice. "No kidding, Joe. I've never met someone from Krypton before."

Joe studied the inside of his coffee cup. "I really don't remember what happened after I sat down at the computer. I'm sorry if I startled you, Rainey."

Rainey bent to kiss his cheek. "Forget that, Joe. Whatever or whoever happened to you, you cracked a secret code and brought up some electrifying, dyno-mite shit."

She finished her orange juice then told Joe that Webster had also informed her about his receiving a psychic impression that Red was still alive somewhere in Area 51. "Do you believe that your reading was accurate, Joe?"

Joe carefully considered her question. "Rainey, the messages and images that I receive from the Jexovah are much more than psychic impressions. When they show me something in my mind, it is three-dimensional and somehow real. Of course that may sound strange to you, but I can't really put these experiences into words."

Rainey had poured a cup of coffee and was sipping cautiously at the steaming liquid. "I appreciate your explanation, Joe. You know, we've talked about these kinds of things for years in the abstract—alien contact, an advanced superscience, paranormal abilities. And then, pow! Suddenly, hey, man, it's really happening."

Blake clapped a hand on Joe's shoulder. "Do you remember at all the explosive information that you uncovered?"

Joe shook his head.

"We have clear proof of a modern conspiracy of governments and certain kingpins within the military industrial complex manipulating the masses and even committing murder to suppress this information," Blake said. "In addition, we have evidence of the alien manipulation of the human species that goes back to the dawn of humankind."

"In short," Newsome interjected, "we have proof of everything that you've been telling us."

Joe sighed, leaned back in the kitchen chair. "So now what do we do with it?"

Rainey jumped up to sit on the edge of a counter, exposing a generous portion of well-shaped leg. "Whatever your next move, guys, think it over carefully. The same Somebody Big who grabbed Red and who blew a large hole in Dr. Farr will quite likely want to shut you up, too."

Blake Webster shrugged. "We know, Hon. It's the same MJ-12 honchos that we've been trying to get to come out from under their rock for years now. I think we all know that they play rough and they play for keeps. We should probably get out of your house, Babe, before you get too far involved in all this shit."

Rainey winked at him. "Hey, listen, the fact that you've always been a muckraker doing your gol-damned best to uncover fraud, abuse, and the government conspiracy to cover up UFOs has always been a major turn-on for me, Lover. You might be dangerous to be around, but I decided a long time ago that I prefer your company to that of an overweight biker with tattoos of Nazis screwing snakes on his chest."

Blake leaned against her on the counter and gave her a kiss. "I love you, too, Sweetcheeks."

Rainey volunteered to drive to the nearest fast-food franchise and bring back some high-calorie, high-cholesterol breakfast for the group. Joe stood and handed her a twenty dollar bill as his contribution to the larder.

"She's a wonderful gal of the nineties," Blake said after Rainey had exchanged the robe for cutoffs and tee shirt and left for the drive-through restaurant. "Her lovely frame and agile mind manifest a nearly endless list of talents and abilities, but cooking is not one of them."

"She can learn," Wayne told him. "If you don't marry her pretty soon, I might decide I've had enough of the single life."

Webster laughed, gave his friend a friendly slap on the upper arm. "I honest to God hope to settle down with Rainey someday. First, though, we've got to deal with the mess that fate has dealt us. Somehow we've got to rescue Red and expose MJ-12 to the American public. And somehow we've got to do our best to come out of this alive."

Joe hadn't completely made up his mind about what their next move should be. He agreed that they were all at grave risk, but he believed that humanity deserved to know the truth about the Jexovah and the secret government.

"Unknowingly and against my will, I have been caught up in a tragic conspiracy all my life," he said. "There could be thousands of other abductees just like me, all carrying a heavy burden, perhaps living tormented lives. Every one of these people deserve to know the truth. I don't care how it affects the government, organized religion, or the world order."

Blake Webster observed Joe Green's mannerisms with fresh vision. The man really had an incredible charisma, he thought. Joe had the kind of presence that only the greatest of leaders have had.

Perhaps Wayne Newsome sensed it too. "Joe, if you want to take on the establishment, I'm just the kind of anarchist rogue that will march right beside you."

"Hey, Joe, I'm with you, man," Blake told him. "But we can't just go to the newspapers or television stations and spill our guts. We have Dr. Farr's notes and some incredible documents that he stole from the government, but the government will just claim that they are all fakes. The murder of Carl Farr has probably already been written off as a hunting accident. If Red won't talk, they can kill him and cover up his murder as an old coot desert rat making a misstep in the hills. If you want to expose the truth, God knows, I'm with you. But we are going to need the proverbial smoking gun."

"Such as?" Joe asked.

"Well, if we could get that alien spaceship that Red photographed to land on the White House lawn, that would do. One of these android biological entities guesting on Ted Koppel's show would be great. Or better yet, one of the Jexovah dudes calling a press conference together with the Pope would be terrific."

Newsome made a wry face at Webster's wish list. "How about a grand miracle of biblical proportions, like Joe parting the Great Salt Lake?"

Blake agreed. "That would do nicely. But without something like one or all of the above, Joe, we'll never convince the masses. And, hell, even if a gray were to knock on every door in America, there will still be the skeptics who will refuse to believe."

Rainey walked in, her arms loaded with a great-smelling breakfast. "Gulp it down, guys. You know this fast-food stuff always smells terrific, but you've got to eat it fast while the illusion lasts. Once this stuff cools off, it reverts to being lumps of cotton and cardboard soaked in hog fat."

Blake shuddered. "My darling, you have painted a word picture of culinary delights that no one could resist."

Rainey sorted the piles of food onto separate paper plates, passed around the necessary utensils, and stood back to survey her handiwork. "Oh, gee," she smiled. "I feel like such a little mother and homemaker."

After breakfast and a bit of small talk, the conversation returned to the serious business at hand.

"You three musketeers are talking about taking on a conspiracy that has been going on since civilization began," Rainey pointed out. "Like Blake keeps pointing out, you've got to have solid evidence or you'll all end up dead or placed in insane asylums to live out your natural lives."

Newsome stood up to get a glass of water from the sink. "The only place we know for certain that more solid evidence exists is at Dreamland, Area 51."

Joe agreed. "Possibly at the Groom facilities. And for sure, the Papoose facilities."

Rainey nodded. "The government has to have massive amounts of data stored on a secure computer system somewhere at one or both of these sites."

Blake leaned back in his chair. "Then we'll just have to break in, rescue Red, and grab the information we need."

"Right! Us and what army?" Newsome wanted to know.

"Let us not be defeatist," Blake admonished him. "Let's say our target is Dreamland. How do we get in? Where in that vast complex do we look? And what precisely are we looking for?"

Newsome sat down with his glass of water. "And what do we do with it when we find it?"

Rainey had a response to the question of how they could get in. "The EG&G Special Projects Division mainframe at our maintenance repair depot here in Las Vegas is networked to our mainframes in Area 51. We would need passwords and decryption algorithms."

Webster spoke up: "Red clued me in on every back way into Area 51. He gave me a map indicating where all of the old mining tunnel entrances and exits are."

Newsome was beginning to see a clearer picture. "My years of surveillance in that region has demonstrated that they only have sensors on the flats, the roads, and the paths leading into Area 51. At night, of course, they also have the helicopters with their infrared detectors."

Joe received a sudden image. He excused himself from the kitchen table, went into the living room, and returned with the box in which Dr.Farr had kept his disks.

"What's up, Joe?" Newsome asked.

Joe opened the box and removed a gold coin. A large gold key and a small piece of cut glass crystal remained in the box. The disks had all been removed and were still at Rainey's computer console.

"This will help us," he said as he set the coin on the table before the others.

Rainey picked it up and held it between thumb and forefinger. "One side has some kind of priest or soothsayer holding a lightning bolt in one hand and a large crystal in the other. He's got an aura or halo around his head and lightning bolts are shooting out of his skull. On the other side, we've got a hand palm-up inside a circle. The palm is holding a crystal with lightning bolts flashing out from it."

Newsome narrowed his eyes to study the coin. "What do you think it means, Joe?"

"This is a *mot du guet*," he said. "It means 'watchword' or 'token' in French."

"Ah," Blake nodded. "A shibboleth."

"Shhh-boom-a what?" Newsome growled.

"It means 'password' in Hebrew," Webster explained. "It's a term used by Mossad, the Israeli intelligence agency."

Joe closed his eyes for a moment as if to more clearly focus on the coin. "The figure depicted on the coin is an oracle. By definition, an oracle is a priest or priestess through whom a deity communicates. In Sumer, it was the Jexovah aliens. This coin will give us the password to enter the computer to which we must gain access."

Rainey touched Joe lightly on the shoulder and whispered in his ear, uncertain whether or not he had lapsed into a trance-state once again. "Joe, we need three passwords to enter the Top Secret mainframe in Area 51. I know, because I talk with our EG&G Special Projects Division technicians. I'm the software manager, and our company, EG&G Special Projects, maintains all of the Area 51 radar, threat sensors, and computers."

Joe knew she was right. He had worked as senior engineer for Lorale, EG&G's primary subcontractor since 1990. Together with Rainey, he explained as briefly as possible what EG&G's role was in the Nevada Test Site and the Nellis Range.

EG&G provided classified research, development, manufacturing, planning, and services for military and government agencies. The company also supplied technical, scientific, and logistical support for nuclear and non-nuclear testing and energy research and development programs. In addition, they provided construction and maintenance for large-diameter drilling, mining, and excavation for underground and mountainside facilities.

It was rumored that EG&G had built the vast underground facilities at Groom, Papoose, and Mercury for the government, which included designing and installing the complex security systems used by the government and military at those bases.

It had been known for years around Las Vegas that EG&G had the DOE (formerly the AEC) contract to supply all phases of support for the atomic testing program at the Nevada Test Site. Huge mine shafts or test wells had been drilled and excavated deep into the desert bedrock, and hidden bunkers, hangars, and observation posts had been constructed into mountains inside the Nevada Test Site and the Nellis Range.

In 1971 through 1973, a massive amount of excavation had taken place at the Groom and Papoose facilities. Most of the subsequent construction had taken place underground.

In 1972, EG&G was granted an indefinite contract called "Project Redlight" to support the AEC and the military. This contract gave them responsibility to assist in the recovery of nuclear materials in cases of mishaps and to provide aerial security for classified government and military sites.

"All right," Wayne Newsome acknowledged, "so this is an impenetrable fortress for which we need three passwords once we do get inside. We never thought it would be easy."

"You think one of the passwords has something to do with an oracle?" Blake asked.

"I'm certain of it," Joe said.

Newsome and Webster nodded. They knew that their friend was somehow receiving communication from the Jexovah.

"The government chose it because it is the acronym for 'Organic Robotic Android Communications Linked Entity,'" Joe suddenly blurted.

"Wow," Rainey laughed. "That's a mouthful!"

"That makes sense, though," Blake told her. "It's what the government calls the Jexovah or the EBE helpers."

Joe had his eyes closed again. "The second password is 'Aurora.' It is signified by the shimmering bolts of energy on the coin."

Rainey left the kitchen to pull a large library-sized dictionary from the bookshelf in the living room. She had just finished flipping the pages as she returned.

"Aurora," she read aloud, "a luminous phenomenon that consists of streamers or arches of light appearing in the upper atmosphere of a planet's polar regions and is caused by the emission of light from atoms excited by electrons accelerated along the planet's magnetic field lines."

Blake snapped his fingers and gave a "right on" whoop. "The MFD, the light, the project, it all makes sense. That's why they chose Aurora as the project name and also as one of the passwords!"

Rainey looked pleased. "Now tell me the third password."

"It's Jexovah," Joe said.

"Of course," Blake agreed.

"By Jove, I think we've got them," Newsome said. "I think we've got all three passwords."

"Rainey can operate any computer once we have the passwords," Blake said.

"And once I'm at the computer, we'll tell the whole fucking world about the Jexovah and the secret government all at once by putting the information on the nets. Milnet, Internet, foreign government nets, and private industrial nets. These computer networks go all the way around the world. Who needs the networks or the wire services? With the unique satellite linkup capabilities that exist in Area 51, we can establish an instant global communications network."

Joe flashed her a smile of approval. "I think she's got it, gentlemen. If we could get to the broadcast satellites for television and other electronic communications, as well as the nets, there would be no way to stop our message from reaching the world. We would be using classified NSA software to link and to control all commercial and government satellites."

"Fan-fucking-tastic!" Webster said with a broad grin..

"Yeah," Joe confirmed. "And I have the strongest feeling that the Jexovah want this to happen and that they will help us make it happen. There's something there in Area 51 that will set their master plan in motion."

Newsome stirred uneasily. "We agree that we can blast the information over the internet whether or not we have a satellite at our disposal. The big question remains: How do we get in?"

"How about getting in the same way security does?" Rainey asked, pausing to make certain she had everyone's full attention. "All security personnel carry a circular laser reflector, about six inches in diameter. In Area 51, all vehicles and personnel that are not under security escort are required to display these reflectors. Security personnel illuminate the reflectors with a laser tuned to a part of the light spectrum that's invisible, and they reflect an infrared signature that can be picked up by their infrared receivers. They've only been using these reflectors for the last six months."

Newsome wanted to get it straight. "So, Rainey, you are obviously suggesting that there is some way that we can acquire such reflectors."

"Remember that my wonderful significant other is the authorization manager for her range maintenance group," Blake said.

Newsome sighed and shook his head in admiration. "The lady has balls!"

"She's got ovaries," Rainey corrected him. "And some day she hopes to use them big time and lay some eggs for Daddy Webster. But I know that's not going to happen until we have done all we can to blow the whistle on the government cover-up of UFOs."

Blake leaned over and gave her a hug.

Newsome applauded. "So while we're giving a big hand for the little lady—Little Lady, how about signing out a vehicle for us as well?"

"No problemo," she agreed with a bright smile. "I can sign out the reflectors, a utility vehicle—and I can authorize a maintenance crew of four to be in the proper area."

Joe placed a hand on her forearm. "Think this over very carefully, Rainey. Are you certain that you really want to come with us? We don't know how many people they've killed to protect their secrets."

"I've thought it over," she answered. "I think it is time that the world was told the truth about alien interaction with the shadow governments. It may be a tough job, guys, but like they say, someone has to do it."

Webster's voice quavered with love and respect. "But, my darling, remember those eggs."

Rainey kissed his hand and brought it up to caress her cheek. "Over the years we've been together, my dearest, I've been by your side when you've exposed the shady dealings of congressmen, senators, and government contractors. But the exposure of the UFO/alien cover-up is the biggest story of corruption and rot that you've ever undertaken. There's no way that you're going to leave me out of this story."

Newsome laughed. "The time should be long past when we stopped calling them the weaker sex."

"Damn right, cowboy!" Rainey agreed.

Joe stood up and started picking up the soiled paper plates and scraps of food. "It's settled then. Let's get to work."

After a brief conference, they decided that they would put together a computer-generated news release. They would use the information from Dr. Farr's files and material from each of their research or personal experiences. They would also assemble a video from the materials at hand. The digital news release would be placed on all the worldwide computer networks.

The video broadcast with pictures and shots of printed files, such as the MJ-12 documents and the autopsy report, would be transmitted via satellite. Joe was certain that he could arrange the "loan" of a communications satellite by utilizing his own considerable skills and the activated mental programming that he was receiving from the Jexovah.

Within three days, they would be ready. It would be showdown time at Area 51.

Chapter Twenty-Three

Dreamland

The four conspirators, Blake Webster, Rainey Roberts, Wayne Newsome, and Joe Green, headed out of Las Vegas around 3:00 P.M. on Monday, September 9. It was their plan to arrive at the Groom facility just as night would be falling. The EG&G Special Projects Division Equipment van that Rainey had checked out from the vehicle compound on West Desert Inn Road stored their computer software, tools, and video. In addition, Rainey had provided them with company identification and coveralls.

When they left Las Vegas, they drove out into the desert hills, dotted with creosote bushes, then headed northwest on Highway 95 past Indian Springs and Cactus Springs. About forty-five miles west of Vegas at a sign that said "Mercury," they turned northwest on a paved four-lane divided road. They were now about sixty-six miles from the turn-off and the Groom facility.

After they had driven about two miles, they encountered a guard shack and gate that blocked the entrance to the 1500-square-mile Nevada Test Site. Here, a guard asked them to get out of the utility vehicle so he could run a hand-held sensor probe inside the van and across each person. Joe suspected that the probe used some type of mass spectometry or gas chromatography to detect explosive materials.

Another guard took their identification and entered the information into the computer in the shack. They would soon know just how good Rainey really was at inputting their cover IDs into the system. The four of them waited outside, afraid to talk, lest they seem nervous.

Apparently Rainey was as expert as she claimed, for the guards seemed satisfied with the results of the computer check and allowed them to proceed.

As they headed north, Wayne Newsome, who was at the wheel, said that they had entered the Mercury Valley. "Ahead lies the most remote and rough terrain in all of Nevada."

Blake adjusted his sunglasses against the glare of the late afternoon sun. "I remember Red telling me about it. I think the landing field with hangars and a few buildings are a couple of miles to the west. I think it's called Camp Desert Rock."

Joe explained that the landing strip was an auxiliary for the Air Force and the DOE. "University and contract research scientists from UCLA, Stanford, and USC, as well as others from Los Alamos, Sandia, and Lawrence Livermore, are flown into the test site at this landing strip. The guests are supported by facilities at Mercury Base, two miles north of the field."

A few miles down the road, Joe switched seats with Newsome and took his turn at the wheel. They had decided that Joe would be the best one to answer any questions from area personnel, since he spoke their lingo and knew the area closest to Groom Lake. Blake and Rainey sat on the seat behind them and watched the billowing trail of dust stretch out endlessly behind them.

"Welcome to Camp Desolate," Newsome said, making a sweeping gesture toward the barren hills and wasteland all around them. "Nothing but scrubby bushes, weeds, and cactus."

The static from the dry desert air caused the dust to coat and to cling to every surface of the vehicle. Even with the windows closed, the filtered air from the conditioner smelled of dust, and the fine particles coated the inside of their noses and mouths and lined their eyes.

"From 1951 to '62, the Atomic Energy Commission tested atomic bombs above ground here," Blake said. "In '62, the International Nuclear Test Ban drove the routine nuclear explosions underground."

Newsome, a lifelong resident of the area, said that he remembered the explosions that shook the desert. "They scattered jack rabbits and wild horses and sent shock waves through southern Nevada—and released radioactive contaminants as far away as Utah. I remember feeling the blast tremors as far up as Tonopah. Mock towns, air bases, and dummy soldiers were constructed for destruction, then blown apart, filmed, and analyzed. There used to be dozens of nuclear test wells and concrete bunkers all over this area."

They drove north on Mercury Road past signs that read Mercury Base, Dell Frenzi Park, and Timpi Site. A blue Air Force pickup truck passed them headed south, and the driver in a white jumpsuit gave a friendly wave.

They were stopped at Checkpoint Pass, northeast of the Mercury Base, and asked for their identification.

"What's your business here?" one of the guards asked Joe.

"We've been called to repair a T-3 threat radar system," he answered with hesitation.

The Wackenhut guard's face was expressionless. "What's a T-3 threat radar system?"

The other three conspirators were grateful that Joe was answering the questions.

"The T-3 was developed by Rome Air Development Center in New York," he began. "It's used to simulate Russian surface-to-air missile tracking radars. It was designed after a Russian radar system captured by the Israelis."

The guard remained expressionless, seemingly unmoved, so Joe continued:

"The T-3 consists of two large tractor trailer vans, two radar dishes that are ten feet across. One radar dish for horizontal tracking is parabolic and the other one is crescent-shaped for vertical tracking. We'll change the software at the EG&G electronics building this evening. In the morning, we'll drive westward toward the eastern Pahute Range and perform modifications to the T-3 system located near Gold Flat at the Nellis Electronic Combat Range."

The guard, who had seemed ignorant of all that Joe had rattled off until that point, suddenly sprang to intellectual life and asked a very pointed question. "That system is about two decades old. Why are they modifying it now that the USSR has collapsed?"

"No, no," Joe responded, momentarily taken by surprise and spinning his mental wheels for a satisfactory answer, "the system isn't changing. The modification we'll be making is an equipment upgrade. Some of the instruments are no longer manufactured or supported by the manufacturer. The circuit cards we have in the van are a new design by a different manufacturer. Would you like to see them?

The guard shrugged indifferently. "No, it just seemed unusual to me that you would be doing this now when a new Green Flag training exercise will start at Nellis AFB tomorrow."

"And that is exactly why we are here on a rush job now," Joe told him. "We didn't receive the modification kits from the Rome Air Development Center until this morning. We'll probably have to work through the night."

"Okay," the guard waved them through the checkpoint. "You'd better get started then."

"I must say that you are certainly well-informed for a guard," Joe said, masking his relief at having bluffed their way through.

The guard accepted the compliment with a barely perceptible smile. "I'm booking for advancement, sir. I don't plan to be stuck at a guard shack forever."

When they were out of earshot of the guard, Joe told his passengers, "Thank God he didn't want to see the modification kits. I don't know what we would have improvised to show him if he had. He was far more knowledgeable about the technology than I ever would have guessed."

Newsome gave him a congratulatory slap on the shoulder. "Good faking there, amigo! You did good!"

"Did you have a little help from your friends upstairs in the UFO?" Rainey asked.

Joe laughed. "No, I bullshitted that one on my own."

Blake called their attention to the test wells and bunkers and the camera stations on the mountain tops.

They drove on along the graded gravel road past an occasional bunker, metal tower, blockhouse, or pumping station. The terrain gradually increased in elevation until they reached Yucca Pass. From the pass they could see a dozen radio towers, scattered railroad tanks, and concrete blockhouses.

"Yucca Lake still has some water in it," Wayne told them, "but it's completely polluted with chemicals and radioactive waste."

Farther north they entered an area marked by a sign that read "Nevada Test Site Area 10."

"Good grief!" Rainey exclaimed. "Look at all the craters, how huge they are!"

"That's where a number of above-ground atomic bombs were exploded," Wayne told her.

They could now see about a dozen huge derrick-like towers dotting the horizon.

"According to Red's map, we've got about ten miles to go before we reach Groom Pass," Blake said. "Then it appears that we're home free to the Groom Air Base facility."

"Listen!" Rainey demanded. "What's that sound?"

The three men heard only the wind and road noise as the van moved down the hard-packed gravel road.

"Don't you hear it?" Rainey was peering out a side window and trying to look up.

"We don't hear anything, Hon," Blake said, glancing at the two other men for any sign of a conflicting opinion.

"Turn off the air and slow down," Rainey told Joe. "There's a damn chopper above us!"

"Jesus, are you sure?" Newsome asked.

The three men looked out of their windows. It was approaching dusk, and the dust-coated glass prevented a clear view.

"I hear it now," Blake affirmed. "Shit, they're on to us!"

"Let's just control ourselves, folks," Joe advised in a calm voice. "Let's see what they're doing."

He looked at the silver reflector disk in its slot pressed against the front window just below the rearview mirror. The helicopter's laser interrogator would read the disk just like a bar code reader at the supermarket. Once again, they were about to find out how good Rainey Roberts was at her job.

Now the black helicopter was visible through the front window. The Apache was equipped with self-dampening sound limiters. The oscillation of the rotor wash could be felt inside the van. The womp womp womp sound of the rotors cutting through the air reminded Joe of the choppers in Southeast Asia.

"Don't worry, guys," Rainey assured them. "I gave us an up-to-the-minute reflector code."

"Jesus, I sure as hell hope you did," Newsome said.

"Come on," Rainey scowled defensively, "the individual IDs worked, right?"

"Right," Blake squeezed her hand in silent apology.

Joe rolled down his window and stuck out his arm. The increased noise coming in the open window filled the interior of the vehicle.

"What are you doing, man?" Blake asked squeezing Rainey's hand a bit tighter than he intended, causing her to wince.

"I'm giving them a nice, big friendly wave," Joe said. "They've read our disk on their interrogator. They're satisfied. Now I'm going to act natural, like I know what they're doing—and what we're doing."

The helicopter dipped in response to Joe's wave and began to move off.

"It worked," Newsome sighed, leaning back heavily against the seat as they watched the helicopter rise in altitude and distance itself from them.

Rainey leaned forward and gave Wayne a light slap on the top of his head. "Of course it worked! I'm good at my job. Have a little faith in me, for Pete's sake!"

Joe complimented Rainey on a job well done. "Now let's all have a little more faith in ourselves—for the sake of our future!"

Chapter Twenty-four

General's Inquiry

It had been five days since General Alex Beauharnais had been summoned to the office of Eli Jerrold and been admitted into the confidence of those self-styled superpatriots who served the MJ-12 committee—and he hadn't had a good night's sleep since he returned to the Groom Lake facility.

Were there truly secret branches of the government working with extraterrestrial intelligences on ultra-modern technology—or were Jerrold and his committee a bunch of nuts? Or maybe they had come up with a bizarre rationalization to foment a rebellion. Perhaps the aliens only existed in Jerrold's wrinkled old brain, and his dementia was driving him to attempt an overthrow of the government.

True, the documents that Jerrold and Colonel Trent had shown him appeared to be authentic, but how could any group in any branch of the U.S. government keep a secret for so long? Since 1947? Impossible!

General Beauharnais's quarters were more like a hotel suite than an apartment. Although hardly spacious, there was a bedroom, a sitting area, a kitchenette, a small dining area, and three fairly large closets. The Groom mess hall served meals to the facilities' employees twenty-four hours a day, but the General took his evening meals alone in his quarters.

Tonight, he had invited his deputy, Colonel Matthew Kingsley, to join him. He had known Matt for nearly twelve years, and he had confided the entire account of his meeting with Jerrold to him within hours after he had returned from Washington. Matt Kingsley might be the only person on the facility that he could trust, and he knew with certainty that he would also be loyal to him and to the government to whom he had pledged his everlasting allegiance.

After a light meal, General Beauharnais poured them each a glass of Chardonnay. He indicated that the colonel should make himself comfortable in a black leather recliner, and he sat opposite him on a matching leather sofa. The general had asked Kingsley for a complete review of the Papoose facilities.

"As you know, the Defense Advanced Research Center is located underground at Papoose Lake," the colonel began. "The DARC personnel are civilian contractors and security. The CIA provides the management of the TR-3 along with the National Reconnaissance Office, and the NSA manages all the research at the DARC facility. All of the facilities have been built underground surrounding the Papoose dry lake. They have their own water and power just like Groom, and the extensive facilities are also underground."

Kingsley took a sip of wine before he continued. "As far as I can tell, I didn't seen anyone or anything that looked alien to me."

"Nothing that appeared just a little too far advanced in terms of known and accepted technology?" Alex asked.

Kingsley laughed and shook his head. "I'm no aeronautical physicist, Alex. There is no question that we do have a number of radical aerospace vehicles, but I am not capable of determining the origin of the technology."

Alex nodded his understanding of his friend's position. "You're simply saying that you saw nothing overtly alien in your opinion. On the other hand, a lot of the advanced technology could have been influenced by alien science."

"Affirmative," Matt smiled. "The SR-75 and the smaller SR-74 are kept at the Groom facilities. The new fighter bomber, the FB-112, looks a lot like the F-117 stealth fighter but is much larger and has no vertical stabilizers or other protruding surfaces. It looks like the bat-plane."

Alex ran his forefinger along the rim of his wine glass. "That's the F-111 replacement vehicle. The one the tech magazines called the A-17."

Matt finished his glass. "Yes, that's it. The A-17 and the TR-3, as well as a number of smaller prototypes are kept at the Papoose facilities. In addition, there are several unmanned aerial vehicles and independently piloted vehicles."

Alex reached over to pour more wine in Colonel Kingsley's glass. "The smallest one, I believe, is called the 'Gnat.'"

Matt nodded and pulled a folder from the leather planner on his lap. "If there is any alien technology involved in the production of these prototypes and if there should be any recovered alien vehicles in the area, then they are based and stored at Papoose."

Matt handed him the folder. "I've made a list for you of each project, the funding source and amount, the type and class of vehicle, and the goal of each particular project."

"Tell me about these vehicles."

Matt considered the question. "Well, they come in all sizes and shapes—conventional to exotic. There are flying wings, delta, triangular, and circular shapes. The TR-3 is the most exotic manned vehicle. The Tier-4B, the 'Fourbee,' is an unmanned or Independently Piloted Vehicle, a smaller version of the the triangle-shaped TR-3. I think that a lot of the so-called UFO sightings are really our own exotic prototype vehicles."

"That's quite possible," Alex agreed.

Matt continued. "I found out that the Gulf Breeze, Florida, sightings were a result of our testing the Tier-4B. The damn thing can move so fast from a standing start that it appears to disappear."

The General rubbed his chin reflectively. "Interesting. But did the super technology that enabled it to move so quickly originate on another planet?"

Matt Kingsley took a swallow of his wine. "Well, the more I investigated that question, the more confused I became. For instance, I was told by one major at Papoose, a Brooks scientist on assignment here, that he could not discuss the intricacies of ongoing projects with me or any other person outside his chain of command or outside the project."

"Really?" The General arched an eyebrow, then frowned.

"He also told me," Kingsley went on, "that he didn't consider the base hierarchy—meaning you and me—or the security assholes to be part of the scheme of things. And he was pretty damn arrogant about it."

"Arrogant is an understatement," Alex fumed. "Didn't you set him straight?"

"I certainly tried," Kingsley said. "When I told him we, the 'base hierarchy,' could have his ass, he just laughed at me. He said his work was SCI, Sensitive Compartmented Information, and we did not have a need to know."

"SCI, eh?" Alex scowled. "We'll see about that."

Matt smiled approvingly. "I wanted to punch his lights out, but I did find out from the computer database profile of personnel that he is a neurosurgeon who works with artificial intelligence and that he is assigned to a project called 'Project Wells.'"

"And what the hell is that, Matthew?"

Kingsley held out his glass to be refilled. "It's a super computer analysis designed to assess the effects and reaction of a culture if the existence of a higher intelligence should be discovered. It's also highly classified and under the control of an unnamed secret agency."

General Beauharnais leaned forward with the bottle of Chardonnay. "And could that be our mysterious friends on MJ-12?"

Matt Kingsley shrugged, careful not to spill any of the wine. "I just think it is strange to have a Black project working on the effect of a superior alien world on our culture on a classified air base in the middle of nowhere."

The general refilled his own glass, then leaned back on the sofa. "It's not strange if aliens really exist, and we are trying to duplicate their technology."

"Then we are back to square one: 'Is there alien technology being tested here on this base?'"

The general excused himself for a moment to put on a fresh pot of coffee. He raised his voice slightly to be heard over the running water. "Let us suppose that it is so. That at his very minute somewhere in the mysterious underground caverns on this base, super scientists are working in secret with flying saucer fragments or whatever. How much alien science do you think they've figured out?"

Colonel Kingsley got up from the recliner and walked into the kitchenette. "Just from looking at some of these aeronautical prototypes—and supposing your hypothesis to be so—one might assume that they've cracked some of it."

"But how much?"

"Well, we still haven't figured out the aliens' language," Kingsley said. "And that certainly inhibits rapid assimilation."

The General wondered what information allowed him to make such an assertion.

"The Research and Engineering Division of the NSA has picked up numerous transmissions along the twenty-one-meter wavelength band," Kingsley answered. "According to a friend of mine in the Foreign Technology Division, who's a member of the NSA's Dundee Society, the NSA began picking up alien transmissions in 1972. It's all highly classified, but he did say that it's more likely that we'll talk with dolphins before we have a breakthrough with the alien language. We can have better luck with the technology through reverse engineering."

"If utilization of alien technology is actually taking place," General Beauharnais smiled, "I would love to get an up-close look at an alien craft. I want to touch something. I prefer my reality in the form of something that I can see and touch."

Colonel Kingsley laughed. "I'll keep investigating. We're both pilots. Maybe we can volunteer to test one of the prototypes."

The General made a wry face. "I'll settle for a close look and a firm touch."

The fragrant aroma of fresh-brewed coffee filled the general's small quarters, and Colonel Kingsley gratefully accepted a large cup. "There's another matter I would like to discuss tonight," he said.

"Of course," the general nodded, as he added one lump of sugar to his own cup.

"It's this new security specialist, Michael Crawfoot. He's definitely not a technical person. And he's downright unsociable. Yet he has a ranking second only to yours. So what's with this guy?"

The General took a careful swallow of the steaming coffee and resumed his seat on the sofa. "I suspect that he has been sent by MJ-12 to kill me if I don't behave."

Colonel Kingsley hoped his commanding officer was joking, but when he looked into his eyes, he saw no mirth concealed within. "You're serious."

"Damned serious, Matt. These boys don't mess around. I was ordered to tighten security against all possible intruders, especially civilians. If I'm not strict enough or give some other indication that I'm not dancing to their tune, I suspect Mr. Crawfoot will be told to shut out my lights."

The colonel had difficulty dealing with what the general was telling him. "They wouldn't dare. You're a general, for chrissakes."

General Beauharnais's voice became a whisper. "MJ-12 will really stop at nothing. I'm convinced of that. When I saw according to Crawfoot's orders that Colonel Ty Trent had placed him as security consultant, I knew that he was sent here to watch over me and to eliminate me if I began to pose too great a risk. Crawfoot is almost certainly a contract killer for the NSA."

"Then we'll throw the son of a bitch in the stockade until we find out what the hell is going on around here," Kingsley said resolutely.

"On what charge do we have him salted away?"

Kingsley held up three fingers. “Give me three minutes, and I’ll have at least a dozen transgressions attributed directly to Mr. Crawfoot.”

General Beauharnais smiled at Matt Kingsley. He knew that the Colonel could be trusted completely and totally depended upon. “We’ll just keep an eye on him for now. I have a gut feeling that something big is going to happen very soon. When it does, we’ll be ready.”

Chapter Twenty-five

A Wake-up Call for Planet Earth

By the time that Rainey Roberts, Blake Webster, Wayne Newsome, and Joe Green reached Groom Base, the sun had gone down and vehicular activity was picking up around the flight line in front of the big hangar. Two black helicopters flew over the base headed south.

The large hangar—called the "Barn" and "Hangar 18" after the infamous hangar at Wright-Patterson AFB that was rumored to hold the remains of extraterrestrials and their crashed vehicles—was 70 feet high and 190 feet on each side. A loud bell sounded continuously as the huge doors slowly opened. A yellow tow-tug backed into the partially opened doors and the runway and flight line halogen lights lit up the surrounding area as bright as daylight.

The four invaders sat in the EG&G Special Project's Division's maintenance van watching the activity with great interest.

"Where do you think they're keeping Red?" Webster asked in a hushed voice.

"In an underground cell," Joe said.

"And you…feel that he's still alive?" Webster asked, wanting to be reassured.

Joe nodded. "I know that Red is still alive."

"Jesus, look at all the lights. There must be hundreds of them," Newsome whispered in awe. "Plenty of troops on duty, too."

"This is our last chance to back out," Joe said. "We can turn around right now and go back the way we came. No one will be the wiser."

"Except us," Webster underscored.

"Knowing we chickened out," Rainey added.

"Knowing we left Red to the wolves," Webster said softly.

"Damn it," Newsome said nervously cracking his knuckles as he spoke. "We've come this far. Let's do it! We know the communications setup here is the best in the world to boom out our message, our call to arms, so to speak."

Joe smiled. "Let's do it."

"What do you think all the activity is about, Joe?" Rainey asked.

"I presume that they're prepping the SR-75."

"Is that the long black thing that tears up the sky when it takes off?" Newsome wondered.

Joe nodded. "It's a sight to behold. I used to work on it. It's built by the Lockheed Skunk Works, the same place that designed and built the SR-71 Blackbird reconnaissance plane."

"All part of the Aurora Project?" Rainey asked.

Joe said that her assumption was correct. "Aurora is the code name of the ongoing project to build and test advanced aerospace vehicles. The SR-75, the mother ship, is called the Penetrator and can fly over eight times the speed of sound. A smaller ship, the SR-74, can actually sit on top of it for some missions. The 75 can launch the smaller 74, called the Thunder Dart, at 110,000 feet, and it can achieve orbit. Look, they're pulling it out of the hangar now."

Joe pointed toward the huge hangar, and they watched as a yellow tug appeared under the nose of a jet black sword-shaped object protruding from the hangar doors. The point of the aircraft emerged first, high up in the air. The belly of the vehicle was at least ten feet off the ground, and the tug was coupled to the front landing gear, which was twenty feet behind the wedge-pointed nose.

"My God, look at that monster!" Newsome exclaimed. Some ninety feet of the SR-75 had emerged from the hangar as the tug gently pulled it forward.

"How long is that mother?" Rainey asked.

Blake was silent, seemingly mesmerized by the sight of the top secret reconnaissance vehicle.

"It's 162 feet long and has a wing span of 98 feet," Joe answered. "It carries a crew of three—a pilot, a reconnaissance officer, and a launch control officer who doubles as the electronics warfare officer."

"Kind of makes you feel like you're watching a science fiction movie, doesn't it?" Newsome suggested.

Blake broke his silence. "You could drive a small car into one of the engine air inlets."

He was referring to the two engine inlets under each wing of the awesome black mother ship. The engine bays hung down seven feet from the underside of the wing and were twelve feet wide. Two high bypass turbojet engines were housed under each wing, and the bays ran some forty feet under the wings, terminating at the trailing edge of the wing.

"Do you think it's getting ready to go on a mission?" Rainey asked Joe.

"Well, they've got the SR-74 mounted on top, as you can see," Joe said, "and they've turned all the lights on. Notice that all the perimeter lights face outward so the craft can't be photographed from a distance. I don't think they would go through all this trouble unless it was going on a mission."

Joe moved the van into forward gear and pulled up to the side loading dock of the maintenance building.

Blake glanced at his watch. "Do you think we can go in yet?"

Wayne Newsome looked around nervously. An ominous feeling was seeping into his bones.

"It's eight-thirty and the last shuttle flight left a little after five," Rainey said. "According to the schedule, all the maintenance personnel should have been out of the building a couple of hours ago."

Joe turned off the ignition. "Everyone all right?"

Blake and Rainey nodded.

"Wayne, you know what to do?" Joe asked.

"I've got the dummy job. I sit here with this portable radio, and if anyone approaches the building, I buzz you three times. If they look like they're going to enter the building or approach the van, I buzz four times. If it's a false alarm, I buzz twice."

"You got it," Joe smiled.

"My manhood is still a little dented, though," Wayne felt moved to state. "Seems like I should be going inside and face the unknown instead of Rainey."

Joe reached over and squeezed Newsome's shoulder. "Except Rainey is our computer whiz, and what you know about computers could fly in your eye and not make you blink."

Newsome conceded the point. "Good luck, gang!"

Joe removed the large equipment bag from the rear of the black Dodge van and handed Blake a smaller utility tool kit. Rainey carried the case with the computer disks and circuit cards.

"Everyone act cool," Joe said. "Act like we're supposed to be here, and we know what the hell we're doing."

There was a small light over the side door to the building. Joe inserted the key card into the code key lock attached to the side of the door.

He swiped the magnetic strip side of the card through the reader and punched in the day code.

Nothing happened.

"What the shit?" Rainey said. "It's supposed to work."

"Now we are fucked," Blake shook his head.

"Relax," Joe said. "I'll try it again."

He swiped the magnetic strip through the slot again, slower, more deliberately, and carefully punched in the six digit code. When they heard the muffled click of the large deadbolt releasing inside, they all smiled in relief.

The thirty-thousand-square-foot building was partitioned inside, housing the EG&G Special Projects Division's shops on the east side, the NSA shops on the south side, and the Air Force avionics and calibration labs on the north side. The EG&G and Air Force took up over eighty percent of the building. Most of the heavy duty repair and maintenance of the test ranges were done at the EG&G Special Projects Division's depot in Las Vegas. The telemetry control and range equipment, as well as the test and mission program tapes, were also kept inside the building that the three conspirators were about to enter.

Dozens of tiny equipment lights sparkled in the darkness of the room they entered as they stepped inside. It was Joe's job to turn on the lights in the breaker box. Rainey was assigned to access the master computer and load the data from the disks they had prepared to transmit to the earth orbit satellite network and the world computer nets. Blake was to stand at the ready to hand Rainey anything she might need to expedite her task.

"How's it coming, Sweetie?" Blake asked after a few minutes.

"I've loaded our report containing our research highlights, Dr. Farr's notes and stolen files, as well as the few photographs we had," Rainey stated in a methodical manner. "I've loaded the program that will send the information out over the national and international computer networks at the proper moment."

Joe looked at his watch. It was a few minutes after nine. At nine-thirty, Rocky Mountain Time, Rainey would have to be finished. Both the computer network and satellite video transmissions would be sent automatically by the loaded programs at that time.

Rainey pushed back from the VAX mainframe computer. "Okay, I'm ready to go to the satellite uplink."

Blake picked up the bag with the other disks and the video tapes.

Joe led them across the room to a three-bay piece of electronic equipment; each bay was six feet high and two feet wide. To the right was a computer console and printer stand. To the left was a large dual tape backup unit.

"This is the Rockwell Satellite Communications Control Station," Joe told Rainey.

She nodded her recognition, pulled up a maintenance stool, and had Blake set the bag on the work surface. Each bay had a foldout work surface about waist high.

"Oh, oh, oh shit!" Rainey suddenly squealed.

"What, Babe, what's wrong?" Blake asked, beads of nervous sweat curdling together on his forehead.

Rainey leaned back and considered the control station. "This bay on the right is the transmit section. The one in the middle is the receive station. The one on the left is the digitizer and control section. Right?"

"So what's wrong?" Blake repeated his question. How the hell would he know which bay was the correct one? Rainey was the expert.

She leaned down and pointed under the work surface on the right bay. "Down here is the intermediate power supply. But the main power amplifier light is not on."

Blake looked helplessly, nervously, under the shelf and agreed that all the equipment lights were off. "So what do we do?"

"We have to locate the breaker box for the transmitter power supply," Joe answered. "Otherwise we can't transmit anything."

Joe raced to a wall studded with electronic equipment. "This has to be it," he said, trying his best to sound confident. He turned on all the equipment associated with the satellite communications control station and waited while the computer ran its built-in test program. Agonizing minutes ticked off.

Finally the computer beeped and the prompt read: "System BIT complete. You may proceed."

"Right on!" Rainey exulted. "We're back in business."

Joe and Blake pulled out the small VHS player from the tool bag along with the rat's nest of cables. Joe hooked up the output jack on the VHS player to the external video jack on the control section bay.

The computer monitor flashed, "ENTER PRIMARY PASSWORD."

Rainey entered ORACLE.

"INCORRECT PASSWORD. FIRST WARNING," flashed on the screen.

"Joe," Rainey bounced anxiously on the chair before the screen, "tell me what I do now!"

Joe held his breath. He had been certain that the first password was "Oracle." If he guessed wrong again now, the system would shut down, an alarm would be activated, and they would be discovered. Their counterattack on MJ-12 would be squelched before it began.

"Aurora," Joe told Rainey. "Enter Aurora!"

"Why the fuck not," Rainey mumbled as she punched in the word.

They all gave a small cheer when the monitor displayed, "ENTER SECONDARY PASSWORD."

"Jexovah, right?" Rainey wanted final confirmation before she punched in the second password.

"That's right," Joe told her.

The monitor responded, "ENTER FINAL PASSWORD."

"Ah," Blake sighed in relief. "All's right with the world. Now it's got to be 'Oracle,' right, Joe?"

Joe nodded. "It has to be."

"Here goes a home run," Rainey giggled as she punched in the letters.

"SYSTEM ERROR. WARNING. IMMINENT SHUTDOWN."

The three of them looked at one another in dumb terror as a piercing alarm sounded from the ceiling and the computer monitor flashed, "REENTER FINAL PASSWORD. SYSTEM SHUTDOWN WILL OCCUR IF INCORRECT."

Joe reeled back against a post. He was confused and dazed. The password sequence that he had been so sure of had not worked. Why the hell not?

Aurora was the technology; Jexovah, the aliens; Oracle, the android helpers. Why hadn't it worked?

"Jesus, Joe," Blake danced nervously from one foot to the other. "That alarm is letting the whole base know that they've got intruders where they don't belong."

Rainey was more to the point. "Shouldn't we be hauling ass?"

Joe would have bet his life that those three passwords were correct. Hell, he grimaced, he probably had done just that—and he had lost.

Joseph Green, we have the answer for you.

Joe spun around, looking for the androids. They weren't there in person, but the alien voice inside his head was clear and direct.

"Joe, what the fuck are we…"

"Blake, shut up!" Rainey shouted. "He's got that look in his eyes again. I hope that his buddies are giving him something we can use right now."

Enter MARSJUPI.

Joe's mental response was pointed and desperate. "That doesn't spell anything. The alarm will go off for sure if I enter the wrong code!"

Enter MARSJUPI. The third password has been changed.

Joe knew they had nothing to lose. He rushed to the keyboard. "Let me try," he said to Rainey.

"You got it," she said as she vacated the chair before the computer.

Joe typed in MARSJUPI and hit the enter key. The computer monitor went blank just long enough for Joe to stop breathing. And then the monitor displayed, "ENTER LAST EIGHT DIGITS OF TERTIARY PASSWORD."

Mentally, Joe called out, "Are you still there? I hope you are. What last eight digits?"

Enter TERPROBE.

When Joe did as the voice commanded, they were at last inside the system. He gave Rainey a thumbs-up victory sign, and returned the computer command post to her expertise.

He was aware of Blake speaking to him, but he wanted to ask the voice inside his head about MARSJUPI-TERPROBE before it left him.

The answer was forthcoming: *It means Mars Jupiter probe. Your government wishes to photograph our installations on Mars. We will not permit that to happen. We have allowed your last probe to land in a remote area of Mars to take pictures of rocks and dirt.*

Joe chuckled to himself. "I always wondered why both the U.S. and Russian probes began to malfunction just as they were to commence taking pictures of Mars."

In regard to the secret committee originally formed by your government to handle information and contacts made by us, they called themselves MJ-12 for Mars and Jupiter. The 12 came from the ancient Sumerian designation for the planet that once orbited between Mars and Jupiter. The term Majestic is not relevant.

We approve of your plan to transmit your message over your world's communications nets. The time has come for your people to know the truth about us. We have prepared supplemental documentation. An alarm on the base has been sounded. You must continue.

Joe sensed that their communications link had terminated, and he stepped back to watch Rainey smoothly and efficiently fulfilling their mission.

"Look at my girl work that computer, man," Blake said proudly. "Isn't she something else?"

"She's terrific," Joe agreed, praying that nothing slowed her down. Area 51 had the tightest security of any installation in the world. Within minutes, armed paramilitary with automatic weapons would probably be breaking down the doors to the building.

Rainey entered the code sequence to cue up the videotape that they had prepared for satellite transmission. Next she entered the code to send another text message out over the computer networks. She started the computer message first and sent it out to Mil-net and Internet with programming commands to retransmit to all user addresses. The programming code that she had prepared would command the Mil-net and Internet user recipients to retransmit automatically the message to all on-line users to their machines. If it worked perfectly, then, theoretically, every computer network user in the world would receive the message.

And she had really gone for broke. The message would keep transmitting indefinitely. The programming code that she had written would infect every computer on a network, just like a deadly computer virus would. In fact, she had modified a computer virus to accomplish the deed. The virus would replicate its own code until each computer would be filled with the message, then the programming code would repeat it over and over again.

The only way that anyone could stop it would be to disconnect their machines from the networks, clear the virus from their machines, then stay off-line and off the nets until every other computer had been cleared. This would take many days, perhaps weeks, to re-establish all of the network links and users.

And just seconds after she had sent the prepared text message out over the nets and the AP and UPI wire services, the satellite uplink transmission began transmitting the video portion of their wake-up call to the world.

Yes, Rainey Roberts had most certainly done her job well.

Chapter Twenty-six

Revelation

General Beauharnais and Colonel Kingsley arrived at the Security Operations building to find it in an uproar. Raul Agabarr was there in his jogging suit and tennis shoes. Michael Crawfoot seemed, as always, calm and composed, as if ice water flowed in his veins.

General Beauharnais requested an immediate status report from Oscar de la Garza, head of security. Armed guards in camouflaged uniforms opened a path for the general and his entourage. It was now nearly 10:00 P.M.

"To put it bluntly, sir," Oscar said, "all hell has broken loose. First the alarm sounded in the electronics building, and then every type of security alarm from here to Tonopah through the Rachel gate went off."

General Beauharnais was very much aware of Crawfoot and Agabarr standing near, catching his every word. He suspected that Agabarr was under MJ-12's orders to terminate him if Crawfoot should fail.

"Oscar," he demanded, "what could cause this to happen?"

"The first was an internal alarm," the security chief explained. "It was set off from inside the building. The alarms along the Groom Range and through Rachel could only be set off by an earthquake."

The general raised a skeptical eyebrow. "An earthquake? Come now, Oscar."

"An earthquake or more than a thousand vehicles moving along the highway that runs from Tonopah to Alamo, through Rachel, to set off all the other alarms," he answered.

Colonel Kingsley emitted a short laugh of derision. "That's hardly likely, is it, Oscar?"

De la Garza hesitated to reply, but things could not really get any worse. "Sir, we've been getting strange reports of a massive caravan of hundreds of automobiles, buses, vans, and RVs headed this way."

Agabarr scowled, then cursed as he looked directly at Crawfoot. "It's probably what we've been warned about. Extreme and dangerous fanaticism from the UFO kooks and nut cases. It's probably some goddam people's revolt headed our way."

General Beauharnais turned to regard Agabarr's strange contribution to the problem at hand. "What do you mean, a people's revolt?"

Agabarr made his answer sound accusative. "That's why we've been ordered to tighten security, sir. UFO kooks and cultists have made Area 51 their Mecca. They've created an entire mythology about this place. That maniac Page St. John has been conducting some kind of weird religious revival ever since Labor Day weekend. Maybe he's bringing his disciples here to pray for a UFO to land and deliver a messiah from a spaceship."

Almost as if on cue, every type of security alarm at the Groom and Papoose facilities, as well as every security sensor in Area 51, was being set off. Bells, whistles, beeps, and the shrill shriek of many types of audible alarms filled the room with a cacophony of electronic sounds.

"Sir," Oscar exclaimed, "the security control computers are jammed, useless..."

Unlike many of the buildings in Area 51, the Security Control building had windows on every side. As the general and the security personnel sat up on the second floor looking out over the Groom dry lake bed, they saw that every runway, perimeter, building, and area light within sight had been turned on. The immediate area around the hangars and dry lake took on the eerie glow of mock daylight.

"Who the hell gave the order to have all the lights turned on?" Kingsley demanded.

"No one," Oscar answered quickly.

"Then shut them off," the colonel ordered. "And turn off those damned alarms before they drive us all crazy."

Within seconds the alarms were silenced, but the outside lights remained bright and defiant.

Oscar de la Garza yelled at a master sergeant to take some men over to the power station and shut off the power to all the outside lights.

"What could cause all of these alarms and lights to be triggered?" the general asked.

Oscar shrugged. "It's supposed to be impossible."

"Is there any natural phenomenon that could cause all of these alarms to go off at once?" General Beauharnais asked.

Oscar said that he doubted it. "Each system is isolated from the other. Each system has its own computer system. And they all send their output data to the master computer right here."

Colonel Kingsley wondered about a malfunction.

"All of our systems were in perfect working order before the alarm went off in the electronics building," Oscar reported.

"Someone must be messing around with the security system," Crawfoot suggested. "Can this system be accessed from the outside?"

"Absolutely no way," Oscar replied.

"Even by some very clever hacker?" Raul Agabarr challenged. "Some smartass hacker who's part of this rebellion?"

"No way," Oscar echoed himself, but his tone carried a trace of uncertainty.

General Beauharnais believed in immediate action at the time of a supposed threat. Philosophizing and second-guessing could come in more leisurely moments.

"Get on the phones," he ordered. "Kingsley, you call the Nellis base commander and have him send all of his available security personnel. Oscar, you handle the National Guard. Tell them to get out and check the perimeter of Area 51. Then recall every off duty military person at the Papoose and Groom facilities. And clear this room of nonessential personnel."

Kingsley scooped up the nearest phone and dialed 9 to access an outside line. After a few moments, he lifted the receiver to his ear. "Sir, the phones are dead."

Oscar de la Garza's confused expression verified that the same was true of his unit.

"Shit," the general shook his head in disbelief. "Are you telling me that the computers are jammed, the security system has gone haywire, the phones are inoperative, and we have no way to communicate with the outside world?"

One of the security personnel, a young sergeant, turned around from the computer console in front of him. "Hey, everyone, you'd better look at this."

Both military officers and civilian security personnel alike were startled to see the incredible data that was scrolling up the computer's screen.

"Where's that coming from?" General Beauharnais asked.

The young sergeant answered from his seat. "Sir, it's coming over Internet. Every network in the world is transmitting this message over and over. Every computer here at the Groom facilities is displaying this message and nothing short of turning off the power to each computer can stop it. It's like a virus."

Colonel Kingsley's brow was knitted with stress lines, and his eyes narrowed their focus. In a harsh whisper, he spoke aloud what the general could see for himself. "This message details everything you've told me about the MJ-12 committee, the Jexovah, the androids—everything that has been discovered about alien technology since the Roswell crash in 1947. Every person in the world will know about this before the sun comes up."

The sergeant seemed unable to take his eyes from the screen. "I calculate that the message is scrolling at two hundred words a minute, just about what the average reader can digest in that time. Holy shit! This stuff is blowing my mind!"

Crawfoot studied Raul Agabarr's baffled expression. "Someone really let the cat out of the bag, eh, amigo?"

"It's those fucking anarchists, Webster and Newsome," Agabarr sneered. "I know those assholes have something to do with this! If only I could have got that old bastard to talk."

General Beauharnais overheard the remark and stared at Agabarr, suspecting the worst.

Crawfoot grinned at his fellow security specialist and shook his head. He had no idea what 'old bastard' Agabarr was talking about, but he loved to push the man's buttons. "If the networks pick up on any of this, the world is going to change right before our miserable eyes, man. We'll be out of a job."

Agabarr was not amused. "You know that certain people will never permit that to happen."

Crawfoot laughed. "So what are they going to do about it now? There isn't a lie big enough to cover all of this."

Agabarr frowned and narrowed his eyes in disbelief. "Bullshit! Once we find who did this, how they managed to get the documents, and where they got the technology to kidnap the satellites, it will be easy to expose them as mad fanatics who created the whole thing as an elaborate hoax. And for frightening the general public in such an irresponsible manner, they will all go to prison for life."

Crawfoot pursed his lips in consideration of what Agabarr had said. "Unless you and me get to them first, huh?"

Agabarr's smile was almost demonic as he nodded and made a slashing movement across his throat with a forefinger.

Oscar was directing everyone's attention to the monitors on the far wall. "We have a satellite receiver that can pick up all of the cable and network broadcasts from all satellites within this region of the globe. The five monitors that you will see," he said, "are tuned to CBS, NBC, ABC, Fox, and CNN." He sat down at a control panel to manipulate a series of knobs and dials

It jarred the senses of the experienced technical and electronics personnel in the room to comprehend that all five networks were displaying exactly the same picture at the same time.

Blake Webster was reading a document detailing the initial alien autopsy after the Roswell crash as the actual MJ-12 script was displayed on the television screens.

This was followed by a list of scientists, politicians, and military personnel that had been eliminated or imprisoned in mental institutions by order of the MJ-12 committee. The information had been taken directly from the files of Dr. Carlton Farr.

Everyone in the room was enthralled with the broadcast—even those who understood that their world was about to make a very sudden and dramatic change.

At the general's order, Oscar switched to other channels. As the television sets received other channels, their screens would flicker, fill with noise lines, then the same transmission would reappear.

It was obvious to all technical personnel in the room that every satellite broadcast around the planet was transmitting the same images.

It was approaching ten-thirty. The room had been silent for nearly thirty minutes as each person watched the series of messages on a computer monitor or television screen.

At last Oscar broke his self-imposed silence. "General, I've just had a thought. The EG&G electronics shop has its own satellite uplink transmitter that is independent of the rest of the facility's computers and communications equipment. Perhaps we could send out some kind of counter message over their system if it isn't being jammed with the same transmission."

"It's worth a try," General Beauharnais agreed. "Let's get over there with some men right away."

Crawfoot stepped forward. "Be certain those men are armed, sir."

Colonel Kingsley wanted to know why weapons would be necessary to check on a satellite transmitter.

"Just a hunch that I have," Crawfoot said. "A few hours ago, our checkpoints gave clearance to a utility van from EG&G with four individuals who were supposed to be checking certain equipment on the base."

"Was there anything suspicious about their identification?" the general asked.

"No, but it just didn't feel right to me that a maintenance run would be ordered without prior notification."

"That's all you have to arouse your suspicions?" Colonel Kingsley frowned.

"Well, here's the thing," Crawfoot explained. "I noticed when they arrived that at first they just sat and watched the experimental craft being towed out of its hangar. They seemed more like tourists than experienced maintenance personnel. When they finally pulled forward to the communications building, three of them went into the building while the fourth sat in the van, like he was a lookout. I can't imagine why EG&G would send four maintenance personnel to do a job that three could do. Unless they're into featherbedding—in which case they should be called on it."

Agabarr supported his fellow security specialist. "It sounds very suspicious to me."

"We can't be too careful," Kingsley said. "If there's a logical explanation, then we can hear it from the EG&G people themselves."

General Beauharnais concurred. "But don't any of you security sharpshooters get carried away here," he warned. "This is has been a bizarre and unsettling evening, but we don't want to get unnerved by the strange situation to the point where we are shooting first and asking questions later."

Chapter Twenty-seven

Why Shoot the Messenger?

Joe Green gave Rainey Roberts a warm hug. "You did it! You blanketed the world with our message. You were terrific!"

Rainey accepted his praise. "But if your space buddies hadn't given us the password, we'd be in chains by now."

Blake Webster was all proud smiles. "I knew my wonder woman could pull it off. But now maybe we should boogie out of here. We've monitored everything for over half an hour, and we are assured that all systems are ripping the lid off the grand UFO cover-up. I think we should split just in case some hostile folks may have heard that alarm before you cut if off."

Joe agreed, but reminded him that they hadn't heard any warning buzz from the van. "They must be going nuts watching the transmissions."

Webster helped scoop up extra wires and cassette boxes into a utility bag. "Joe, I'm not going to relax until Rainey and I are on a plane headed for parts unknown to lay low for a while."

Just as Rainey opened the door to the outside, a white Jeep Grand Wagoneer with a blue star next to the Nellis AFB decal on the windshield pulled up beside their van. Within moments a blue Air Force six-pack extended cab pickup pulled in next to the Jeep. Six armed men in camouflage uniforms and automatic weapons jumped out of the pickup.

Bzzzz, bzzz

Wayne Newsome got off two quick punches on the radio button before it was snatched out of his hands.

"Shit!" Rainey exclaimed. "The bad guys are here!"

Blake pulled Rainey back inside and bolted the door with the sliding steel bar.

"What's going on?" Joe asked.

"There are at least seven or eight armed men outside. They've got Newsome," Blake told him. "It must have been that fucking alarm."

The door rattled slightly, and they turned their attention toward the noise. They could hear the key code latch disengage, and someone try to pull the door open. It didn't budge.

"The bar should hold them for a while," Blake said, the tension in his chest making his breath come in shallow gasps.

General Beauharnais watched as the men unsuccessfully attempted to open the door to the EG&G building. "Crawfoot," he spoke sharply, "you're the security expert. What do you recommend that we do next?"

"Secure the premises," Crawfoot answered. "I think we can assume that the people inside are responsible for the unauthorized transmissions."

Colonel Kingsley wondered about the intruder who had been waiting in the van.

Raul Agabarr was grinning broadly. "A marvelous catch, sir. It's Wayne Newsome, one of the notorious rabble rousers that we have been pursuing for so long. We can be certain that Blake Webster is one of those inside and that they are responsible for the trash being broadcast over the nets."

"As I was saying, sir," Crawfoot continued, "we can't negotiate with them because the phones, computers, and radios are jammed. I think we should cut power to the building, then blow the door and take them by force if necessary."

"Colonel Kingsley?" General Beauharnais wanted to know his fellow officer's assessment of the situation.

"I concur with Crawfoot, sir," he replied. "I'll send Oscar to get some of our explosives and demolition people to be ready to blow the door. Sergeant Epstein can summon Dr. Quinlin in case there are any injuries."

General Beauharnais nodded. "Force should not be necessary," he said firmly. "These are civilian protesters, not terrorists."

For the first time in many years, he was uncertain of what was the right thing to do. He knew his by-the-book duty; however, he also acknowledged that while the people inside might have broken a dozen federal laws just getting into Area 51 and seizing the building, they had also exposed MJ-12's conspiracy to cover-up alien intervention through humankind's history. For such a valiant feat, they should be given an A for their efforts—even though MJ-12 would probably patch up the leak quite easily with their usual tactics of character assassination, physical intimidation, and overt threats against life, limb, and family members. He wished that there was some way he could get the four watchdogs safely away from the turmoil in which they had embroiled themselves.

He thought of the months that he had endured the torture, starvation, humiliation, and ceaseless propaganda that were served up daily at the infamous Hanoi Hilton. He had served a tour in hell and survived, but he would never completely trust in his government again. He had vowed that should he live through his imprisonment and continue to be a military officer, he would never again compromise his values.

If he weren't in the military and he was an ordinary citizen, what would he want? The answer came quickly: He would want the truth, no matter how painful.

The MJ-12 committee of patriotic leaders feared that the public couldn't handle the truth, that such knowledge would undermine the very fabric of society and the essential tenets of all Earth's religions. But when was the last time that the government told the people the truth? When was the last time that the best interests of the government coincided with the best interests of the people?

The EG&G electronics room went dark. The lights, the equipment, and the monitor all went out at the same time. Joe could not see them, but he knew that Rainey and Blake stood within a few feet of him. He heard them gasp as a loud pounding began on the security door.

"Is this where it all ends?" Joe asked himself.

And then the frightened words of Rainey and Blake and the thuds of the violent pounding began to fade away. Once again, he heard the Jexovah speaking to him inside his head:

Government troops will confront you. Be at peace. The majority of people of the world will react favorably to the information you have transmitted. In not many of your Earth years, the governments of the world will be forced to change, to seek peace, to make compromises, and to form a one-world government. Because of the coming transitions, large numbers of humans will die in the years to come, but many will be transformed in the Rapture.

"Why will the transition cause the deaths of so many people?" Joe asked mentally.

Those humans with defective genes will no longer be able to generate offspring. They will be sterile. By the year 2009, sixty-two percent of the world's population will be sterile and will die of natural causes. You, Joseph Green, are the catalyst for the Chosen. Some will call you the Antichrist and will try to destroy you. You must prevail. You are the catalyst that will begin the Rapture.

Joe nearly laughed out loud. Prevail? They were as good as dead.

Death is a place of transition. The human spirit is indestructible. The mass collective unconscious is the network that holds all that has ever been and all that ever will be for the human species. You will never cease to exist.

The security door gave way on its hinges with a sudden resounding boom. It bounced off the wall and fell to the floor with a clang that nearly deafened the three occupants.

A dozen security and military personnel with automatic weapons raised entered the compound in an orderly rush. The beams of the laser targeting devices attached to the weapons filled the huge room with pinpoint lines of overlapping light. The armed personnel searched through the sea of infrared images, watching for movement, listening for any sound.

Rainey and Blake froze the moment the door fell, afraid to move, to talk, or even to breathe.

Joe got to his feet and called out to the men. "We're unarmed. Don't shoot. Don't harm us."

The lights flickered on for about two seconds before the breakers tripped and they went back off. The sudden flash of light caused the soldiers' infrared goggles to bloom with blinding brilliance before the surge gain control could adjust to the unexpected illumination. With Joe's movement and the distraction of the lights, the lead Wackenhut paramilitary soldier fired in reflex at the moving infrared hot spot.

Simultaneously with the flashing of the lights, Blake reached up and tried to pull Joe down, fearing for his safety. The selfless action on his part caused him to take the first bullet in his right shoulder.

Raul Agabarr hated to miss out on any firefight. He saw one figure spin to the floor, but a clear target was left standing. His rifle bullet caught Joe in the middle of the forehead and penetrated his skull.

Rainey's scream of terror and rage pierced the darkness.

"Hold your fire!" Crawfoot shouted. "Hold your fucking fire! I didn't give any order to shoot!"

Crawfoot moved forward in a crouch and watched for movement where the two men had fallen. The soldiers kept their place and allowed him to take the point position. He edged forward, a few inches at a time—and saw a foot sticking out from a prone body.

"You assholes!" Rainey denounced them in a shrill voice. "He tried to tell you we were unarmed. You've killed him. Goddam you all to hell!"

At that moment the lights came on. Crawfoot ripped off his goggles in time to see Agabarr leveling his weapon at the cursing woman. He reached out with cobra quickness and knocked the barrel of Agabarr's rifle off target.

Agabarr cursed, swinging the rifle toward Crawfoot. Then he regained control and laughed. "You're right, Crawfoot. It'll be more fun interrogating her."

In the next moment, Agabarr took a good look at the wounded man she was cradling in her arms. "Will you look at who we have here. It's Blake Webster himself, the blabbermouth with the microphone we just saw on all those television monitors. When we nabbed Newsome outside, I just knew this scumball had to be near. Oh, Mr. Webster, you don't know how long we've wanted to get our hands on you!"

"Bastard!" Rainey screamed at Agabarr. "He needs a doctor."

"The wages of sin, bitch!" Agabarr shot back. "What's your name?"

"You already said it, asshole," Rainey countered. "It's Bitch."

Colonel Kingsley edged forward through the men crowded around the wounded intruders. "You're right. It's the man we just saw on the satellite transmission."

"Blake Webster, sir," Agabarr said. "He's a known enemy of the government. We've been trying to track him down for a long time."

Colonel Kingsley would have to take Agabarr's word for the man's notoriety. The name meant nothing to him. "What about the others? The dead man?"

"Jesus Christ!" Oscar de la Garza exclaimed. "It's Joe Green. He works here. He's an engineer—and a damn brainy one. What the hell is he doing here?"

Crawfoot's memory banks responded quickly. Could it be the same Joe Green who had suffered the rapture of the deep under mysterious circumstances during their assignment in the Gulf of Tonkin?

"Shit!" Crawfoot spat as he stepped closer and verified his memory. "What the fuck is going on here? This guy is one of ours!"

"Was," Agabarr corrected. "And how is it that you two know a subversive agent who has just violated a dozen laws breaking into this place?"

Crawfoot scowled his displeasure at Agabarr's interrogation. "I served with him on a special mission. He's a stand-up guy."

"And I eat lunch with him," Oscar said. "He works here. He must have had a damn good reason for being here tonight. I think we just made a terrible mistake."

"These invaders made the mistake," Agabarr reminded them. "They breached security and transmitted a message of rebellion against the government."

Rainey was cradling Blake's head in her arms and crying. He was moaning, wincing at the pain. "Where is the goddam doctor?" she shouted. "This unarmed man you bastards shot needs a doctor!"

Crawfoot knelt beside Joe. He was surprised that his eyes showed movement. There was no chance that he could survive a wound like that. Blood was pouring from the hole in his forehead. What appeared to be bits of skull of brain were splattered on his collar.

Joe's open, staring eyes recognized his old buddy from the gig in the Gulf of Tonkin, and his mind spoke, even though his lips could not. *Mike Crawfoot! It really is you. Better hurry if you're going to pull me back into the boat this time. I feel like I'm sinking fast. Going to rapture again.*

Crawfoot had a sudden flash of recognition. It had been Joe that he had seen at Dr. Farr's place at Medina Lake. "Joe Green! What the fuck is a straight-out guy like you doing involved in this mess?"

Joe smiled. *It's my destiny. It was the right thing to do. The people have to know the truth. Don't you remember how we used to talk about how the government was always screwing over the little guys? The truth had to come out!*

Crawfoot could not believe that Joe was still alive after sustaining such a wound. "Hang on, Joe. A medic will be here any minute."

Joe's mind began to drift. He was floating in a sea of peace. Maybe he really was back in the ocean.

Joe began to ride a river of energy, moving rapidly down a tube of light, sensing the spirit of collective humankind flowing past him at a dizzying pace. A tendril of his mind searched for a safe point to probe the energy as he became aware that the wrong move would cause him to be sucked into a vortex of infinite energy that somehow contained the everlasting spirits of all sentient beings that had ever lived.

If you enter the void, Joseph Green, you cannot return. Hold onto your awareness of the now. You have not completed the plan. You are the Catalyst for the Chosen Ones.

Joe did not wish to be chosen for anything. "I'm no one. What's so special about me? It is so peaceful to be near the energy. I want to be one with it."

You have not completed the plan. You are special because you are the Catalyst for the Rapture. The combination of your spiritual energy and your genetic structure is unique among humankind. Very soon, you will begin the Rapture.

Because of your transmitting the messages of our existence, the world now knows that there are intelligent, peaceful aliens observing them, watching over them. The influence of Jexovah on humankind has been explained. The governments of the world are now powerless to explain away the mass of evidence. We have prepared the way for you to fulfill your part in the plan.

Joe told them to do whatever they had to do without him. How could he make a difference?

One human can make a difference. One human can change the world. With our help, you can make a difference, and you can change the world. The time is at hand.

Joe remained unconvinced. "I don't want to be a part of billions of people dying. How can you ask me to do something that will cause so many deaths?"

Almost one hundred million humans die on your planet every year. Some die of natural causes and from accidents. Most die from starvation, disease, war, and crime. Starvation, disease, war, and crime can be stopped. It will be stopped after the Rapture is completed.

"I need to rest," Joe told the voice. "No more talking. Please."

Dr. Quinlin looked up into Crawfoot's grim face after completing a brief examination of Joe Green's condition. "There's nothing that can be done."

General Beauharnais stood waiting for the doctor's reading of the situation. Dr. Quinlin said that it was just as it appeared to the layman. One man was dying with only minutes to live. Another had been wounded in the shoulder.

"All right, Doctor," Colonel Kingsley said. "Take the injured man to the infirmary and patch him up. As soon as the other dies, put him in the cooler until we decide how we're going to handle this situation."

"Crawfoot," General Beauharnais demanded, "who gave the order to open fire on unarmed civilians?"

Crawfoot's fists opened and closed in mute frustration as he studied the bloody visage of his dying friend. "It wasn't me, sir. That bastard Agabarr overstepped his bounds."

The computer notebook that Oscar de la Garza carried in a thigh holster started beeping in a high-pitched tone. Apparently communications were no longer jammed. He slipped it out and stepped a few paces back from the others. After a hurried conversation, he approached the general, pale-faced and shaken. "General, we're being invaded! Guards at the north gate say that there are thousands of vehicles entering the area."

Colonel Kingsley scowled his disbelief. "How is this confirmed?"

"Our guards can see them from the towers," Oscar told him. "Thousands of lights coming across Groom Lake from Rachel. Thousands of vehicles moving toward us."

Chapter Twenty-eight

Prophet, Heal Thyself

Page St. John's bus led the motor caravan around the north end of Groom Lake. The number of pilgrims in the gathering had reached over thirteen thousand, fitting themselves into over two thousand vehicles. They had come from all over the United States, Canada, and Mexico—all touched by the message of the Celestial Prophet that the Chosen One would appear somewhere near Rachel, Nevada, during St. John's crusade and set the Rapture into motion.

From the West Coast, the East Coast, the Midwest, the South, hundreds upon hundreds of cars, pickups, trucks, buses, campers, recreational vehicles, and motorcycles joined the caravan as its tendrils moved out toward Reno, Salt Lake City, Denver, Phoenix, then all converged toward Rachel.

Within a few minutes of the alert received by Oscar de la Garza from the base's restored communications system, Page St. John's golden Glory Bus was pulling up beside the Groom Lake security building. The vehicles in the massive automotive caravan of the Celestial Church were parked along the taxi-way and the dry lake bed.

Among the first things that Colonel Matt Kingsley noticed about the incredible sea of mixed humanity moving toward them was the great number of television cameras bobbing up and down among its waves. Even a cursory glance told him that every major network and dozens of television stations were represented.

Among the first orders that the Colonel issued were to the Wackenhut security officers to lower their weapons. He certainly had no intention of killing any more civilians that night. "We must assume that while highly illegal and unsolicited, this assemblage is peaceful in intent," he said. "But be watchful and alert."

Page St. John emerged from his bus, issuing a cheery greeting to the military officers arrayed before him. "We come in peace, sirs, to welcome the Chosen One, whom God has told me awaits us here on this base."

General Beauharnais stepped forward from the soldiers who flanked him. "Are you aware that you are illegally on a secret Federal facility and that there is a very stiff fine and imprisonment for trespassing?"

St. John, a big man with a deep, commanding voice and piercing green eyes, bowed his full head of white hair in a gesture of submission. "I am but a pawn of God, General. I go where He commands and directs."

"I know of your group, Reverend," Oscar de la Garza told him. "I've even heard you on the radio a couple of times late at night."

"Then, my friend, you may be aware that we are standing on hallowed ground, the very place where the Chosen One will lead the true believers from the revelation to the Rapture," the minister said. "He will lead us to the new tomorrow, a tomorrow filled with God's chosen children."

General Beauharnais had no idea how he would handle this most unusual situation. Nothing in his vast military experience had prepared him for Page St. John and the Celestial Church.

"Hasn't all this already been done?" General Beauharnais asked. "The Chosen People of God already made the trek across the desert with Moses, several thousand years ago. And what makes you think that your so-called 'Chosen One' would be on a secret military base, anyway?"

St. John was unhesitatingly direct. "It is not I who decide such things, General. The voices of God and the angels directed me. They named the place where we would find him. Besides, haven't your communications people been watching the television networks and monitoring the computer nets? The message of the Jexovah and the government cover-up of their presence has been broadcast all over the world—from this very base! That's the work of the Chosen One."

Raul Agabarr could be silent no longer. "That was the work of subversive elements. You mistakenly credit to your God the deeds of misguided and deceitful men."

St. John cast Agabarr a baleful look that would have wilted a less aggressive man. "Woe be to the one in error who distorts the righteous work of the true Children of God."

Crawfoot decided he would just sit this one out and watch the others trying to handle an extraordinary occurrence. What the hell were they going to do with thirteen thousand religious fanatics seeking their so-called Chosen One and determined to invade their base? This would be like thirteen thousand shepherds invading Bethlehem all at once to pay homage to the Christ child at the manger.

Colonel Kingsley wondered how St. John would know the Chosen One if he saw him or her?

"I do not know why he is here, Colonel," St. John answered honestly. "As I told you, the voice of the angel of God told me he would be here. Who will he be and what will he look like? The voice said to me, 'You will know him by his suffering, and he will fill your minds with truth.' "

General Beauharnais knew that it would be fruitless to stand there and debate theology with Page St. John. All that would remain would be an unprecedented situation and over twelve thousand citizens to deal with.

"Would you please tell your people to stay with their vehicles until we have some time to decide how best to deal with this, ah, unusual situation?" he requested. "No one must wander around this base. This is a highly classified installation, and I am responsible for it. I must insist on some semblance of order until we sort all of this out."

"Certainly, General," St. John said. "We shall comply with your request. Our initiated Celestial Servants, our priests, will see to it that order is maintained among our pilgrims."

The reverend glanced at his watch. "It is now just a few minutes past midnight. Let us say that dawn arrives at around six o'clock. We will give you nearly six hours to provide us with access to the base so that we may find our Chosen One. That seems most reasonable to me."

A few minutes later, back in his office, General Beauharnais asked what they knew about Page St. John and the Celestial Church.

Raul Agabarr volunteered that they had quite a file on the man. "His father was a Protestant chaplain in the Air Force who served in WW II and the Korean War. He became disillusioned with orthodoxy and developed a more liberal approach to theology, which his son Page picked up. When he became a seminary dropout in the 1960s, he became a popular hippie preacher among the flower children. We suspect that he has been a long-time communist sympathizer."

Oscar de la Garza had more to add, but first he wanted to moderate his colleague's view. "Agabarr smells a Red under every bed. There's no reason to suspect St. John of being politically subversive. He wrote a religious bestseller in the late '80s entitled *The Celestial Prophet,* in which he attempted to extract the basic moral highlights from all of the world's leading religions. That's when he decided to start a one-world religion."

Agabarr interjected with the charge that anything having to do with a "one world" theme was probably communistic in nature.

"Well, be that as it may," Oscar continued, "the direction St. John went next was not likely to earn red stars in the Kremlin. He started to preach that the human race is descended from aliens that came to Earth during the dawn of civilization. He also believes that every spirit is reincarnated until each individual spirit has achieved enough goodness and wisdom to rise permanently to the next plane of existence. All forms of ESP and psychic phenomena, as well as UFO sightings, are explained by these beliefs. Furthermore, all mystical experiences are an aspect of Oneness with the spiritual universe."

Agabarr clucked his tongue in derision. "My goodness, Oscar, how do you know so much about this religious fanatic's church? Did you become a member?"

Oscar sighed in acceptance of the reality that he had to tolerate Agabarr because the man had been placed on the base on the authority of some unknown higher command. "For your information, I am a Roman Catholic. But, you see, I read newspapers, watch a little television, listen to the radio, even read an occasional book. All these are marvelous sources of information about our contemporary culture."

General Beauharnais thanked de la Garza and Agabarr, indicating that he had heard enough about Page St. John. Now he wanted to know more about Joe Green and the other intruders.

"Green and Webster are under Dr. Quinlin's care." Crawfoot responded. "The last I checked, Green is still alive."

"Incredible," Colonel Kingsley marveled. "How could anyone survive even a few seconds with such a head wound?"

Crawfoot continued. "We learned that the woman is Lorraine 'Rainey' Roberts, an employee of EG&G."

Agabarr snapped his fingers. "I knew it had to be an inside job. Both Green and Roberts, fucking traitors."

"The other man is Wayne Newsome…"

Agabarr interrupted again. "Newsome is a well known environmental activist and conspiracy buff. He's been scouting our classified bases here in the desert for years. A real pain in the government's ass."

Crawfoot nodded agreement. "We are detaining both Roberts and Newsome until the best course of action is decided upon."

Agabarr smiled like the fox that has found the henhouse door wide open. "I'll interrogate them and find out how wide a ring of conspiracy is involved. There's no way that these four could have pulled this off by themselves."

General Beauharnais slammed his open palm down on his desk. "You'll do no such thing, Mr. Agabarr. The citizens remain in Crawfoot's custody until I decide how I'm going to handle this mess. Is that understood?"

Agabarr would not easily surrender his fresh victims. "Sir, your most recent orders advised you to tighten security and to get tougher on citizen trespassers. My God, if there was ever a clear-cut case in which…"

General Beauharnais narrowed his eyes and pointed a forefinger three inches from Agabarr's nose. "You heard my order!"

Agabarr turned first to de la Garza, then to Crawfoot for support. Both men looked away from him. "Yes, sir," he hissed in open contempt. "Your order will be obeyed."

Although Dr. Quinlin had sought to keep him heavily sedated, Blake Webster sat at the side of Joe Green's bed and wondered what miracle was keeping the man alive.

Joe was oblivious to the outside world, and he had no desire to return to it.

The Rapture came slowly at first, ever so slowly. Joe's psyche was an observer to the outwardly unseen genetic change enveloping his being. He felt a touch here, a probe there. Blood clotted. Cells rejuvenated. New bone formed over torn and ruptured bone. Proteins, enzymes, and chemical nutrients worked their own unique functions.

Joe floated in a place located somewhere in the farthest reaches of his mind. A flash of memory, then a string of neurons firing. There were moments when he felt as though his psyche was the center of an intense cornucopia of mystical stimuli, a frenzied psychedelic fireworks show. His very essence was suspended in time, a time without form, a time outside of time. It was as if he could perceive whole universes contained within his mind. He was surrounded by a field of energy that was made up of billions of spirits of humans who had once lived.

And then there was an unseen stranger near him, a powerful alien mind that had the power to dissipate his life forces with the passing of a millisecond. Joe felt no sense of fear. He knew somehow that this was no mere Jexovah android, but a god with power unknown to mere mortals. Euphoria enveloped him, and he felt at peace with All That Is.

You are experiencing the Rapture. You are the Catalyst for the Chosen Ones. Your body has been injured. We have repaired your injured bone and tissue. In the future, your body will be able to heal and repair itself. When you awaken, you will be ready to bring about the beginning of the Rapture. It will then engulf nearly half of all humankind.

Speak the truth to all those you meet. Seek to encounter as many humans as possible. Your special talent will be touching those who would Rapture. Your special knowledge is the truth.

Joe wondered where he would find those who wished to Rapture.

They will come to you. They will be all around you. They will find you, and they, the vanguard of the Chosen, will in turn touch others who will Rapture.

Many will be awaiting you when you awaken. They have been following a signal broadcast from this area on a frequency that only certain of your species can perceive. This area, the one you call Dreamland, was once a base of the Jexovah, many Earth centuries ago. Far beneath the earth at this place there are machines and implements whose purpose would as yet be incomprehensible to your science.

Rest now, for many await your catalytic presence when you awaken.

Dr. Quinlin re-entered the small intensive care room next to the infirmary to check on Blake Webster. Two Wackenhut guards stood at the door to prevent the patient from checking himself out of the doctor's medical supervision.

"Hey, Doc, put Joe on a life support system," Webster said. "Don't you guys still take that oath to cure people?"

Dr. Quinlin frowned in disbelief, bent to look closer at Joe. "I didn't expect him to live two minutes when we brought him in here. It's been nearly four hours."

"That's what I'm talking about, Doc. Shouldn't you at least go through the motions of giving a shit?"

Dr. Quinlin shot Blake a dirty look, then positioned his stethoscope to listen to Joe's heart. "What the hell?"

"What?" Webster insisted on knowing.

The doctor looked confused, pale. "It's not possible."

"What? Tell me what's happening here, Doc."

One of the medics had wrapped a bandage around Joe's head wound. Dr. Quinlin gingerly removed the blood wrapping and emitted a sharp gasp of complete shock.

"There's no wound," he said, wiping Joe's forehead with a swatch of cotton. "There is absolutely no sign of the head trauma. No entrance or exit wound."

Webster ignored the pain from his shoulder wound and edged the doctor aside. "Holy Mary! You're right, man!"

"Of course I'm right!" Dr. Quinlin shouted. "I'm a doctor. But how is it possible?"

Webster shook his head. "You tell me. Remember, you're the doctor!"

Dr. Quinlin excused himself and called for an orderly to remain with Webster. His head was swimming. He was a rigid man of science, devoted to the logical, the rational—and the predictable. Nothing in his medical experience had prepared him for what he had just witnessed. By everything that he understood about the material world and its physical laws, what had just occurred to Joe Green was completely impossible.

And then, although Dr. Quinlin had never believed in such things as intuition, he suddenly received a mental impression that he knew that he must fulfill.

He called another orderly to his side. "Crim, that prisoner that we've been carrying for in the holding cell. Take another man with you and bring him up here to the infirmary."

Crim hesitated, recalling the grim visage of Raul Agabarr. "Do we need any other authorization?"

Dr. Quinlin shook his head. "None at all. Now please be quick about it."

Somehow the doctor knew that the man that Agabarr had so terribly tortured was connected with these men. Somehow he knew that the wretch lying in that underground cell needed to be in the presence of Joe Green. It was as if something deep inside his mind was telling him these things.

Dr. Quinlin shouted for one of the guards, Sergeant Beckwith, to get General Beauharnais, on the double.

When Sergeant Beckwith arrived at the general's office, he found that Page St. John was in the process of making an appeal.

"...But the voices told me emphatically, sir," St. John was saying. "I have just been told that the one we seek lies in the infirmary."

General Beauharnais had not been at all pleased when the reverend had blustered his way into his office. It seemed that some loose-lipped security officers had told him about the invasion of the base and revealed that two of the intruders had been wounded.

"I'm only asking that you grant me permission to see for myself if one of the men is our Chosen One, the Catalyst who will begin the Rapture," St. John pleaded. "Send a dozen armed soldiers with me. I'll not do anything disruptive."

Colonel Kingsley burst into unrestrained laughter. "Not do anything disruptive? What the hell do you call bringing thirteen thousand unauthorized citizens to a highly secret military base?"

"Under God's orders," St. John readjusted the charge.

Sergeant Beckwith took advantage of the pause in the heated dialogue. "Sir, Dr. Quinlin has asked me to bring you to the infirmary at once."

General Beauharnais frowned, "Surely the doctor knows that I am very busy just now."

"Yes, sir, I'm sure he does, sir. But I think something really important has happened."

Colonel Kingsley shrugged. "The engineer Green died."

"No, sir, he hasn't."

General Beauharnais was taken aback. "The man is still alive?"

"More than that, sir. I really don't wish to say, but from what Corporal Sneed and I could hear from the door, I think he's gotten better."

Page St. John was back on his feet in triumph. "There it is! Don't you see? This Joe Green must be the Chosen One."

General Beauharnais leaned back in his chair, suddenly uncertain of nearly everything. "At the very least, he's a medical miracle."

He reached for his telephone and quickly punched in the numbers for the infirmary. After three rings, an orderly answered. After another wait of nearly two minutes, Dr. Quinlin was at the other end of the line.

"Dr. Quinlin, what is Sergeant Beckwith suggesting?"

"He shouldn't be suggesting anything unless he was eavesdropping more than I thought."

"Then you tell me what's going on over there."

"Quite simply, sir, the fellow that was brought in here with a fatal head wound is not only still alive, his vital signs are perfect."

General Beauharnais paused a moment to consider what he had just heard. "So you are telling me that a man who was shot in the head and should, by all rights, be long dead is now recovering?"

"General, what I am telling you is that I can't find anything at all wrong with him."

"It can't be. What about his massive head trauma?"

"There is only the slightest of scars to indicate where the wound once existed."

General Beauharnais shook his head in disbelief. "Dr. Quinlin, I'm on my way over there to see this for myself."

Dr. Quinlin was not expecting such a large entourage to accompany the general to the small infirmary. Colonel Kingsley, Michael Crawfoot, and Page St. John had accompanied Sergeant Beckwith to observe the medical miracle that had occurred at Groom Lake.

"Doctor," the general wanted to know, "if some miraculous healing event has taken place, then why is he still unconscious?"

St. John answered before the doctor could state his medical opinion. "He will awaken at dawn. He is the Chosen One. He's the one that the aliens have called the Catalyst, the key to the Rapture."

The Reverend stepped forward and gently touched Joe's forehead. "Yes, yes. I can feel his energy. This young man will change the world. I have been told that in my visions."

Crawfoot looked at his old friend and saw for himself that the head wound had disappeared. "I always knew him to be a pretty tough hombre, but this is beyond belief."

"He will awaken at dawn and begin the Rapture," St. John said again.

General Beauharnais excused himself, saying that he had to get in touch with the Director at the NSA to get some objective input on how to handle such a strange, unprecedented occurrence.

Blake Webster sat up in his bed next to Joe's. "Joe was always taking about the Rapture. What the heck is it?"

Page St. John chuckled. "You'll see for yourself tomorrow, friend. You know, I've preached about it for nearly thirty years, but I never really thought that I would get to see it for myself."

Only minutes after General Beauharnais and Colonel Kingsley left the infirmary, orderly Crim and a security officer wheeled Red Redding into the room where Dr. Quinlin, Page St. John, and Mike Crawfoot stood beside the bed of Joe Green.

"Here's the patient you requested, sir," Crim said. He could not imagine why the doctor would want this tortured wretch of a human shell on view in the infirmary. It seemed to him that such a terrible example of Agabarr's monstrous skills would be better left hidden in the underground cell.

Dr. Quinlin nodded, dismissed the orderly and the security officer.

"Merciful, Father," Page St. John cried out. "What happened to that man?"

"It's Red," Blake Webster gasped. "Oh, dear Jesus, Red, what in God's name have they done to you!"

Red's eyes seemed sightless as his head rolled from side to side on his shoulders. Spittle flowed from a corner of his mouth into a matted tangle of beard. The hospital gown that covered his nakedness was stained with urine and feces.

Dr. Quinlin inhaled sharply, feeling a fresh rush of guilt for his role in the brutal interrogation of the man. Somehow he had known that the "desert prospector" was connected to Webster.

Webster struggled to his feet, gritting his teeth against the pain in his shoulder as he left the hospital bed. Tears stung his eyes, and he made no effort to hide his anguish.

"Red, Red. This is all my fault. I never should have let you stay in the area after…" Webster knelt to embrace his friend with his good arm. "I'm sorry, Buddy. Oh, God forgive me, I am so sorry."

Crawfoot was bending over Red, conducting his own silent inspection. "It's Agabarr. Some day I'm going to give that bastard a taste of his own medicine."

Dr. Quinlin picked up one of Red's wrists to check his pulse. He had two medical curiosities to examine. A man with a fatal head wound who would not die and who was defying all medical truths by healing himself, and a man who had literally had his brains fried and scrambled and who stubbornly clung to scattered shreds of a reality that also lay beyond medical science.

Suddenly Red's head stopped its back and forth motion. His eyes seemed to focus for the first time since he had been wheeled into the room. A spark of recognition seemed kindled by Joe's supine form in the bed nearest him.

Dr. Quinlin could not suppress a shiver that ran up his spine. This was amazing, and yet he had received a premonition that the mentally damaged prisoner needed to be near Joe Green. Perhaps one miracle might create another.

Red leaned forward in his wheelchair and reached out to touch Joe's hand.

"Does Joe know this guy?" Crawfoot wanted to know.

Webster cleared his throat as he wiped his eyes. "Only casually, but recently Joe established kind of a mental linkup with him. That's how we knew Red was still alive."

Crawfoot and Dr. Quinlin looked quizzically at him, but Webster scowled back at them. "It might sound weird to you guys, but it just happens to be true."

Dr. Quinlin shrugged. After this bizarre evening, he would probably hang up his shingle and become a witch doctor.

"Joe is touching this man's soul," Page St. John said. "As the Chosen One, Joe has many such abilities. They are blending together in spirit."

Everyone in the small room was astonished when the seemingly unconscious Joe Green opened his fingers to accept Red's hand in his own.

Dr. Quinlin stepped over to Joe and placed a stethoscope over his heart. "He keeps getting stronger, but he still appears to be unconscious…"

"But aware," St. John interrupted. "He's more aware on the soul level than all of us put together. He's aware of everything happening around him in this world and in the world beyond."

Red coughed twice, then shook his head as if awakening from a deep sleep. He looked around him in momentary confusion and smiled when his newly regenerated eyes focused on Blake Webster. "Hey, man," he chuckled, "I have been on one really weird trip."

Chapter Twenty-nine

Rapture the Chosen

At 7:00 A.M. on September 10, Joseph Green stepped out of the Groom Lake infirmary and faced the crowd that had gathered to await the appearance of the Chosen One that Reverend Page St. John had promised them. There were people of all ages, all ethnic groups, all faiths gathered to greet the beginning of the Rapture. The sun had just cleared the mountains, and it was a cool, dry morning.

Broadcast and print journalists from all over the country had been given special clearance to land at the classified area and their civilian helicopters sat out on the dry lake bed. Within minutes of establishing a satellite feed signal from Groom Lake, the major networks of the nation and the world awaited the arrival of the person that the Church of the Celestial Prophet called the Chosen One.

Ten hours after he had received what should have been a fatal head wound, Joe Green appeared in the white slacks and white shirt the doctor had given him to replace his blood-soaked clothing. As he strode purposefully toward the area where Page St. John stood, Joe was followed by General Alexander Beauharnais, Colonel Matthew Kingsley, Rainey Roberts, Blake Webster, and Wayne Newsome.

Just a few feet behind them in a wheelchair pushed by Dr. Quinlin was Red Redding, smiling broadly at the sun that he had not seen for over a week. Within a few minutes of contact with Joe, he was well on the path to a full recovery of his mental and physical capacities.

The grim-faced military officers had been advised by the NSA to allow the religious passion play to expend its energy naturally. The Director believed that General Beauharnais had greatly exaggerated about the alleged miracle cure, but he advised him that it would be most unwise to use any kind of force on any assembled group of citizens of such magnitude, especially if their motives were religious in nature. Besides, with the news media there in droves, it would be exceedingly bad public relations to expel the people forcefully. Let them be, the Director stated. Once they saw their Messiah was just an ordinary man, they would disband on their own. And then, damn it! Tighten security so that a lizard couldn't get onto Area 51 without special clearance!

Raul Agabarr moved closer to Michael Crawfoot and spoke in a low voice. "It's up to us now, Crawfoot."

Crawfoot frowned his disgust with the man. "What are you talking about?"

Agabarr nodded toward the crowd. "These fools have all been taken in by this mystic mumbo-jumbo—and that includes Beauharnais and Kingsley. It's up to us to instill some order into this chaos."

Crawfoot studied the man silently for several moments before he responded. "What do you have in mind?"

"Our original orders have been somewhat revised. MJ-12 wants you to take out the general, and I'm to hit Green and Webster."

Crawfoot moved his arm away from Agabarr's touch. "Fuck off. I told you Joe Green was a friend of mine."

Agabarr's eyes narrowed in surprise. "You're disobeying orders? A pro like you? I talked to Trent just an hour ago. He repeated your original order to erase Beauharnais if he should demonstrate weakness and a reluctance to follow the orders that MJ-12 dictated to him. The Committee added Green and Webster as threats to national security."

Crawfoot had nothing but contempt for the man standing before him. "Screw those orders," he told Agabarr.

Agabarr was astonished. "MJ-12 will eat your ass for breakfast."

Crawfoot shrugged. "I just resigned. And if you try to carry out those orders, I'll smoke you where you stand. If you make one wrong move toward Joe Green, I'll blow you in half."

Agabarr's hand seemed involuntarily to move toward the holstered automatic on his hip.

Crawfoot smiled at the man's reflexes. "Want to go for it, scumbag? Right here and now? How about our own gunfight at the OK Corral? Go ahead. Count three, draw your piece."

Agabarr lips twitched nervously.

"Well?" Crawfoot challenged. "Want me to give you a head start?"

Agabarr knew that Mike Crawfoot was a professional killer with ice water in his veins. His own skills lay more in the interrogation of prisoners than in gunfighting. Without another word, he turned on his heel and disappeared into the crowd.

As Joe Green walked through the mass of expectant humanity, journalists and broadcasters talked into their microphones and cellular phones, explaining that this man standing before them was someone extraordinary. He had been repeatedly abducted by aliens, and he had been one of the key instigators that had broadcast previously classified information about the aliens and the U.S. government to the world. The night before, he had suffered a fatal wound to the head, and now it appeared that a miracle had taken place and he had been completely healed.

To the thousands of men and women assembled there that day, such a miracle was taken as proof that the Chosen One had appeared. This was a happening that had the momentum to change the world as they knew it.

A light breeze carried whispers and quietly spoken words throughout the crowd. Dozens of camera crews from the networks and area television stations frog-walked and crouched beside Joe as he moved slowly through the multitude. He could feel an ocean of faith and love emanating from the people. He felt the new energy that filled him with each breath. He had never felt so alive, so full of peace and happiness.

Although someone had handed Joe a cordless microphone, he returned it with a smile of thanks. He didn't intend to preach to the crowd, nor did he wish to remain aloof or distant from the anxious faithful and hopeful. He moved through the people with ease and confidence, touching, hugging, shaking hands, making contact with all who reached out to him.

Each time Joe made contact with a new individual, the energy flowed from him to that person, beginning the change in humanhood that would forever be known as the Rapture.

Slowly the transformation began in the majority of the people with whom he had contact, and as they touched others, they also effected the same manner of change that Joe Green had begun in them. The power spread throughout the crowd in concentric waves.

A tall African-American of about forty-five with a high, receding hairline stepped forward holding his eight-year-old daughter in his arms.

Joe knew that the man, Melvin Perkins, was a successful attorney in Newark, New Jersey. His wife, Clara, was an elementary school teacher. They had put their lives on hold to make the journey to Area 51 with their daughter Gena, who had muscular dystrophy in both legs, because Page St. John had promised that they would find the Chosen One in the desert.

Joe held the little girl's hand for a moment and kissed her forehead as he moved on.

Susan McIver was maneuvered through the crowd in a wheelchair by her sister, Deliah. Susan had broken her back when a drunk driver had plowed into her station wagon five years ago. She had been living with Deliah and her husband George Dickson. She had received the call to come to see the Chosen One, and she felt the healing energy enter her when Joe stopped to give both her and Deliah a hug.

Joe saw that there were a number of handicapped people in the multitude who had heard the call. Orville Sims, a veteran of the Korean conflict who had been blinded by an ordnance explosion forty-five years ago, was escorted through the crowd by a young woman in a red dress. Joe said a few encouraging words to Orville and his daughter Cissy before he was pulled away.

There were so many others, such as Theresa Mueller, a young doctor who had told her professional friends and family members that she had been abducted by aliens. She had been committed by her family, and her friends had testified against her to the state medical board, which suspended her license to practice medicine. Had it not been for an old boyfriend who was an attorney, she might still be confined.

Some of the people in the crowd had Bibles, others had copies of *The Celestial Prophet* in their hands. They had been called. They had come. And each of them hoped that they might be able to touch or to talk to the man

Page St. John called the Chosen One. Joe sensed many in the crowd who had been touched in some way by the Jexovah at some time in their lives.

He had progressed only a few steps farther when he heard Melvin Perkins shouting that his daughter Gena could walk. Although others near Perkins began an excited murmur and delivered shouts of praise to the Chosen One, Joe was also able to hear Susan McIver's scream of joy that her broken back had been healed and Orville Sim's cries of jubilation that he could see.

It was no surprise to Joe, who could divine each person with whom he came into contact, who would be the ones who would Rapture. And he knew that each person who received the Rapture would become mentally and physically whole. The individual miracles were caused by each person's faith and genetic ability to Rapture. Their newfound strength would grow daily, and over a period of time, new insights and abilities would come to each of them.

Joe also perceived, in a rush of awareness, that over eighty percent of the people assembled there that day would Rapture. After all, it was a very select audience.

Not everyone in the crowd was vibrating with love and the expectancy of entering the Rapture. Joe sensed a threat to his well-being approaching him from behind.

Joe turned suddenly to face Raul Agabarr as he was pulling his pistol from its holster. A news cameraman captured both Joe and Agabarr in his lens as the gleam of the stainless steel pistol pointed toward Green's chest.

Unexpectedly, Joe reached out and grabbed Agabarr's gun hand. He didn't try to take the weapon from him, he just held it while it was pointed at his chest. His assassin seemed frozen, unable to pull the trigger or even to breathe.

Joe looked deeply into Agabarr's eyes, and the energy flowed from him into the would-be murderer. A woman screamed. A couple pushed away from the gunman. The newsman pulled the camera closer to the confrontation.

The moment the surge of energy flowed into him, Agabarr felt something deep within him shatter. He didn't resist when Crawfoot relived him of his weapon.

"You murdering bastard," Crawfoot snarled as he pushed his way through the crowd to stand next to Joe. "I warned you."

"That's the crud who shot Joe in the head," Wayne Newsome shouted. "I heard some of the security guys talking. It was Raul Agabarr."

Red shook his head sadly from his wheelchair. "That man is a devil. He loves torture like a drunk loves booze."

The crowd was milling around, shouting for the assassin to be delivered into their hands.

But then Joe and the men and women who had Raptured or been healed by his touch lifted their right hands in unison. "No violence," he declared, and all those who had entered the Rapture echoed his words. "We have moved beyond that, brothers and sisters."

The crowd stepped aside to allow General Beauharnais and his men to catch up to Joe and the subdued assassin.

"Agabarr, what the hell did you think you were doing?" Colonel Kingsley demanded.

Raul's eyes narrowed in contempt. "You're all mad and under this man's spell. It's some kind of mass hypnosis."

Joe knew that Agabarr would not Rapture. The depravity within him was too deeply entrenched. And when they had briefly intermingled energies, Joe sensed that the man had knowledge of a horror nearly beyond the parameters of the darkest imagination.

Suddenly he had a clear picture of the monstrous evil within Raul Agabarr's mind. "General," Joe shouted, "you must evacuate this base at once! There's an air strike on its way!"

General Beauharnais was stunned. There were too many things happening at once. "An air strike! What are you saying?"

Agabarr's eyes widened in surprise, then he laughed and shook his head in wonder. "I don't know how this witch doctor does it, but he's managed to hit the bull's-eye. Not that this knowledge will do you any good now."

Crawfoot grabbed Agabarr's upper arm in a powerful grip. "What the hell is going on?"

Agabarr tried to shake off the vise that held him, then he sneered openly at Crawfoot before he spoke to General Beauharnais. "I telephoned MJ-12 several hours ago and reported to Colonel Trent what was happening here at Groom Lake. That's when he gave me orders to eliminate Green and Webster. Crawfoot here was supposed to take out General Beauharnais for not following his orders from MJ-12."

"The air strike!" Kingsley prompted. First things first, but now he was also keeping one eye on Crawfoot.

"Once we had hit our men, Trent warned me to get off the base as quickly as possible," Agabarr explained with a triumphant fervor. "Eli Jerrold has ordered an air strike to destroy the Celestial Church movement."

"A direct attack on defenseless and innocent citizens?" Kingsley's mouth dropped open.

"And on a classified base of the United States Air Force," General Beauharnais added incredulously. "MJ-12 is prepared to murder thousands of unarmed citizens and destroy a military base with all its personnel in an attempt to keep its dirty little secrets!"

Crawfoot dropped his customary cool. "Secrets that Green and Webster and their gang have already broadcast around the world! What would they gain—except revenge?"

"You must give an immediate order to disperse, to evacuate the area," Joe said. "Some people might still make it out alive."

The general was feeling lightheaded, disoriented. "Yes, yes, of course. We must at least attempt an evacuation." Could all of this truly be happening? "How…how long do we have?"

Agabarr was clearly enjoying watching them attempt to deal with the knowledge of their impending death. "I don't know," he shrugged. "And I could give a fuck."

Crawfoot took a menacing step toward him.

"I really don't know," Agabarr insisted. "Maybe hours. Maybe minutes. The cover story is to be that Groom Lake was overrun by anti-American terrorists. The military then had no choice but to destroy the base, even if it meant blasting military personnel along with the terrorists."

"The monsters on MJ-12 have to be insane," Crawfoot said. He felt disgust that he had been their tool of death for so long, and he felt horror that he had believed that he was somehow acting in the best interests of the nation. Just an obedient, unquestioning soldier following orders, however distasteful.

Webster laughed sardonically at Crawfoot's sudden realization of the evil machinations of MJ-12. "I've been trying to tell everyone that they were monsters for years now. Damn shame they have to prove it to some of you by killing us all."

Colonel Kingsley glowered at Crawfoot. "So Beauharnais' suspicions about you were accurate? You really were sent here to take him out if he didn't comply with MJ-12's directives."

Crawfoot didn't deny the accusation. "That's why I was sent here, Colonel. But as I earlier informed that asshole Agabarr, I have resigned as MJ-12's hired gun."

General Beauharnais raised his voice. "None of this matters now! We must see to an immediate evacuation."

Agabarr laughed at the chaos and fear around him. "You're all going to die! Accept your deaths like men."

"And what about you?" Crawfoot growled, shaking Agabarr in the grip he maintained on his arm. "You're going to die with the rest of us."

Agabarr seemed resigned to his fate. "I had intended to make my escape after I had offed Green and Webster, but a good soldier is always prepared to die for his masters."

Crawfoot cursed, pushed Agabarr away from him as if he were ridding himself of a sack of garbage. "If I'm going to die, I don't want to be in the company of a prick like you. Get the hell away from me!"

Agabarr complied, offering Crawfoot an obscene gesture before he doubled over and made a sudden move for his ankle.

Crawfoot knew in a sudden flash of realization that Agabarr was going for a second gun, perhaps hidden in an ankle holster.

"Joe, hit the dirt!" Crawfoot shouted, unholstering his own weapon.

Colonel Kingsley had been on guard ever since both Agabarr and Crawfoot had confirmed General Beauharnais' supposition that they had been assigned to the base by MJ-12 to remove him if he did not fulfill their orders. Crawfoot's sudden unholstering of his automatic pistol triggered a similar movement on the part of the colonel. Crawfoot's slug punctured Agabarr's heart only a second before Kingsley's slammed into Crawfoot's own chest.

Crawfoot spun crazily into Joe's arms. He had time to ask his friend only one brief question before his breath left him forever. "Have you got room for me in your boat, Joe?"

Red Redding shouted angrily at Colonel Kingsley. "Why the hell did you shoot Crawfoot? He was going for that sick fuck Agabarr! He wasn't aiming for the general!"

Kingsley seemed dazed, momentarily uncertain what to do with the pistol in his hand. "I didn't...I thought..."

"It's over," General Beauharnais said firmly. "And if what Agabarr said is true, these two professional killers may have been granted more merciful deaths than we are about to receive."

Rainey edged her way through the crowd, moved next to Webster, and put her arms around him. She knew that the bullet wound in his shoulder was nearly healed after Joe had touched it. "What's wrong? What's happening, honey? Those shots?"

Webster held her, but did not answer. He didn't want to tell her that they had won the battle, but lost the war.

An explosion rocked the mountain and a fiery plume rose skyward as the communications tower above Groom Pass exploded. The F-4 Wild Weasel came over the pass and made a radical maneuver away from the explosion created by one of its laser guided missiles. Some of the crowd screamed and began surging in different directions, confused, frightened, uncertain.

"They're attacking without warning, sir!" Kingsley shouted in utter disbelief. "Agabarr was right!"

"Those men up there are just following their orders," General Beauharnais answered grimly. "They believe the base is overrun by terrorists. And they've knocked out our communications tower so we can't even try to convince them otherwise."

Six F-15 air superiority fighters from the 57th Tactical Fighter Wing swooped toward the Groom facilities from the south.

"Well, folks," Red said stoically, "it's a good day to die."

Joe Green shook his head as he lowered Mike Crawfoot's body to the ground. "Not just yet. They are here!"

As the F-15s and the single F-4 approached, the light from the bright, clear morning sky dimmed, then flickered. The roar of the fighters' engines coughed, then stopped mute.

At first the low frequency hum couldn't be heard over the noise of the approaching aircraft's dying engines; but within seconds the hum became louder and a huge, silver-blue triangular starship appeared as if from nowhere and hovered above the crowd. There was no doubt among those who witnessed its arrival that it was an alien vehicle from another world.

A thin silver line of light glowed around the circumference of the ship that must have been at least as wide as three football fields in diameter.

"Praise the lord," Newsome sighed in relief. "It looks as though somebody up there still likes you, Joe."

Joe nodded, allowing the tears to flow unchecked.

"It's beautiful. It looks just like the one that Red managed to catch on film," Webster said, referring to the clip that had been telecast on "Exploring the Unknown."

Red laughed excitedly from his wheelchair. "That's the same one, all right!"

"Isn't it the most beautiful thing you've ever seen?" Webster whispered in awe.

"Like the angels made it," Rainey said.

Newsome agreed. "It looks just like I always knew it would."

"My god," Kingsley gasped. "It is the one they showed on television. The one they said was a fake, a mock-up. They fucking lied. This one's for real!"

"Yes," Beauharnais nodded. "It's true. Everything that MJ-12 has been hiding, everything that Green and his friends broadcast over the world is true. They are really here."

Everyone's attention was focused on the ship until a flash of brilliant light encircled the massive craft, unnerving the observers on the ground. A halo of shimmering energy engulfed the starship as the brilliance dimmed.

Then seven fireballs of glowing light flared out from the perimeter of the craft and were projected at an extreme rate of speed toward the seven distant aircraft that were approaching dead stick without controls and without power. Hundreds of people on the fringes of the crowd started running, hoping to distance themselves from what appeared to be an inevitable series of crashes.

The fireballs, one at a time, intercepted the oncoming fighter aircraft and exploded in a burst of multicolored light, reminiscent of a Fourth of July fireworks display.

The already decelerating aircraft, falling at a great rate of descent, stopped in midair. Free floating, the aircraft slowly rotated and tumbled from some unseen, but powerful, force. The negative gravity zone of the alien spaceship attracted the aircraft, and each one floated closer and closer to the massive ship.

The mysterious starship perimeter shimmered in and out of focus with iridescent silver-blue colors. Within three minutes, each of the fighters hung motionless under the huge alien craft. The surreal sight appeared to those below to be a giant mobile, as the aircraft slowly dangled and shifted without any visible means of suspension.

Next, tubes of light encircled the starship in concentric rings around its outer circumference, emitting peculiar chirping sounds as the different colored lights pulsed. The pulsating circles of lights and unusual rhythmic tones mesmerized and calmed the crowd.

Thousands of laser-thin light beams fired from the bottom center of the alien craft, sweeping the multitude, touching each person for a few seconds.

Everyone became fascinated by the light beams sweeping, probing, touching. Each light appeared to intermingle with the others in a medley that constantly shifted in frequency, intensity, and color. People raised their arms, trying to touch the light beams. Joe knew that the Jexovah androids were searching for those who were in the process of Rapturing.

Joseph Green, we will destroy the intruders that meant to harm you.

Joe could tell that the voice could be heard by all those who had Raptured. He lifted his arms and beseeched the Jexovah: "Do not harm those men. We forgive them, for they did not understand what their actions would do to the future of humanity."

Thousands of voices rose as one from the Raptured. "Forgive them. Forgive them."

Would it not be best to destroy them? They may try again to harm you.

"You must release them!" Joe said. "The whole world is watching through hundreds of television cameras. It would be wrong to start the Rapture with such violence."

Once again, thousands of voices echoed Joe's plea: "Release them. Release them."

You did not initiate the violence. These craft carried nuclear devices. You would all have been killed. Many others in the surrounding area would have been killed. The radiation would have done great harm to the environment. The Rapture would have been ended. The Great Plan would have been set back thousands of your Earth years.

"These men were only following orders," Joe answered. "The evil, greedy ones who sent them will now have their power taken from them. The entire world has observed their ruthless attempt to destroy the innocent and to bury truth. The whole world now knows that the Rapture has begun."

"The Rapture has begun. The Rapture has begun," the voices chorused in ecstasy.

It is as you wish. The Rapture has truly begun.

As the crowd watched in astonishment, the seven fighter planes floated down to the Groom Lake runway as though they were giant leaves spiraling down from a great oak tree.

Joe Green lifted his arms and clasped his hands as if in prayer. "Thanks," he shouted toward the starship. "Thank you."

In the next moment, the massive space vehicle was no longer there.

General Beauharnais sighed and wiped tears from his eyes. "Now we damn well know that we're not alone."

"Wow!" Rainey Roberts gasped. "In and out of our dimension in the blink of an eye. It's going to take our eggheads quite a while to catch up to that kind of technology!"

"And if they ever do catch up with them," Colonel Kingsley said, "they had better share that technology with all of Earth."

Wayne Newsome shrugged. "Maybe we're not supposed to catch up. You know, it's not so bad being an earthling right here on good old terra firma."

Blake Webster indicated the thousands of people Rapturing around them. "And I have a strong feeling that things are going to get even better in the next few years."

Page St. John had at last made his way through the crowds to embrace Joe. "You've done it, Joseph Green. Like the prophets before you, you're touching the hearts and souls of the masses. You've started something that will change the world. You've started a holy fire here today that will continue to burn brightly for future generations to see."

"I didn't do anything except be," Joe protested. "They—whoever they really are—did it to me for reasons I am certain that I will never fully understand."

Joe Green knew that, in time, there would be an end to wars, and humankind would at last learn to live in peace. He also foresaw an in-between time of great turmoil and chaos. MJ-12 would be certain to conduct a massive disinformation campaign in an attempt to negate the worldwide transmission of their secrets and to squelch the impact of the unexpected cosmic drama that had occurred when the huge starship intercepted the mission of destruction that would have annihilated Area 51, its military personnel, and thirteen thousand citizens. Undoubtedly, key officers would be removed, retired, or transferred. Civilian experts would be called upon to debunk the entire episode as a hoax. And it was not out of the question to suppose that certain of the central players in the perpetration of the "hoax" might be marked for assassination.

But Joe also knew that it was all over for MJ-12. Too many people had seen the incredible display of alien intervention and would believe. Too many people had read the previously secret documents that betrayed the shadow government's involvement with aliens and their technology. The time of the secret superpatriots had gone, and Joe hoped that they realized it.

He knew with complete certainty that he would continue to interact with those men and women who were ready to embrace the Rapture. He would not perform this function in the role of a pope, a messiah, or an avatar. He would live quietly, and he would always be accessible to the sincere seeker. He would be an enhanced, transformed Earthman, living a balanced, fulfilled existence, establishing the pattern for the new humans who would have the power to shape their own tomorrows.

Joe understood clearly that there would be those who would deny the truth and campaign against those who would Rapture. But in the end, it had been revealed to him, the last generation of humans with distorted alien genes would die off and leave Earth to those who had reclaimed the birthright of humankind.

Joe knew that the Jexovah had no desire to rule or to guide their creation after the Rapture. They were like doctors in that sense. They had begun the healing process, and it was up to the human species to forge its own path out into the stars and claim their right as equals with the countless other races that had preceded them.

The Jexovah would watch, as gods sometimes do, and ponder their creation. Had they made the right choices and decisions for humankind? Time would tell, for even gods of infinite wisdom sometimes make mistakes.

Would they continue to manipulate the affairs of humans? Nothing they had ever told Joe revealed whether or not humankind would ever meet face-to-face the cosmic creators who had formed them, guided them, and finally healed them of their ills. For the present, it was enough to understand that the Rapture had begun.

As the Chosen One, Joe was aware that what seemed to be the end of a prophecy was only the beginning of a revelation.